Luca Veste is a writer of Italian and Scouse heritage, married with two young daughters. He studied psychology and criminology at university in Liverpool. He is the author of five novels, *Dead Gone, The Dying Place, Bloodstream, Then She Was Gone* and *The Bone Keeper.*

Find out more at www.LucaVeste.com or follow @LucaVeste on Twitter and Facebook.

Praise for *Then She Was Gone*

'A page-turner'   ***Sunday Times* Crime Club**

'Veste's Italian and Scouse heritage has produced an intriguing hothouse flower'   ***Financial Times***

'I loved it – I was gripped from the start and by the end I couldn't leave it alone! A chilling story of power and revenge that made my blood run cold'
Jenny Blackhurst

'Luca Veste's Murphy and Rossi series hits the very pinnacle of modern crime fiction. Totally compelling'   **Steve Cavanagh**

'Socially incisive, emotionally fraught and utterly gripping, *Then She Was Gone* is another triumph from Luca Veste and marks the coming of age of the Murphy and Rossi series'   **Eva Dolan**

'Four books in and Murphy and Rossi's Liverpool is as dark as the Mersey. With missing children and dodgy politicians proving Veste's grip on social issues remains bang on the money, it's all tied up in a breathtaking and satisfying plot'   **Nick Quantrill**

Praise for *Bloodstream*

'This is a twisty, psychological crime debut in a gritty setting: a new favourite for police procedural lovers'   **Clare Mackintosh**

'Luca Veste is leading the new wave in British crime fiction'   **Jay Stringer**

'A dark, thrilling ride. Murphy and Rossi are getting better and better'
Stav Sherez

THE
BONE
KEEPER

LUCA
VESTE

**SIMON &
SCHUSTER**

London · New York · Sydney · Toronto · New Delhi

A CBS COMPANY

First published in Great Britain by Simon & Schuster UK Ltd, 2018
A CBS COMPANY

3 5 7 9 10 8 6 4 2

Simon & Schuster UK Ltd
1st Floor,
222 Gray's Inn Road
London WC1X 8HB

Simon & Schuster Australia, Sydney
Simon & Schuster India, New Delhi

www.simonandschuster.co.uk
www.simonandschuster.com.au
www.simonandschuster.co.in

A CIP catalogue record for this book
is available from the British Library

Paperback ISBN: 978-1-4711-4141-6
eBook ISBN: 978-1-4711-4142-3
eAudio ISBN: 978-1-4711-7374-5

Typeset in the UK by M Rules
Printed and bound by CPI Group (UK) Ltd, Croydon, CR0 4YY

MIX
Paper from
responsible sources
FSC® C020471

Simon & Schuster UK Ltd are committed to sourcing paper that is made
from wood grown in sustainable forests and support the Forest Stewardship
Council, the leading international forest certification organisation. Our
books displaying the FSC logo are printed on FSC certified paper.

This one's for Emma.
My wife and best friend.

I wouldn't want to share this
life with anyone else.

Author Note

All of the locations found in this book exist; however, some minor details have been changed or expanded to better tell this story.

The Bone Keeper's coming.
The Bone Keeper's real.
He doesn't stop.
He doesn't feel.
He'll snatch you up.
And make you weep.
He'll slice your flesh.
Your bones he'll keep.

Before

Her story begins in the tunnel.

The soft ground underneath her feet as she walked through. The calm swoosh of air, lightly caressing her face. The sounds coming from the darkness. The echoes. Rage. The smell of death, clawing at her skin.

That's what she'll always remember.

The tunnel.

Four of them would walk through it. Silent and alone. One after the other.

Three would come out.

Before the tunnel, it had been a different evening. Crisp autumn air swirled around the group as they walked into the woods. She was eleven years old, following her brother Matty. He was three years older, but not much wiser. Two other kids shuffled alongside them, Lee and Faye, her new stepdad's niece and nephew, around the same age as them. It was nothing more than a game, an adventure of sorts. They weren't supposed to be playing out this far away from the house, but it was half-term in October and they were kids.

They were invincible.

'Come on,' she said, taking the lead and walking with what she wanted to look like confidence. 'Let's get this over with.'

She passed the sign that said 'Dibbinsdale Nature Reserve' and the picnic tables on the right and followed the path into the trees. Overhead, it was growing even darker. Black clouds gathering. If they had come a week later, it would have been almost night already, but there was still some light left as the evening drew on.

It wouldn't last.

'It's going to rain.'

'Don't worry,' Matty said, catching up to her. 'We've got the trees. Nature's umbrella.'

She saw the grin appear and then vanish. A last remnant of the pre-teenage boy she used to know. They crossed a wooden bridge, Matty and Lee throwing small, thick branches into the water as they did so. She paused, watching the water bubble and quiver occasionally.

'Think there's any fish in there?'

'Nah,' Faye said, standing beside her as she rested her hands on the old wood. 'They wouldn't survive.'

The bubbles came up and made concentric circles in the water. She stared at it a little longer, squinting as the light continued to fade around them. Then she followed the rest, as their voices continued on the path. The path became a little wider, before shortening up again as they followed it around tall reeds, sunk into marshland.

It became slushier underfoot as they approached the place they'd come there to see. She brushed her foot against a single grey feather, slowing her pace.

'This is the place.'

A hush fell over them. The wind rippled unseen trees,

leaves and branches coming to life. The air grew colder as they came to a stop ahead of her.

'You think it's real?' Matty said, trying to sound jokey and brave. She knew it was an act now. The previous confidence slowly evaporating, as reality set in.

'The Bone Keeper lives here,' Lee replied, his whisper almost lost in the movement of the trees above them. 'People have seen it.'

She reached the other three, standing on another wooden bridge looking away from her approach. The tunnel came into view as she stopped beside them.

'Who's going in first?' Matty said, the bravado slipping from his voice now they were there.

'I reckon it should be Matty,' Lee replied, turning to look at the other teenager. 'Ladies first.'

She shivered as a slow breeze came through the trees and the air grew colder still. A few raindrops fell in the water, the pitter and pat breaking into the suffocating silence.

'Why should it be me? Are you scared?'

'You think I haven't done this before?'

'Yeah, right,' Matty said, a smile creeping across his face. 'You would never dare do anything like this . . .'

'I'll go first.'

They turned towards Faye, eyebrows raised at the small voice suddenly piping up. If she'd had to bet, she would never have guessed it would have been the little waif of a girl, a year younger than even she was, who would have volunteered to go through first.

In front of them, a short walk from the end of the bridge and a stone path just like all the other paths before, were two tunnels. One half was bricked up, the other . . . the other was not.

It's called Otter's Tunnel, Fake-dad had said to her earlier that day. *Used to be water running right through it and they reckon otters lived in there once upon a time. Couple of hundred years since then though. Now, it's just a few bats and maybe a couple of rats.*

She'd shuddered at the thought then and did so again now. Matty gave her a look, so she rubbed her arms as if she were cold.

'I'm going through it now,' Faye said, beginning to walk away. 'Can't be bothered standing around just looking at it.'

She watched as Faye continued to walk towards the path, Matty and Lee exchanging looks and then shrugging.

'You're really going to let a ten-year-old girl do it before you?' she said, suppressing a giggle. 'Yeah, you two are dead hard.'

Matty and Lee shot her a look, disgust and annoyance. A little fear still there too, just on the edges. They waited for Faye to leave, each taking up a position almost in single file.

She went through the tunnel third, after the other two idiot kids went first. She would have happily done it sooner, given how stupid the entire thing seemed to be. No excited shrieks or howls of fear. It was a little boring, if she was honest. It seemed to be a short walk, given the muted shouts she heard once the others had made it to the other side.

Then, it was her turn.

She stepped towards the tunnel, straining to see the pinpoint of the exit at the end of it. Only dim light was around them now, as the evening drew in. The darkness beginning to take hold, sunlight disappearing and making the air thin and lifeless.

'Are you scared?'

She turned towards Matty, who was swaying from one foot to the other. 'No, of course not.'

'Why are you just standing there then? It's your turn.'

'Do you want to go first?'

Matty smiled back at her – that sickly one he always used when he had the upper hand. 'And leave you on this side alone? Bet you wouldn't like that. Just get going. We'll have to go back soon.'

She didn't know the time, but she expected it was past that magical time parents had, when it suddenly went from being fine to being *FAR TOO LATE*. She tried to work out how long it would take them to get back from where they were, but couldn't remember the length of the walk now. They would probably have to come back through the tunnel as well. Maybe all together this time, although she expected the boys would take the opportunity to make it appear more scary than it actually was.

'Come on, are you going to do it or not? Getting bored now.'

'I'm going, I'm going,' she replied, her voice echoing around the silent woods. 'You're just scared yourself, that's all. Want me to back out, so you don't have to do it.'

'That's stupid, I was happy to go first, if those two hadn't wanted to show off.'

'Yeah, I believe you. Honest.'

'What do you think of them?'

She studied her brother, recognising the way he had thrust his hands in his pockets and was kicking the ground. This was Matty wanting to know if things were going to be okay – whether he should be worried about what was to come.

He was the older brother, but more and more it seemed like she was supposed to look after him.

'They're annoying Wirral brats,' she replied, a grin appearing on her face. 'They would last five seconds on our side of the river. But, they're all right. I suppose. Not like we have to spend too much time with them.'

'I hope Mum isn't thinking of moving over here,' Matty said, still looking towards the ground rather than at her. 'Not sure I could deal with that.'

'We've been through worse.'

This time Matty did look up at her, a pained, scrunched up look on his face as he shook his head. 'I don't think so.' Then he gave her that smile she always looked forward to.

'Come on,' he said, taking his hands out of his pockets and pointing towards the tunnel. 'Let's get this over with.'

She turned and began to walk, allowing herself to cross the threshold into the tunnel. At first there was still some light behind her, so she could see where she was walking. It didn't take long for that to change. The light disappeared, making it difficult to keep her bearings, as the darkness within the tunnel took hold.

The water beside the path was still, no sounds coming from that direction at all. She concentrated on walking forwards, squinting into the distance to focus on where she expected the exit to appear.

She was halfway there when the smell hit her.

It turned her stomach, making her gag. She stopped walking, bending over with her hand over her mouth. It was a revolting stench, her eyes watering instantly. She shuffled forwards, ready to have a go at the two little brats who hadn't warned them of it.

Then she heard a noise.

A shift, nothing more. A small sound, which would have been unnoticeable outside. Inside the tunnel, it was as loud as a roar.

For a moment, her body betrayed her. She stopped in her tracks, unable to move. Her heartbeat increased tenfold, a churning feeling in the pit of her stomach. The small hairs on the back of her neck stood on end, whipped up by the draught of breeze that came through the tunnel.

The sound came again. Turned into a whistle. A breathy tune.

A tune she recognised.

The Bone Keeper's coming. The Bone Keeper's real …

'Lee,' she whispered, too afraid to raise her voice any louder. 'If that's you I'm going to kill you.'

The whistling stopped, replaced by another sound. A growl? A laugh? She couldn't tell anymore.

This time, her body obeyed her and she found herself able to move. She didn't think twice, breaking into a jog, hoping she was facing the correct direction. She could feel the ground beneath her grow softer, muddier, as she moved along it. She was worried about slipping, but couldn't stop herself now.

If she fell in there, she wouldn't know what to do.

She imagined the sound was following her, but didn't stop moving in the direction of the pinpoint of light, now growing larger.

There was something in the tunnel. Something watching, lurking in the shadows. Now, she could almost picture whatever it was following her as she broke into a run. Could hear it slithering along the path, ready to catch her.

She burst out of the tunnel, collapsing to the floor in front of the other two children and dropping at their feet.

She turned back around, expecting there to be someone emerging. Ready to catch her, now her legs had finally given way.

'What's up?' Lee said, grabbing her by the arm. 'Got scared, did you?'

She couldn't speak, breathing heavily, long gasps of fresh air. Instead, she stared towards the tunnel, unable to see anything within.

She wanted to scream Matty's name. Warn him, tell him what she had heard, seen, felt.

She couldn't make a sound.

Couldn't tell Matty to stop. That something was in there.

Warn him not to go through.

Warn him that it wasn't safe.

She would never see her brother again.

Now

It is as if the world shifted in its sleep, and one of its ideas escaped and became real.

Steve Mosby, *Black Flowers*

One

Louise Henderson was sitting in her car, trying to breathe, when the call came in.

She didn't believe in fate or being able to see the future. Yet, it was almost as if her body had known what was about to happen. That it was trying to sound a warning to her. Maybe she knew on some level that it was coming.

A *danger ahead* sign, which she always seemed to ignore.

At that moment, she just wanted to be able to breathe properly. A simple act – something that goes unnoticed until you suddenly can't do it.

Is this what dying feels like?

Before her mobile had cut the radio off mid-song, ringing over the speakers in her car, she had been sitting at the side of the road. Parked up, the engine idling as she gripped the steering wheel; the sun disappearing behind grey clouds, as if it was playing its own part in her drama.

She had been thinking about fire. That was the reason she'd pulled over. When the smell of smoke and ash assailed her. A flash of light, red and orange, then black. Then, in seconds, she was gasping for air. It was as if someone had their hands around her throat, a weight on her chest. Her stomach churned, a thousand butterflies taking flight inside her. Cars passed by in a blur, a couple of people walked on the pavement beside her, as she closed her eyes and tried to breathe in and out. In and out. Calm. She was safe, nothing could harm her. Not now.

Not now.

You're okay. Nothing is wrong.

The soothing tone of her inner voice helped a little, but it could barely be heard over the roar of so many other thoughts running through her head.

It was getting worse. These moments were becoming frequent; the bouts of terror and of not being able to breathe threatening to become the norm. The night before, she had stared at the glow from her mobile phone screen, lying in bed unable to sleep. Scrolling through a list of counselling services in the local area.

As if she needed it.

She didn't, she'd decided. No one ever did, she'd thought, lying to herself. It was all a con, a ruse, a way of extracting cash from your wallet. Money for old rope. The idea that any of it would make the slightest bit of difference to her life was beyond any logic she could recognise.

Yet, she was beginning to think it was the only way. The only thing that could help at that moment. Telling a stranger your deepest and darkest feelings. Bringing out forgotten and suppressed memories.

No.

She had shut off her phone at that point, stared into the dark and shook her head. It would be a meeting filled with pointless questions. Making her examine feelings and all that rubbish.

She was better than that.

Yet it was becoming more difficult to ignore what was happening to her. What had always been there, beneath the surface. Or that it was getting worse. It wouldn't be long before people at work started to notice. If they hadn't already, of course. She had no idea if people were talking behind her back. If she was the subject of gossip being passed around.

She thought Shipley would have told her if that was the case.

The sound of the phone ringing still filled the car, as her focus came back. Reality began to sharpen, her breathing returning to normal, as she pressed on the screen and answered. Wished she'd checked who was calling before she'd keyed the button.

'Hello?'

'It's me,' said the voice on the other end of the phone. 'Are you on your way down?'

Louise bit down on her bottom lip before responding to the detective sergeant. 'On my way where?' she replied, catching a glimpse of herself in the rear-view mirror as she checked behind her and pulled back into a gap in the traffic.

'No one else has been in touch yet? Bloody hell . . .'

'What's going on?' Louise said, cutting off the beginnings of what sounded like an oncoming rant.

'A woman found wandering the streets in Melling. She's been assaulted and paramedics are working on her now. Doesn't look good. You need to get yourself down here.'

'What's the address?'

DS Paul Shipley reeled off the road name. 'How long will you be?'

Louise looked around her, the unfamiliar street she was

on not exactly helping. She tried to remember where she'd been heading before she'd pulled up, but was struggling.

'I'm on my way, sir,' Louise said, and ended the call. She continued to drive in as straight a line as she could, hoping to find a familiar landmark or road sign. Eventually she gave up and pulled over again. Pressed the address into her satnav and got back on the road.

The radio had kicked back into life, some mindless, soulless track playing. She ignored it, concentrating on what was in front of her. Anxiety was quickly being replaced with anger, the two emotions more interchangeable than ever, it seemed.

She hoped the person who had attacked a woman on the street was still around when she got there. That would be helpful.

Another twenty minutes and she was arriving at the scene. All previous thoughts disappeared from her mind – professional mode kicking in. Boxed off her personal feelings and focused on what lay ahead. The crowded street, the multiple vehicles, police livery stark and on show.

Her job.

A residential area with a few shops scattered here and there. The old corner shop, now a Londis. Post office next door. Old-style zebra crossing, globular lampposts on either side. Waddicar Lane, which Louise enjoyed whispering to herself as she sat in the car.

Waddicar.

She left the car parked up on a side street, half on the road, half on the pavement. She could already hear someone standing outside their house grumbling at her arrival as she made her way towards where the main hive of activity seemed to be concentrated. She pulled her coat tighter around her body as the wind picked up and swirled around her.

'DC Louise Henderson,' Louise said to the closest uniform to the crime-scene tape still being strung up. She held up her ID for him when he gave her a withering look. 'Victim still on the scene?'

The uniform gave her a nod, then looked towards the ambulance parked up nearby. 'They usually take people in her state with them when they go back the hospital.'

Louise stopped herself replying with a similarly sarcastic remark, and instead made her way towards the figure standing a few yards away, ending the power trip the uniform was displaying for no one's benefit but his own.

'Sarge?'

'Louise, finally,' DS Shipley replied, glancing in her direction and then back towards the paramedics she could now see more clearly. 'Start taking statements from the closest witnesses. I don't trust these uniforms to catch everything. And get that lot over there to stop bloody filming everything we're doing.'

Louise looked across the road to where a group of people had gathered. A few had mobile phones raised up, pointed in her direction. She instinctively raised a hand in front of her face, but dropped it before – she hoped – Shipley noticed.

'What have we got here?' Louise said, trying to work out what exactly was being asked of her. 'Just so I know what to ask.'

Shipley breathed heavily through his nostrils and placed his hands on his hips before crossing his muscular arms over his chest, all in one supple movement. He was taller than

Louise – him being just over six foot, her in the mid five range – but he didn't loom over her as other superiors had in the past. He was lean and simply unthreatening. 'Young woman, found walking up this road. She's in a right state. Paramedics were on the scene first. Looks like she collapsed right around here. Someone has done a right job on her. Beaten and stabbed by the looks of it. There's a trail of blood up the road. They're trying to stabilise her now.'

Louise scanned the surroundings, trying to spot anything out of the ordinary, but it couldn't have looked more usual if it had tried. A normal road, lined with houses. White double-glazed bay windows at the bottom, a double pane above them. Red bricks and a patch of grass in front of most of them. It would be idyllic at another time, but now, the police vans and cars, an ambulance and a bunch of onlookers spoiled the quiet.

'What's her name?'

'No idea,' Shipley said, already eager to get on, she thought. He uncrossed his arms and ran a hand through his hair, mussing it up a little, the side parting not settling quite right. 'She didn't get to the point of introducing herself to us.'

Another sarcastic remark, Louise thought, but didn't show any reaction. This was how it always was. Everyone hid their true feelings from each other.

As coppers – detectives – they were better than most at doing that.

Without saying another word, she left him to it, walking towards the group on the other side of the road. Not before she took a short detour, past the paramedics working on the woman. She couldn't see much, but enough to know it was bad.

Ripped clothes, torn and almost shredded. Blood on the ground beneath her, but not enough to pool – just spots, patches. Her eyes were closed, but she could see the rise and fall of her chest, which seemed non-erratic. The paramedics kneeling beside her worked in silence, the occasional murmur of support almost whispered into the woman's ear.

Louise looked away, scanning around her, looking for something. Anything that might give her a clue how the woman had ended up there. She had a vague sense of the area, but wasn't as familiar with it as she now wished she was.

She stared up the road, imagining the woman's journey to the place where she collapsed. Ahead, she could see houses stretching into the distance, the look of the road not changing dramatically. Behind those, she could see green fields. Trees.

Woods, she thought.

She will have come from the woods.

Two

A light breeze rippled the police tape strung up across the road as Louise crossed over to the other side. More people were turning up at the scene. Some she guessed had just been passing by and wanted to see what was going on. Others would have been told about it and had come specifically to see what was happening on their doorstep. As she crossed she had caught herself before she looked both ways, realising there wasn't any traffic able to travel down the road at that point. Not with all the police vehicles blocking the way. It took seconds to reach the growing number of people gathered there, all of whom were beginning to look a little uncomfortable. A uniform she recognised fell into step with her.

'That's enough now,' Louise said, holding up her hands to the various members of the public standing around. 'Going to need you to move further back over that way and stop filming.'

'It's our right, isn't it,' a voice said from the back. 'Can't stop us doing it. We've got rights. It's a public place.'

'Just listen and let us do our jobs,' the uniform next to Louise said. PC Robertson, she thought. Her first name came to her mind just as easily. Andrea. A tall, stocky woman in her mid-thirties. Long, dark hair, tied back out of her way. 'Let's not create more of a scene.'

Louise was about to speak again, but the loudmouth towards the back piped up again.

'Can't force us to do nothing. We're not doing anything wrong. What's the matter, you worried we'll see you doing something you shouldn't be?'

That's how it was now, Louise thought. Every move recorded, scrutinised. The victim didn't matter to these people, just what they could capture on video or in pictures. They were more interested in posting on social media and gaining as many shares, likes, comments, whatever, as they could. They didn't care who was affected.

'Come over here,' Louise said, her eyes growing darker. The tall lad at the back gave a quick smirk to one of his mates, then peeled away from the group and made his way over to the side where she was waiting for him. 'Put that down for a second.'

The lad couldn't have been more than twenty, the cocky air of the young and foolish surrounding him. Black tracksuit pants on, one of the legs tucked into a faded white sock. He was holding his phone up, pointing it at her. 'Don't see why I should.'

Louise smiled at him, which had the effect she wanted. A flush of red rose in his cheeks as he lowered the phone, switching it off and placing it back in his pocket.

'Listen, we're just trying to give her a bit of dignity,' Louise said, her voice low so she couldn't be heard by the rest of the people gathered. 'You understand, right?'

The lad hesitated, quickly looking her up and down. He grinned as his eyes rested on hers again. 'You're fit for a copper you know.'

'Did you see anything, at least? Make yourself useful to me.'

'I got here the same time as the first ambulance,' he replied, his voice thick with accent and entitlement. 'Just the bird on the floor, that's all.'

Louise tried to ignore the *bird* word, clenching her jaw to stop herself from saying something she'd regret later. 'Are you going to stop getting in the way and back to whatever you usually do?'

'What do I get out of it?'

Louise could feel herself losing control of the conversation as she glanced back across the road, to the main hive of activity. She imagined grabbing the lad by the throat, slamming him into the ground. Smashing his head off the pavement, watching him cry, beg, plead for mercy. The images flashed through her mind in an instant. An explosion of violence she couldn't control. She'd often heard it described as red mist descending – usually from some no-mark defendant in an interview room – but that wasn't how she experienced it. It was more like darkness. The world turning black, punctuated by pockets of light, which contained horror within them.

'I'll tell you what I'll do,' Louise said, blinking away the images and remaining calm. 'I won't search through your pockets and find the weed and whatever else you have on you.'

'I'm not stashing anything—'

'Save it,' Louise replied, stepping closer to the lad now. 'You reek of it. Just do us both a favour, get on your bike and bugger off out of here. We've got enough to deal with.'

The lad thought about it for a few seconds, then walked away, jerking his head to a couple of the other men who'd been standing at the back of the group watching them intently. Louise waited for them to round the corner and then started breathing again.

The rest of the group milling round looked back across the road as she returned to them. The phones had disappeared now, but she knew they wouldn't wait long to start up again. It would be too late anyway, she thought. They would have enough to get as many likes and retweets as their hearts desired.

'Can we help?'

Louise turned to the two uniformed officers who had been waiting for her to come back. She looked them up and down, wondering how much use the dozy-looking pair would be, and shook her head. 'Help Robertson there move the tape back. At least out of sight of the ambulance.'

She didn't hear their response, her attention drawn to the shop opposite. A few feet from where the ambulance was parked up, yet seemingly ignored. A figure stood in the doorway and caught her eye as she looked towards him, then turned away, disappearing into the shop. Louise frowned, then crossed back over, leaving the uniformed officers to sort themselves out. A few seconds later, she was stepping into the shop.

'Hello?'

There was no answer, so she continued to walk further in. It was a convenience store, which seemed to contain everything anyone could ever need for any eventuality. An alternative to one of the bigger supermarkets, which she knew were a hell of a walk from there. She imagined it was a favourite for the old dears who probably made up a high percentage of the local populace.

'Hello?' she tried again, raising her voice a little more. 'I know you're in here. I saw you in the doorway. I just need to ask a few questions, that's all.'

As she reached the counter, Louise heard the laboured breathing from behind it. The man she'd seen in the doorway was standing off to the side, hidden by the oversized scratch-card dispenser.

'Hello,' the man said, shuffling towards the counter now. He was older than she'd expected, face creased by lines and age. Leathery skin, which kept going back from his forehead, grey unkempt hair sprouting from the sides of his head. There was an almost imperceptible shake in his hands as he raised them and pointed towards the outside of the shop. 'I don't know what's going on out there.'

'Have you been here all morning?' Louise asked, ignoring his plea. 'You saw what happened?'

The man shook his head, the shake in his hands becoming worse the longer Louise looked at them. 'Please, I don't know anything.'

He had the look of someone from her past – an old guy who had run the local corner shop. Weathered and dishevelled. 'There's no trouble here,' she tried, cocking her head and smiling tightly. 'We just need to make sure we don't miss anything, okay? We want to help. I'm Detective Constable Louise Henderson. What's your name?'

'George,' the man replied. It was clear from his tone that that was all she was going to get at this point.

'Okay, George, we just want to help the woman who's been injured, now—'

'I can't help you.'

Louise stopped smiling, working hard to keep herself from giving the man a good, hard shake. 'Why don't you just tell me what you saw before we arrived. What happened?'

The man shook his head, more forcefully now. 'I don't want to get involved, I've already told them I didn't see anything. I've heard the stories. You ask for my help and then suddenly I'm a grass, a snitch. Next week, they'll put stuff through my windows and I can't have that. You're only placing me in danger. I'm not going to speak to you.'

'What are you talking about? I don't understand—'

There was movement at the back of the shop, a sound like something shifting on one of the shelves. 'Are you hiding someone back there?' Louise said to George, who didn't respond. She looked at the doorway quickly, then turned back in the direction of the noise. She walked towards it, waiting for any more movement or sound.

A head poked around the door, saw her coming and disappeared again. Louise straightened up from the bent-over crouch she'd been walking in. 'You can come out now, I've seen you.'

A small boy, no older than eight or nine, peered around the shelves and then withdrew, but not as quickly this time.

'I won't bite,' Louise said, stopping a few feet short. 'I want to make sure you're okay, that's all.'

The boy shuffled out, staring at his feet as he did so. She could see some resemblance to George, who was still behind the counter but watching her intently.

'What's your name?'

The boy didn't answer, so Louise squatted down, finding his eyes and not looking away. 'Mine's Louise. Are you okay?'

He thought for a moment, then nodded his head.

'Shouldn't you be in school?' Louise asked, trying not to sound like a teacher as she did so.

'Teacher training day,' the boy replied, his voice soft, a

slight trace of a local accent, but nothing like some of the kids of that age she'd dealt with in the past.

'You can check with the school,' George said, appearing behind them. 'They'll tell you he never misses a day. I'm just helping out my daughter, that's all. She can't take him into work with her, so he's come here to be my helper.'

Louise ignored the interruption. 'Have you been back there this whole time?'

The boy shook his head. 'I was in the doorway when the woman went past.'

'So you saw her?'

'Yes. She was bleeding.'

'She was, but we're helping her now. Did you see anything else?'

'No,' the boy replied, shaking his head. He was small, but stocky for his age. A hardness to his posture. 'She was singing.'

Louise felt her legs begin to protest as she continued to squat on her heels. She wasn't ready to stand up yet, though.

'What was she singing?'

The boy's eyes flashed to his grandfather's, a watery film appearing over them and then being blinked away. Louise turned to George and met his stare. He gave a nod to the boy.

'Was it a song you know?' Louise said, prompting the boy now. 'A pop song, or something like that?'

The boy shook his head. 'Not that kind of song. It's one the other boys in school say in school, to frighten everyone.'

Louise frowned, wondering what the hell she'd got herself into. *Never take the word of a child*, she heard DS Shipley say in her mind.

'What's the song?' Louise said, ready to give up and go back outside and make herself useful.

'The Bone Keeper song,' the boy replied.

Louise rocked back on her heels slightly, but didn't show any other reaction. She remembered the song; it came to her mind quickly and easily. The familiar rhyme, the sound of the voices that had sung it all that time ago. She hadn't heard it in years, but just this reminder was enough for it to replay clearly in her mind.

'The Bone Keeper song?' Louise said, wanting to be sure.

'Yes,' the boy said, his eyes now locked on his grandfather's. As if he were scared of his reaction, or maybe just wanted his approval. 'She was saying it over and over. Then she fell over, just outside the shop.'

There it was in Louise's mind. The song, being sung offkey. A child's voice, thick with scorn, trying to scare her. The horrible rhyme, full of death and fear.

'Did she say anything else?'

The boy looked back at the floor, scraping his shoes against the linoleum. 'She said he was coming back for her. That he was going to get her. I ran away and hid at the back of the shop.'

Louise stood up, her knees clicking as she did so. She turned back to George, who was standing behind her, arms folded, but unable to keep the fear from his face. She looked back at the boy, who had shrunk further into himself.

'You did good, lad,' she said. For some unknown reason she had the urge to ruffle his hair, but she resisted. 'Thank you.' She turned back to George, giving him the same smile she'd given the boy, but he didn't return it. 'Don't worry. I won't tell anyone you said anything.'

She left them there, her mind racing as memories flooded back to her. Children's voices, singing and playing. The squeak of swings and the braying of boys' laughter. The sounds you only hear deep in the woods, as the trees become closer together and the wind struggles to dent them. One single thought came through more than any other.

Why would a grown woman be singing that song?

Three

Louise stood in the hospital corridor, a bored-looking detective sergeant opposite her, pacing up and down and muttering to himself. She couldn't make out what he was saying, but she didn't imagine it was anything good. Her experience of DS Shipley told her that he was annoyed and that he wouldn't calm down any time soon. They had only been there for an hour, but already it was beginning to feel as if it had been ten. Nothing to do other than stand, lean against the wall and wait.

Waiting was the worst part.

'This is the part they leave out in training,' Shipley said, looking at his watch for the hundredth time since they'd arrived. 'All this standing around doing bugger all.'

'Someone once said to me that the job is ninety-five per cent boredom, five per cent actual stuff happening,' Louise replied, remembering the old inspector who had passed on that nugget of wisdom to her. He was dead now. Heart attack two years after retirement. She still remembered the look of disbelief on his widow's face at the funeral, as if she couldn't understand what she had done to deserve it. 'You wonder why they don't tell us that sooner.'

'Probably worried about putting people off. Not that I would have walked away at that point.'

'Neither would I.'

She had never questioned her decision to join the police. It had just been the logical conclusion; given how mixed-up her childhood had been, and the trouble she'd got into as a teenager, it had seemed only right that she would finally find a home in the police service.

No one had told her it was just as dysfunctional as real life.

Now, she found herself staring at a wall, trying to work out what colour it was. Anything to take her mind off the smell. Was it white or cream? Off-white, maybe?

'Not going to make the gym tonight at this rate,' Shipley said, interlocking his hands in front of him and stretching. 'About time I just put some equipment in the flat and stopped pretending this was a nine-to-five job.'

'You're getting addicted to the place anyway.'

'I just like the way it makes me look,' Shipley replied with a smile. He checked his phone again as Louise looked away. He was looking better for it, she thought. He'd never been overweight, but had been getting podgier in his mid-thirties. In the past year he'd joined a gym, shed the extra pounds and looked younger and better for it.

The only issue was that he wouldn't shut up about going to the damn place.

'I don't know why we're even getting this involved, now I think about it,' Shipley said, walking slowly over and coming to a stop near her. He folded his arms and leaned against the wall. 'Yeah, it looks bad, but odds are, a partner or an ex has beat her up and tried to properly mess her up. That'll be all. We could do first statement tomorrow morning, instead of waiting around this late.'

'Yeah, well, you're probably right,' Louise replied, not believing her own words. 'But you tried that line on the boss and it didn't work then either. Your instinct back at the scene was right. We were always going to end up here.'

Shipley didn't answer, just made some sort of guttural noise and resumed pacing up and down again. As if that was helping. He fiddled with the phone in his hand, turning the screen on, stopping to scroll through something, then pacing again.

'Why don't you just stop for a second?'

'I don't like this place, Louise,' Shipley replied, coming to a stop next to her. Louise looked down at the phone in his hand as the screen came to life. He caught her looking and smiled. 'Nothing substantial on the *Echo* website yet, just the bare bones. They've got a live update page going, but it just seems to be some reporter with a phone taking pictures of our vans.'

'I'm sure that'll change soon enough. Something more interesting will happen and they'll move on.'

Louise went back to staring at the wall, knowing she was stalling. She wasn't allowing herself to remember the words the young boy back at the shop had said to her. Wasn't going to allow those thoughts to return.

History to come flooding back in.

It was no use, of course. As much as she thought she was ignoring the thoughts, they were still there. Lurking behind a facade of carefully constructed bricks. A wall she had built purposefully, over a long period of time.

She was an adult now. She didn't believe in fairytales or myths anymore.

They were fake memories, made into something more by a young mind, desperate for any sort of magic, or just attention. She couldn't trust them. Louise felt her hand ball into a fist, banging against one leg, as she stood with her back against the wall. She uncurled it, glancing in Shipley's direction to ensure he hadn't seen what she'd been doing. His back was to her, his head shaking slowly from side to side as he checked his phone yet again.

Louise turned back to the opposite wall. More beige than white, she thought. That was as close as she could think.

It wasn't real.

It was another hour before they were allowed into the room. Somehow, even with hospitals as they were, they had managed to keep her off a ward for now. In her own private room in the A&E department of the largest hospital in the city. A nurse was still there, scribbling notes on a clipboard before placing it over the end of the bed.

'She's still quite out of it,' the nurse said, speaking to Louise after taking a tired look at Shipley. 'Not sure how much sense you're going to get out of her.'

'How is she doing?' Louise said when it became clear her DS wasn't going to ask. 'What injuries does she have?'

'It's bad, I can tell you that much. She's in a right state. Beaten black and blue, bruised ribs . . . that's not the worst of it though.'

Louise affected a look of concern, which she hoped didn't convey her true thoughts. *Just get out of here so I can ask her who did this.* 'What's that then?'

'She lost a lot of blood. He sliced into her,' the nurse replied, almost spitting the words out. 'Cut off the skin from different parts of her body. Like he was flaying her alive. Unbelievable what someone can do to another person.'

'Don't worry, we'll catch whoever did this to her,' Shipley said, moving closer to the bed and standing over the woman lying there. 'That'll be all.'

Louise eyed the woman in the bed as she slowly opened her eyes. She wondered how much she had heard as they had stood there, talking as if she wasn't in the room with them.

The nurse was about to say more, but moved towards the door instead. She turned as she got there, still only talking to Louise. 'Make sure you do. Not sure I want to see what someone like this does next.'

The door closed behind her, leaving Louise still hovering behind Shipley as he looked down at the woman lying in the bed. She could see some effort had been taken to clean her up, but there were still the remains of dried blood on her face. The room was stark in its blandness – a single window giving a little light, but not much, through the closed blinds. A couple of notices on the walls, a sink and a seemingly empty hand-soap dispenser. There was a single chair for visitors, but neither of them sat down, Louise choosing to make her way to the other side of the bed. She squeezed some alcohol rub onto her hands from the bottle hanging at the foot of the bed and covered her hands in it, being careful not to touch any of the equipment surrounding them.

'CSI have already taken what they could,' Shipley said, looking across as Louise continued to rub her hands. He shook his head at her. 'Hopefully it gets us something useful.'

'Maybe we should ask her first,' Louise replied, raising

her eyes towards the woman in the bed, who was now staring at Shipley. There was a translucent quality to the look, as if her eyes were unfocused, seeing right through him. 'If it is someone she knows, it'll make this much easier.'

'Can you hear me?' Shipley said, looming closer to the woman. His voice was unnaturally loud in the small space, almost echoing off the walls. 'What's your name?'

The woman continued to stare at Shipley, seemingly trying to work out who he was. What he was saying. He looked across at Louise, giving her the nod to try herself.

'Hello, I'm Detective Constable Louise Henderson, this is Detective Sergeant Paul Shipley,' Louise said, waiting for the woman's head to turn in her direction. 'We're here to help you, okay? We just want to ask you a few questions, then we'll get out of your way and let you recover.'

Louise heard a sniff from the other side of the bed, but ignored it. Sometimes, it was left to her to work out the best way of approaching things, but she knew what Shipley would be saying as soon as he got back to the station. She imagined 'woman's touch' would feature in that monologue.

The woman was now staring at Louise, blinking up at her. Her eyes became more focused as she seemed to understand who they were. Why they were now on either side of her bed.

'What's your name?'

The woman opened her mouth, then closed it again. She tried once more. 'Caroline,' she said, her voice a whisper. It seemed to take her a lot of effort to speak, but Louise could see she was ready to do it. 'Caroline . . . Rickards.'

'Hello, Caroline,' Louise said, trying to give her a

reassuring smile, even as she registered the pause before she'd revealed her surname. 'Do you know why we're here?'

Caroline frowned for a second, looked past Louise and around the room a little. 'I've been hurt.'

'Yes, you have. We just want to ask a couple of questions about that, for now. Nothing major. We'll let you recover a little more first. Is that okay?'

Caroline gave her a small nod, her movement crinkling the thin pillow beneath her head.

'What do you remember before getting here?'

'I . . . I don't know.'

'Do you remember the ambulance?'

A shake of the head from Caroline. 'I was running.'

'Do you know where you were running?'

'Down the road,' Caroline replied, breaking her gaze from Louise's and staring up at the ceiling. 'I was hurt.'

'Yes, that's where you were found. What about before then? What do you remember before then?'

Caroline's face began to crumple, but no tears appeared. 'There was grass and mud around me. Trees. It was there. It was hurting me.'

'Who was, Caroline?' Shipley said, ignoring Louise's pleading looks to let her carry on. He was a battering ram sometimes, when what was needed was a light knock. 'Who did this to you?'

'It was him, it was him,' Caroline replied, her voice rising to a shout now. 'It's real.'

'Was it your boyfriend or husband, Caroline?' Shipley continued, placing one hand on the bed next to her. 'An ex or something? What's his name?'

Caroline ignored Shipley, turning back towards Louise.

'It's real. Everything they said was right. It lives there. In the woods.'

'Okay, take it easy, Caroline,' Louise said, reaching a hand out towards her. 'Take your time.'

Caroline's right hand shot out and clutched Louise's, with a tighter hold than she'd been expecting. The skin on her wrist shouted in pain as it was twisted in the woman's grip. The room grew colder as Caroline forced herself closer to her, gritting her teeth with the effort.

'It was the Bone Keeper. It did this to me. It's real. And it's going to come back and find me.'

Four

Louise rubbed at her wrist, glancing down at the redness that had sprung up there, silently admonishing herself. Caroline had been through something horrific, yet still had the strength to grip her wrist hard enough to leave a mark.

It had been too soon, they should have known that. The two of them going in there asking questions was probably the last thing she had needed.

Still, that was the job they had to do.

'Bloody lunatic, if you ask me,' Shipley said, driving back towards the north of the city with little care to the rest of the road users. 'She'll be sectioned and we'll never know who did this.'

'Maybe not,' Louise replied, rolling her sleeve down and trying to ignore the stinging sensation she still felt. 'Maybe something happened out there. There's farmland and woods all around that area.'

'What, you believe her?' Shipley said, punctuating his point with a laugh. 'She's gone doolally, that's all. Someone has beat the hell out of her and cut parts of her skin off.'

'The kid in the shop—'

'We're not going to take that kid's word for it, are we?

So what if she was singing about the bogeyman? She wasn't exactly in the best frame of mind, was she?'

'I'm not saying she was, but the kid wasn't lying. And she said as much back there. She thinks she was attacked by . . . by *whatever*. We can't exactly ignore that,' Louise tried, knowing what the reaction would be before it even came.

'Yes we bleeding can,' Shipley said, then leaned on his horn as the car in front didn't move away quickly enough from the lights they'd pulled up at. 'Just the babblings of a mad woman. Don't get sucked in, we've seen this loads of times. It'll be some bloke who couldn't handle a break-up or something. It'll be off our desks by tomorrow morning, I bet.'

Louise didn't answer, instead thinking of the fear that had been emanating from Caroline, lying helpless in that hospital bed. Scarred for life, but lucky to be alive. She wasn't as certain as Shipley that this would be shifted over to some unlucky team to deal with, along with all the other domestic incidents they had to investigate.

'They'll have found CCTV by now,' Shipley continued, shifting into a higher gear and overtaking a slower car in front of them on the dual carriageway. 'That will clear things up more.'

He carried on talking but Louise stopped listening to his droning voice, preferring to stare out of the passenger-side window. The green fields, as they moved further out of the city, towards the wide-open spaces no one realised existed in Liverpool. The various woodlands and farming areas. The greens and browns replacing the grey and white of the city buildings.

'. . . and you should have seen his face,' Shipley was

saying as Louise tuned back in. He pounded the steering wheel a couple of times as his laughter grew louder. 'Honestly thought he was going to die or something.'

'Hmmm,' Louise replied, wondering what she had missed.

'You can make kids believe anything. Especially with a story as good as that one. Haven't thought about that in a long time. Poor lad wet his pants, he was that scared. I'm telling you, the woods were great for that sort of thing.'

'What type of thing?' Louise said, turning towards Shipley.

'Were you even listening?' he asked, shaking his head at her. 'I'm talking about the time we made some stupid kid who used to follow us everywhere think he was about to be caught by the Bone Keeper.'

'Sorry, mind had wandered, that's all.'

'Well, it's not as funny when I have to repeat myself,' Shipley said, almost pouting at the gall of her not listening. She liked this side of him. The injustice he felt about her ignoring his braying. It made him more human. 'Anyway, there's this little kind of cave thing, in the middle of Sefton Park. We took this kid there and told him that's where the Bone Keeper lived. You have to squeeze through these metal bars to get inside. Once you're in there, it's pitch black. Anyway, we let him go through first, then ran off shouting we'd seen him. You should have heard him squealing. We couldn't stop laughing.'

He was laughing now, but Louise didn't join in. Instead, she thought of a frightened little boy in the dark. Feeling those walls closing in on him, the fear of the darkness and what it could hold. What horrors lurked in the unseen.

Shipley wasn't to know. To him, it would have just been a childish prank, playing on the fears of others.

She was aware he had stopped laughing and was instead looking at her.

'What's the matter with you? It was just a little joke on some kid. You're not going to start crying over that, are you? That's the last thing I need.'

He grinned at her, showing he wasn't being serious. It did nothing to quell the feeling bubbling inside her. Louise started to answer, but decided against her first instinct. She took a second instead. 'Sorry, I wasn't listening properly. I was just thinking of that woman in the hospital. What she's gone through.'

'Oh,' Shipley said, his voice growing quiet. The reality of the situation coming back now. 'Listen, we've dealt with this kind of thing before. It's probably exactly what it always is. Some horrible little scrote of a boyfriend, who's decided to do a number on her. She doesn't want him arrested, so makes up a story instead. Same old, same old. I don't think it's going to be some fairytale we used to tell each other as kids, do you?'

'Suppose not,' Louise replied, but she didn't trust her own words. 'What's the plan then? We just ignore it, or do we at least look into her claims?'

'We'll take a look around, but from the word I've received from the ground, the blood trail didn't lead any further than the road. Not into any woods or the like,' Shipley said, after thinking for a few seconds. 'Not that we'll be able to see much at the moment. Not in this light. If we hadn't been stuck in that hospital for hours, maybe we'd have had time. I'll let uniform know it's an area of interest for now. Do a proper search in the morning.'

Louise went back to staring out of the passenger window as the streetlights began to slowly disappear. The road went from two normal-sized lanes to the less wide country lanes. She knew the scenery outside would have become more interesting too, if she could have seen it.

She thought of what the woman had said. How scared she had been. As if everything she had ever considered to be real had been stripped away.

Louise knew that feeling well.

'What are we going to be looking for exactly?' Louise said, filling the silence between them. 'There's not likely to have been much left behind, if she was telling the truth—'

'She isn't telling the truth,' Shipley cut in, his tone probably an attempt to lighten the mood, but just coming across to Louise as patronising. 'She can't be.'

'What if she is though? What if someone was keeping her somewhere and she escaped?'

'Well, I bet he panicked. Left everything behind and went on the run. Which means there'll be evidence – wherever the scene is. If she's telling the truth, we could be looking for a needle in a haystack and I don't like our chances. Given how little she's actually told us.'

Louise took her phone from her pocket, bringing the screen alive, then tutting when she saw the percentage of battery remaining. She left a finger over the home button, allowing the phone to read her fingerprint, then clicked on the Maps icon.

'Tracing her steps?'

'Something like that,' Louise replied, finding the road where Caroline had been discovered wandering, then scanning back down to where she guessed she had walked from. 'There's a number of fields nearby, but they wouldn't give you much privacy. I think we'll be looking more for some kind of woodland. Trees to give you cover, if you're keeping someone captive.'

'Could have been a back garden for all we know. It's not like we can rule out the idea that she may have been confused.'

'Here,' Louise said, zooming in on her phone to the closest wooded area she could find to where Caroline was found. She had been right. No more than a mile from the spot on the street where she'd collapsed. 'Next to the canal. Drive to the bottom of Tithebarn Lane, near the Bootle Arms pub. You can access it from there.'

Once the road had widened a little Shipley pulled the car over, then looked at the phone screen as Louise pointed it in his direction. 'I know that area,' he said after a pause, turning back to the road and pulling away again. 'There's no chance we can cover any of that alone. Not to any useful extent. We'll have to wait until morning and get a few uniforms sent that way.'

Louise said nothing, just moved around the map on her phone a little more for show. Silence fell on them once more, until Shipley turned in her direction again.

'You're not going to argue.'

It was a statement, rather than a question, but Louise chose to answer anyway. 'No, you're right. It wouldn't really be a good idea to go traipsing around in the dark now. We wouldn't find anything and if there is something there, we could end up missing it.'

'Still, it's unlike you not to argue against doing something like that.'

There was a slight tremble to Louise's hands as she keyed the lock button on her phone and placed it in between her legs, so it didn't fall to the floor of the car. 'I'm tired, that's all. It's been quiet recently, as you know. Not used to being out this late. I'll be fine.'

'I'll drop you off,' Shipley said, checking his mirror, then turning around in the road. 'We'll need a few hours' kip before the morning, if we're going to be spending tomorrow looking for that needle. I'll ring through to the uniforms still around. Get them to make a start on the search. You should get some rest.'

Louise was about to argue, but decided against it. There was a finality to his tone that she recognised as being useless to argue with. She eyed him from the corner of her vision. The few-days stubble, dark with patches of grey. The tanned skin that she now knew to be natural, rather than from a bottle or bed. The two-inch white scar that ran down the side of his neck, almost invisible unless you were looking for it.

The memory of how it had happened came to her then. As it did often.

Pounding steps on concrete. Her legs screaming in protest, as she desperately tried to keep up with Shipley ahead of her. The guy they were chasing even further ahead. Disappearing around a corner out of sight.

She wanted him to slow down, wait for her before rounding that blind corner, but she didn't say a word. Simply kept running, trying to keep up.

A shout.

A sound. Thud. A body dropping to the ground.

She had slowed as she reached the end of the alley, turning the corner away from the wall.

Shipley was on the ground, lying still, his chest rising and falling hard. In the distance, the suspect was becoming a dot on the landscape. She only glanced in that direction, instead focusing on the figure over Shipley. His hand to the side of his neck. Holding a knife against the skin. He was shouting at Shipley, but she couldn't hear the words. She was only focused on the blade, piercing his skin. His neck.

Shipley began to struggle, as blood appeared, but it didn't matter.

By that point, Louise was already on him.

Louise remembered the fear she'd felt as she had caught up to Shipley, seeing him lying on the ground, the blade against his skin.

The fear, then the anger. Some bloke waiting around a corner as they chased his brother from a crime scene. Angry, or stupid, enough to think stabbing a detective would allow his brother to escape. Both of them ended up locked up for a long stretch. Shipley received some kind of award for it all, but hated talking about it. She shook the memories off and concentrated on the road ahead of them.

Ten minutes later, she was standing at the edge of the path outside her house, waiting for Shipley to peel away from the kerb. She gave him a wave, sensing him having an internal battle about whether to wait until she made her way inside or to play it cooler. She turned her back, took a few steps and then stopped as she heard the car's engine kick in, then fade away.

She listened for any sound, her breathing coming in short bursts. She wanted to close her eyes and control it, but the darkness was too much.

Louise tried to recall the last time she had been afraid of going inside her own home. A ridiculous feeling, but one she struggled to ignore. Still, she stood there on the path, listening to her own breathing. No other sound, other than the wind as it rustled the small hedge around the edges of what she laughably called a front garden. There was no light within her house that she could see. She willed herself to walk a few steps, feeling more confident with every movement. Her keys were out already and when she reached the door, she took another breath, then unlocked the door and watched it swing inwards. Waited a few seconds on the doorstep, then stepped inside.

Louise flicked on the hallway light, feeling better as soon as the darkness was eliminated. Took off her shoes and began shedding the detective costume she wore during the day. She moved upstairs, filling the wash basket with the clothes she'd been wearing, then walked into the bathroom and turned on the shower.

The house was silent. Devoid of any noise other than the ones she made.

After she'd washed away the day's events, she sat on the edge of her bed, holding her mobile phone in her hand. A few months earlier, she would have called someone. Just for a chat. Simply to hear the sound of someone else's voice in the quiet of her small home, even if it was only on the other end of the phone.

Now, she was alone. The last non-police friend she'd had not answering her calls any longer. That's what she did. She got close to people, then found a way to destroy it.

The contacts list in her phone was filled with them all.

Carla – Two years since they had spoken. Fell out over who had bought the most drinks in a pub. Louise could still easily find the anger at being taken for a fool over that. Like she didn't always end up paying for most of the rounds on a night out.

Harriet – Going on four or five years. Louise had told her the truth about her boyfriend. How he'd tried to feel her up in the kitchen at a house party, which was how he'd really ended up with a broken wrist. Harriet hadn't believed her. Another friendship dead.

Sarah – Six months. She hadn't appreciated Louise's tone of voice when someone had cut them up in traffic. Or the fact she'd got out of the car and pounded on the bonnet of the car in front, when they reached the same set of lights seconds later. It wasn't Louise's fault that Sarah's baby had been in the backseat and started crying as soon as he'd heard the raised voices.

Louise thought about deleting all these memories of not being alone, but instead she locked her phone and tossed it onto the bed beside her. The closest person she had to a friend now was Paul Shipley, which was a sobering thought. She thought about the man as she dried off and changed into pyjamas. The way he looked at her sometimes, the jokes he would tell the others in the office. He was a mix of old-school and new man. Someone who wanted to do right. Someone who would enjoy putting his boot through a door, but listen to every word the person on the other side would have to say afterwards.

She thought of the others at the station. The way people would think they would be like a family. All the men and women in blue, together as brothers and sisters.

It wasn't really like that, of course, but it was the closest she was going to have right then.

Her family was dead. The last one – her grandmother – had gone three years earlier.

She was the only one left.

Five

There was a sense of an atmosphere change overnight among the uniforms, now spread out across the land near where Caroline had been found the previous day. A possibly thankless task, which Louise could see was being made more difficult by the fact that there were very few of them doing it. She could see three from where she was standing; others, she assumed, might have made it further into the undergrowth.

'We're not going to get very far without being given a better indication of where this place might be,' Shipley said, sidling up to her and handing over a Styrofoam cup of what she hoped was coffee. 'Could have been the other way for all we know. She might have got turned around somewhere and become even more confused. That's if she was in the woods at all, of course.'

'She seemed pretty adamant that's where she was.'

'Yeah, well, who are we to argue,' Shipley replied, removing the lid on his own cup and blowing on the liquid inside. 'Except being detectives who have heard stories like this for years. You know, if that counts for anything.'

'Why do I get the feeling you're not exactly invested in Caroline's story?'

Shipley took a swig of his drink, pretending he hadn't burned his mouth doing so as he turned towards Louise. 'It seems straightforward to me, but the rest of it ... no. I get it, I do. Young woman found badly assaulted. It's not like we haven't seen that kind of thing before. It just becomes much harder to deal with when they make up a story. Are we supposed to believe everything she's said so far? The Bone Keeper is suddenly a real-life person, who she escaped from? Come on.'

Louise kept quiet, wrapping her hands around the cup and staring into the fields in front of her. She knew they would be going back to speak to Caroline soon enough. She would let him talk for now. He'd picked her up that morning – her car was still parked near the original crime scene – without needing to be asked. It had become the norm more recently, him picking her up on the way to work.

She hadn't complained or questioned it, despite her knowing it wasn't exactly on his way.

'Besides, it's hardly rocket science is it,' Shipley continued, turning away a little and blowing on his coffee again. 'We know how these things usually end. We'll pick up some bloke, who'll say she had it coming or some such rubbish. I know it and so do you. What makes you so sure this time is different?'

'I never said I was,' Louise said, lifting the coffee cup to her mouth and risking a taste. 'We need to be thorough though.'

Shipley snorted in response, but didn't argue with her any further. She was glad of that. She wasn't sure she could take any more arguing that morning. She stifled a yawn, hoping he didn't notice.

'Didn't get much sleep last night?'

No such luck, Louise thought. 'Not really, no. I was thinking about all of . . . this.'

'We've been working together how many years now?'

Louise turned to Shipley, eyebrows raised, waiting for the punchline. He didn't continue, so she prompted him. 'Three. At least.'

'Right, three,' he replied, nodding his head. 'We work together well, don't we?'

The question was so out of the ordinary, Louise was stumped for a few seconds. They had been shoved together a few years earlier, when Louise finally made detective. He was the rank above her, but never made that apparent. Instead, he'd looked out for her over the years. Kept her sane, without ever realising that had become his role.

She knew he would stare at her every now and again, running through scenarios in his mind. She'd seen the looks before, many times. Only occasionally did she succumb to them.

Sometimes, she needed to feel normal.

'I think we complement each other,' she said eventually, when the silence became too much. 'I'm the one who likes to do things thoroughly, you prefer to go off half-cocked. We meet in the middle and that's usually the best way.'

Shipley said nothing for a second, then smiled. 'You're probably right with that assessment.'

'What makes you ask?'

She watched as Shipley thought for a few seconds, wondering what was going through his mind. He sighed, then took another sip of his coffee.

'I don't really know anything about you,' Shipley said finally, turning back to her. 'You know, outside of work.

Your family, your friends. After this long, you'd think I'd know that much by now.'

'There's not much to tell,' Louise replied, looking away, over the field. 'Can't imagine you would be very interested.'

'I am. That's my point. We've been working together, side by side, for at least three years, and I don't know the first thing about your life, other than the fact you live alone and never mention anything personal. What about your family, friends ... boyfriend?'

'Maybe there's just nothing to tell.'

'I doubt that,' Shipley said, a short laugh escaping his lips. 'We all have stories to tell. You know I'm from a large family. You know about my brothers, their wives, their kids. You know my parents are getting older and more annoying. What about yours?'

'Maybe there's nothing to tell because they're not around to be annoying,' she tried again, hoping he would drop the subject. She knew the moment the words passed her lips that it wouldn't.

'You've lost your parents?'

Louise thought for a second, wondering if it was the right moment to let him in. He was right – they had shared so much professionally over the years, but she had never really talked about anything other than work with him. She, of course, had listened to him drone on for hours about his own family. 'Yeah, both gone. My grandparents brought me up.'

'Brothers, sisters?'

'No,' Louise replied, feeling the familiar feeling in her chest. The tightening, restricting, choking sensation. Air slowly dissipating around her, thickening the atmosphere.

She bit down on the inside of her lower lip, experiencing the pain through the fog.

Fire burned around her for a split second, before she closed her eyes for a moment and then opened them again to reality. She could feel the air lighten around her, once more easing into her lungs without effort.

'No siblings,' she said, knowing it had only been a second or two, but also feeling as if it had been much longer. 'It's just me.'

'And you're enough,' Shipley replied, smiling at her. 'See, wasn't it nice to share after all this time.'

'Maybe you've just never asked before.'

Shipley shrugged his shoulders, the smile fading as he stared out across the grassland stretching out in front of them.

Louise stared at the side of his face for a moment longer, then turned back to face the open fields. Thankfully, they hadn't been asked to join the search. She wasn't sure she could face traipsing through the woodland right at that moment.

Knowing what could be out there.

Instead, Louise waited for as long as she thought was necessary, before pulling Shipley aside and saying it was time to go and speak to Caroline again.

The nurse on duty looked as harassed as they usually did. There was a sense of familiarity between them – not that Louise had ever dealt with her in the past; just the sense of *we do the same kind of job* she felt when talking to anyone in any of the three emergency services.

Louise kept a lid on the part of her that wanted to scream *no we don't, you have no idea what I've seen outside this hospital. The people I've met. The evil I've dealt with.*

'We've kept her in the same room,' the nurse said, making notes on a clipboard as she spoke to them. 'Didn't think she would do well on a ward. Poor lass is still suffering. Night staff said she didn't sleep much, until they gave her morphine. That gave her a few hours' rest at least.'

'Has she said anything more?'

The nurse looked from her to Shipley with a raised eyebrow. 'You mean other than the bogeyman coming to get her? No, not much else. Not that I've been in there very often. Just to keep an eye on her. She needs rest more than anything. Poor girl has been through the mill, that much is true.'

Louise had to find another lid, in order to stop herself from saying something about the use of the word 'poor'.

'We won't be in there too long,' Shipley said for them both, stepping out of the way as people passed by them in the corridor. 'We just need to ask a few more questions.'

The nurse didn't have anything else to add, leaving them to walk into the room alone. Louise felt as if it had grown darker in there in the hours since they'd been there last. The figure in the bed diminished somehow.

'Hi Caroline,' Louise said, forcing herself closer to the centre of the room. 'Do you remember us from yesterday? DC Louise Henderson and DS Paul Shipley?'

Caroline's head turned in her direction, then settled back to her original position. Staring up at the ceiling, blinking sporadically. 'Yes, I do. Have you found it yet?'

'What?' Shipley replied, taking up the space Louise vacated as she moved to the other side of the bed.

'You know . . .'

'Let's take it from the beginning,' Louise said, before Shipley could speak again. 'Do you remember a bit more about what happened now?'

Caroline nodded, so Louise continued. 'When did this start?'

'What day is it now?'

Louise gave Shipley a quick glance, which she hoped would convey one word to him. *Quiet*. 'Tuesday.'

'It was two days ago,' Caroline said, eyes still locked on the ceiling. 'Sunday. I was walking somewhere. I can't remember why. Probably for no reason. I sometimes do that. I don't remember why I walked that way, but I think I wanted to look at the canal.'

Louise had been right; Caroline was talking about the same woodland she'd pointed out to Shipley the previous night. The same land that was now being searched by uniformed officers.

She decided it wasn't the time to say *I told you so* to her superior.

'What do you remember about that walk?'

Caroline closed her eyes for a few seconds, then opened them and looked at Louise. 'It was getting dark. I couldn't really see where I was walking. There weren't any lights on the canal path. I was starting to get further from the road, so I decided to head back. That's when I could sense something.'

'What did you hear?'

'It wasn't a sound. Not in the beginning. I could smell something first. I can't describe it. It was horrible. It made me gag, almost like meat that's gone off. Rotting or something. I couldn't see where it was coming from, thought maybe an animal had died somewhere. A fox or whatever. I was retracing my steps when I heard my name being called.'

Louise tried not to react, but a quick glance in Shipley's direction told her she was being studied. She ignored it. 'Your first name? Being called?'

Caroline nodded, her hands shaking on the bed now. Her bottom lip joined in a second later. Quivering, as if it was acting on its own accord. 'It was a whisper at first, but it was so quiet on that path I heard it easily. I turned, but there was no one there. I thought I'd imagined it, so I kept walking. Then I heard it again. Louder this time. When I turned this time, something was there.'

'A man?'

Caroline didn't respond, but she didn't need to. Louise could see she was in the right area. And not, at the same time. The lip quivered more, then tears sprang to Caroline's eyes. 'Yes . . . but it wasn't like anything I've seen before. It wasn't dark, but I couldn't really see what it was. It didn't look real. It was just . . . black.'

'A black guy?' Shipley said, louder than the two women had been talking. He seemed to realise he'd broken into something and lowered his voice. 'He was a black man?'

Caroline didn't look away from Louise, but shook her head violently on the pillow. 'No, no. I don't know. It wasn't anything human. It was just darkness. Black, horrible darkness. Like a black hole, only real.'

'What happened when you saw him, Caroline?' Louise said, leaning closer to her.

'I wanted to run, but I . . . I couldn't move. It was like I was stuck there. My feet wouldn't move. It seemed to get even darker, so that I couldn't see a thing. Something moved towards me and . . .'

'Go on, Caroline,' Louise said, as Caroline's words faltered and her chest began to hitch. Tears were now flowing more freely down her cheeks as the memory of what had happened to her seemed to take hold. 'You're safe now.'

'That's it. That's all I can properly remember. Just … flashes. There was pain, so much pain. No words, no nothing. I could see eyes though. I'll never forget them. They were lifeless, soulless. There's nothing else.'

Louise caught something, a flash across Caroline's eyes as she shook her head. She recognised that moment, when a memory was suddenly there but was pushed away. Ground down into nothingness, as her mind tried to protect itself. She noticed movement in her peripheral vision; Shipley was shifting away from them – a quick glance in his direction showed him backing out of the room. She ignored it and kept talking. 'What happened in those flashes, Caroline? What do you remember?'

'Trees, woods. Being tied down. Or up, I can't really remember. I couldn't scream, even though I wanted to. There was something over my mouth.'

There would be more details in time, Louise thought. Caroline would spend months remembering small details, building a picture of what happened to her in the twenty-four hours she was held captive. The memories would perhaps resurface, or she would spend years battling to never remember. For this moment however, Louise was glad she couldn't remember all that much.

The memory would begin to hurt more over time. The helplessness, the vulnerability. Losing whatever power she had before. Those feelings would only be compounded by time.

That was how it worked. Louise knew that better than she cared to.

'How did you get away, Caroline?' Louise asked, not taking her eyes off the woman in the bed. 'How did you end up on that road?'

Caroline shook her head, blinking away more tears. 'I don't know. I don't remember. I was just suddenly . . . out. I must have broke whatever was holding me.'

There were a few seconds of silence, as Louise considered how to try to question that part of her story more.

She didn't believe her story. Something didn't feel right, especially how she came to be there in the first place. Caroline didn't look the sort to just go for walks by a strange canal. Not alone, in a place she didn't really know all that well. She was someone with a job, Louise thought. A family who would be worried about her.

Before she had a chance to say anything, Caroline spoke again.

'It wasn't there. I know that.'

'You didn't see him? He left you there?'

'No,' Caroline replied, looking back towards the ceiling now. Her voice became stronger, more sure of itself. 'No, not that. I just know. It was going to kill me. There's no way it would have let me go. No one ever gets away from it.'

'Caroline,' Louise began after a few moments of silence, bracing herself for an answer she didn't want, to a question she never liked to ask. 'Was there anything else he did? Anything—'

'Sexual?' Caroline cut in, almost whispering. 'No, nothing like that. It wasn't that kind of thing. I don't think so anyway. I felt strokes, on my arm, my stomach. Nothing else.'

'You must have had some visitors since yesterday,' Louise said, changing the subject as quickly as she could. 'Lot of people worried about you? A partner?'

'I'm single . . .'

'Your mum and dad then? Brothers and sisters, friends?'

Caroline shook her head, but didn't say anything.

'We can contact people for you, if you like?' Louise continued, refusing to believe Caroline really wanted to be alone in that place. 'The hospital really should have done that already—'

'No,' Caroline replied, her voice forceful, strong. Louise moved her hand instinctively, still remembering the way the other woman had grabbed her wrist the previous day. 'I don't want anyone knowing I'm here. I'll be fine on my own.'

'Are you sure?' Louise said, wondering how far to push this with her. 'You shouldn't be going through this alone.'

'I'm fine, honestly. I'd rather just heal up and forget this ever happened. I don't want to worry anyone.'

She knew they had been looking into Caroline's circumstances and had found very little information about her. Nothing in the system to say she'd been in contact with the police previously. Nothing that flagged up any issues, domestically or otherwise. Just a normal woman, going about her normal life. Louise made a note to check to see if workmates had been spoken to, then opened her mouth to continue asking questions, but was stopped by the door opening with a loud smack. Her head shot up, seeing Shipley standing in the doorway beckoning to her. Caroline was looking the same way as she turned back to her and mumbled an apology as she crossed the room towards him.

'They've found something,' Shipley said as she reached him, barely able to keep the glee out of his tone. 'Looks like you were right. There was a reason to find those woods.'

'What is it?' Louise replied, suspecting she knew the answer.

'A body.'

Six

Louise and Shipley were back at the woodland within half an hour, but it looked like most of Merseyside Police had beaten them to it. The place was crawling with uniformed officers, marked vehicles looking abandoned in the small road area which lay behind the Bootle Arms pub. They stretched along Rock Lane towards the church further up, where the road became even narrower.

Another CSI van pulled up just as they got out of the car. The increased presence had attracted a small crowd of bystanders closer to try to see what was happening. Louise pulled the nearest uniform towards her, indicating the roadside. 'Make sure there's crime-scene tape up as far back as here.'

The uniformed officer gave her a nod, his brow furrowed and sheened with sweat.

'What have we got then?' Shipley said to another detective constable, who had appeared as Louise moved around the car.

'Body in a shallow grave,' the DC replied, almost breathless as he tried to hide his excitement. 'Dog unit found it. Another uniform identified him pretty quickly.'

Shipley's eyes lit up. 'Really? That's good luck at least.'

'Whole scene is weird though,' the DC said, looking back in the direction that the new CSI unit was walking towards. 'Seems like whoever it was had cleared the space to do who knows what. If the woman you found yesterday was there, looks like she had a lucky escape.'

'Who's the body? And how was it identified so quickly?'

'Nathan Coldfield. Apparently the uniform had dealt with him a few times in the past. Tattoo on his forearm of his mum's face, that's how he knew it was him. Once the dog started digging, he found his arm first. Not sure if lucky is the right term in this instance, but it's definitely made our job easier.'

'Where's the site?' Louise said, earning a questioning look from the DC, who then turned back to Shipley.

'About two hundred yards into the treeline up there,' the DC said, pointing in the direction of the woodland. 'There's farms on both sides, separated by these woods. You wouldn't even know they were there from the roadside.'

Louise knew that to be the case. There were hundreds of areas like this in the city. Thousands, maybe. Hidden pockets, where anyone could disappear and never be seen again. Or found. The thought chilled her bones, the idea that there could be anything out there, in the city. Disappeared, never to be found.

Your bones he'll keep.

'We best go and have a look,' Shipley said, not waiting for Louise to follow as he started moving. 'Not that CSI will let us get too close.'

'Won't be a problem,' the DC replied, leading the way. 'There's enough other stuff to see.'

It didn't take long for them to walk across the field, Louise stepping carefully as she moved. She wondered which direction Caroline would have run once she was released. She imagined it was the opposite way from where they were walking, towards the more noticeable buildings in the distance. Disorientated, she would have looked for lights. Signs of life. The direction from which Louise and the other two detectives had walked would have looked dark and uninviting even that early in the evening.

She wouldn't have wanted to go towards the unknown.

There were uniformed officers moving towards them, but they paid them no attention. Focused only straight ahead, to what lay within the trees. What was hidden from view.

A few minutes later, Louise was ducking beneath a branch, searching for a path that wasn't there. 'People don't usually come into these woods,' the DC said, falling back and walking next to her. 'No paths or anything. We've been trying to keep to one place when walking, just in case.'

'Lead the way then,' Louise replied, stopping and waiting until the DC was ahead of them. She fell into line at the rear, glancing to either side as they walked further in, the trees becoming thicker around them.

'We'll have to wait here, but you can see through can't you?'

Shipley took up the space vacated by the DC, moving a low-hanging branch away a little and revealing a small clearing. The available space was being taken up by various people in forensic suits, as the operation began to take hold.

'What am I looking at?' Shipley asked the DC, but Louise didn't need to be told. She had already spotted the markings on the trees opposite them.

Inverted crosses, marked into the trunks of two or three trees. Then, more, as she continued to scan the wood. Louise held her breath, feeling her heart beat against her chest as she looked across the clearing. The horror of the scene in front of her.

'He's real,' she whispered. Shipley shot her a questioning look, but she shook her head. 'What are those marks?' she said, diverting his attention as she could see him trying to work out what she'd said. He turned in the direction she was pointing.

'Don't know, but it looks like some kind of circle.'

Louise absent-mindedly rubbed the top of her thigh as she struggled to take her eyes away from the marks.

'It's something inside a circle,' Shipley continued, turning back towards her. 'What the hell is this?'

'Nothing good, sir,' the DC said from Louise's side. 'Looks to me like some kind of devil-worshipping thing. They look familiar though.'

Louise wanted to disagree, to tell him he was wrong. She had seen the marks before. Carved into school desks, onto the front of exercise books. They had been everywhere when she was younger. She imagined Shipley would recognise them eventually, he had surely experienced them before as well. Instead, she moved forward a step, bringing into view more of the clearing. There were more marks on the tree trunks surrounding the small area; the earth on the ground in the middle was well-trodden. Muddy and turned up.

'How long until they remove the body?'

Louise continued to scan the clearing as Shipley and the DC talked, looking for something she felt was missing. A sign that he'd been there. More than the marks. Some scent left behind. She thought of what Caroline had described. The rotting meat smell. She imagined it settling on the ground, the bark of the trees. Being absorbed and becoming one with the surroundings.

It wasn't there.

'No idea, sir. I'll get a CSI over.'

She moved a little further over, but it was no use. There was no way of seeing any more without stepping into what was now a crime scene and incurring the wrath of some CSI.

'Louise, are you coming?'

'Yeah,' she replied, forcing herself to tear her gaze away from the clearing and what lay there. 'Sorry.'

'That's okay,' Shipley said, softly as they traced their steps back towards the larger field. 'This is turning into something unexpected. I guess we're looking at a completely different case than I thought.'

'I guess so. It's about time you were wrong about one though.'

'Doesn't happen very often,' Shipley said with a laugh. 'Let's get a move on before Major Crimes gets involved. We'll be sidelined when they eventually turn up. You know what they're like.'

Louise murmured agreement, wondering if that was something she wanted or not. Whether being taken away from the case would be a good thing, or if she needed to stay close to it. To know what was happening at every step in the investigation. It was already moving in a direction she hadn't really expected. A body found, without warning. What had begun as a young woman being found on the street assaulted, saying that name over and over, was now looking like a murder investigation.

She could feel excitement within her, the chance to do something at last.

'Are we going to do the death knock then?' Louise said, once they were out of the woods and on the farmland. 'Even with just one uniform's possibly dodgy identification?'

'There'll already be liaison officers making their way to the address,' Shipley replied, that strong jawline of his tensing. 'We can tag along and see if we can get a head start.'

'Okay, I'm with you.'

'Those marks . . . I know where I've seen them before.'

Louise held her breath, waiting for Shipley to work it out. 'Yeah?'

'The crosses and circles,' Shipley continued, stopping as they reached the end of the field. 'That's supposed to be his mark, right? What he's supposed to leave behind?'

'That's the myth,' Louise replied, shrugging her shoulders, but battling against the excitement and dread growing inside her. 'All part of the same story.'

'Maybe there's more to it than I thought. I'm not saying the bogeyman is real, but it's starting to look like someone is trying to make us think it is.'

Louise didn't reply, instead leaving Shipley to think about it more. She walked away, knowing he'd follow her. After reaching the roadside once more, calling over the uniform who had identified the body and getting the details from him, they got back in the car. The radio was repeatedly crackling into life as the news of the discovery began to take hold. It seemed as if nothing else was happening in the city – the only story being discussed was what was happening in that small patch of woodland.

Louise wondered if this was the beginning. Whether there would be more bodies to be found. She had seen it etched on the faces of all those in the woods. The fear, the excitement. She could see it written all over Shipley's face now as well. The idea that they had stumbled into something.

She wondered how long they could contain it for. When the outside world would begin to talk about the local legend as a real threat to them.

Within half an hour they were pulling up outside a nondescript terraced house, on a notorious council estate twenty minutes out of the city centre. This was the other side of Liverpool. One she saw less often now, since she'd left her days in uniform and moved to work further north in the city, where it was more affluent. The streets of graffiti-laden walls and unkempt grass verges. Metal gates at the end of alleyways, piles of broken furniture behind them. Net curtains twitching as yet another strange vehicle turned up.

They parked behind a marked police car; there was another that she knew to be an unmarked one in front of that.

'They've moved quickly,' she said, snapping off her seatbelt as Shipley pulled up the handbrake. 'Not messing around.'

Shipley went to answer, but a cry from the doorway of the house closest to them made them both look that way instead.

'I'm guessing someone has just been told the bad news.'

Louise could only nod her head as Shipley grimaced, then looked back towards the house.

Seven

Louise rocked on her feet, waiting for the uniformed officer to finally leave the room. When he was gone, she let out a long breath. There was silence now; the mother of the man they had found in the woodland had been taken to the morgue, she guessed. Waiting for her son's arrival there. She found herself thinking about how the woman would be feeling at that moment. Whether she could see something of herself in there. She'd been a part of so many death knocks over the years, but could never really find a normal response.

She knew the answer was different for everyone. No one ever dealt with these moments the same.

Some would cry and wail. Scream and shout. Others would retreat into themselves. Some would find God, praying for a different outcome or for some peace.

Then, there were the ones who would try to never even think about the act or what had happened to their loved one. They wouldn't want to know the truth. They would simply pretend it had never occurred. That the person they had loved and lost had never existed. That the loss didn't have any effect on them.

The room was still, sun bleeding through the net curtains in the bay window. Louise walked towards the light, picking up a photo frame from the sill. An unseen draught rippled the nets a little as she lifted up the photograph. She traced a finger over the face of the young boy pictured there and wondered if it belonged to the body currently being unearthed.

The look of innocence, before age ripped it away.

'At least we didn't have to break the bad news.'

Louise jumped at the sound of Shipley's voice, then placed the photo back down in its place. She turned and gave him a tight smile. 'Small mercies.'

'She's got another child,' Shipley said, seemingly not noticing her reaction. 'Anna, thirty years old. So, I'm guessing most of the pictures are of the victim.'

He held her stare for a second longer, then broke away, looking around the room. Louise followed his gaze, seeing the multitude of photographs on every available surface. Four on the walls above the leather sofa. More on a sideboard. A couple on the mantelpiece. All from different stages of his life. School images, dressed up in uniforms which probably fit well at the beginning of the year, but looked more uncomfortable by the time the pictures were taken.

'She's not taking it well at all.'

'Would you?' Louise replied, a little more harshly than she'd intended. Shipley didn't seem to notice, so she kept talking. 'He's obviously the golden child. There's barely any pictures of the daughter. I bet you anything he was always in trouble, her little rogue. The daughter will have been nice and normal – just enough to slip under the radar and never get any attention.'

'He was living here off and on according to the uniforms who got here first. He would just turn up unannounced and stay a few days.'

'Then disappear off again,' Louise said, finishing the thought. 'Heard this one before. Transient lifestyle, relying on the backup of a parent when things get a little too tough.'

'Probably why he wasn't reported missing. She didn't know anything had happened to him. Going to be tough creating a timeline because of that. We don't know the exact day he disappeared or was taken, unless we can find associates willing to talk. Or when he died, without the post-mortem, of course.'

'Did he have his own room?'

Shipley nodded, extending an arm towards the doorway and up the stairs beyond it. Louise took the lead, taking the steps up two at a time, reaching the small landing area in seconds. She waited for Shipley to catch up and then opened the closest door. She moved on, as she revealed nothing more than a bathroom, then reached for another as Shipley made it onto the landing. The main bedroom door had been left ajar, easily and instantly recognisable as the sleeping quarters of an older woman. Louise removed gloves from a packet in her pocket and placed them over her pale hands.

'She said he keeps some personal stuff up here, but nothing she thinks will help,' Shipley said, waiting behind Louise as she checked another room. 'She's been through it all before. We might be able to spot something that wouldn't make sense to her, I suppose. Probably need to put on gloves.'

'Of course,' Louise replied, turning to Shipley and revealing her hands already adorned. 'Always thinking ahead, sir.'

Shipley smiled at her, showing teeth which were almost perfect apart from a couple of minor crooked ones on the bottom row. 'How many times do I have to tell you? Don't call me sir. I'm not that old. Makes me feel middle-aged. I'm only a few years older than you.'

At least five or six, Louise thought, but didn't say it aloud. 'I'm supposed to call you Shipley? That doesn't feel right.'

'How about you call me Paul, like I've asked you to a million and one times?' Shipley replied, his face relaxing as he stopped smiling. 'That is my name, after all. We've been working with each other long enough for you to call me by name.'

Louise hummed a reply, turning her back on Shipley. 'Paul it is,' she said, pushing open another door. She stepped within and blew out a surprised breath. 'Christ, we've just travelled back in time.'

'It's like a museum.'

Hanging on the wall, one side drooping down a little – the Blu-Tack holding it there had finally given up the ghost – was a poster featuring the Gallagher brothers in typical Mancunian gurning pose. Next to that, an Everton team photo from almost two decades earlier. On the wall opposite, a poster for the film *Trainspotting*.

'How old was he exactly?' Louise said, moving into the room. 'I realise I should have asked that earlier.'

'Thirty-two apparently,' Shipley replied, standing in the doorway with his hands on his hips, shaking his head as he looked around the room. 'I'm not sure he's lived here at all since the nineties, looking at this place. It's like Britpop threw up in here.'

'Obviously just never got around to updating his decor.

Or just enjoyed the nostalgia of it all. Maybe it was a reminder of better times.'

'I could be in my own teenage bedroom here,' Shipley continued, crossing the room and picking up a Stereophonics CD from the bedside table, then placing it back down. The alarm clock sitting beside it blinked numbers in red light, showing a time that would have been correct nine hours earlier. 'Make a start on that chest of drawers there. I'll see if there's anything in here.'

Louise turned and moved over to the chest of drawers, which stood opposite the bed. There was the sound of a drawer opening in the bedside table and a quiet exclamation followed quickly. Louise continued with her own search. She bent over, removing the bottom drawer and placing it on the floor. She dropped to her knees and began rifling through what was inside, going through old receipts, a *Loaded* magazine from almost two decades earlier, scraps of paper with various scribblings on them. Phone numbers that would have to be checked but which she imagined were probably out of use now. Landline numbers from back when everyone used them instead of mobiles.

A few packets of Rizlas, yellowing with age. A box of filter-tips, a squashed cheap cigar and a few old coins.

'Anything over there yet?' Shipley said.

Louise began separating what she'd found into piles. 'Just a load of rubbish probably.'

'Just old underwear and T-shirts over here. About what we'd expect, I suppose. You haven't found anything about the Bone Keeper then?'

She could hear the lightness in Shipley's tone; he was trying to show that he was joking, but she knew he would be having second and third thoughts about his initial feelings. 'Nothing jumps out at me.'

'He'd be the right age for when it was at its height, I think,' Shipley said, his voice growing quiet, almost as if he was remembering his own history with the local myth. 'It was huge in the late eighties, through the nineties. Makes you wonder if they still talk about it now?'

'I imagine so,' Louise replied, knowing from an earlier search online that it was true. She would eventually lead Shipley to look at it himself, but for now she was content to let it bubble under the surface. 'Kids aren't really that different these days. They'll still be finding ways to scare each other.'

'True. It's an old story though. You'd think they would have moved past it onto something else by now, surely?'

'The old ones are the best. Most people our age have probably passed it down to their kids by now.'

'When did you first hear the story?'

Louise paused, thinking back to the time her brother had first mentioned the name.

He's called the Bone Keeper. He hides in the woods and takes people away. You remember Dennis, who lived in the road behind us?

They moved, didn't they?

That's what the grown-ups want us to think, Lou. He went missing and never came back. They were so scared that they moved to get away from the Bone Keeper. He was going to come after them next.

You're lying . . .

Why don't you go into the woods on your own then? If you think I'm lying, go and look for yourself.

Louise smiled to herself, remembering her brother's

impish grin as he tried to cajole her into believing in the
legend. She had so few memories of him that the ones she
did have she held onto with a vice-like grip. She never had
gone into the woods alone though. Not even as she grew
older.

She hadn't needed to.

'Must have been at school,' Louise said eventually, not
turning to look at Shipley in case he caught the lie. 'Same
way as everyone else. There was something in the woods.
He would take people away. Make them disappear. Almost
as if they'd never existed. He'd slice your flesh and keep
your bones. That old chestnut. You wouldn't hear him
coming, almost like a ghost—'

'Or a monster,' Shipley said quietly, then shook off the
word with a shudder, as he seemed to recall a time when
he thought of those things.

'Right. Only, we don't believe in ghosts or monsters do
we? Things that hide in the woods and make people disappear? We grow up and realise it was all just stories we
used to scare each other. It's just a story.'

'Those markings on the trees . . . probably kids, right?'

'Would be some coincidence if they were. I mean, in the
same place as we actually found a body?'

She didn't get a further response, so took the next
drawer out and continued her search. The sun suddenly
decided to show its face, blaring through the single-paned
window between her and Shipley. Dust motes danced in
the air in the space between them, becoming increasingly
abundant the more the pair moved things around in the
bedroom.

The second drawer didn't yield the same results as the
first, containing instead a few old annuals – *Beano* and

Match – an old *Guinness Book of World Records* and a couple of knackered electronic toys. Unwanted Christmas present drawer, she thought to herself with a smile, remembering that she'd had something similar when she was a teenager. Usually filled with cheap hair straighteners, ropey perfume and various other bits her grandparents had thought would count as something she'd actually want. Another thirty minutes of searching the room didn't produce anything more.

'One day, I'm telling you, the answer will be left on a whiteboard for us,' Shipley said, standing up from checking behind the small radiator. 'It'd make things much easier. Wouldn't have to go through someone's underwear drawer, for a start.'

'That actually happened to me once.'

Shipley stopped in his tracks and turned towards Louise, eyebrows raised. 'Really?'

'Yeah,' Louise replied, looking around the bedroom for a stone left unturned. 'Well, not a whiteboard, as such. I was looking into the welfare of someone when I was in uniform. A young girl, can't have been much older than seventeen. She was living with an older man and the parents didn't approve. Probably right to, considering what happened. Can't remember her name now. Anyway, we go to the last known address and don't get an answer. Sergeant gives us the okay to break in and we get through the door quite easy. In the hallway, propped up against the stairs, is a chalkboard. Says on it "She's in the shed. She wouldn't stop arguing with me. Please bury us together."'

'Well, that was nice of him.'

'We expected to find him dead, but he was lying on

the bathroom floor holding a razor blade. Couldn't bring himself to do it, could he? Turns out she wasn't dead either. Just locked in the shed, with a blanket thrown over her. He thought he'd killed her during an argument, but he'd just fractured her skull.'

'Do you ever think our job would be boring without domestic violence? Like we wouldn't have much to do?'

'We're here now, aren't we? This doesn't look like a couple who've had an argument and the bloke has done his partner in.'

'Unless Nathan was seeing Caroline and she's just confused, of course.'

'Yes, that's usually what happens. People have an argument, then you kill yourself and bury your own body in some woods.'

'What if it was the other way around?'

'So, Caroline slices herself up after burying her boyfriend? If we find a link between the two of them maybe, but I have a feeling these two will never have met before.'

Shipley clearly couldn't disagree with her, so turned his back instead and pulled away the chest of drawers Louise had inspected from the wall. She moved out of his way, still thinking about the long list of domestic incidents she'd investigated over the years. One day, she wanted to work out the percentage of her cases over the years that had been the result of arguments which had 'got out of hand', as her least favourite phrase went.

She imagined it was high.

She'd thought about how someone could be pushed to that point of no return. How love could turn to hate in an instant, the desire to hurt overwhelming a person in one moment and changing lives forever. The level of toxicity needed to snap in that instant, wanting to hurt the one you supposedly loved more than anyone.

Frustration boiling over and turning to violence.

Was any killer different? Did everyone have that capacity for brutality within themselves?

'There's nothing of interest behind these drawers,' Shipley said, breaking into her train of thought. Louise welcomed it, a brief reprieve from the muddled thinking that was beginning to invade her mind. 'Or anywhere else in here.'

'There's a few bits and bobs in the bottom drawer, but nothing that screams evidence to me. Give me a hand with moving this bed. Let's see if there's anything better underneath.'

Shipley shook his head and mumbled something under his breath, but still moved to help her. Probably at his own mistake of not checking himself. They lifted the bed and moved it closer to the door, revealing what was underneath. Old magazines, scattering as they moved the furniture which had held the pile in place. Louise could see from the covers that they were more explicit than the copy of *Loaded* she had found earlier. Old tissues had been stuffed down the side of the bed, now disseminated alongside the magazines, matted together. Louise decided not to move them any further.

The smell was murkier now, dissipating and rising around them.

Shipley stood up fully and wrinkled his nose as the smell reached him. 'Quite usual for a teenage boy's room, but this guy was much older. No excuse. Still, at least it's in keeping with the rest of the room.'

Louise didn't reply, instead getting down on her haunches and lifting a few magazines up to inspect the covers. 'These aren't *Razzle* or *Playboy* though,' she said, lifting one up and showing Shipley. 'I don't read Dutch or German, or whatever language these are in, but I don't think you can get these in this country.'

She waited for Shipley to realise what she was showing him, then felt better when he shook his head in disgust. '*Bloedschande*. I know what that means.'

'Go on . . .'

'Incest. And these girls don't look over the age of consent, if you ask me. I'm guessing they haven't exactly been brought in legally.'

Louise nodded and leafed through a few more of the magazines, seeing similar images peering back at her. She created a pile of them and shoved them to one side. She moved further over and spotted something in the corner that must have shifted when they'd moved the bed. She lifted the photograph up, scanning the image. She recognised the place pictured.

'What have you got there?'

Louise didn't respond, instead looking more closely at the photograph. She turned it over, reading the words printed on the reverse, her heart beating faster as she did so. She tried to control her breathing, but was unable to stop the shaking that started up in her hand.

'Come on, what are you looking at?' Shipley said, harder now. He dropped to his haunches next to her, giving her no opportunity to hide the photograph.

'Looks like the same guy from the pictures downstairs,' he said, taking the photograph from her hands. 'Bit older, of course. Probably quite recent as well.'

Louise continued to stay quiet, waiting for Shipley to turn over the photograph.

'The place looks familiar, but I can't work it out ...'

'South of the city,' Louise whispered, then cleared her throat. 'I mean, it could be anywhere, I suppose.'

'No, I think you're right,' Shipley said, bringing the photograph closer to him. 'Not sure what's significant about it.' He turned the photograph over and froze.

Louise waited as Shipley read what was written there and then snapped his gaze towards her.

'Well. This changes things a fair bit.'

On the reverse side of the photograph, in scribbled letters, the letters TBK, then, underneath, RD, and one word. *Real.*

Eight

There was a moment just before it happened. A pause, just before he was taken, which could have changed everything that happened after. If he could go back to any moment in his life, it would be that one. The chance to change what was to come. An opportunity to save himself the pain and agony that followed.

It wasn't the way he was supposed to die. Not in pain. Not this soon.

Carl Groves knew how people described him. He was a bum, a waste of oxygen, a stain on society. Someone to be ignored, rather than noticed. It didn't matter what had happened in his life, he was to be judged on his current state and that was it. He was bothered by it less and less now. Screw everyone and their opinions. They were no better than him or any of the thousands of other people in the same position. They were all one bad decision away from being sat outside an ATM or shop begging for spare change. That was how easy it was for anyone to end up in the same hole he found himself in.

For Carl, things had taken a lot longer than one bad decision. For the most part, it was a range of terrible decisions, made by other people who were supposed to be looking after him, that had done the job.

That's how he found himself at nineteen years of age, trying to scrape together a few quid so he could buy himself some tobacco and scratch the itch he'd been feeling since he woke that morning. The shelter he'd been staying at provided food – for what it was worth – and water, but he had spent his dole money within a couple of days, so was forced to do the usual. It always amazed him what people threw away in the street. In a hurry, trying to catch a bus, chucking half a cigarette away without thinking. A half-empty bottle of juice, or something more substantial, to tide him over until they served a meal back at the shelter.

Wandering through the streets wasted time. That was all he had, after all. Hours upon hours, with nothing else to do. No plans or places to go. No friends to meet up with. Nothing to do, other than walk. And walk. And walk.

Sometimes he wouldn't have the energy to go as far as he'd like to, but almost every day he made the same circuit. The shelter was in a built-up area in the city, but if you walked five or ten minutes in any direction you were suddenly on country lanes, green fields and trees at each side. Barely any traffic, as he shuffled slowly alongside grass verges, stepping up any time a car passed him by.

It would fill his time every day, simply doing the same walk. Kicked out of the shelter at 9 a.m., back at five or six in the afternoon; he needed something to fill those hours.

Nineteen years of age and already the future looked bleak. It could have been worse though, he thought as he continued his usual walk. He could have been dead already. He had escaped abuse and violence; his mum hadn't been as lucky. He hadn't gone to the funeral. It was too difficult. Nobody should have to be fourteen years old and grieving for a lost parent.

He wasn't sure how long his dad had got sentenced for. Wasn't interested. He had left the city of his birth and moved south, to Liverpool, looking for a better life. Ended up on the streets, of course, as it was never easy to leave the past behind you.

There was still no moment other than that single instant of time, just when he sensed the change beside him. Just before the darkness came. Nothing before that he could have changed even if he had tried. His life was set from birth. He supposed he could have gone back and tried to stop his own arrival into the world, but that was a stretch. No, it wouldn't have been any other point in time.

Carl could have been somewhere else. Anywhere else. Maybe, if his reflexes had been better, he could have seen it coming. As it was, as the sun dipped behind the clouds on its way to the other side of the world, he didn't even see the darkness before it swallowed him whole.

Only a dull thud. No instant pain, or scream of agony. A single flash of light suddenly encroaching on his world, then his legs giving way. Things had become blurry then, as something moved his body, dragging him away from the lane. Into the bushes and what lay beyond that.

He had tried to lift his head, but it didn't respond. He remembered more flashes, more blows. There was a slow pulse in the back of his skull. Still no pain.

That would come later.

He had slipped into unconsciousness easily, without warning. When he came to, he couldn't move. Every limb screamed as he tried to move it, every movement of his head sending shockwaves of pain flashing through him.

His head slumped forward; he was coughing with the agony of it. Bile rose in his throat, spewing out of his mouth without warning. His entire body was racked with hurt. He opened his eyes and tried to look around, but it had become dark while he'd been out cold.

Confusion surrounded him. Nothing made sense. What had happened, where he was. As his head cleared a little more, he tried to work out how he had ended up there. It didn't help that he didn't know where *there* was.

The sky above him darkened a little more, and then he realised a shadow had fallen across him. Only, that didn't work logically, as it was dark. It was evening. No sun to make a shadow.

That was when the smell hit him.

He had experienced that odour before. On the streets in the city centre. In the middle of the night, trying to find somewhere he wouldn't be moved on from. An alleyway in town, nearby clubs finally winding down their noise levels. Unsuspecting fellow young people, stumbling away in search of a taxi or night bus home. Never knowing what was only a few feet away.

That odour had been in the alleyway. The undiscovered body of someone who had finally given up. He had expected the body to be stiff as he rifled through pockets and took what he could, but it had been soft and pliable. There a couple of days, he thought. The smell would soon lead people to him, but he had got there first.

Two quid and five cigarettes.

It was the stench of death. Standing over him. He couldn't see the face, or any features at all. It was just darkness, looming, looking at him, as he lay helpless on the floor.

Hard floor. Ground. Outside. Wind brushed through leaves, so it was somewhere in the nearby fields, he guessed. The hidden countryside in the major northern city.

No one would hear him if he shouted. Not that he could. He realised his breathing was shallow, blocked from being able to take enough oxygen into his lungs.

Something had been placed over his mouth.

Why me? Carl thought. There were so many other people who deserved to be in this position, rather than him.

The shadow looming over him moved slightly, giving his eyes another chance to focus on his surroundings as much as they could. He squinted into the darkness, trying to hear any movement, but it was silent all around him. Only the wind, sporadically, rustling against whatever foliage was nearby.

The voice, when it came, was unlike any he had ever heard. It startled him, wet in his ear. Whispered, full of intent. Inhuman. Stripped of anything that was recognisable.

It wasn't real. It couldn't be.

'I've been waiting for you.'

A song exploded in his head. Back at the shelter, there had been talk of this . . . thing who lived in the woods. Of other homeless people going missing, never seen again.

Of a local myth, who was waiting for them in the darkness.

The Bone Keeper's coming. The Bone Keeper's real. He doesn't stop. He doesn't feel . . .

He could feel the tears falling down his cheeks as the first cut was made. The skin on his stomach being sliced into, a stinging sensation that quickly grew. He opened his mouth to cry out, but something blocked his shout. He tried to struggle, but he was pinned to the floor, able to move only his eyes around to catch glimpses of what was happening to him.

He'll snatch you up. And make you weep ...

Carl could hear the voices of those other waifs and strays at the shelter. Talking late at night, in hushed tones, of the ghost that walked among them. The legend of their childhoods. Their voices had been light, but he knew now they'd been scared.

They had known to be afraid of what lay out there. Waiting for them.

He'll slice your flesh. Your bones he'll keep.

Nine

The room was cold, the single radiator not sparking to life for a reason Louise couldn't work out. Not that it seemed to bother Shipley. He was sitting behind one side of the table, making notes in silence, an impassive look on his face. She leaned against the wall to his side, studying him in profile.

There's trust between them. A bond. That's how it works in the police. It doesn't need to be voiced. They are there for each other, no matter what. They're a team, a screwed-up family.

Not a family. A family has secrets.

They're not supposed to have those.

Louise wondered if there was anything he was keeping from her at that moment. Everyone had secrets and she was curious to know what Shipley's were. There was something going on behind those dark, almost Mediterranean features of his. He was pleasing to look at, the character in his face, the scars and marks telling their own stories. She looked for any tell, a moment when he would give himself away. A flash of clarity which would reveal his inner workings to her.

There was nothing, of course. She wasn't Derren Brown.

Louise wondered if Shipley kept things from her, the same way she kept things from him. Whether that was just the human condition. Never telling the entire truth. Lies growing with little work, becoming the norm.

'You're staring at me again,' Shipley said, without looking up from the notes in front of him. 'It's becoming disconcerting.'

'Sorry, mind was wandering,' Louise replied, lifting herself away from the wall and walking away to the small window. She faced away from him, hoping he didn't see the blush rise to her cheeks. 'Any plan for how we approach this with the mum?'

She heard the chair scrape back a little, then a sigh from him. 'Well, now she's positively identified him, I guess we have to find out the usual. Let's forget the woman—'

'Caroline.'

'Yes, I know her name, Louise,' Shipley replied, a little abruptly. Louise could hear the grin behind the tone, however. 'We've been to her house, looked into her life. We can't find any connection to Nathan Coldfield at all. In fact, it doesn't seem like she has any connection to anyone. She's a loner. A boring life, exactly as she described. Just a lonely woman, who happened to stumble across something, by the looks of things. What I'm saying is, let's treat this as we would any other murder. See who his closest acquaintances are, where she saw him last, etcetera. Then we can move onto the other aspects of this.'

Louise turned around, hoping the colour in her face had returned to normal. Shipley had already gone back to writing up what they'd learned up to then, so it mattered little anyway.

Nathan Coldfield's mother had met her son's body at the morgue near the city centre, IDing him within seconds, they had been told. They had also been informed that this was now a murder investigation, which wasn't exactly surprising. Major Crimes Unit would be getting involved soon enough, Louise guessed. She thought that they would stay involved with the case, given the dwindling resources available across the city, but she could still feel the tension emanating from Shipley.

He didn't want to be left behind.

They were waiting for Nathan's mother to join them in the room, so they could question her further. Louise had done this numerous times before, but the atmosphere felt different now. More charged, less familial. It had been a while since they last investigated a possible murder, so she put it down to that.

The looming presence of a local legend didn't help matters.

Louise pulled out her phone, flicking through various news stories, finding the scant information that had been released about the unfolding one she was a part of now. It was more newsworthy for the local press, but the national websites had smaller pieces, with little detail. Something told her that wouldn't be the case for very long, though. She pressed the home button and clicked on one of the social media apps she kept on the home screen. Fake name on her account, like so many others in the police did these days. Twitter opened and she searched for mentions of the body's discovery. Scrolled through a few tweets and then opened the search box again.

She typed *The Bone Keeper* and began scrolling.

'Didn't take long,' she said to herself softly, still staring at the screen but sensing Shipley looking up at her. 'It's already being talked about on Twitter.'

'I hate that thing,' Shipley replied, but didn't look back down at his notes. 'What's being said?'

'Just a few mentions about the Bone Keeper possibly being responsible. People wondering if the guy was murdered in the woods because he stumbled into its home or something. Some jokes. Memes. Nothing substantial.'

'That'll change if it gets out that victims have talked about it.'

A knock disturbed them both, Shipley jumping to his feet as the door opened. Louise stuffed her phone back in her pocket as a uniform led Nathan Coldfield's mother through without a word, knowing they were waiting for her. A thin-faced woman, who from the way she carried herself didn't seem to have ever had anything good happen in her life. Light blonde hair, through which grey roots were showing. Lines creasing her face, yet her eyes were blue and welcoming.

There were a few pleasantries exchanged before they got to the point all parties knew was coming. Louise could see she was still in the shocked state most family members found themselves in after something like this had happened. Eyes widened, trying to take in everything around her, which would only be a blur in a few hours' time. She was never surprised by their varying reactions; everyone was different, after all. Barbara Coldfield was on the normal end of the spectrum, from what she could tell. The paleness, hands shaking almost imperceptibly, eyes that wouldn't – or couldn't – fix on them. They finally fell on the wall to the side of them, and she was seemingly lost in her own thoughts.

Louise preferred this type, for the most part. When they began to wail and cry and blame everyone in their path, things were more difficult. Similarly, when they had too many questions, for which she usually couldn't provide an answer, it only served to make her uncomfortable.

'Are you okay to answer a few questions, Mrs Coldfield?' Louise said, leaning forward and closer to the older woman. 'We won't keep you much longer.'

'It's not like I have anywhere else to go,' Barbara replied, eyes wandering slowly over to where Louise was sitting. 'It's not Coldfield anyway. Not anymore. But you can call me Barbara.'

'Thank you, Barbara,' Louise continued, putting on her usual soothing tone. It always seemed to work with people of a certain age. 'Do you remember when you last saw Nathan?'

'It's been a few weeks. He's in and out, if that makes sense. Towards the end of September, I know that much. If I'd known it was going to be the last time . . . I don't know. Maybe I would have paid more attention to the date.'

Louise listened to Barbara's soft Liverpudlian accent, wondering if she was from the city originally or had lived elsewhere in her childhood. It was difficult to tell now.

'And you didn't report him missing? Was this normal behaviour?'

'Yes, that's right,' Barbara replied, her gaze drifting to the wall behind Louise, then back to her. 'He would do this constantly. If he had ever gone missing, I'm not sure I would have noticed. Not for months anyway. Although . . . he did miss my birthday. Last week. He's never done that before. Even with all his troubles.'

Shipley gave Louise a quick glance, a look she interpreted

as being a request to continue in the same vein and not expect him to jump in this early. That had been the agreed plan: she would deal with everything light, he would deal with the trouble. She continued to ask further questions, but learned little more. It was soon his turn.

'Has anything else happened to make you think there was a reason he may not have been in touch?' Shipley said, providing his own attempt at a soothing tone. It wasn't as perfect as Louise's, but then, he'd always been better in different scenarios.

Not that she hadn't proven herself in that department more than once.

'No contact from friends,' Shipley continued, making notes as he spoke. 'Other family members or anything like that?'

Barbara shook her head, which seemed to take more effort than it should have. 'No, nothing at all. I don't really know anything about his friends. No one else in the family had heard from him either. Not that he kept in close contact with any of them anyway.'

'What was he like on the last day you saw him? Anything out of the ordinary?'

'Nothing at all from what I can remember,' Barbara said, a hitch in her breath as she spoke. She swallowed, still hanging on and not breaking down. 'He was the same as he'd always been. Especially in those last few years. He came home a few days before that, was fed and watered, slept a lot. I don't think he'd slept much in the weeks before he'd come back.'

'Did he do that a lot? Go away for a while then just turn up?'

'Yes, that was the way he was. Wouldn't see him for

weeks, months even. Then he'd show up out of the blue like nothing had happened. I never questioned him about it. Maybe I should have done.'

Louise could sense that their time was limited now. The reality was beginning to set in for Barbara. The sudden knowledge that what she had dreaded was true. She decided to jump in now, before it was too late. 'When you said troubles, earlier, what did you mean about that?'

'I didn't pay much attention. I just wanted him to be safe.'

'But you knew he had been in contact with the police on a number of occasions,' Shipley said, cutting in after Louise's set-up. He turned over a page of the file on the table for the first time since Barbara had entered. 'Multiple times, for a whole range of offences.'

'He was a good boy. Never in trouble growing up. He just got mixed up in the wrong crowd.'

Shipley went over the dates of Nathan Coldfield's arrests, listing some here and there. Louise could hear his tone of voice change, as he struggled to hold back from saying what he wanted to.

The obvious. Almost twenty years of breaking the law was a long time to be mixed up in the wrong crowd.

'Did you know about the things he was accused of doing over the years?'

Barbara fixed him with a stare now. 'I'm not sure what this has to do with what's happened to my son, detective.'

'We have to cover everything, Barbara, I'm sorry.'

She gave a long sigh and a shake of the head towards Shipley. 'He would sometimes call me, but he would never let me go to court or anything like that. He used to say that he was always just in the wrong place at the wrong time.

That once you're thought to be a certain type of person, then you'll always be a target. An easy one.'

It was becoming increasingly shaky ground, but Louise listened as Shipley pushed on regardless. 'Some of the offences were minor, but there are some more serious ones on this list. Is it possible that he got himself mixed up in something he couldn't control?'

'I think the fact I've just had to identify his body would say that was right,' Barbara replied, a steel that hadn't been there before now present in her voice. Louise realised Barbara was just the same as most of the parents she had encountered. He wasn't a *bad lad* or a *criminal*. Those things happened to him, rather than him making the choice to do them himself.

Normal then, Louise thought. Typical.

'Someone has killed my boy,' Barbara continued, her voice quieter now. 'I don't know if that's because he got himself into trouble now and again, or because someone else saw him as an easy target, just like your friends in uniform did. I just want you to find out which it is.'

'Was there anyone in particular Nathan was close to before his disappearance?' Louise said, changing tack before she was forced to promise something she couldn't.

Something crossed Barbara's face, a darkness, an anger almost. 'This one guy. Nathan said his name was Rhys or something. Nathan wouldn't stop talking about him. Started a few months before the last time he visited. I didn't like the way he spoke about him. I tried to tell Nathan that, but he wouldn't listen. He said it was someone he met on the street one day. He said this guy was helping him. Was going to set him right.'

'Did you ever meet him?'

There was a pause, a moment of hesitation before Barbara spoke. 'Once. Not properly. He was outside, at the end of the path. He'd walked with Nathan, on one of his visits home. He didn't come inside or anything though. Nathan knew better than to invite people back to my house.'

'You never spoke to him?'

Barbara shook her head. 'I didn't need to. I knew what he was like just by looking at him.'

'And what was that?'

'He was dead behind the eyes. Like looking into two dark tunnels. There was nothing there.'

Louise bit down on her lower lip with her teeth, bringing the skin together so it began to sting with pain.

Eyes like tunnels. Dark, without soul. Without life.

She had known eyes like that before.

It never ended well.

Ten

When Val heard the announcement, time seemed to stop.

A body found in her city would do that at any time. Especially one they didn't name.

She waited expectantly all day for the knock at the door, feeling that it was going to happen any second. It was just a matter of time. That was all. They were finding him now, identifying him, knowing he was her boy. Her son.

More details sneaked out. The woods where the body had been found. The other side of the water from where her son had disappeared. Different woods, but it wouldn't have mattered much to her anyway. Anyone in the city was a possibility. Even further afield than just Liverpool. She had travelled to Manchester and Preston before then to identify dead bodies which had turned out not to be her son.

Her boy.

It was almost the twentieth anniversary of his disappearance. Everyone thought that day would be worse than any other. They were wrong. It was only a few weeks until what should have been his thirty-fourth birthday.

Those days were worse.

Christmas, birthdays, New Year's. The *event* days were when she felt the loss most keenly. That's how grief worked. You missed the times you should have spent together. As a family.

Now, they were fractured. Incomplete.

No knock at the door. No answers suddenly appearing.

No peace. No resolution.

Val forced herself to watch more and more as the drama unfolded. The local newspaper had a page dedicated to live updates on the story. She waited for each new item to appear, holding her breath as the website paused and then revealed the nothingness it usually delivered. The various postings on Facebook and Twitter were the same – although it didn't stop her looking for any further information that wasn't being reported. It seemed to be the case that they were now linking the two incidents together – the woman who was found wandering the streets in Melling, and now the body discovered in woodland nearby.

Most people seemed to think it would be whoever attacked the woman. Killed himself rather than face justice.

If we had the death penalty, maybe we could have done the job for him.

Saved us some money. Pure evil.

People commenting without any idea of what had actually occurred.

Val thanked a deity, not for the first time, that social media hadn't been as popular when her son had gone missing. She didn't think she would have been able to cope with reading all those people's opinions. She had read enough about missing-child cases since, the vitriol levelled at the parents left behind, to know she never would have survived that examination.

It would only have been a mirror to her own feelings. Her own sense of guilt. The ill-informed scribblings of the masses would have been too much for her. Of that she was sure. Her son going missing ruined her marriage, her family – having everyone talk about her from a veil of anonymity would have ruined her soul.

She knew some believed that he had done a runner and she actually knew where he was. That the entire disappearance had been a ruse. A secret plot to divert attention from a bigger crime. There was no truth to that, of course. Not that anyone would listen. When her husband had brought that question into her house, it had been the final nail in a coffin on which construction had begun months earlier. It was already being gently lowered into a grave by that point; he just brought the end a little sooner than she had thought it would be.

She reached for the phone again, wanting to call her daughter. Not that she could have if she wanted to. The last time they'd spoken – all that time ago – had felt final.

She was stuck in a distortion. A moment in time, trapped for decades. Her son's bedroom still existed in its past form upstairs. She went in every week or so, dusting off old toys and electronics which he would never use again. Even if he did return. Technology now out of date.

Untouched for all that time, other than by her own hand.

She had kept it pristine, awaiting his return.

Sometimes, she would forget what had happened. Early in the morning, half-awake, catching herself pushing open the door expecting her teenage boy to still be under the covers. Waiting for her to wake him up for school. She was transported back to a simpler time, when all she had to worry about was his tendency to be silent, getting into minor trouble.

It would take a few seconds for reality to hit her. That she was twenty years older and her son had vanished without a trace.

Now, she was content to disappear into the world on her laptop screen.

And watching the local news websites update every few minutes, on a story which – it became more and more apparent – was nothing to do with her missing son.

Until the first video arrived.

The blurred form of a woman, staggering down the middle of a road she didn't recognise. The image wobbled and turned as the person holding the camera tried to get closer. It was almost as if they didn't want to. That if they'd got too close then they would somehow become a part of whatever was happening.

The sound was more important.

Val could hear the woman singing, screeching. Seemingly using the last of her strength for it before she collapsed to the floor. The song was one she knew. An old rhyme, one most people in the city knew.

The Bone Keeper's coming. The Bone Keeper's real.

Val's hand went to her mouth, covering the noise which threatened to escape.

The questions she had.

The fear that wanted to break free.

Eleven

Louise was standing at the evidence table, scanning the various scraps of paper removed from Nathan Coldfield's bedroom. Every receipt, every screwed-up ball of rubbish, was now suddenly of great interest.

She wondered what people would think of her tendency to keep receipts for everything if they ever had to do this for her. If some poor DC would be told to work out the value of a five-year-old receipt for a hairdryer which had broken three years earlier. Instead, it was Louise going through the detritus. Trying to find meaning, or something of value, among the mess.

The picture she had found underneath the bed was in the centre, seemingly now of utmost importance.

'Just anything,' Shipley said, lifting a bus ticket in the air and staring at both sides. 'We have a name, but it means bugger all at the moment.'

'We could just track down every Rhys in the city. Ask them all what they were doing two nights ago.'

Shipley didn't laugh, but he smiled at least. 'Can you imagine the overtime claims for something like that ever being agreed to?'

'There'll be something, in among all this here,' Louise said, beginning the process of separating out each scrap of paper on the table. The accumulation of modern life, screwed-up pieces of forgotten trips, things bought and consumed without thought.

'You really think so?' Shipley replied, unable to keep the pessimism from his tone. 'I doubt it.'

Louise shook her head towards him, then returned to examining the contents of Nathan Coldfield's entire bedroom, laid out before her. 'It's here. Something will be here.'

'It's obvious what he's done. He's been back every few weeks, emptied the pockets on the one pair of jeans he wears, got his mum to wash them, then buggered off again. It'll all be pointless.'

'Maybe, but you never know,' Louise replied, knowing Shipley was just voicing his annoyance with the situation. 'Did we find out anything at all about Caroline? Family etcetera?'

'No, nothing yet. She has a flat, but there wasn't anything of note there when uniforms went over. And I mean, not a thing. The place was spotless. Almost like a show home, was how one of them put it. No personal touch to it whatsoever.'

'So, no closer to finding out if there's anything more to her story then?'

'I guess not.'

Louise thought about the woman lying in a hospital bed a few miles from them. About what she had gone through, what she would be feeling. She could feel the anger rising within her as she thought about the kind of man that would do this. Felt her breathing become heavier as she did so.

She clenched her jaw and concentrated on slowing her breaths. Tried to focus on what was in front of her.

There had to be something there.

Eventually, they found it.

Louise stood outside a seemingly normal semi-detached house, on a quiet street towards the south of the city. Garston, only a few miles from the last town before Liverpool turned into another city. Speke only a mile or two away, the last leg on a journey towards Runcorn and Widnes. A cul-de-sac, the name of the road showing marks of graffiti that had been removed.

Rows of houses on each side, almost bearing down on her as she took them in, all similar in build and shape. Each containing a different class of person than the more notorious council estates on their doorsteps. Working people lived there, only a few scant parked cars in the middle of the day, with newer number plates than would be found in those other places. Care had been taken with each house's front; new paving stones in small driveways, tiny porches erected so there was an extra entrance rather than just a wooden front door. Bushes, well tended, in the few which had patches of grass in front.

They had found what they had been looking for within an hour. A full name for the mysterious 'Rhys' character. His surname was Durham and a long-gone mobile phone number accompanied the name scribbled down.

The 'RD' on the back of the picture had been the key. Once they'd paired that with the name Rhys, and the phone number, things began to move. It hadn't taken them much longer to link the phone number to an actual Rhys Durham, despite it being a throwaway pay-as-you-go SIMcard.

Louise sometimes feared the power they had now. The ability to find out information with so little in hand.

'This is really the only relative he has?'

'She's the only one in this area, put it that way,' Shipley replied, pulling the car to a stop at the side of the road. 'And she's listed as his next of kin, going from the last time he came into contact with any authorities.'

They had tried his previous known address, but the current occupant hadn't been able to provide them with help in any way. A quick chat with the landlord over the phone gave them little more, only that he hadn't lived there for some years.

Louise was beginning to think Rhys Durham didn't want to be found.

Shipley left the car, waiting for Louise to close her door before keying the automatic lock. A train rumbled past somewhere, causing both Louise and Shipley to look up at once, then at each other.

'Well, that would get annoying quickly,' Louise said, waiting as Shipley made his way around the car and next to her. 'Which station's round here?'

'West Allerton up that way,' Shipley said, pointing back towards where they'd come from. 'Liverpool South Parkway the other way. Wasn't there when I lived near here. Nearest station was Hunts Cross. Still is, actually. That's if you want to walk from the train station into Speke. Used to be a pain in the backside, getting the train from town home. It would take three-quarters of an hour to walk home from the train station. When we were kids, it felt like three hours.'

'Bus was better then?'

'Yeah, when it was running properly. Used to be hit

and miss, back in the eighties and nineties. That's why we barely ever left the place. Not that we needed to.'

'You lived round here for a while then?'

'Only about twenty years,' Shipley replied, giving Louise a smile that reached inside her somehow. 'I've told you this before. We were on the outskirts, for the most part. Used to pretend we weren't part of the proper estate in the centre. Nearer the airport entrance, so it was almost a self-contained place. Not part of the main town. Lot of new builds round there. My mum used to look down on those from the proper estate in Speke, but we were no different really.'

'Sounds a bit like my mum,' Louise replied, trying to replicate the smile he had given her. She didn't think she pulled it off as well. 'She always wanted better for us.'

'What was your mum like?'

Louise pretended she didn't hear him and changed the subject. 'What's the plan here then? How much do we say about why we're on her doorstep?'

'Let's play it by ear,' Shipley replied, standing just behind and letting her take the lead. 'We're obviously not going to say too much. Mainly because we don't know an awful lot.'

'You've got that right.' Louise was up the path ahead of him in a few strides and knocking on the door within seconds. The sound echoed around the street, and she imagined a few blinds being parted by the more nosy neighbours living there. Shipley stood a few steps behind her. She gave him a quick glance, but he was looking towards the upper floor of the house itself. He then stepped to the side, looking up the small path and back gate that lay there.

'Probably should have had someone watching the back,' Shipley said, seemingly to himself. 'There's only train tracks back there, but still.'

'You think someone in here killed Nathan Coldfield and attacked Caroline?'

Shipley shrugged at her, stepping back onto the path behind her. She looked at him for a few seconds more, then turned back to face the door. She thought about the body they had pulled out of the woods. About Caroline lying in a hospital bed. The dark dead eyes of Rhys Durham.

Probably should have come with backup.

Louise ignored the voice in her head, straightening herself up, ready for whatever lay behind the door in front of her.

She didn't have chance to mull it over too long; the door opened in front of them, revealing an older woman, struggling to pull the door back and keep a dog from rushing out towards them.

'Get inside, Rufus, what are you like?'

Louise stepped to the side as Shipley moved instinctively backwards away from the opening door, away from the bark which was becoming louder and more insistent by the second.

'Get down, what are you playing at?'

Louise shook her head mockingly towards Shipley, then turned back to the door and extended her ID in front of her. 'Hazel Durham? I'm Detective Constable Louise Henderson and the guy disappearing down the path behind me is Detective Sergeant Paul Shipley. Can we have a word, please?'

The dog seemed to be more under control now, but was still being held tightly by Hazel Durham as it strained to get away from her. 'Do you have a warrant?'

'Do we need one?'

'Depends what you're after.'

Louise thought for a second, then tried a disarming smile. 'We just want to have a quick conversation about your nephew, Rhys. Won't take up much of your time.'

'Haven't seen him in years. Don't know why you would think I have.'

The smile hadn't worked, which Louise wasn't exactly surprised by. It was obvious this woman had dealt with police in the past. Possibly more than a few times.

That fact didn't bode well for them.

'Well, we wouldn't mind asking you a few questions about him, if you don't mind,' Louise continued, risking an extremity and stepping closer to the door. 'Just to clear up some things in an ongoing investigation.'

Hazel Durham didn't flinch, but eventually subsided and allowed them past. Louise went first, Shipley coming slowly behind her. He speeded up as Hazel Durham opened another door from the hallway and shoved the dog inside. She closed that door, then shut the front door behind Louise as she showed them the way into the living room.

'As I said, I haven't seen him in years. I'm not going to be much help.'

'You don't know what we're going to ask yet,' Louise said, taking in the living room in one quick glance. Shipley hovered in the doorway, allowing Hazel to pass him before disappearing into the hallway without her noticing. 'When was the last time you saw him?'

'Must be more than two years ago now. We didn't exactly see eye to eye on most things, but he took it too far.'

'Took what too far?'

Hazel moved to stand across the room from Louise, one foot tapping as she folded her arms over, standing near a white mantelpiece. She couldn't look more the part if she tried, Louise thought.

'He wasn't the brightest spark. He thought I wouldn't realise, but I did. I put it all together. He took too much this time.'

Louise was beginning to lose patience, but took a breath and asked her again. 'What did he take from you?'

'Everything,' Hazel replied, her arms dropping to her sides with a slap. 'He took everything from me. He took my son.'

Louise was about to answer, but didn't get the chance to as Shipley appeared at the living room door. 'You're gonna want to come and see this.'

Behind Shipley, Louise could hear the dog still yapping away, but her focus was on her DS.

And the look on his face.

Twelve

There was a couple of seconds when Louise couldn't see why Shipley was excited. Then she spotted it on the wall, just as she crossed the threshold and entered the bedroom. The darkness of the ink, the way it appeared to almost lift from the wall. The artistry, the horror of it. She blinked, but could still see it in her vision.

It could have been Nathan Coldfield's bedroom, if he had been born a decade later. Hazel Durham was a little more house-proud than Nathan's mother Barbara had been. It looked as if she tidied and dusted more often. A shrine kept absolutely pristine. That didn't mean there wasn't a musty smell lingering in the air. The aroma of a room that hadn't been entered in a while. A coolness to the air, empty of life.

Not that the condition of the bedroom was the first thing you would notice. On one side, old posters and faded wallpaper. On the other ... well, if Shipley wasn't sure, Louise knew.

'This must have taken some time. What do you think it is exactly?'

Shipley was still looking pale, but had regained some

of his colour. 'I don't know what it is, but it's freaking me the hell out.'

'Pun intended?'

'It wasn't intentional.'

The main visage was a close approximation of a devil mask. A giant drawing, etched directly onto the wall. In black marker, faded in places but still as effective. Shaded in red around the mouth and eyes. Strands coiled from the features like tendrils, springing forth from the hateful mask onto other parts of the wall, smaller illustrations of the same kind dangling from them.

Above the image, the letters TBK seemed to bleed from the wall itself. Underneath the Devil, and the words 'He's real'.

'Rhys's work?' Louise said, turning to the doorway, where Hazel Durham was now standing. She was looking at the floor rather than the two of them.

'No, of course not. He couldn't do something like this. He doesn't have the talent to do something as artistic. He'd probably struggle to do a stick figure, never mind anything like ... this. My son did it.'

'What's his name?'

'Jon,' Hazel replied, quietly as though it were an effort to say the name. 'His name was Jon.'

Louise caught the change. The past tense. 'Was?'

Hazel shook her head, gave a tight smile that disappeared and was replaced with a scowl. 'He died a year ago. I ... I don't come in here often. It's too painful.'

'What do you know about this?' Shipley said, pointing towards the wall. 'What does it mean?'

'I don't know, but I knew it wasn't anything right. He thought it was art. I had to agree with him. He would get into something like this, some kind of subject, and it would be difficult to get him off it. It was all he would ever talk about, if he spoke at all. He was always in this room, working on his computer or writing stuff down.'

'What is it?' Louise said, moving closer to the drawings and other marks on the wall.

'It's the Devil,' Hazel replied, as if Louise had asked a ridiculous question. 'Can't you see that?'

'Of course,' Shipley said, through gritted teeth. 'It's not something I usually see drawn on someone's bedroom wall, that's all. Why did he do this?'

'In the months before he ... before, he became obsessed with a story. Would talk about him as if he were real. That stupid one we all heard about as kids. Another bogeyman to keep us scared. The Bone Keeper.' Hazel shook her head and looked away. 'I think some kids took advantage of the way he was and filled his head with rubbish. He struggled with that kind of thing. He didn't understand it was just a story, that it wasn't real. I just put it down to being a bit isolated, later on. He would spend hours on his computer, playing games. Never really left the house, not once he'd finally finished school. I couldn't really get any sense out of him. Then, that stupid story captured his imagination.'

'The Bone Keeper ...' Shipley replied, and gave a heavy sigh. Louise was looking at the wall, but she could almost see him shake his head and place his hands on his hips. A look of incredulity as the name came up again.

'There's a few notes here talking about sightings,' Louise said, cutting in before they lost Hazel for good. She pointed at the scraps of paper on the top of a chest of drawers next to the wall drawing. 'Places he had appeared and been seen by people. Different versions of the story. They're all here. Did he talk about this, Hazel?'

'Only all the time,' Hazel replied, a thin smile appearing on her face. 'He was obsessed with finding him. There's a bunch of binders down there full of the same thing. He couldn't let it go. He wanted to find him and make him stop. I remember him watching superhero films and taking notes, as if he was going to really stop this evil monster that didn't exist. Rhys took advantage of him.'

Shipley stepped forward, then stopped short as Hazel shrank back a little. 'What happened with Rhys?'

'That's where things really went wrong,' Hazel said, after a few seconds of silence. 'When he got involved, that's when it went from bad to absolutely terrible. It's my fault. I should never have asked him.'

'Asked him what?'

'To try and get him out of here,' Hazel said, leaning against the doorframe. 'I thought he could snap him out of it. Jon had looked up to him as a kid, and I wasn't getting anywhere with him. He was ... different. To other boys his age. They never quite worked out what was wrong, but he wasn't like other teenagers. He was very young. In the head. He looked eighteen, but really, he was a little boy. Rhys was supposed to make him come out of his shell a bit more. He'd struggled at the same age, not surprising seeing what happened to him.'

'What happened to Rhys?'

'I thought you knew? His parents died within a year of each other. Drugs, they said. My sister – his mother, he didn't have his father's surname – was a different person once she met his dad. I never liked him. He led her astray, but she seemed glad to be led. She went first, heroin overdose. He followed a year or so later, running away from police because he had drugs on him. Got hit by a train. Rhys seemed to be okay, so I thought he could help Jon as well. Jon never knew his dad and he missed that male influence in his life sometimes, I thought anyway. Instead, it just got worse. And now all I have left is this room.'

'Jon ...' Louise began, then crossed the room to get closer to Hazel. 'How was Rhys involved with Jon's death?'

'He was a good boy, my Jon. He would have grown out of this ... this obsession. He would have found something else. Something to make of his life. He was too good for this.'

Louise could sense that Hazel was about to shut down, becoming lost in her memories. 'You need to help us understand here Hazel. We need to find Rhys. If he did something to Jon—'

'He killed him. As good as, anyway. Filled his head full of bad thoughts and Jon couldn't get away from them. They found him near Oggie Shore.'

Louise felt a jolt at the name of the old shoreline that lay at the bottom of the Mersey. Another link to the south of the city. 'What happened?'

'They said he killed himself. That was the official word, anyway. I never believed it. They found him with the empty pill bottle beside him and a note. That was enough for them. I know the real story though.'

'And what's the real story, Hazel?'

'Rhys forced him to do it. Somehow. He filled his head with all this rubbish and look where it got him. My son – my Jon ... he was a good boy. He would never have done any of this, if it wasn't for Rhys. He knew how to get inside his head. Make him think things were real that weren't.'

Louise looked back at the mural on the wall. The black eyes of the devil mask staring back at her. That's how the story was told sometimes – the Bone Keeper had a devil mask, or was the *real* Devil.

All parts of the same story, just with a variety of embellishments and fractured memories.

She began taking photos with her phone, being careful to make sure each item was captured. She did so without thinking, without wondering. Without listening to the voice inside her shouting to be heard.

How much of this story is real?

Shipley was still talking to Hazel, who Louise knew was lost now. She would still speak, but it wouldn't make sense. Not to anyone who didn't speak the language of grief. Of loss.

Louise listened as Shipley continued to try, although she wanted to put a hand on his shoulder and tell him not to waste his time.

'Hazel, what happened to Rhys? Where did he go?'

'I don't know,' Hazel replied, slumping down the wall and coming to a stop when she reached the floor. Both of her hands ran into her hair, fingers interlaced with the strands, pulling lightly. 'I never saw him. Not after the funeral. He wasn't wanted around here, he knew that. Not after what he said.'

Louise knew Shipley was used to prompting, but she could see he was becoming more and more annoyed at the shorter answers, the things left unsaid. 'What did he say?' he asked, trying to keep the impatience out of his tone.

'He said it had finally got Jon. That the Bone Keeper

always gets what it wants. Then he just stood there with a horrible grin on his face. Like he was happy about it. I couldn't even say anything back to him. I was just stunned. I told you lot about it, but there was no evidence, they said. Nothing that showed it was anything more than a suicide. I always knew though. Even if Rhys wasn't there at the time, he as good as found the pills and forced them down Jon's throat. It was all his fault.'

Louise turned back to the wall as Shipley continued. He may as well have been talking to the wall behind Hazel now. She wasn't in any fit state to tell them anything more. The sobbing emanating from the woman was becoming louder, filling the small room with its despair.

Louise read the notes on the drawers near the devil mask. Took some photographs, but they would be taking them away that day, she assumed. 'He walks among us, bathed in a deathly glow,' Louise said, quietly to herself, reading the uppermost note. She turned her attention back to the wall, the icons next to the mask. Most were almost illegible; random words and symbols which meant little to her. A few stood out and jarred among the more random markings.

There was something about the symbols, the way they flitted around the wall surrounding the mask. Various colours, but mainly red and black. Her eyes settled on a picture, a blurred image which felt familiar.

It didn't take long for her to recognise it properly. The same woods as in one of the pictures found in Nathan Coldfield's bedroom. On the outskirts of the city, only a few miles from where they were standing.

Louise waited for Shipley to usher Hazel Durham back down the stairs and for him to return. She continued taking pictures, pulling the binders from their small cub-byhole, leafing through them and taking pictures.

They would have to take them away. There was just too much information in them to read and make sense of it all here. Most seemed to be longer thoughts on the more brief and brash headlines scrawled on the wall behind her. There were more pictures. Various woodland areas, maps, places circled in red.

She wondered if there really could be a link. A woman escaping death, a body found in the woods she'd fled. An old myth, passed around for years, now being considered as possibly having something to do with it.

It was ridiculous.

Still, there was something about the ritualistic way in which both victims had been marked. In Caroline's case, Louise had no doubt she would have ended up in the same position as Nathan Coldfield. Yet, she had managed to get away.

How? He became distracted suddenly, right in the middle of slicing into her? That makes no sense.

Louise shook her head, ignoring the voice in it.

'I've put a call into a family liaison,' Shipley said from the doorway, then moved into the room to stand at her shoulder. 'Wasn't sure what else to do. She's pretty upset.'

'I think we've opened some old wounds.'

'Beginning to think they were never closed. Anything in there that might lead us to Rhys Durham?'

Louise looked again at the pages in the binder, the reds and blacks on the pages. The violence, the hate, the dread dripping from every page. 'I don't know. I think Jon was a troubled boy, who got mixed up in a story. We can take this with us and see if there's anything, but I doubt it.'

Shipley stared at the page, shaking his head as if he couldn't understand the words written there. Louise knew it wasn't that. It was the fact that they were now looking at something much more than they had been expecting.

'If this case wasn't weird enough before . . .' Shipley said, exhaling loudly after his words, as if the rest didn't need to be said.

Louise didn't respond, her attention snatched once more by the wall. The dark, dead eyes at the centre of the mask. The horror that lay there, the evil which loomed over them.

'Just a story,' she whispered finally. 'It's not real.'

Thirteen

There had been more of these meetings than she cared to remember. Louise was usually quiet, letting everyone else speak while she listened.

Today, it would be different.

The case had taken a turn now and she wasn't sure what it would mean yet. The binders from Jon Durham's bedroom, along with the mural, didn't amount to much really. At least not after they had left the house. Louise hadn't managed to direct Shipley's attention away from what she supposed was the more pressing matter of Nathan Coldfield's body and the attempt to make Caroline into another victim.

No amount of talk was going to drive anyone to see the path she herself could sense ahead.

The Major Crimes team were now on the periphery, waiting to take over from the small operation she and Shipley had been running up to that point. A couple of representatives sat in on the meeting – sitting with smug looks on their faces, as no doubt they silently judged Louise and Shipley.

Let them, Louise thought.

'Settle down everyone,' Shipley said, standing up and clearly resisting the urge to tap a pen against his mug of coffee to get everyone's attention. 'As you all know, we're here to discuss the latest developments on the Coldfield case.'

'Should be a short meeting then—'

Shipley turned his head in the direction of the now reddening face of the uniformed copper near the back who had spoken a little louder than he'd probably intended. They needed to make the others realise how serious this was – and quickly.

'As I was saying,' Shipley said, eyes boring into the uniform who had interrupted him. 'The body of Nathan Coldfield was discovered in the woodland near the street where the young woman Caroline Rickards appeared after being brutally assaulted. He has been positively identified by a family member and preliminary post-mortem results show death was probably caused by blood loss. Preliminary reports of time of death put it at about twenty-four hours before Caroline emerged on the street.'

As he spoke, Louise changed the photographs appearing on the screen behind him. Remote clenched in her hand, trying not to look at the body flitting through the images.

She wasn't usually skittish around death.

This was different.

'Louise will take you through what we've found so far, so you're all up to date.'

Shipley sat down, taking the remote from Louise as she stood up. He turned the fob over in his hand and rested his thumb on the correct button, looking up at her expectantly.

'We've spoken to Nathan Coldfield's mother, who hasn't

seen the victim in a few weeks,' Louise said, taking over now. 'She has confirmed the victim was acquainted with a person of the name Rhys, who we subsequently tentatively identified as a Rhys Durham, who has now become of primary interest.'

She waited for Shipley to key the button. The photograph on the screen flicked to the next one – an old mug shot of Rhys Durham, around five years out of date. She glanced over her shoulder, making sure it was the correct image. Thin-faced, sunken cheekbones, but the unmarked face of someone only in their early twenties. He could have been any shaven-headed lad, only recently thrust into the throes of adulthood before he'd intended. Still walking around town with a baseball cap on his head and a swagger in his step.

He looked normal.

'Rhys Durham, aged thirty. He was an acquaintance of the deceased, one his mother suspected of being a bad influence on her son, even if she never directly met with him. She didn't like him, basically, and probably had good reason not to. He has a record.'

A hand went up from the chairs in front of her. 'What was he banged up for?'

Louise tried to pretend the interruption didn't bother her. *Like I wouldn't have told you.* 'Many things over the years. Violence, mostly. Also, he raped a fourteen-year-old girl when he was seventeen and got probation for it. Because she led him on, apparently, according to his defence and a soft judge. We've spoken to the woman involved and her family. They've not seen or heard from Durham since the trial. The only family member of Durham's we have been able to locate is an aunt. Hazel Durham. His parents were both drug addicts, dead before Rhys was eighteen. He was getting into trouble before then, but his violent offending increased following their deaths, before seemingly coming to a stop two years ago. The aunt also hasn't seen Rhys in a long time, but that may have something to do with what happened to her son.'

Louise explained what she and Shipley had found at Hazel Durham's house and her son Jon's room in particular. Shipley flicked to the photos taken the previous day of what they had found on the teenager's wall. Now, she could see the expressions in the room change.

'These were done by Jon, Rhys's cousin. They depict something most of the locals in the room will recognise.'

There were a few murmurings from the group, whispers going around. She spotted a few confused faces, but most seemed to know what it meant.

'I know some of you will be wondering what the scribblings of a young man with a history of mental health issues has to do with the case. Well, this story has come up a number of times already.'

'So, the Bone Keeper is real and killing people?'

Louise stared at the uniform who had interrupted Shipley earlier and was now smirking away near the back. 'Why? Are you scared? Want to ring mummy?'

The uniform stuttered a reply, but Louise was already moving on. 'The Bone Keeper, for those in the room unaware, is a local myth. There have been stories about him for a long, long time, but nothing has ever been found to be true. He's the local bogeyman, with various stories attached to him. Usually the stories concern a strange *thing* in the woods, who takes people and makes them disappear.'

'Basically, every missing person in the city during the past few decades has been attributed to this ... story,' Shipley said, loosening his tie a little. 'But no one has ever found anything tangible.'

'And he has his own song,' another voice said and started to sing it, until Louise put her hand up.

'Thank you, but that's not necessary. We've all heard the stories; they go back a few decades now. People going missing, never found. There's always someone ready to say they were seen near some woods and perpetuate the myth. We've never had a single sighting of anyone or anything to suggest these aren't just the normal missing person's reports we see all the time. Obviously, this is one avenue of enquiry at the moment, but there are many.'

Louise continued talking, but she could see she wasn't getting through to them. They were still just stories to these people. They couldn't see the pattern. Not yet.

'Regardless of the "Bone Keeper" angle, this is another death that involved Rhys Durham. In what capacity, we can't be sure yet. We've looked into the death of Jon. Everything pointed to suicide. Body was found near to Oglet Shore, in the south of the city. Random dog-walker, pill packets next to him. A note was also discovered on his person. Post-mortem revealed he died of an overdose.'

Shipley pressed the button in his hand, but an image of the note didn't appear, only a photograph of Oggie Shore.

Louise didn't glance over her shoulder this time.

'The note read "*The Bone Keeper finally found me*".' She waited as the group caught up, visibly now beginning to see why she had brought up the local legend. 'The coroner couldn't determine if he had intended to cause his own death, so it was an open verdict. Most probably suicide.

Jon's mental health problems were depression, anxiety, all the usual. He had become obsessed before his death with the story of the Bone Keeper. At the inquest, this was attributed to a major depressive episode.'

More raised eyebrows now, people shaking their heads, incredulous at the path they were seeming to take. She'd lost them again.

'Rhys Durham was asked by his aunt to spend some time with Jon,' Louise continued, looking down at the notes she was holding. 'He was supposed to try and lift him out of the misery Hazel thought her son was feeling. Instead, she contends that he made the issue worse. Fed his fears.'

'The picture we're getting of Rhys Durham isn't a pretty one,' Shipley said, without rising from his chair. 'Which is why we're eager to track him down and find out where he's been hiding.'

'And there's been no sighting of him in over a year?' the DC from the woods said. Louise had finally put a name to the face. DC Stuart Cavanagh. 'Any clues at all?'

They had already considered this. Over and over. 'Nathan Coldfield's mother seems to recall him hanging around a month or so ago, but since then no, nothing. But we haven't looked hard enough yet. He's not been reported missing or anything like that. Simply disappeared off the radar. Our job is to get him out of his hidey hole. Details of Rhys Durham will be released to the press this morning. There hasn't been much national coverage of the discovery of Nathan Coldfield's body yet, but that could change at any moment. Hopefully someone out there will recognise this guy and we'll have him in custody shortly. Meanwhile, I want everyone looking into every single acquaintance Rhys Durham has ever had. I don't care how tenuous the link. He's our main focal point right now. We find him and hopefully all this ends.'

'What about the woman?'

'We've gone over her life,' Shipley replied, shooting a quick glance at Louise before facing the room again. 'Seems like she was in the wrong place at the wrong time is all. She's not allowing any visitors in to see her in hospital, but we think that's out of embarrassment, or privacy maybe. We've spoken to her boss, who says she comes in, does her work, goes home again. Never any problems. Nothing on file about her and there's no links to Nathan Coldfield that we've found. As I said, she's stumbled into something that she shouldn't have. That's as best as we can tell.'

He began delegating responsibilities to the assembled men and women, each clearly aware of what was being asked of them. Louise could see the weight of the matter begin to drop on every shoulder as they contemplated what lay ahead.

Finding one man. Someone who hadn't been seen in a long time. With only a single family member, seemingly, and no real friends. It wasn't the most difficult job, but still ... things could have been easier.

They waited for everyone to leave the meeting room, the air settling around them now they were left alone. The photograph of Rhys Durham was still on the screen behind them, almost staring straight at them. Judging their performance. Judging them, it seemed.

Nathan's mother had been right. His eyes looked black, piercing through the photograph and into her head.

She imagined looking into them in reality, rather than just on a screen. Tensed up at the thought.

'Do you think he's our man?' Shipley said, disturbing her thoughts, though she was glad of it this time. 'Reckon he's attacked Caroline in the same place he killed someone else a day earlier?'

'I think it's possible Caroline disturbed him while he was returning to the scene of the crime. We still have nothing from forensics to link him to the murder,' Louise replied, avoiding his gaze, sliding paper into a folder and closing it over. 'He could go no-comment in the interview and we'd struggle.'

'Full forensics haven't come back from the body yet,' Shipley replied, attempting a conciliatory tone. 'And there's probably enough circumstantial evidence to prove it.'

'I'm not sure about that. We've had stronger cases fail.'

'At least he'd be off the street,' Shipley replied, following Louise across the room to the now closed door. 'God knows what he's been up to in the last couple of years.'

Louise stopped in her tracks as she reached the door, folder under one arm, one hand on the door handle. 'What about all this business with the Bone Keeper thing?' she said, trying to keep her voice light. A *just asking* tone. 'We have a few things now, which all seem to come back to that. Are we just going to ignore it?'

'What do you suggest we do? Start going around looking for people wearing devil masks? It'll be Halloween soon, we'd fill the cells with people.'

He waited for Louise to reply, but she stared him down instead. Shook her head and turned away.

'Look, hang on,' Shipley said, moving around towards the opening door and in front of her. 'I admit, it's pretty bloody weird that this thing we used to tell each other as kids has now been mentioned numerous times. I just don't know how it links in at this point. And neither do you, otherwise you'd have told me by now. Fear does strange things to people. Maybe Rhys was going around telling people that's who he was, but it was just a cover. If it's him, he's just a sick bloke, who likes to kill. Nathan was probably his first victim. Caroline disturbed him and was almost killed for the trouble.'

'And he also knows her name? Remember, she said he'd said it before he attacked her.'

'I think she was just confused, that's all. At the moment, we have one victim and one person we think might, possibly, have done it. When we find Rhys Durham, we can ask him, okay?'

Louise nodded, but said nothing, as they left the room. She wondered when Rhys Durham had moved from being a person of interest to a murder suspect.

She supposed it was better a real person than a myth. She stopped, turning around to face Shipley again. 'Sir—'

'What have I said?' Shipley interrupted. 'Don't call me that.'

Louise opened her mouth, wanting to say more. Tell him her fears. That there was more to this than either of them could comprehend. Yet, she couldn't, not now. It wouldn't be anything but her own dread that would come out. The thought of it constricted her chest as well. That now familiar feeling, as she felt the weight of her fears begin to crush her from within. The room growing smaller around them, as she contemplated telling him what was hidden inside her.

Instead, she shook her head.

'Nothing, sorry.'

Fourteen

The street was in darkness by the time Shipley parked the car up outside her house. He let the car idle as Louise fiddled with her seatbelt, unable to find the release, the bag on her shoulder getting in the way.

'Here,' Shipley said, flicking on the overhead light. 'You'll be there forever otherwise.'

'Cheers,' Louise replied, finally getting free. She was about to open the door when Shipley put a hand on her arm to stop her.

'Louise, what's going on?'

She didn't turn to face him, but also didn't move away. There was a moment of silence, just the sound of their breathing filling the car.

'Nothing,' Louise said eventually, twisting his way and giving him a fake smile. 'Just tired is all.'

'I can sense something isn't right,' Shipley continued, as if she hadn't responded. 'You've been snappy all day. Not with me, before you start protesting, but I noticed it with others.'

'There's nothing to worry about. It's only this whole thing blowing up overnight. I just keep thinking about Caroline, lying in that hospital bed alone.'

Shipley settled back in his seat, his hand leaving her arm. 'I know, it's unbelievable really. Why wouldn't you want people around you at that point?'

Louise knew what Caroline was thinking. The shame of it, the need to punish herself for other people's actions.

'Who knows how close she came to being killed,' Shipley continued, as Louise began to make a decision. 'How did she get away? That's what I want to know. He's already murdered someone else in those woods, then lets the other one go accidentally? I'm not buying that.'

Louise murmured an agreement, thinking about Caroline and how she'd escaped. How she was *allowed* to escape. That was her feeling now. There was more to that aspect than they could see at that moment. Had to be. It made little sense otherwise.

'You'd tell me if something was bothering you, wouldn't you?' Shipley said, his forehead creased with concern.

'Of course.'

'I care about you – you know that, right?' Shipley said, his face softening now. She could still see the strain there, the almost earnest nature of him. 'Plus I don't want us to screw this up – the case, I mean.'

'We won't,' Louise replied, staring into his eyes, hoping he could see how much she believed that. 'We'll find him.'

Shipley stared back at her, opened his mouth as if he was about to say something, then closed it again. He looked away ahead of him, towards the dark street outside. 'Let's hope so. You're best getting in. Can't imagine it'll be any less hectic tomorrow.'

There was a moment when Louise almost asked him inside. A slight wavering, a massive leap into the unknown.

She caught herself, smiling and saying goodbye before she had the chance to think about it again.

Louise wanted so much for things to be normal. For her life to be something else. 'I'll see you tomorrow,' she said, exiting the car and closing the door far too hard behind her.

She stopped at the end of her path, looking back towards the car and giving a quick wave. It was dark inside now, so she couldn't see Shipley's face. She knew he'd be staring at her though, trying to work out something he couldn't.

The car suddenly came to life, taking off from the edge of the road and becoming a blur within seconds. She looked at the field opposite her house, bordered by small trees scattered at the edges. She felt something pass through her, but shook it off. Turned towards her house and strode confidently towards the door.

Louise could still smell the faint aroma of his aftershave swirling around her like a mist she was walking through.

Normal. It would have been that, to invite him into her home. Her living room. Her kitchen.

Her bedroom.

She couldn't do that. Not now. There was simply too much to consider, too much to lose. Instead, she let herself into her empty house, a blast of cold stale air hitting her as she stepped inside. Into the silence, the sound of the distant ticking clock in the kitchen her only greeting.

Normal. You just want to be normal. That's all.

She continued to ignore the voice in her head, removing her jacket and shoes and walking through into the kitchen. Busied herself finding something to eat, ignoring the feel of Shipley's hand on her arm and the look on Caroline's face as she looked up at her from the hospital bed.

Ignored them and the anger which built up inside her as she thought about Caroline. And Nathan Coldfield. The reason for them being there. For her knowing they existed. The reason she'd heard the name she'd been happy to avoid for so many years.

The Bone Keeper.

The hatred and disgust she instantly felt about the moniker. The myth. The story.

She stared at her knuckles as they turned white against the grey of the fridge door handle. Louise released her hand, an imprint of the handle now embedded into the skin of her palm. She looked at it for a while, watching it fade and return to normal.

Someone was using the name. That's all. Some evil, screwed-up killer had assumed the mantle of a local folk-tale and was passing himself off as someone he wasn't.

That was all.

He wasn't real.

Louise stood in the kitchen and made a snap decision. She didn't have to be alone.

The hospital corridors were quieter than they had been when they'd visited last, in the daytime. Less foot traffic, fewer people milling around. The lights seemed dimmer, as if at night someone had decided they would hit a switch and bathe them in a pale glow.

Louise paused at the door, wondering if she was doing the right thing, then decided to ignore her worries. She pushed down the handle and went inside. The room was almost in darkness now, but she could hear the soft noise from the television hanging on the wall.

She made her way closer to the bed, trying to keep her

movements quiet just in case, but she knew it wasn't necessary really.

'Hello,' Caroline said, shifting herself up in the bed, grimacing at the effort. 'I didn't think you'd be here this late. Has something happened? Have you found something?'

'Sorry, that's not why I'm here,' Louise replied, pulling over a chair closer to the bed and sitting down. 'I thought you could use some company, that's all.'

'Oh, right,' Caroline said, confusion sweeping across her face before being replaced by a slight smile. 'Thank you. I have been getting a bit bored stuck in here.'

'I bet you are. Late-night TV is awful. And it's not like you get hundreds of channels of choice on these things.'

'I never thought I'd miss Netflix this much,' Caroline said, a chuckle escaping her lips, before a sharp intake of breath at the pain that followed. 'Sorry, I won't be much fun. The painkillers take the edge off, but I'm still quite sore. Probably best you don't make me laugh.'

'I'm not much of a comedian anyway,' Louise replied, leaning over to Caroline's bedside cabinet and handing her the bottle of water sitting there. 'Are you feeling any better at all?'

'Loads, weirdly,' Caroline said, swigging quickly from the bottle before twisting the cap back on and leaving it lying close to her on the bed. 'I know it doesn't look like it, but honestly, I didn't think I was going to ever feel normal again. I'm getting there. Slowly. The skin will heal, they reckon. No need for skin grafts hopefully.'

'They'll leave some amazing scars though. You'll have something to talk about forever.'

'True. I'll never be the boring one again. Kind of wish I'd taken up juggling or something instead though.'

Louise looked over at the television, watching the flick-ering images of a film she didn't recognise. 'Have you slept at all?'

Caroline shook her head. 'A couple of hours here and there. Bit difficult when people come in and check on you every five minutes. I'm looking forward to getting out of here and getting a good night's sleep at some point.'

'I hear you.'

'Although, I don't know if that'll come easy. I keep find-ing myself back in that . . . place.'

Louise didn't say anything, glancing back at Caroline, who was now looking towards the ceiling. Now she was closer to her, dark rings were visible under her eyes.

'I didn't think you could be that scared and still live, you know,' Caroline said, her voice faltering a little. 'I thought my heart would have given out at some point. I've never felt anything like it.'

'We can live through more than we ever give ourselves credit for, I've found. We all have that sense of survival instinct within us.'

'That's just the thing,' Caroline replied, moving her head down to look at Louise. Her eyes were green and had the sheen of coming tears across them. 'I didn't want to survive. I wanted it to be over. All the pain, the agony . . . I was so scared. I just wanted it to stop, but it wouldn't. I was ready to die.'

Louise kept silent, letting Caroline get the words out. Allowed her training to take over, when everything within her wanted to reach out to the woman and tell her it was going to be okay.

That she was going to find whoever did this to her.

'You must have seen things like this before,' Caroline

said finally, sniffing back emotion. 'Probably all the time in your kind of job.'

'We get our fair share,' Louise lied, deciding to make her feel a little comfort that she wasn't the only one out there to have gone through something as horrific as she had. 'It doesn't mean we treat it any different. We treat every case the same.'

'I wasn't suggesting—'

'No, I know what you mean,' Louise said, interrupting her before she could finish the thought. 'I just want you to know we're working hard to find who did this to you and make sure he can't do it again.'

'That's good to hear,' Caroline replied, relaxing back into her pillow. 'Although, I don't think I'm the first this happened to, or the last. It was too calm. Like it was planned out. I keep remembering little things, but I never saw a face. Just a presence. I'm just sorry I can't be more help.'

'Don't worry about that. You just concentrate on getting better.'

'It just sounds so ridiculous, you know? I think about what I'm telling you about what did this to me and it's just . . . stupid.'

'You've been through a lot,' Louise replied, wondering how much Caroline believed her own words. How confident she was about what she'd seen. What she'd encountered in those woods. 'Don't worry about how you sound to us. It's your experience. Just keep trying to remember. Any little detail could be key to stopping whoever – *whatever* – did this to you.'

'I'll try.'

'Have you thought more about getting in touch with

people? Letting them come in and visit? The company might help.'

'No, I don't want anyone seeing me like this. It's all they'll ever see whenever they look at me in future. I don't ... I don't want to be only ever seen as a victim, if that makes sense?'

It did to Louise, so she continued to sit by Caroline's bedside, even as the anger grew inside her. The thought of whoever – whatever – had put Caroline in that bed, and who had placed Nathan Coldfield in a shallow grave, still out there. Consuming her thoughts, until all she could see was a man with no face, lying on the ground at her feet. A blade in her hand as she sliced into his skin.

The idea excited her.

Before

The world spun, as she lay on the ground watching. Waiting.

She felt as if she were in a dream. The sky above her black and orange. White tendrils reaching across her line of vision, as she willed her body to move.

It remained there, broken and still.

The previous moments were a blur, her pre-teen mind unable to order her thoughts coherently. She couldn't comprehend what had happened. What she had allowed to happen.

The air grew thick, her body reacting, finally, and coughing up nothingness. She willed her limbs to make any sort of movement, but they didn't respond. Instead, they seemed to dig in further, not wanting to obey her commands.

As if they knew that by lying there, by not moving, she could pretend that people weren't dying near her and she was doing nothing to stop it.

She continued to lie there, the soft ground beneath her cold and unforgiving. Objects in her peripheral vision turning and becoming distorted. Inhuman.

'*This is what you wanted.*'

The voice was low, gruff, a growl. As if something animal-like had peeled out of the bushes and prowled towards her unseen.

'*You wanted them dead. Didn't you?*'

She couldn't move, couldn't answer the voice. One so familiar, but now alien and distant. Unconnected to what was happening around her.

'*This is it. This is where you are born.*'

She wanted to scream, lift herself from the ground and do something.

She wanted to believe the voice. To go towards it. Accept it entirely and do its bidding.

'*They're dead and it's your fault. You wanted this. You needed this.*'

There was a part of her that knew the truth, yet she struggled to accept it. That the words meant nothing, they were lies, designed to put her on a different path.

Or, to guide her on the one she always knew was hers.

'*You have to walk with me now. We have to move on from here. You have to come with me into the woods and live your new life. Become just like me.*'

She refused to move. Shaking her head, as the world she'd known collapsed around her. Burning to the ground, until all that was left would be ashes. A life once so tangible and real becoming something dead and destroyed.

Gone.

All that was left was her. Lying on the ground, unable to move, unable to follow the voice into the darkness. Waiting for nothing to happen. For her life to end, just the same as the others.

To not be alone.

She closed her eyes, even as she could hear herself screaming into the night sky.

'No. *I don't want this. I didn't want this to happen. I want to die. I can't live with this. LEAVE ME ALONE.*'

The voice disappeared at the sound of her scream, leaving her alone, lying on the ground, eyes closed to reality. A weight on her chest as she lost consciousness, truth leaving her on a stream of wind and smoke.

She knew this was the end. That she would never live this day and night again. It was already disappearing, becoming nothing but a faded memory. One she would never remember clearly. Placing the events in a box and shifting it to a corner of her mind she would never explore.

She heard the song as she drifted away, waiting for her own life to be taken.

The song of death.

Now

Fifteen

Three hours.

That was all the sleep Louise had been able to manage after she'd finally left Caroline at the hospital. She had closed her eyes at 4 a.m., just as dawn began to break outside. Exhaustion taking over, despite her having felt that she would never sleep again.

The body can trick you into anything.

She had been thinking about the woods. The ones she'd seen in the pictures, back in Jon Durham's bedroom. The familiarity of them, the way she could almost remember the feel of the trees as she lightly danced her fingertips across the bark of the trunks. A faded memory, one she couldn't exactly trust.

Outside of the estates, the built-up areas, dissected by roads and motorways in the city, there were pockets of those woodland areas. She had been to many of them over the years. Vanishing into the silence. Looking for answers to questions she couldn't remember.

Those thoughts had crowded her mind while she tried to sleep.

The woods and fire.

She had driven into the car park bleary-eyed, stopped and stared straight ahead at the brick wall in front of her. Allowed the red and brown colours to merge, blur.

She could feel it coming now. The constriction in her chest, her breathing becoming more ragged. Shorter. Tighter. The world disappearing around her, as her body began to shake. She couldn't breathe, but the inside of the car was filled with her exhalations.

Panting, sucking in oxygen, as if it were about to run out. Edges appearing in her vision.

The world was becoming dark. Darker. Darker still. She screwed her eyes tight shut, gripped the steering wheel and concentrated on her breathing.

In. Out. In. Out.

She could feel herself relaxing slowly. Thoughts flew through her mind. She was unable to pick out any single thing as important. Instead, she tried forcing herself to empty her mind.

It was impossible, but it did allow her to keep concentrating on her breathing.

In. Out. In. Out.

Don't force it.

It felt like hours, but when she opened her eyes it had only been a couple of minutes. It hadn't been one of her longer lasting ones, but the panic attacks were becoming more frequent.

Eyes stinging, headache brewing, Louise dragged herself up to the office that housed her department. She ducked into the toilets before going in, checking herself in the mirror once she'd made sure no one else was in there. Ignored the dark lines under her eyes, the sallow look of the skin of her face. Those things came with the territory and wouldn't be remarked upon. Instead, she was looking for any sign of anything unusual.

Looked deep into her eyes, the flare of her nostrils. Opened her mouth, checked her teeth. Anything she felt could give her away and see her distanced.

She had to be on this case now. She couldn't afford to be pulled away now.

She needed to know.

There was nothing she could see; not that she really knew what she was looking for anyway. It wasn't as if she was walking around with something etched into the skin on her forehead. Permanent marker, *I'm not sure I can do this*.

She looked as normal as she ever did, she decided.

Louise made her way into the open-plan office, walking straight to her desk and taking her jacket off. Slipped her bag under the desk and switched on her computer. Shipley was already seated on the opposite side of the room and Louise could feel his eyes on her as she sat down. She ignored him, fixing her eyes on the computer monitor and waiting for it to come to life.

There were a couple of fellow detective constables on her bank of desks, but they hadn't tried to engage with her. They never did. Not that she was too bothered – she had always preferred her own company.

More so as she had grown older.

Fragmented ideas, thoughts, words, images flashed through her mind, without her wanting them to. Louise pushed a fingernail into her thigh, wincing at the sharp pain that followed; but it worked – she snapped out of her head. There wasn't time for any of this. She couldn't put it off any longer.

The thought had come to her overnight. The woods, the secrets they held. A hunch, if she was going to be truthful. A hunch predicated on some base facts, of course, but a hunch all the same.

It had to look right.

She couldn't just drop it into conversation, as if it didn't matter. She didn't think Shipley would take it seriously. Not in the growing mood he was getting into the further the week went on. He was eyeing Major Crimes, which meant he was being too careful. She needed a plan.

She stared at her screen, opening random emails and reading a couple of lines of each. Pretended to herself that she was acting normal, when everything within her didn't feel that way. The opposite.

This was a gamble. If she was wrong, when Major Crimes turned up Shipley wouldn't bother bringing her along with him. She would be damaged goods. Someone with a ridiculous idea, wasting time they didn't have.

There was something in those woods. She knew it. There had to be.

Louise watched the clock on the computer screen ticking off the minutes. She decided five would be enough.

They stretched into eternity.

She still had no plan.

Three minutes went by. She imagined Shipley was looking her way less often now. There didn't seem to have been any new information overnight, so she guessed the investigation was much as it had been when she left. All scurrying around, looking busy, but not really getting anywhere.

Each question they answered seemed to generate another six in its place.

Rhys Durham was the main focus now. They wanted to find him and hoped that the search would end there.

'Louise, everything okay?'

She didn't jump, but Shipley's voice was still a little startling. She realised she had been staring at the monitor for at least two minutes. Maybe three.

And she was still doing so.

'Yeah, sorry, just miles away there,' Louise replied, quickly looking at Shipley then averting her eyes. She wanted to plant another fingernail into her thigh, but decided against it. 'How's it going, anything new?'

'No, nothing. We're still trying to track down this Rhys Durham, but no luck so far. Did you see the news at all?'

'Yeah, it's not gaining as much traction as I thought it would.'

'Probably because of the victim,' Shipley said, folding his arms across his chest. 'If we could put Caroline out there a bit more—'

'I don't think she's ready for that,' Louise said quickly, thinking of the way she'd been the night before. Still full of fear of what she had escaped back in those woods.

'You're probably right, but I imagine she'll have to come forward at some point. The more I think about things, the more he sounds like our guy. Obviously he had an issue with Nathan Coldfield – a falling-out or something – and that's how he ended up buried in those woods. Caroline was just in the wrong place at the wrong time. That's all. We're going to speak to her soon, see if she recognises the name or the photo. Hopefully that'll clear it all up.'

'Right. Sounds like we're almost done with this then.'

'Hmm.'

Shipley sounded about as convinced by that as she was.

He was more wily than she had first thought. 'Still, probably best to explore every possibility in the meantime?'

'Yeah, we're going over what we pulled from Nathan
Coldfield's bedroom now.'

Now she had to tread lightly. 'What about Jon Durham's?'

'What about it?'

She took a breath, still trying to work out exactly what
she thought might work best. 'I'm just thinking, it couldn't
really do any harm to see if there's anything in that wall
display he had going on. Might give us a possible route to
finding Rhys, if anything.'

'Not sure I follow you. It was all random rubbish really.
He wasn't right in the head.'

'There might still be something there,' Louise replied,
trying to keep any semblance of eagerness out of her tone
of voice. 'Wouldn't take long for a couple of us to go
through it all. We found Rhys's full name doing the same
thing. Makes sense to try the same thing now.'

Shipley didn't say anything at first, just looked down at
her as she leaned back in her chair. In her mind she was the
epitome of nonchalance. Just trying to be helpful, nothing
more than that.

'Go for it,' Shipley said eventually, uncrossing his arms
and tapping his pen on her desk. 'Just don't take too
much time. Want as many people on trying to track Rhys
Durham down conventionally as possible.'

Louise waited for him to leave, then breathed a sigh of
relief.

She had her in.

It didn't take long to bring up the photos they had taken
the previous day, enlarging them on her screen and taking
screenshots. She felt for sure she knew the locations, of

course, but she had to make Shipley see them as well. Recognise them. That was key, if she wanted the story to hold its weight.

She couldn't just tell him. He had to think he had been led to the place by his own path.

She decided an hour would be enough for her to go to him with a simple query. Presented without fuss, just a quick question maybe. See if he bought the first part, before she turned the screw a little more. It was tricky; this wasn't the normal way of doing things.

This entire situation wasn't normal though. It wasn't as if they investigated murders every day. Or even every week. Things were usually very different.

Louise closed her eyes for a second, hunching behind her computer monitor so no one else would see her. Breathed in and out a few times, settling her nerves, then stood up and walked over to Shipley.

'Got a second?'

Light and breezy, Louise.

'Yeah, what's up?' Shipley replied, not looking away from his own screen.

'Just going through these pictures from Jon Durham's wall,' Louise said, placing a few images down next to Shipley. 'Does this look familiar to you? I'm sure I've seen it before.'

Shipley looked at the image she had laid on top, frowning at it, pulling it towards him for a closer look. 'I'm not sure. Could be any woodland area, for all we know.'

Come on, Paul, Louise thought, trying to telepathically emit the correct answer towards him.

'What about this one? Any idea?' She slid the next photo his way, knowing Shipley now had to put the two things together. The second image was much like the first one, but it contained a small clue. She wouldn't have known it was there if she wasn't looking for it.

In the top right-hand corner, almost hidden by what was pictured in the foreground, was the grey wooden slats that indicated the bottom of a small building. She knew what it was now, but without having first-hand knowledge of the area, she wouldn't have known to look for it.

She was counting on Shipley seeing it for what it was. A memory of it. The familiarity he surely had with the area, having grown up nearby.

Shipley squinted some more at the photograph, covering the image with his index finger, moving along it.

'There's something really familiar here,' he said softly, staring intently at the photograph.

Louise's heart beat against her chest, but on the outside she exuded calm. She was battling against her natural instincts, but doing a good job of doing so. Everything within her wanted to shout and point at the part of the photograph she wanted him to recognise. Instead, she waited, holding her breath.

'Hang on a minute . . .'

Yes, Louise thought, *come on*.

'This can't be what I'm thinking it is. It's been years.'

'What is it?' Louise replied, hoping she sounded genuinely intrigued. 'Something you recognise?'

'I think so,' Shipley said, scratching the back of his head with his free hand. 'He needed to be almost invisible, but close enough to do these things. He's just moved from one part of the city to another. That's all.'

Louise jumped as Shipley smacked the desk with one hand in triumph.

'There is no Bone Keeper, Louise,' he said finally, turning to face her fully, a broad smile on his face. 'But there is someone living rough in those woods. Probably scaring kids still, and possibly a lot more.'

'Which woods?'

Shipley stopped smiling, but puffed out his chest a little. 'Ever heard of the Big Mummy in Speke?'

Louise wanted to sigh with relief, but kept calm instead.

They were going to get this guy. He was there, in those woods. Keeping the story alive.

Now, they would stop him.

Sixteen

Blood had pooled around the body of Carl Groves. His skin now slashed and torn.

The woods breathed life for him, as his body was still and lifeless.

The glint of the sun broke through the trees above the broken man, catching the blade of what looked like a knife, as it twirled and bounced on the surface of the unmoving body.

Carl would have been glad not to be alive now. To not feel the pain of each slice into his skin.

The woods grew silent, in reverence almost. As if they knew what was happening within its clutches.

As if they were aware of what had taken them over.

If you were walking through the woods at that moment and closed your eyes to the scene of death, nature would explode in your ears. Every small movement in the undergrowth apparent, breeze rippling through the trees almost like waves crashing on the shore. Whispers of the unknown, the forgotten.

If it was never found, Carl Groves's body would slowly decompose in these woods. Left to become just another part of the ecosystem. A lifeless presence there, making the atmosphere around it thick and substantial. The smell would become a part of the scenery, eventually coalescing and becoming natural.

His last breaths had been in agony. His jaw clenching, his efforts to scream into the darkness. All in vain. Nothing there that would save him. That *could* save him.

Carl's life had been cruel and hard. His death was no different.

The woods were now home to more than just natural beauty. To the animals that had made it their own.

There was something else in there now.

Young people would go there and scare themselves. Less often than they had used to, but they came now and again. Their harsh laughter breaking through the trees and branches. Disturbing the quiet.

They wouldn't come as often after today.

The sounds around the clearing where Carl Groves lay on the ground changed. Natural sounds replaced by an outside presence. Footfalls on fallen leaves, breaking them down, crackling like logs on a fire.

Someone had found the secret the woods had been hiding.

Seventeen

Shipley pulled the car to a stop near a field which led into the woods themselves, as Louise fiddled with her seatbelt, eager to get moving. Within minutes, they were walking in step across the field towards the treeline ahead.

'It's about ten, fifteen minutes' walk. That's if I've remembered it right.'

Louise mmhmmed a reply, trying to remember the time she had been there before. The vagueness of her memory of it, mixed in with a multitude of other teenage recollections. Escaping her grandparents' house to drink cheap cider with a group of people who would never amount to much.

'It's much bigger than you'd think,' Shipley continued, his voice low. They weren't bathed in sunshine, but it was much lighter than it had been recently. The clouds above had lifted overnight, so the dusky fog-like atmosphere wasn't surrounding them now. The ground was soft under-foot, a consequence of the rain that had been a feature of the previous week. It wasn't until they broke through the trees and found the path within that she realised how ethereal the light around them was. Almost as if someone had taken a sepia-toned photograph and brought it to life. It grew quieter still within the woods, the sounds of traffic from a nearby A road being lost in the density of their surroundings. The trees there, old and dark brown. Almost grey in places. The bark would break off and crumble if Louise had reached out and taken a piece. She kept moving, following Shipley as he moved further in.

'It's not until you start making your way into it, or see it from above, that you realise why we called it the Big Mummy woods,' Shipley said, his voice lower now. Louise could barely hear him now, as if the surroundings were having an effect on the way he wanted to speak. 'You could get lost quite easily in here. You'd eventually find your way out, but you could end up in Hale – or worse, Widnes – before you realised it.'

'It stretches that far?' Louise asked, watching her step carefully as the path ended and they began traipsing through thick leaves yellowed and brown with age.

'Yeah, but it turns into fields before you get there, I should say. Surprising though isn't it, considering where we are.'

'Did you come here a lot when you were younger?'

Shipley didn't say anything for a while, probably considering his response, Louise thought. He wouldn't want to say the real reason, but she was wondering how close he would get to the truth.

'Not really. It wasn't technically allowed. All our parents had heard the same stories we had. We moved here when I was about five or six. Even when we were a bit older and braver, we didn't tend to come this far out. It's a bit of a walk from the estate.'

'What kind of stories were they?'

There was a hefty sigh as Shipley stepped over a thick fallen branch. The trees were old; Louise imagined during heavier storms they would no longer stand up as well as they had done in the past.

'*His* stories. You know.'

Louise didn't know how to respond. She knew who Shipley meant, but wasn't sure how far to push it. 'Oh . . . of course.'

Shipley stopped, almost causing Louise to walk directly into him. He turned to face her, tilting his head slightly to one side and frowning. 'Look, I know it sounds ridiculous, but we were kids. It's not like I still believe it's true. Despite what everyone keeps saying the past few days.'

'I understand,' Louise replied, as if she was accepting his explanation. He seemed to buy it. 'What was the story round here then?'

Shipley looked at her for a little while longer, then turned around and continued walking. 'He supposedly lived in these woods. In a little shack, which was hidden deep into them. I didn't think the hut even existed until I saw it one day.'

'You came looking for the Bone Keeper,' Louise said, her voice a whisper on the breeze. 'What did you find?'

'Nothing,' Shipley replied, his voice dripping with derision. 'There was nothing to find. That didn't mean we couldn't all get riled up though. We were kids – must have been no older than eleven or twelve. All trying to wind each other up. Before we'd even got this far in, we'd lost half the group. Only a few of us remained when we broke through to where it was supposed to be. There was an older lad with us – Eddie, his name was. We all looked up to him because he was a young amateur boxer, with a fair few trophies and that's what we all wanted to be back then. That, or a footballer. Anyway, he was leading us all to see this place and said we could peek inside the window and see where the Bone Keeper lived. It was too big an opportunity to miss.'

'I'm guessing the story was more involved round here than where I grew up. With the woods on your doorstep almost. Must have been exciting as well. Like an adventure.'

'Oh, yeah,' Shipley said, almost breathless now. He couldn't hide the excitement in his voice as he remembered. Louise felt a wave of affection for him suddenly crash over her. It was gone almost as suddenly. 'We all thought we were in *The Goonies*, or *Hook*, you remember that film? It was the nineties, so that's all we knew, those old kid-adventure type of films. It was either that, or we'd be playing Ghostbusters on Damwood Road. Watching the planes coming into Speke Airport and pretending they were bringing in ghosts and that sort of thing. We were young. We made up stories.'

'What happened when you came here then?'

'We didn't see a thing. Didn't get close enough, I suppose. Just caught sight of it, then got scared and ran away. Didn't stop us telling people that we'd seen him and that he'd tried to get us, of course.'

Louise had heard similar stories over the years. Everyone growing up in Merseyside seemed to know the tale. It was a rite of passage, it seemed. There were numerous different takes on the same legend. It had been the local evil. Something to keep children in line, keep them scared. That's the way of things everywhere.

The only discernible difference seemed to be that this myth was suddenly being used by someone real.

'What about you? Didn't you ever go searching for the Bone Keeper?'

'Not really,' Louise replied, not wanting to tell him that she didn't really know. That her memories of her childhood were almost non-existent. 'Probably once or twice. I tried to ignore it as much as possible. All a bit too creepy for my liking.'

'Not far now,' Shipley said, slowing down considerably. Louise wasn't exactly sure what he expected to find there. It seemed like he had wanted to experience his childhood again – that sense of danger, of excitement. He had been almost giddy when he'd decided they should come down and check out the area. She wondered if it would have been better to wait, to see if they could have possibly come with more officers and detectives, rather than just the two of them.

'I think we've come the more difficult way, sorry,' Shipley said, coming to a stop at the bottom of a small trench. Ahead of them, a raised bank of earth that ran a few metres in both directions. Trees lay at the top, beyond which Louise knew was the back of a small shed, or shack.

'It's just up here,' Shipley continued, checking his belt for ease of access to what he had insisted they both come with. An extendable, telescopic baton and handcuffs. She suddenly had a premonition that they wouldn't be using them.

She thought of the last time she'd been in these woods. Fear coursing through her veins, scared and frightened. The smell of sulphur in the air, assaulting her senses. The sound of the teenager at her side, breathing heavily, but trying to hide his own fear. Putting up a front, so she didn't see what was obvious. How scared he'd been.

The past has a way of pulling you back, nostalgia a

masked assassin. She had to ignore it, put her head down and keep moving.

Louise took the lead, walking up the small bank, which turned out to be steeper than she'd anticipated. Fifteen, twenty years ago, she would have leapt up something like this, but now age was slowing her down somewhat. She planted her feet, bending over slightly for balance, careful not to put her hands down on the ground and into the damp earth.

Shipley followed her, making more noise as he hefted his bulk up through the muddy bank.

Louise stopped at the top, already able to spy the hut through the trees, the sight of it bringing her to a halt. Shipley appeared in her peripheral vision, but she couldn't take her eyes off what was in front of her.

A childhood memory, come back to life. A blurred distortion of a reality she had remembered down the years, now real again.

'There it is,' Shipley said, sounding almost in awe of it. 'God, it hasn't changed at all.'

Louise moved her hand slowly to her side to grip the baton at her side. This suddenly felt very wrong. Like she had been led into a trap, easily, without any real effort. An unseen force guiding her there of her own volition.

This was a mistake.

Going there was her fault.

'There's someone here,' Shipley said, his voice a whisper. He ducked down a little and moved forward slowly. 'I can hear them.'

There was a pause, then Louise could hear the same noise. A shuffling, almost like water running. The smell became more powerful as it drifted towards them. She began to feel her chest constricting as the fear of what was near them grew. She tried to concentrate on her breathing, but the odour of death seemed to increase with each inhalation she took.

'We need to get closer,' Shipley said, looking over his shoulder towards her. He was still crouched over, baton in his hand, seemingly oblivious to the cloying stench. 'He's round the front. We need to separate and go around each side. Block him in.'

'Shouldn't we call for backup?'

'No time,' Shipley replied, breathless as he moved swiftly across the ground to the corner of the hut. The grey slats of wood were more aged now she could see them better. Brittle and broken. The passage of time marked along each piece.

Louise moved to the opposite corner. She heard another sound and turned to where Shipley had been standing, but he had already disappeared out of sight.

Over to her left she heard a slight noise, but there was more sound coming from around the front – branches snapping, leaves being pushed aside. But she followed Shipley's lead and moved around the side of the hut.

The noise grew, along with a new odour. Crackling, as she placed what it was she had detected in the air.

Burning.

There was a flash of something in her vision – a memory, or a sensation of one – which disappeared in a blink. More movement off to her side, but her focus remained on the hut, the sounds emanating from within. The growing heat in the atmosphere around her.

Fire.

The hut was burning down.

Eighteen

It was a mistake.

Being in those woods.

Being drawn to the fire.

They rounded the corner of the hut just as the fire really took hold. The heat from it, scorching across her face, turning the air around them black with smoke. The smell of burning flesh came next, before the assault on her senses became too much. The memories it conjured up, the past and present blurring together.

The hut is in flames. Now. It's the present and you're here.

For now, Louise listened to the voice.

'Call for backup,' Shipley said, shouting over the sound of splintering wood and the roar. 'There's someone in there.'

Louise didn't hesitate, taking the radio out of her pocket and making the call for the fire service. She looked back up to see Shipley trying to get closer to the hut. 'Don't, it's no use,' she said, her words coming out high-pitched and desperate. 'Stop, it's too late.'

'We can't just watch them burn,' Shipley said, then

stopped talking as he looked over Louise's shoulder. She spun around as the world shifted and turned dark.

She needed to get out of there. Away. Away from the fire.

She couldn't do this.

Her breaths were coming in slow pants, as the weight on her chest tightened. Louise staggered up the hill, moving through the broken branches and allowing the trees to swallow her from view. She continued moving forward, even as she felt the air leave her body, breaking down the bracken in her way. She didn't stop to think about what direction she was going, concentrating on moving her legs in time.

One, two . . .

Louise felt as if she could hear the sound of branches snapping, leaves being disturbed, rushing into her ears and making her stumble. Off-balance, as the world spun around her. Blurred and misshapen. She caught her breath, panting hard, bent over at the waist. The sounds were still there, as though there was something else in the thick of the woods with her.

She moved onward, stepping over a fallen log, not breaking stride, the only other sound that of her heavy breaths.

'Stop.'

Her shout echoed back, breathless and laboured. She stopped for a second, coming to a halt in a break in the trees. Tilted her head, to hear any sound.

There was silence.

She continued to move forwards, faster now, as she tried to cover the ground quicker. She imagined it was only a few feet away, just hidden by the thickness of the woodland around her. Adrenaline took over as thoughts flashed through her head, of getting her hands on whoever was in these woods with her.

She burst through tightly packed thin branches and found herself near the field they had crossed when they had arrived.

Louise spun around, looking for something that would prove she'd heard something human in the woods. A blurred figure. A man dressed in black running away. A shout or cry of escape.

There was only still, unbroken air around her.

Louise was standing on the edge of the field, her breath just about returned to normal, looking towards the woods again. They looked less impressive from this angle – as if they only went back a few acres, rather than the large expanse she knew they covered, stretching out of sight.

She considered her story. What she would tell Shipley and the others, when they began asking questions. Why she'd left him there.

It had been so long since she'd been into those woods, yet she could have still been exactly the same person. The familiar feelings of fear and anger were there. The fight or flight response coursed through her, just as it had all those years ago. She remembered the place being more impressive in the darkness – full of nooks and hiding places. She imagined what it would be like spending hours within the bracken, worried about being lost forever in the confines of the trees and bushes. Or purposefully trapped, with no chance of being free.

A field on one side of a road, lined with trees at the end of a small grassland, within which lay a hundred or so acres of woodland, then fields beyond. There was more traffic noise than she remembered, but she knew that disappeared when you made your way through the treeline. They had moved too quickly for her to stand and appreciate what was there. What she could feel. The darkness that was only a few steps away.

'What did you say this was called?' DC Cavanagh said, the passenger-side door closing behind him as he made his way around the car towards where Louise was standing. He looked out of his depth – more so now than before. A small, stockily built man, who she couldn't be more than a year or three older than, but looked much younger.

'DS Shipley called it the Big Mummy,' Louise replied, smiling for a split second at the term before remembering why they were there. 'Big Daddy was the other end of Speke, nearer the airport. It's only used by dog-walkers now, he says. The scrambler kids keep to the fields, pretty much.'

Another car came to a stop on the other side of the road, another detective out of the vehicle almost before it was parked. Shipley joined them, pocketing his phone, not saying who he had been calling.

'What is this place then?' DC Cavanagh said in Shipley's direction. 'Louise reckons you know all about it.'

'Grew up round here, didn't I,' Shipley replied, firing a smirk in DC Cavanagh's direction. 'Proper Scouser, me. Unlike you.'

'Whatever, I'm happy being from Cheshire. Less chance of my car being nicked.'

Shipley seemed to ignore the comment, as Louise watched the two men speak between themselves. 'There's a few places growing up in Speke that everyone knew about,' he said. 'Well, the kids, mainly – they were the ones who used them most. This is one of them. This is Big Mummy.

Big Daddy is at the other end of town. Separated by the length of the two main roads that run through here.'

'Which roads?'

'Damwood Road and Hale Road. Big Daddy is closer to the airport. Silly names I guess. Childish. Which is how they got the names, I suppose.'

'Big Mummy. Doesn't look all that big.'

'Looks can be deceiving,' Shipley replied, a cloud crossing over his expression. 'I suppose they're not as big as the ones further north of the city. Formby and that. Or out towards Skem – that's Skelmersdale to you, Cheshire lad.'

'Oh, don't start calling me Cheshire—'

Shipley ignored the plea and continued. 'There were other places we spent more time at. The Venny for one. That was an adventure playground – well, it was really just a collection of climbing equipment. Would never pass a health and safety check these days. All of them were painted in bright colours, just to further the illusion. The parade and the market as well. Or just on the roads, playing footy on whatever scrap of grass we could find. Playing kerby in the side roads. Made-up games, all of that. Probably the same as anyone else, whether or not they lived on one of the most deprived council estates in the country.'

To Louise, it sounded like something she had never really had. A community. A group of languishing council estate kids, looking for something to do when there were only four channels on the television and kids' programmes lasted for a couple of hours after school.

'I'm guessing we're going towards the smoke?'

Louise looked past DC Cavanagh to the smoke rising through the trees. They had been too late to stop the hut from burning to the ground. She wondered why the sight of it burned and broken didn't have the same effect on her as the fire itself had.

'We couldn't do much with the tiny fire extinguisher in the car. All we could do was call for backup and watch. Louise almost caught the bugger, but he was long gone by the time we got out of the woods.'

'He could still be in there,' DC Cavanagh said quietly, standing up straighter as he realised what Shipley was suggesting. 'Although I'm sure you knew that.'

'Uniforms are combing the woodland now,' Louise replied, saving Shipley the bother of coming up with a cutting reply. 'I heard something and didn't think twice. Just bolted after it. Didn't take long to break out onto the field. I'd have seen him if he was still there.'

She would have, she thought. There was no doubt about that. She had spent another half an hour walking back through the woods, listening to every sound she could hear.

There wasn't anything in those woods now.

There was something in there though. And you were too busy trying to breathe properly to find it.

'Here comes the air support,' Shipley said, shielding his face as he looked skywards. The helicopter appeared above, the distant sound of dogs barking instantly being quietened.

When Louise had finally got back to the hut, it was almost completely destroyed. Shipley had been standing a few feet away, pain etched across his face. His hands were black, his breath coming in short, sharp pants.

He was alone.

They had made their way out of the woods within minutes, worried about compromising what could be a crime scene.

The fire crew would do enough of that for them.

Louise hadn't pointed out the markings on the trees to Shipley before leaving. She would leave that for him to discover.

Off to her left, a fire engine lay idling, waiting as backup. Across the field were tyre marks. Another truck lay in the distance. 'We'll let them finish first. They'll tell us if there was someone in there.'

Once the fire had been extinguished, she knew pretty quickly that something had been discovered. A couple of uniformed coppers, sent ahead to assist on what they had probably assumed was an easy job, broke through the treeline and were making their way over to where she was standing. Shipley appeared, giving her the nod to follow him as he crossed the field towards them.

'What's happening?' Shipley said, his voice carrying over the hundred yards between them. He closed the distance quicker than Louise, but she was walking as quickly as she could. Determined not to miss anything. 'What have they found?'

'I . . . I don't know,' the cop on the right said, shaking his head. Louise couldn't be sure he wasn't always this pale, but she began to think he probably wasn't. Whatever they had found near the hut, she knew it wouldn't be good. Or normal. 'Nothing good.'

'What do you mean?'

'I think it's best you check it out for yourself,' the second cop said, his hands shaking as he straightened out his jacket. 'I don't think anything we say is going to help.'

Louise followed Shipley, leaving the uniforms with the other DCs making their way closer to the entrance to the woods. As they reached it, three firemen emerged, expressions giving away nothing.

'What's going on in there?' Louise said, her heart beating against her chest again now. She could feel her breathing becoming more laboured by the second, blinking away spots in her vision.

Not now. Not now. She turned away slightly, concentrating on her breathing. Shipley's words drifted her way, but she focused on getting through the next ten seconds.

'What was it?'

'We've done our job, now it's your turn,' one of them said, stopping to speak to Shipley as the others carried on past them. Louise swallowed a few times, feeling a little better each time. She turned back towards the men, taking in the fireman who had remained. His uniform looked like it was straining against the body within in it; lines creased his skin. The guy looked as if he could grout his own face and not have any left to finish doing the bathroom tiles. 'Looks like a body inside to me, but I'm only guessing. Fire had spread a little, but we got it out. Who's in charge?'

'Detective Sergeant Shipley, at your service.'

Louise allowed Shipley to have his moment. It wouldn't be him in charge from here on out. She knew that for sure. Not when another body was on the horizon. It would be too many for the top brass. Major Crimes would be taking over.

'Yeah, well, it won't be my service. This is your wheel-house. Our sarge is through there. You need anything, I'm sure he'll help you out.'

They left the fire officer behind and made their way back through the trees. This time, it felt different. More people were on the scene now, giving her more of a sense of control. It was an illusion, but she held onto it tightly.

The smell increased the further they walked, the burning and smoke filling the atmosphere. There was something else there as well. A scent she recognised well, having dealt with similar incidents in the past. Unmistakable, when she thought about it. Flesh, burned and broken. It was there, underneath the surface, but she could sense a change.

Shipley stopped to look at some of the markings on the tree trunks. 'These weren't here when I was a kid,' he said, his voice low. He almost sounded like he was admiring the scenery, rather than looking at evidence. 'Same ones as from the other woods.'

'He's continuing the story,' Louise replied, looking at another set of marks. An eye in a triangle, upside-down crosses, pentagrams. A mishmash of occultist and anarchist symbols, merging into one. 'They're probably not anything other than his way of marking his territory.'

They continued to walk, getting closer to the hut now. Off to the side, the smoke still drifted in short trails, the hut blackened and fallen in on one side. Already, she could see that inside were charred remains she could almost identify as human.

It could wait.

It was the area they hadn't reached yet that seemed to be the real hive of activity. A uniform spotted them and beckoned them over. Shipley broke into a jog, then remembered he was at a crime scene and slowed, allowing Louise to catch up.

'What have you got?'

'Shallow grave, sir,' the uniform said, his cheeks flushed red, excitement in his voice. 'There's a body.'

Louise looked past the uniform to the tree behind him. The clearing here was smaller, but it was still big enough to see what had been discovered. She turned around, looking down at the earth at her feet. The quality of it, compared to the rest of the woods. A thought came to her, suddenly, which she tried to dismiss; but it was no use. She knew she was right.

They were standing on a graveyard.

Nineteen

Louise was experiencing a feeling of revulsion mixed with admiration. She had felt it before, but never in a setting such as this. Everything about what she was looking at was horrifying, but there was also a sense of wonder. The time and effort it must have taken to create something of this magnitude.

They had to stop this. There was no doubt about that.

'I count eight,' Shipley said, barely moving from the spot he was occupying. 'If they're all here, they're going to be busy down at the morgue.'

Louise didn't answer, still struggling to take her eyes from the vision in front of her, trying to make some sort of sense of it.

It was only a small clearing, but she thought she remembered it. A memory dancing on the edge of her mind.

It's the fire. It's playing tricks on you.

'It's just dates though,' Louise replied, blinking her way back into the present, and considering the numbers carved into one of the trees. 'It could mean anything.'

'You said it yourself. This could be a graveyard.'

'So ... we have a serial killer?'

Shipley didn't answer her, instead moving around, being careful where he stepped. He'd dismissed the uniforms so they didn't compromise the scene any further, leaving just the two of them there and the CSI techs doing the more interesting work.

While through the trees were bigger, more open clearings, she imagined it was in these tight spaces that the kids had played. Maybe not here, so deep into the wood, but surrounded by the trees, blocking out the light just enough to make it more gloomy than it should have been. The black features of it were stark against the yellowing leaves surrounding them. Autumnal colours, clashing with the darkness of the clearing. A breeze swept through the trees, almost dying as it reached them.

'More CSI are on their way,' DC Cavanagh said from behind them, loud enough for the few techs already there to hear too. He stopped before coming into the clearing proper. 'Everyone is, to be honest. Station will be empty I think. If this is what it looks like, well, I think that's probably wise.'

'Scene is secure?' Shipley said, nodding to himself despite the question. He knew what was coming, Louise thought. That his moment in control was about to come to an end.

'Of course,' DC Cavanagh replied, shifting from one foot to the other. 'Place will be crawling within a few minutes. Anything we can do before then?'

Louise watched Shipley shake his head, look down at the ground, then stick his hands in his pockets.

'We'll let CSI do their job, but I want a list of these dates. That's where we start.'

'Are we going to continue then?' Louise said, tentatively

hoping for a positive reply. She wanted to be involved. Had to be.

'Damn right we are,' Shipley replied, flashing that grin of his her way. 'Until we're informed otherwise, this is still our case. We got this far, didn't we?'

'Provided there's actually something under here,' Louise said, turning back to the ground beneath them. 'Could just be an elaborate game. Takes focus off the poor guy in the hut over there, doesn't it? Could have nothing to do with anything.'

'And the body lying there?'

Louise didn't answer, but looked at the shallow grave a few feet away. A year maybe. Eighteen months tops. The body was beginning to waste into nothing, but she could see the mottled skin, the inhuman colour of it. Some attempt had been made to wrap her in bin bags, it seemed, but they didn't cover her entirely.

She couldn't have been older than twenty or so, Louise guessed from what little of her face was on show. Her hair was dark, matted. Dried blood still clinging onto the skin in places, merging with the soil and turning black.

'I think we've stumbled our way into something much bigger than we'd anticipated two days ago.' Shipley paused and looked around slowly. It was as if he had heard a sound and was trying to pinpoint its location. 'This isn't somewhere people come very often. It's too far in. More difficult terrain. Apart from some enterprising dogs off their leads, you could be here and never see another living soul for a long, long time.'

'There's a whole row of houses back there,' DC Cavanagh said, pointing back to where they had entered the woods. He meant off the road, but it could have been just a few yards through the branches, rather than the hundreds it was, for all they could see of them. 'Not sure they'll have seen anything from all the way over there, but worth a shot. I'll get people knocking on doors, shall I?'

'Yeah, go ahead,' Shipley replied, turning back to face the clearing as DC Cavanagh left him and Louise alone again. 'Let's look at this logically—'

'First time for everything.'

'Smart alec,' Shipley replied, shooting her a quick grin. 'We've found two pieces of evidence pointing us towards this place. Nathan Coldfield and the photograph in Jon Durham's bedroom. Only locals would know about the place though. It's probably not even got a name on Google Maps.'

'It doesn't, I checked.'

'Right,' Shipley said, turning and looking at her. She held her breath for a second or two, waiting for him to speak again. 'So,' he went on, 'that means someone with local knowledge is involved. Nothing in Rhys Durham's record – basically the only thing we know about him – puts him anywhere near here. Not this far south of the city.'

'Apart from his aunt.'

'That's still miles away. No, this is something only those from round here would know about. How did Rhys find out about this place, that's key.'

'We don't even know what we're dealing with yet. We're probably getting ahead of ourselves.'

Shipley murmured an agreement, but she could see he didn't mean it.

He knew exactly what this was.

*

Another hour went by, but it was all beginning to feel like much longer. When you're just sitting around doing little to nothing, time drags. Louise could feel the beginnings of hunger pangs returning, but tried to dismiss them. Simply remembering the blackened and charred body in the clearing a few hundred yards away should have been enough, she thought; an image like that was difficult to forget. Never mind the dead woman in the shallow grave.

There had been time to take in the scene one last time, before more CSI techs arrived and they let them get on with their job. She had been glad to get out of there and leave them to it. Simply leave the scene behind for a little while.

She usually didn't believe that places had a sense of darkness about them. Of *evil*. She was now questioning that idea. An unnerving quality had surrounded the scene through the treeline ahead of her. It was as if it could feel the borders around them closing in. Keeping the scene sacrosanct, like it knew what was hidden there.

'How long until we know if anything else is buried under there? Can't imagine that's going to be a quick job.'

Louise turned to Shipley, who was pacing back and forth behind her. 'Hopefully not long,' she said, placating him, knowing he was starting to become aware of how little time they had left as lead detectives on the case. 'They have all kinds of technology now, don't they? I'm sure they'll know if there's more bodies under there soon enough.'

'Not sure I want to know,' Shipley replied, stopping in his tracks and looking past her. 'Think we're about to get some kind of information though.'

Louise pivoted to where he was looking and began walking towards the treeline again. A CSI tech in full protective gear was making his way towards them.

'What have we got?'

'We won't know if anything other than the one body is buried underneath for a few hours yet,' the CSI tech said to Shipley, coming to a stop a few feet from them. Louise recognised the face, as much of it she could see anyway. His head was mostly covered, but the features were recognisable. Mind, she wasn't the best for remembering names anyway, so it hardly mattered.

'What have you got so far?' Louise said, hoping for something they could work with at least. Anything to keep Shipley happy, even if only for a few more hours. 'The last body we dug up was identified within minutes, so I'm hoping you can make it as easy as that was?'

Louise waited for him to speak, but it looked like he wanted to make a performance of it. She imagined strangling him, wrapping her bare hands around his throat and watching the life drain from him. She blinked and the vision disappeared, annoyingly. Sometimes she enjoyed the bursts of imaginary murder she thought up.

'The body has been there at least a year, but we're guessing it was in the process of being moved. It was a shallow grave, so we're thinking it could be the same for any others possibly buried there. We don't want to disturb any evidence, so we're going to take our time. We'll try and go as quick as we can though. Hopefully you'll be able to find out who she is pretty quickly. She's in good condition, considering.'

'Good condition?' Shipley said, before Louise had the chance to say something similar. Maybe with an added expletive.

'You know what I mean.'

'Right, of course,' Shipley replied through a clenched jaw. The CSI tech took the hint and left them to it.

They turned back to the road behind them, knowing there was little else they could do there now. Some traffic was being allowed to pass down the road, given the actual scene was a good walk away, but with the number of both marked and unmarked vehicles now taking up space, it wouldn't be long before they'd have to come up with an alternative plan. Louise stopped, once Shipley had moved far enough away, so that she was standing on her own in the field. She turned in a circle, thinking about the location, the history of the place. Face one way, you're looking at the outskirts of a council estate in south Liverpool. The other way, it could be old English countryside, anywhere in the northern part of the UK. In the distance she could see the town of Hale, only a couple of miles away but not counted as part of Liverpool. Almost as if it were on a hill and they were currently sat in a valley at its base.

The air around her stilled and she could almost hear the laughter of the other kids who would come to play here. The excited shouts, the jibes being passed between them. That would be how it would have been usually.

She wondered what had become of them all. The children who would tell each other stories, filling this now empty field with laughter and frivolity. The streets were now more deserted than when she'd been younger. She wondered if places like these would forever be tainted for her now. Whether that be woodland, fields, parks . . . all those places that had held so much wonder to her as a child, now turned to something else.

Where something dark and unseen lurked within every shadow, without her ever realising. She found it difficult to picture this place being used for something else. For evil. She turned towards the trees again, the thickness of the woods there. Louise could see it all playing out now; how easy it would be at night to fall into darkness and not be discovered. Live for years as a myth within those woods, no one ever brave enough to discover the truth – being able to hide if anyone ever was.

Lived in the woods? Are you crazy? It's not real.

'Think you were right about the possibility of tyre marks,' Shipley said, walking back slowly towards her, looking at the ground beneath him. 'If there were ever any here, he's got rid of them. Covered his tracks, if you'll excuse the pun.'

'You are excused,' Louise replied, still staring towards the woods. 'You don't just stumble across somewhere like here. There's no reason to drive down this way, unless you're going somewhere or know someone who lives here. Or, you grew up close by and knew about it.'

'I agree, for what it's worth,' Shipley said, now standing next to her and staring into the same empty space she was. 'I didn't even know about this place until I was an older kid. Maybe nine or ten. It just wasn't really talked about.'

'These places exist all over the city. Little clumps of nature. Most people don't even notice them. Which makes them good places to do things like whoever our guy is. Little patches of tranquillity.'

'Quite nice really, if you forget about the dead people a few hundred yards away.'

'Do you think it's Rhys Durham – the burnt body, I mean? I never really got a look at who or what I was chasing. Could have been a fox or something stupid like that,' Louise said, voicing what she knew Shipley had been suspecting. She guessed he hadn't wanted to say it out loud. He liked finality to an investigation – a chance to question a suspect and find out their reasons for committing whatever crime it was.

'I don't know,' Shipley replied with a weary sigh. Louise watched as he rubbed his fingers against closed eyes. 'We need to identify him as soon as possible. That burnt body could be important. Whoever was in those woods set that fire in order to make our jobs more difficult.'

'Or her,' Louise replied, sniffing and scuffing a shoe along the grass in front of her. She was becoming better at affecting a cool exterior, even as her body tried to rebel. She hoped it wouldn't happen again, knowing it was a futile wish. 'It's not like we could tell all that much from what we could see. Don't think we got there in time. Probably not going to be enough left to get a quick ID. He probably set the fire so he could get away. A distraction.'

Shipley nodded an agreement, then turned and made his way back to the road, leaving Louise alone again. She took her phone from her pocket, checked for any messages, unsurprised when it didn't show any. Who would call her anyway? She could feel her chest becoming constricted again, hands shaking. They became clammy, the phone sliding from her hand as she thrust it into her pocket. She could feel sweat peppering her brow, so she wiped her sleeve across it. Closed her eyes for a few seconds, fighting the urge to scream and shout. Fall to the ground and thrash around. Feel her arms and legs hit the earth, the pain shooting through her bones.

Instead, she opened her eyes and walked back towards Shipley and the others.

Powerless, that's what she was.

She didn't enjoy the feeling at all.

Twenty

A knock at the door.

Val always thought she would know the moment it changed. When she would sense he was gone. Ceased to exist. Mother's intuition and all that went with it. She was supposed to know if something had happened to her son.

In twenty years, she had felt nothing but emptiness. A sense that her world had shifted and would never be righted. Even if he reappeared now, after all this time.

Two decades ... Had it really been that long? Time had stopped the moment he had gone. That moment of realisation that he wasn't simply missing for a few hours. Those hours becoming days becoming weeks becoming months becoming years. On and on. The hurt the same every day.

There had been other times, when he had been younger. Moments of dread when she had lost sight of him in a shop, or in the park down the road. When horror dropped into the pit of her stomach for a few seconds, before he suddenly reappeared in front of her. Every parent recognises those moments.

You have one job. Keep them safe until they can keep themselves safe.

She had failed.

Now, she waited. For them to arrive and tell her they had found him. The idea of doing anything else was unthinkable. That's all she had now. An interminable wait for the truth of what had happened.

Her daughter seemed to be dealing with the loss better, on the surface, but Val knew she hurt as much as she did herself. Just as hard. That her life had suffered because of her brother's disappearance. She remembered her little girl back then, growing up before her eyes. A teenage girl in an adult's body. On the cusp of leaving and finding her own path.

Her brother going missing had fractured that natural process. Made her grow old overnight. An adult before her time, forever tainted as a result. Her daughter wasn't the same woman she would have become without that. Living with a mother who had dedicated her life to finding her lost brother. A stepfather who disappeared just as quickly, as suspicion had rained down around them.

A real father who was never there. Not even when his son had disappeared. Making a show of being concerned for five minutes, before rushing back to his comfortable life, where nothing bad ever happened.

Left to pick up the pieces alone.

She wondered what her daughter looked like now. Whether the years would have been kind to her or not. Whether she would still see that loss etched across her features, like a second skin.

Would either of them cope if they finally found out what happened?

She could hear footsteps outside, but was lost in her own thoughts, staring at the television screen in the corner of the room.

Wondering, considering.

Was this the time?

Was this the moment she would find out?

She suddenly didn't want to know. She wanted to continue her life as it had been. Left in limbo. The mother of a missing child. A failed parent. He was gone. Still gone.

Nothing was going to change that. It didn't matter if they found him now, she would still have been an unsuccessful mother. Unable to do her job properly.

The knock came again, but she made no move towards the door. She found herself stuck to the couch, unable to stand.

Still staring at the screen. Watching the news ticker run along the bottom of the screen.

BODIES FOUND IN SOUTH LIVERPOOL

She didn't want to know. Not now. Ignorance *was* bliss.

The knock came once again, more persistent now, and she buried her face in her hands. Shaking her head and moaning the word 'no' over and over again, as if that would be enough to send them away.

This wasn't how she wanted reality to hit. She wanted to continue to live in this stasis that had become her reality. Never knowing the truth. If this was it, they could keep it. She would happily live her life never finding out what happened to her boy. Safe in the knowledge that she would never know what his last moments were really like.

She didn't want to know anything. No more.

Not like this.

A knock came at the window, banging, insistent.

Val rose to her feet, checking her reflection in the mirror, then crossed the living room and went into the hallway. Reached for the door, ready to open it up.

To allow the truth, whatever it was, to rush in and devour her.

Twenty-One

The mood at the station was different now. News of what had been discovered in the woods – what was still being discovered – had filtered through the entire building. The pointed looks from other officers she passed on the way to her boss's office said all she needed to know.

Rather you than me.

They knew how things would change for everyone connected to the case.

What had started with one woman running away from an unseen danger had now become at least three dead bodies. Far too swiftly for her liking. She had read enough about serial killers to know what all of this meant.

The word she hated even more than 'moist'.

Escalation.

Louise reached her detective inspector's office, knocking once and entering before there was any answer. She was already late, having spent far too long in the bathroom trying to compose herself. She took a seat next to DS Shipley, who gave her a quick look, but snapped his attention back to the conversation that had already begun.

'We don't know if they're connected,' DI Hardy said,

barely acknowledging Louise's arrival. He had been usurped from his usual chair, a new face sitting there instead. Louise knew who it was, of course.

DCI Peter Sisterson, from the Major Crimes Unit. The city's top team. And Sisterson looked the part. Silver at the temples, immaculate suit. She guessed his shoes cost more than her monthly mortgage payment. His eyes were blue, piercing through anyone they encountered.

DI Hardy was attempting to remain calm, but she could see that events were moving too quickly for him as well. 'We're believing a fairytale here.'

'It would be one hell of a coincidence,' Shipley replied, exuding calm from every pore. He'd been waiting for this, Louise thought. Now was his opportunity.

'Whoever did this knows we were getting close,' Shipley continued, directing his explanation towards the DCI. 'He was in those woods. We almost had him. He can't be too far away now. He's running out of options for where to go.'

'How are we getting on with identification?'

'The bodies are being processed at the moment,' Louise said, taking her cue from Shipley's look to join the conversation. 'Shouldn't take too long if they were reported missing. We haven't ruled out that the body in the hut was Rhys Durham, or whoever this turns out to be. We have a list of dates, carved into a tree, but we're not entirely sure what relation they have to the bodies we have found so far. The last date was yesterday, which would make sense if the individual found burnt was killed then.'

DI Hardy sighed audibly, for effect, Louise thought. He obviously wasn't happy that two of his detectives were already handing things over to the DCI from the larger — and more important – unit.

Power games. Louise had never liked them.

DCI Sisterson interlocked his hands, resting his elbows on the desk. He ignored the DI and kept his eyes on Louise and Shipley instead. 'What are we looking at here? The story being real?'

Shipley gave Louise a quick glance, but she looked away, settled her eyes on the window. She could barely see through the blinds, but the view had been blocked anyway. Another office building built, waiting to be occupied. She knew it was the same in the city centre, where the DCI had travelled up from. She didn't go into town often, but when she did, there was always something either newly built or in the process of being put up.

'I think the story is still a story,' Shipley said finally, which caused Louise to tune back into the conversation. 'Someone is just using it. Building up their own myth, as it were. All these things are connected. Rhys Durham is still the main person of interest and that's all he is. A person. We find him, we find our answers.'

'If he's willing to talk . . .'

'Oh, he will be,' Shipley replied quickly, gripping the arms of his chair. Louise wondered what he meant by that. Whether he had the same kind of anger inside of him that she buried within herself.

'We need to go more public, which probably won't be as difficult now.'

'No, three bodies in as many days is enough to grab the national attention, it seems.'

Louise looked over at DI Hardy, who seemed to have taken a sudden vow of silence. He had been defeated quickly, without fanfare. She had never liked him much – she'd thought of him as someone who believed they should be followed without question. Now, she could see the weight of expectation beginning to weigh heavy on his shoulders. He was nearing sixty, which seemed to affect every decision he made now. Professional, yet always looking over his shoulder. Cautious of what could be coming up behind him. A thin-faced weed of a man. She had no idea how he had survived any time in uniform.

Not for the first time, she made the decision never to take on more responsibility than was absolutely necessary. She was quite happy at the level she was right now. With great responsibility comes greater sleepless nights and culpability.

Unless you managed to get right up to a certain level.

'We're going to use the press in order to get more information on this Rhys Durham,' DCI Sisterson said, sliding a hand back over his hair. Perfectly coiffed, the silver at his temples blending naturally with the rest of it, as if he dyed it on top only. Looked like a professional job, which didn't surprise her. More money the further you moved up the ranks.

'I know that's been tried already, but I want his face absolutely everywhere,' Sisterson continued.

'So, you are taking the case off us,' DI Hardy said, leaving the question mark off the end of his sentence. It didn't require one.

'I don't think there's any other option, do you?' DCI Sisterson replied, deigning to look at the DI now. 'This sounds like a major crime to me. And that is my forte.'

'So we need to smoke him out,' Shipley said, uncrossing his legs and sitting forward. 'He's not been seen, other than by the first victim's mother, for a long time. Nothing pops up from forces around the country, so if he has moved, he's kept himself out of trouble. I suppose though, if he's not been seen around this area, chances are he's been in other parts of the country.'

'And now he's come back?'

'Exactly,' Shipley said, wagging a finger in DCI Sisterson's direction. He sat back slightly, seemingly pondering something. Louise thought about that scenario. Wondered how long it would take for them to realise it wasn't the case.

'Why now though?' Shipley continued. In Louise's view, he was enjoying himself. It had been a while since he'd had the opportunity to be listened to by top brass. As a DS, and working with her, an even lower DC, he was usually the dogsbody.

'He would've had to have been following the news around here to know Nathan Coldfield's body had been discovered quickly, and he has to think that the woman was talking about him as well. And even then, it wasn't like the address was released.'

'Yeah, but the *Echo* named the pub nearby,' Louise said quickly, in response to Shipley's stumble towards the truth. 'He knows we found that place and now we've disturbed him in a different patch of woodland.'

'He's going to be on the run.'

DCI Sisterson held a hand up, to stop the back-and-forth. 'Who knows how he found out about it. I think it's pretty obvious, for what it's worth. And now, if he has been in hiding, he's back out in the open. He's not exactly hiding in plain sight. He's apparently living in a hut in the middle of some woods. If the two are connected, of course. Either way, we have the possibility of a serial killer. We also have to face the possibility that we might never know the truth. That whoever did this burned in that hut in the middle of the woods.'

Louise ignored DCI Sisterson's comment about the two cases being connected. She knew everyone was on the same page now. No one would buy the idea of a coincidence, given enough time to think it over.

'The way I see it,' Shipley said, clearly in control now. DI Hardy had been forgotten, which Louise knew wouldn't sit right with him. 'All roads lead back to that story. The Bone Keeper. Caroline – the first person to be found, alive, says his name ...'

'This Caroline, what's her story?'

Shipley looked at Louise, prompting her to answer the DCI's question. 'She seems clean. Never had any cause to be in touch with police before, by the looks of it. Wrong place, wrong time. Uniforms visited her address and neighbours didn't even know her name. Seems to keep herself to herself. Works for a homeless charity of some sort. The boss didn't have a bad word to say about her. We can't locate any family, and she's not been helpful on that score. Listed her next of kin as an elderly neighbour who didn't even know her surname. She wants to be left alone. No visitors or anything like that. Bit of a lonely life, by all accounts.'

'Keep in contact with her. See if she remembers anything else that could help us.'

'We've looked into the contents of Nathan Coldfield's bedroom more as well,' Shipley said, taking over from Louise. 'There's a picture with the initials RD on the reverse, which we think is of the woods in Speke. Then, we found Rhys Durham's full name and an old number on another scrap of paper. So, it looks like they were in

contact for some time. On the wall of Jon Durham's bedroom, we have a mural in reference to the Bone Keeper
and pictures of the woods in the south of the city. And
now, someone sets fire to a body and we find another one
buried. And, the same marks on the trees as were there at
the first crime scene. Only, this time there were also dates
on the trees. He wasn't exactly hiding by doing that. He
wants to do something.'

'Confess?'

'No, I don't think so.'

'I'd like the two of you to join our team on this one,' DCI
Sisterson said, a finality to his sentence. 'If that's okay with
you, DI Hardy?'

'They're grown-ups, suppose they can make their own
decisions.'

Louise wondered if DCI Sisterson would rise to the
undisguised hostility, but he seemed to ignore it. 'You
two have been involved in this case from the beginning.
It makes sense to keep you on board. I want you on the
ground, moving around. Just get me something to work
with. I don't care if we need to contact every last copper
in the country, I want to know if anyone has seen Rhys
Durham. I want to know what he's been doing all this time.
We also need to find out if this burnt body is Rhys Durham
and if not, put an end to this story.'

They were dismissed, leaving DI Hardy still in his office
with the DCI. Outside, Shipley gave Louise a quick look.
A nod and a smirk. He'd got what he wanted, at least.
Louise wasn't sure if she could share his excitement. They
wouldn't exactly be at the forefront of the investigation,
that seemed clear. Scut work and pounding the pavements,
like they were back in uniform. That seemed to be escaping

Shipley's thought process, however. For him, she guessed, it was all about being there. In the city centre, a seat at the top table.

She needed to remember these moments the next time she wanted to jump on him when they parked up outside her house at night.

As they made their way back, DC Cavanagh shot upright from where he'd been perched on the edge of Shipley's desk.

'Been waiting for you,' DC Cavanagh said, a piece of paper flapping in his hand. 'Thought you'd want to be the first to know about this.'

Shipley held his hand out for the paper. DC Cavanagh handed it over and crossed his arms, waiting for a reaction. Louise stood quietly beside Shipley, wondering what could be coming next. He read the details it contained and swore under his breath.

'It's not Rhys Durham. The body.'

Louise frowned at Shipley. 'Who is it then?'

'Look,' Shipley replied, handing over the single sheet to Louise and sitting down at his desk. 'Guess we're not as close as we hoped.'

Louise read, and saw the issue instantly. 'The body is that of a man in his late teens, twenty tops, apparently. Plus, while his body was burnt quite extensively, his facial features were intact enough for them to rule out Rhys Durham as the victim. I don't think Rhys could be mistaken for someone as young as this guy looks. How old was he in that last mugshot?'

'About mid-twenties'

'He looked ten years older at that point.'

'That's not all,' Shipley said, clicking his computer

awake and typing in his password. 'Have a look at the prelim on the woman.'

'Flayed skin, cut open and removed from the body,' Louise said, swallowing back her revulsion. 'So we're back to square one.'

'Not quite,' Shipley replied, swivelling in his chair and facing Louise. 'We know his name and what he looks like. We're one step ahead of where we usually are in stranger murders.'

Louise wanted to feel as excited about this as Shipley, but couldn't. There was something that didn't make sense about Rhys Durham being the man they were looking for.

'The earliest date on that tree . . . what was it?'

'2001, I think,' Shipley replied; he carried on grinning for a second, before his face fell a little. 'He would have been about fourteen or fifteen. Plenty old enough to do something like this, right?'

'Still, a little young don't you think? Plus, he was getting into petty trouble after that. Hardly the way a serial killer would be working.'

'You'd be surprised,' Shipley said, but Louise could see his mind turning now.

'I'm not sure . . .'

'Look, it's the closest we've got. We don't even know if there's any bodies buried there that are that old, do we? Could be just more madness.'

Louise nodded, but she didn't accept the explanation. Not just about the madness part – that wasn't all there was here.

This was more than that.

Twenty-Two

Normal people. Normal lives. All crowded together at the tape, the closest they could get without stepping into what the police had decided was a crime scene.

They chatted together. Coming up with theories for what was happening. Right there, on their doorsteps. They had a right to know, that they could all agree on. Yet, no one was telling them anything. The occasional grunt from some bloke in a uniform who was standing watching them.

The locals passed information around, as if they knew anything. A large woman, cigarette dangling from one of her chubby fingers, took a drag and pointed towards the woods with the glowing ember. 'It'll be some paedo I bet. Or some druggie. God knows what goes on in those woods at night. I never go near the place.'

'I want to know what's hidden in those woods,' another woman said. No cigarette or exposed stout flesh on this one. She was almost painfully thin, protruding cheekbones jutting from her pale face. 'Why all these police have come here. It's always drugs usually. A meth den or something inside there.'

There were around twenty or thirty people gathered

now, all watching nothing but an empty field. Normal
people with normal lives. Without anything better to do
at three in the afternoon than this.

Any of them could have been a victim.

A young girl, no more than twenty, thin-faced and
scarred. Her pockmarked belly could be carved open. A
look of surprise on her face, as blood dripped from her
skin and bones.

An old man, who smelled faintly of cheap whisky and
damp. Wisps of hair protruding from every facial orifice.
Grey and wiry. Clothes that would have fit him a fair few
skipped meals ago. The folds of skin at his neck could be
compressed, his eyes bulging as the struggle for oxygen
became too difficult.

Something didn't belong among this crowd.

'I bet it's nothing,' a young lad with protruding front
teeth and pale skin said. 'Just a waste of money as usual.
Either that, or a bunch of foreigners setting up camp.'

There was tutting from a few of the crowd, but their
attention didn't waver.

Something watched them all without them knowing.
Something abnormal and malformed.

Something they wouldn't recognise.

They thought they knew evil.

They had no idea.

Twenty-Three

It was late afternoon by the time they reached the hospital. It was perfunctory at best, Louise thought. She didn't expect Caroline would be able to give them any more information than she had already, but it was the first task their new boss had assigned them, so it had to be done.

She wondered how long this would last. Whether they would be sidelined as soon as the case became Major Crimes' lock, stock and barrel. There would be many other detectives more than happy – and experienced – to take up the slack.

They could go back to burglaries, domestics and assaults. That would suit her much better, she knew. Yet, there was a big part of her that needed to be there now.

'I keep thinking about that poor guy burned to death,' Shipley said, turning the steering wheel and entering the hospital car park. 'If I could have got there sooner, or maybe . . . I don't know.'

'There was nothing you could do. It was too late. There was obviously some kind of accelerant used. We had no chance – and anyway, he was probably already dead. It's not like we heard any screaming.'

'So you don't think it was just some animal in the woods

then? That you were chasing someone through those trees? Maybe even Rhys Durham?'

'What do you think?' Louise said, a grin stretching across her face. Shipley snorted in response. 'I don't know what I heard in there. It all happened so fast. I was only covering all angles. Even before we had a possible age of the victim.'

'I want to be in and out here,' Shipley said, pulling the car to a stop and turning to Louise. 'We know there won't be anything else she can tell us and I want to be in the first briefing in the city.'

'Won't get any argument from me.'

'Should be easy enough. Show her the mugshot of Rhys again and get the same answer. *She can't remember, it was dark.*'

'Still, doesn't hurt to check she hasn't had some sort of epiphany overnight.'

Shipley shot her a look, wincing at the suggestion, but then nodded. 'I know, I know. I just think she's told us everything she can. If she'd seen more, she would have said by now.'

'I agree with you, but we have our orders.'

Those they did have. DCI Sisterson was quite firm about what he wanted to know before moving on to the next part of the investigation. Louise wasn't quite sure what that next part would be, but she was just being pulled along now. In a daze, almost.

Her entire life had become a daze.

There was a part of her that hoped the past few days had been a dream. That the ghostly quality to her vision was a by-product of that. That nothing was real – just the feverish dreams of a sick woman. Memories colliding with her current life and creating a new reality.

It would be so much easier that way.

She hadn't been prepared for any of this.

Louise followed Shipley's lead, getting out of the car and walking behind him as they reached the hospital entrance and took the lift up to the room where Caroline had spent the previous few days. When they reached the correct floor, they were buzzed in by a nurse after a few seconds' wait. She checked the board to make sure Caroline was still in the same place and then ushered them through.

Louise had seen more of these hospital corridors than she cared to over the previous few days. Not that the place was alien to her – as a police officer, this wasn't exactly a foreign country. She still remembered the countless hours she'd spent in various hospitals in the county while she still in uniform. 'You know, part of the reason I applied to become a detective as soon as I could was to avoid these hospitals,' she said.

'You spend far too much time in them as a uniform,' Shipley agreed. 'It's a struggle to make much of a difference.'

'Just putting sticky tape over cracks in the ceiling.'

'I always thought of it like I was balancing plates on a stick, always watching for something about to fall. Always reacting, trying to keep the peace.'

Louise nodded slowly. 'Instead, you wanted to provide justice.'

'Exactly. What about your family? Any of them coppers?'

'No, not that I know of,' Louise replied, her mood dropping even further. 'I'm probably the first one.'

'You never talk about your family. Why is that?'

'Nothing to say,' Louise replied, hoping he would get the hint soon enough. 'I don't have any left to talk about, so it seems pointless. I had a nice childhood, got up to the

usual teenage hijinks, but that ended quickly. Now, I tend
not to think about them more than I have to.'

'Too difficult?'

'I . . . I don't exactly remember them all that well. I was
young when I moved in with my grandparents.'

'After it happened.'

Louise looked at Shipley for a second, wondering if he'd
looked up her past since they last talked. Whether curiosity
had finally got the better of him. Delving into a past she
couldn't remember. Didn't want to remember.

'Yeah, after it happened.'

Shipley stared at her for a few seconds, before she
averted her eyes from his.

'I'm sorry, I shouldn't have brought it up,' Shipley said
finally, and sighed. 'I don't know when to shut up sometimes.'

'Don't worry,' Louise replied, wanting to keep talking
to him. Open up about her past and what little she remembered about it. Tell him things she'd never told another
person before. She wanted nothing more than to walk
away with him there and then. Take him somewhere else,
quieter, more discreet, and just talk. For hours and hours,
before doing what she'd wanted to since first meeting him.

She knew he felt the same. Maybe had done for as long
as she had.

Instead, the moment passed by in the blink of an eye.

The room was brighter than before, blinds open and
sunlight streaming through the now bare windows. It
also meant Louise could see how still the air was; nothing
fluttered in the light trails, as it would in any other room.
Caroline looked a little brighter than she had the previous
night, although she was still lying horizontally. The bruising

to her face had started to colour – angry blacks and purples.
Yellow tinges to some parts. Her jawline was also more
swollen than Louise remembered, but then she hadn't really
concentrated on what Caroline had looked like.

'Hi, Caroline,' Shipley said, taking the lead here too, it
seemed. 'Won't keep you long, we promise.'

'I'm glad of the company, to be honest,' Caroline replied,
sitting up a little in bed, which seemed to cause her some
discomfort. She winced as she pushed herself up, but then
settled, a few inches more vertical. 'Getting a little bored
watching daytime telly. Same old stuff as it always was.'

Louise gave her a look that she hoped Caroline understood. *Don't mention I was here last night.*

'We just have a couple more questions for you, that's all.'

'Go for it,' Caroline replied, shooting a grin towards
Louise as she did so.

Shipley stood aside, allowing Louise to move past him
and closer to Caroline. She hesitated, standing at the side
of the bed, then looked around and pulled up the chair
lying there. She sat down, pulling out her notebook. 'Have
you remembered any more since we last saw you?'

Caroline shook her head. 'Nothing substantial anyway.
I've been having dreams, but I can't really trust them. For
one, it always catches me in them.'

'Was he there when you escaped?'

'I don't know,' Caroline replied, screwing up her face
as she tried to remember. 'It's all a little fuzzy, that part.
I remember it in flashes, standing over me, hurting me . . .
I'm sorry, it's just hard to think about.'

Louise waited as Caroline composed herself. It took less
time than she'd expected. 'What do you remember about
your time in those woods?' she said once the tears had

subsided a little. She didn't want to push her too hard, but they had orders to find out everything they possibly could.

'Not much, sorry. I thought a couple of days would help, but it's all just a blur. I remember parts of it, but it's all just a mess.'

'We won't know for a few days if you were given any drugs,' Shipley said, picking up a card from the cabinet next to the bed. He placed it back down, shaking his head at Louise. 'It's possible that's why your memory isn't proving to be helpful.'

'Do you think I was drugged?'

Louise hesitated, then opted to change the subject. 'Have you had anyone in to visit yet?'

'I had a card from work.'

'And family?'

Caroline shook her head. 'There's no one. I ... I don't keep in contact with any of them.'

This was new, Louise thought. Before, she hadn't wanted them to see her in this state. Now, it was a different reason.

'What happened? Why isn't there anyone you want to come in?' Shipley said, leaning against the cabinet with his arms folded.

The tears had gone now, but it was still a surprise when Caroline turned towards Shipley and spoke in a hard tone. 'There just isn't, okay? Is that against the law or something?'

'I was just wondering, that's all.'

'I don't want to have any contact with those people.'

'A falling-out?'

'Why does it matter?' Caroline said, her tone not softening. 'It has nothing to do with what happened to me.'

'You need me to be the judge of that.'

Caroline fixed Shipley with a stare, a few seconds pass-ing by in silence. 'We fell out a long time ago. The last thing I need is for them to come in here and start *judging* me. I'm fine on my own. I haven't seen them in years. Wouldn't even know how to get in contact with them. They're miles away. That good enough? Because it'll have to be.'

Subject closed, Louise thought. She could understand that feeling though. She made a mental note to ask Caroline about her family more if she visited alone again. They might have more in common than she'd first thought.

'Sorry, I'm just . . . this has all been very hard,' Caroline said, turning to Louise and giving her a smile, soft but devoid of warmth. 'I don't want to open padlocked doors if I don't have to. They reckon I can go home soon.'

'Why did you walk near that place, Caroline?' Shipley said, before Louise had a chance to reply. 'Is it somewhere you go often?'

'Every now and again, I suppose,' Caroline replied, turn-ing back towards Shipley, the cold smile falling away. 'It's nice round there. Used to be, anyway. I can't imagine I'll be going back there in a hurry. Peaceful. You can hear your-self think. It's difficult to find places like that these days. It's all cars and people everywhere. Noise. I like the quiet.'

Louise frowned at this response. Something about it niggled at her, but she couldn't quite work out what it was.

'And you've never seen anyone else there before?' Shipley continued, drawing closer to Caroline. 'Bumped into people, that sort of thing?'

'Only people walking dogs, couple of joggers every now and then. Nothing out of the ordinary. It's not the usual place to go for either really. As I said, it's usually pretty quiet.'

'Ever had the sense you were being watched or followed?'

Caroline shook her head. 'Nothing like that. Do you think he's been watching me or something?'

Shipley held out his hands, trying to placate her. 'Just covering all the bases, best we can. That's all. We need to build a complete picture.'

'Is it true, what they're saying?'

Shipley didn't answer, his mouth left hanging open. Louise took over when the silence went on for a few seconds too long. 'Is what true, Caroline?'

'That they've found bodies. You've found bodies, I should say. Is this whole thing linked with what happened to me?'

'We can't really say at the moment,' Louise replied, without pausing. One of those sentences you get used to having to say. Over and over, so it loses all meaning. 'Anything you can tell us would be a great help though, Caroline. You're the only one who has seen him.'

'I'm sorry, I just can't remember,' Caroline said, screwing her eyes tightly shut and turning her head away. 'I wish I could. I don't want anyone else to end up in this position. Or worse. By the sounds of it, I got very, very lucky. I could have been . . . you know.'

Louise did know. Shipley too. The woman in the bed was the only one to have escaped, by the looks of things. There hadn't been any other reports of someone calling themselves the Bone Keeper committing this sort of assault and the victim living to tell the tale.

Which meant there was something different this time around.

No one was supposed to escape.

Twenty-Four

It was almost evening by the time they arrived at the first house. There would be similar visits made right across the city, Louise imagined. A couple of faceless detectives, knocking on the door and changing the lives of those living behind them.

Three more bodies had been unearthed in the woods that afternoon.

She didn't think they would be the last.

Two had already been tentatively identified. One was a missing man from Northumberland. Louise had wondered how they had ended up this far down the country, but then considered the usual victim in cases such as these. The types of missing people that would be found buried in forgotten woodland and left to rot. No major task force looking for them throughout the borough. Simply forgotten.

They were just outside the city centre, in Bootle, waiting for a door to open. The second body possibly identified that day had led them to it. A scruffy-looking terraced house, deep in the middle of a council estate. Next door seemed to have decided to have a car boot sale in their front garden, but had no customers. A stained leather sofa, one of the seat cushions missing, pushed up against the fence. Next to it, a washing machine lying on its back. Various children's toys scattered about. A purple wheelie bin with no lid, graffiti scratched into its sides.

The other way, a well-maintained patch of grass, nice porch attached to the front of the house.

In the middle of that, the house they were still standing outside. Scruffy, but not overly so. White trims on the window awnings, the paint peeling away in places, staining the red brick below it. There was a gas meter cupboard attached to the wall next to the door, its door swinging open every time a burst of wind hit it.

'I hate doing this,' Shipley said, rocking on his feet as they waited. 'I can never get used to it. Telling someone the worst news imaginable. How do you ever get used to giving this sort of news?'

'The way I see it,' Louise replied, sliding a finger across her hair to get it out of her eyes, 'you hope you never do.'

'Shall I try again, or give up?'

Louise gave Shipley a shrug, then stepped forward herself and rapped on the door a few times. She smacked the letterbox down as well, just for good measure.

They could hear swearing from behind the door, a deadbolt being shifted and finally the door opening.

'William Scarrow?'

'Who's asking?'

Shipley lifted his ID, giving the old guy standing with his hand still holding the door a chance to inspect it. 'Detective Sergeant Paul Shipley. This is my colleague, Detective Constable Louise Henderson. Can we come inside please?'

'Got a warrant?'

'We're not here for anything like that, Mr Scarrow,'

Louise said, allowing him to look her up and down. She could almost feel his eyes crawling over her. 'We need to speak to you about your daughter.'

William Scarrow must have liked what he saw; he stepped to one side and allowed them to enter the house. The smell of mould and damp hit Louise as soon as they crossed the threshold, almost making her gag. Alongside that, a wave of something she couldn't quite place at first, but then it hit her. The sickly sweet smell of a class B drug. Shipley failed to stifle a cough, which told her she wasn't the only one suffering.

'Excuse the mess,' Scarrow said, picking up some news-papers off a threadbare sofa and gesturing for them to sit down. He plonked the papers on the floor next to it, exploding a cloud of what could have been either dust or someone's ashes as he did so.

Shipley gave Louise a look, knowing they should sit down to deliver this kind of news. Neither of them wanted to, but they did so anyway, carefully, lowering themselves down slowly and almost in sync.

'So, which daughter of mine has got herself into trouble then? I'm guessing Angela. Or is it our Julie? Has to be one of them.'

'I'm afraid we've got some bad news, Mr Scarrow . . .'

'Please, call me Bill,' he said with a dismissive hand wave. 'Now, what's happened? One of my girls got them-selves into something bad, no doubt.'

'It's about Eleanor.'

Bill Scarrow hadn't been expecting that name, it was clear. He rocked a little, then allowed himself to fall back-wards in his chair. 'Have you found her?'

'Yes,' Louise said, giving Shipley a nudge to move over

an inch so she could lean towards Bill. 'I'm afraid we believe we've found her body. We've matched the finger-prints from a body to one in our database. To Eleanor. I'm really very sorry.'

Bill didn't react, simply staring at Louise. He lifted his hands, interlocking his fingers and resting them on his head. Blew out a long breath. 'Are you sure?'

'We'll need you to identify her,' Shipley replied, opening the folder on his lap and removing a single sheet. 'We have a photograph with us, but a more formal identification will need to be made.'

Bill took the proffered image, printed out in high reso-lution. It was of her face only, decay thankfully minimal due to the fact the body had been wrapped like a mummy in bin bags.

That wouldn't help all of them, Louise thought. If the dates carved into the tree were correct. Some of the bodies would have been buried for a number of years. She dreaded to think of the forensic investigations which would need to take place over the coming days. 'That's her,' Bill said, keeping hold of the photograph. He looked at it for some time before handing it back over. 'What happened?'

'We're still investigating the exact circumstances behind her death, Bill.'

'Is this to do with the bodies found in Speke?'

Louise glanced at Shipley, who gave her a nod. 'It's still an ongoing investigation, but she is one of those we have recently found.'

'I don't even know why she'd be that far south of the city,' Bill said, tutting and shaking his head. 'Then again, what the hell would I know about her life. Never did. Never will now, I suppose.'

'Forgive me, Mr Scarrow,' Shipley began, seemingly hesitating over his words. 'But you don't seem too shocked.'

Bill shook his head, gave a small shrug of his shoulders. 'To be honest, I've been waiting for this day to come for a while. I ... I can't say I'm surprised she's ended up dead, because that's what I always thought would happen eventually, you know? The other girls, they got into trouble, sure. Eleanor was different. It was like she went looking for it.'

'When did you last see her?'

'Must be five years now. Maybe even six. Long time, either way. I don't really remember the exact date. She was always flitting in and out. One day, she just never came back.'

'What happened when she disappeared?'

'She was a bit of a tearaway,' Bill said, a rueful smile appearing on and quickly disappearing from his face. 'Back when she was a young 'un. All our girls were. Once their mum died, they all went off the rails a fair bit. I had kids late, but their mum was young when she died. Understandable, I guess. Eleanor was just ... not there anymore. She was the oldest, so I suppose I leaned on her to help out a little more, you know, with the younger ones. I don't think she ever liked that.'

'How many daughters do you have, Bill?'

'Four. No boys. And not one of them liked football, can you believe that? Just my luck.' Bill chuckled, but there was no feeling behind it. Louise could see him holding back the emotion now, his broad chest rising and falling faster by the second.

'And how old was Eleanor when her mum died?'

Bill made a show of thinking about it, but Louise guessed he actually knew all the details without having to consider. 'Must have been about thirteen or fourteen.

She was gone three years later. Sixteen or seventeen and thought she could look after herself.'

It was always different, that was what you learned quickly doing these death knocks. There wasn't a normal way of reacting to being told someone you loved was never coming home. Still, Bill had been more prepared than most of the people she had done this with.

It didn't make her feel any better. Any less angry.

'Do you know anything about where she was before she went missing?'

'Not really,' Bill replied, sitting forward, his hands clasped together almost as if in prayer. 'We heard she was possibly in a hostel, or homeless. We weren't really sure. Someone once said they had seen her begging in town, but when I went there, she wasn't around. I did try looking for her, but it seemed she didn't want to be found.'

'More likely, Bill, she couldn't be found.'

Bill looked at Shipley, seemingly searching him with his eyes. 'You're probably right, mate. Maybe I didn't have a chance.'

The room filled with a choking silence, the smells becoming more noticeable again. Desperation and despair pouring out of every surface. Louise looked around the room – the clutter, the mess. The giant television in the corner, a brand she didn't recognise. Untidy wires, protruding from behind it, snaking around to its front.

There was an old photograph on a cluttered mantelpiece, but that was the only one she could see. It was a younger Bill, fresh-faced and thin, but still ten or fifteen years older than the young woman he had his arm around. He was smiling from ear to ear.

Time hadn't been kind to him.

'What happens now?'

Louise turned in Bill's direction, wondering what the answer to that question should be. Shipley seemed similarly silent on the issue, even though they had both faced it before.

'We'll be joined soon by someone who will be able to talk you through the specifics,' Louise said, thinking of the liaison officers who would soon become the support for the family. 'Is there anyone you can call to come round now? Your other daughters?'

'Yeah, that's probably a good idea,' Bill replied, as if he had only just considered the possibility. 'I'm sure they'll want to know. Phone's been cut off though.'

'You can use mine,' Shipley said, digging into his pocket and removing his mobile. 'We'll stay with you until someone gets here.'

'Thanks,' Bill said as Shipley handed over the phone. He stared at the screen for a few seconds before handing it back. 'Can't work the new ones. Can you dial for me?'

Louise drifted away again, looking around the room. The normality of it killing her slowly. This was the reality of things. Those left behind. All those bodies, those people. The lost ones. She knew what kind of victim this . . . *Bone Keeper* would be looking for. The ones who lived on the edges of society, scraping by and barely living.

Ones who wouldn't be missed.

These people wouldn't be found staring out at you from the front page of some tabloid. The tearaways, the drug addicts, the drunks. The forgotten missing, who were allowed to slip silently onto the streets, to be ignored by those passing them by, as they held out a styrofoam cup begging for change.

Those were the people the Bone Keeper preyed upon.

Who he enjoyed taking control of, whose lives he enjoyed ending.

The teenagers with troubled home lives. Abused or neglected. Or just misunderstood. No one was surprised when they disappeared. No one cared.

It was simple in her mind now. Someone had become the mythological figure of their childhood and was picking his victims off one by one. Whether it was Rhys Durham, as it looked likely to be, or someone else. Louise understood it all now. Not that it made it any easier to listen in as Bill made his phone call to one of his daughters. She could hear the reaction, the scream of anguish, as he told her what had happened.

Within minutes, there was a rap at the door. She watched, Bill as he remained unmoved, seemingly preparing himself for the emotion about to enter through the front door. Louise was about to get up, to let him sit for a while longer, but he held up a hand to stop her.

'Best I answer,' he said, lifting himself out of the chair. He seemed to have aged even more since they'd arrived. Deep lines appearing in his face, yellowed skin and teeth. 'They'll want to see their dad.'

'You reckon they'll all be like this?' Shipley asked, once Bill had left the room. He kept his voice low, meaning Louise had to lean in further in order to hear him. 'All the victims, I mean?'

Louise went to answer, but was stopped by the sound of the door opening and a cry from the hallway. They sat in silence for a few seconds. She was suddenly scared to say what she really thought.

Instead she gave Shipley a look, gazing into those soft eyes of his. Then, she silently nodded.

Twenty-Five

He had to take a deep breath and be calm. Had to be careful, if he didn't want to be caught before he had the chance to go inside the house and do what he wanted.

There were many places he could find someone easily enough. Spend enough time hiding in the shadows and you came across similar people in the world. Those who hid from the light the world provided, whether by choice or not. It didn't matter who they were; all of them were targets. Even those who felt safe and sound, locked in their houses, sitting in their cars, walking through busy towns and shopping centres.

It started, as it always did, on the streets.

There are many towns in the city, each different and similar in many ways. Some more rich than others, more working people, more educated residents. Nice houses, newer cars parked outside them.

It was one of those houses he was standing near now.

Darkness had fallen a few hours before, some lights remaining on, dotted around in the homes on the quiet street. He could see houses either side, lights coming on in various rooms, then switching off. He wondered how thin the walls would be. Whether anything could be heard through them. The air was still, no sounds other than the occasional rustle of leaves as a cat searched for something to do in the black of night.

And him.

It hadn't taken much to hop a fence and gain access to someone's back garden. To stand there, waiting. There was no light in the garden, but nonetheless he kept as still as he possibly could. Waiting, concentrating, as he stared at the back of the house, the door and window, wondering if they would notice him crouching in the bushes. Cloaked in darkness, an animal ready to pounce.

A light came on in the kitchen, the back door opening with a creak, a man stepping out and closing the door behind him. The flick of a lighter, the red glow and loud exhale. The man's face illuminated by the mobile phone in one hand, fingers cradling a cigarette, pausing between inhalations to flick at the screen.

He watched him, holding his breath and wondering how the man's blood would look as it dried on his hands. Watched, as he smoked his cigarette and looked at his phone. He could kill him there, on his back step ... but something kept him still, just watching the man in the darkness.

The door opened again, the kitchen light flicking off moments later.

He waited a few more minutes. Then, a few more. Allowed them to settle back in, safe in their home again; then he walked towards the back of the house, moving across the small garden. Past the tired-looking furniture, the uncut grass, the muddy patches. Towards the door, cupping his hands around his face to look into the darkness inside. He opened the door slowly, moving into the dark kitchen beyond, wondering why anyone would think leaving the back door open would be a good idea. Not with things like him out there. He could hear the television playing in the living room, through the closed door. Canned laughter, the occasional grunt of appreciation from someone sitting watching. He stood near the living room door, listening to normal life from within. The hallway was dark, but his eyes had become accustomed to that. He waited there for a few moments, closing his eyes and imagining everything behind the door. The young couple he had been watching for days without their knowledge. The furniture, the television they were glued to. The way her legs curled up against his, the familiarity of touch which was so alien to him.

He slipped past the living room door, the couple inside still chuckling, and made his way soundlessly up the stairs and found their bedroom.

There was a moment of movement downstairs. He slipped his hands around the knife in his pocket and held his breath. He left the room; seeing a guest bedroom on the other side of the landing, ducking inside and waiting for them to finally come to bed.

And waited.

He could have saved himself the trouble. Stayed outside until they were safely tucked up in bed. Broke into the house and slaughtered them in seconds.

This way had appealed to him more.

There was something about wanting to watch them sleep. To watch them at their most fragile, most vulnerable. When they were least expecting anything to happen to them.

When it was safer.

He waited. An hour, possibly longer.

He listened in the darkness, waiting for any sound other than his own breathing. Then, there was movement. He smiled to himself as the voices grew closer, enjoying the sound of their routine. Heard the sink in the bathroom.

He wondered if he would hear anything else, once they were in bed.

Another hour.

Then, in the dark and silence, he slipped out from underneath the bed and took a deep breath. Left the guest bedroom and walked across the landing. He stood outside the door of the main bedroom, listening to the soft sounds of breathing from within. Waited, for any sign they were still awake.

Then, he opened the door slowly and went inside.

Twenty-Six

Louise was going through CCTV images, frame by frame, hoping to catch sight of something, anything, which would point them in the right direction. This was the deal now they were over in the Major Crimes Unit; smaller cogs in a larger machine. At least they were still involved, she thought. The case could have disappeared and they would have found out if they caught anyone at the same time as everyone else.

As it was, she was still a part of the large machine. Which meant she could help in some way. Willingly putting herself through torturous hours of monotony, in the hope of finding a single face that didn't fit. Someone returning, to see what was happening. The hope that he wouldn't have been able to help himself, coming to watch as they trawled through his hiding place.

She paused the images flashing past on her screen as Shipley perched himself on the edge of the alien desk she was sitting at.

'Latest report from the woods is five bodies found,' he said, picking up a pen from the desk and twirling it between his fingers. 'They reckon there'll be more as well.

Quite the operation going on. DI reckons they'll be there for days.'

'Any identifications yet?'

'Just a couple. One should be familiar. Adam Porter.'

There was a moment before she recognised the name, but then it came to her clearly. 'Oh no . . .'

'Couldn't believe it myself,' Shipley said, unable to hide the excitement in his voice. 'He's been gone what, ten years?'

'Pushing fifteen now,' Louise replied, feeling that familiar dread in the pit of her stomach. The feeling that she had managed to get herself involved in something that was too much for her. The anger was back as well. The thought of the young teenager, his face so recognisable to the local populace, even if his name was harder to recall. Left to rot under the ground. 'Must have been 2002, 2003 when he went missing,' she found herself saying. 'It was huge news for a good few months. His mum still pops up every now and again, usually around the anniversary of him going missing.'

'Yeah, well, the date seems about right. The body they dug up was in bad shape. It was only because he had his name on him that we can say it's him at the moment. You never know, we might get lucky and it's someone else.'

'Any other names?'

Shipley stopped twirling the pen in his hand, took a piece of paper from his pocket and laid it out in front of her. Three names, listed underneath the ones they already knew. Seeing them there, just written on a piece of paper, it lost some of its grandeur. She thought of all the families linked to those names. The people left behind, never knowing the truth.

'I don't recognise anyone else here. How about you?'

'Possibly,' Louise replied, extending a finger and tracing down the names on the list. She could smell Shipley's aftershave, a trace of it lingering even after all the work they had done in the previous few hours. 'Maybe that one?'

'Nicola Borthwick,' Shipley said, as if he were testing the name, seeing if it jogged his memory. 'No, don't recognise it.'

'Maybe I'm mistaken.'

'Do we really think Rhys Durham was killing people that far back? A teenager as a serial killer?'

'I don't know what to think any more,' Shipley said with a sigh. The stubble on his face was getting longer with each day. It made a noise as he swiped a hand across it, like a hard brush scraped along concrete. 'He's the only lead we have.'

'I suppose so,' Louise replied, feeling unconvinced. She hated the idea of focusing on one person, when it could be someone else entirely. 'He could be a victim, that's all I'm saying.'

'Keep on with what you're doing,' Shipley said finally, tearing himself away from her desk and standing up fully. 'Until we find anything that says otherwise, we have to try and find Rhys Durham. I'll show my face at the press briefing.'

'There's another one?'

'I get the feeling there'll be a fair few before this thing is out.'

Louise watched him leave, her eyes lingering on his diminishing figure as it retreated, then turned back to the paused screen in front of her. She preferred to stay there, rather than be anywhere near the news cameras, which she assumed were increasing in number with each passing hour. The television perched on the wall in the corner of the office said as much. Sky News, now running the story as breaking news. She was better off being left in the unfamiliar office of the Major Crimes Unit in the city centre. The dull brown-brick building, looking out onto student accommodation and the river. It would have been a nice view a couple of years before, she thought. Now, it had been blemished by the unending desire to keep building and building.

They had pulled CCTV from the Ford Road – and everywhere else they possibly could – near the woods, going back to before they'd had cameras and uniforms on scene. The crowd which had gathered nearby, watching and waiting for any news – those who had possibly not had their details taken down by anyone. She had suggested going through it, earning a frown from Shipley but a nod from DCI Sisterson. They had heard enough tales of perpetrators of crimes returning to the scene for it not to be out of the question to check. Not a waste of time, rather a covering-all-bases check.

She hummed the tune from her childhood without thinking, the words running through her mind.

'The Bone Keeper's coming. The Bone Keeper's real. He doesn't stop. He doesn't feel. He'll snatch you up. And make you weep. He'll slice your flesh. Your bones he'll keep.'

Louise looked back at the names on the paper, wondering whether they had heard that tune themselves.

Whether the Bone Keeper was really out there somewhere.

She decided to carry on looking at the list of names,

to allow her eyes a little rest from the CCTV images. As before, they didn't really ring any bells for her – other than that of Adam Porter. She wondered why that one was different. Why he had been chosen. Whether the Bone Keeper had purposefully strayed from his usual modus operandi, or had simply chosen wrong.

Adam Porter. She typed his name into Google. The youngster's face immediately popped up. An almost ridiculously angelic-looking young boy, dimples and freckles to boot. That was the image most circulated around the time of his disappearance, but Louise knew there was a more apt one. A more dour, shaven-headed appearance, in a photo taken a few weeks before he went missing.

There had been rumours for years that he'd got mixed up in the wrong crowd, but his mum wouldn't have any of it. She had shouted from the rooftops that he was a good boy, one who could do no wrong, and she'd had the media behind her from day one.

Teenagers go missing all the time, but some are more missed than others.

He'd been fourteen when he disappeared – it looked like he had ended up always being that age. She was glad she wasn't going to be the one doing that death knock. She felt sorry for the officers who would be tasked with that one. Especially as it would be one of the more decayed of the bodies buried in the woods. Adam's mum wouldn't accept the news in any way, if Louise had read her right.

That's how they were, the mothers left behind. The fathers tended to be more pragmatic. They didn't have a 'father's intuition' breathing down their necks. Mothers were supposed to know what had happened to their children. Somehow. In Louise's experience, though, no one had any clue what happened until someone like her knocked on their door.

Louise searched the official police database for more information, safe in the knowledge that it wouldn't be odd if her name appeared on the search records. The detail was extensive, but ultimately pointless. A number of people had been interviewed – some under caution – over the years, but no one could ever be linked to Adam's disappearance. She looked for the last address he'd lived at before he had gone missing, and felt a jolt of recognition at the name of the road which came up. She worked out how far it was from where she'd grown up, quickly realising it was only a few minutes.

Was that the Bone Keeper's old stomping ground, she wondered. Her adopted hometown when she was a teenager? There were woods in the area; Otterspool wasn't a far walk from where her house had been. She imagined they would be too small for him, though. He'd prefer somewhere easier to get lost in.

The south of the city wasn't far away.

Sefton Park was even closer, but she thought that would be too populated for it.

She shook her head, admonishing herself for thinking of this man as something mythological. He was simply someone who enjoyed killing people. He wasn't some sort of spectre hiding in the woods.

He was just a man.

Had to be.

She thought about fire. The images returning with ease. Louise began rubbing at her thigh absent-mindedly, almost able to feel the heat again. Then she blinked her eyes rapidly, returning to the present, her present, and went back to watching the CCTV. She kept her eyes on the screen, watching a new angle now that showed the group of people who had arrived to watch the developing scene. The camera was so far away that she couldn't see in any great detail, but it might give them something, she supposed. The crowd had started out small – just two or three people – but had quickly grown in size. Within fifteen minutes, there were at least twenty people there. Word travels fast in the small towns. Old communities. Might be that they hadn't had cause to speak to their neighbours for the previous year, or longer – but Louise imagined they'd be talking now.

She imagined walking among them without anyone knowing she was there. Judging them, silently and savagely. Picking apart each of their lives and deeming them worthy or not.

She shook her head, pulled a few folders closer to her and started reading.

Tiredness was beginning to take over now; she read the same line in a witness report three times. She glanced at the clock, wondering where Shipley had got to. Wondering if he'd offer her a lift home, as he always seemed to do now. She knew he didn't do that for everyone and that there was something different about the way he felt about her.

She didn't know what to do about that.

Louise closed everything down and waited for Shipley to return. For now, she had to stay focused on not screwing this up by allowing the edge she was always teetering upon to drop from beneath her. Ignoring the small voice in her head, the anger bubbling inside her.

She thought of fire and how it destroyed everything.

Even memories.

She thought of what might be hidden in the woods. What might have lived there for decades without being seen. Only a story passed around from child to child, adult to adult. A legend, which people would laugh off, never acknowledging how it really affected them. How they wouldn't venture alone anywhere near where someone said they'd seen the monster.

She thought of the marks on the trees. What they meant, what they symbolised. Whether they were just carved into the trunks by kids wanting to extend the myth, or actually signified something.

Louise could feel the heat grow around her as she recalled the fire in the woods. The way the reek of it seemed to seep into every pore in her body. A thousand showers not enough to get rid of it. The path of destruction it might take.

She leaned back in the unfamiliar chair, at the unfamiliar desk, in the unfamiliar office. Everything had moved so quickly, she hadn't had a chance to breathe.

There was too much to think about. Too much to take in. She could feel her chest constricting with the weight of it all. Her breathing becoming more shallow, rasping, as if she were underground. Buried under a mound of earth. Sucking in soil instead of oxygen. Butterflies flew in her stomach, turning it into a cauldron, a swirling, twirling mess of anxiety.

Close your eyes. Count to ten. Count to twenty. Count to thirty.

She could picture herself, buried with all the other bodies discovered in the woods. That could have been her. Desperately trying to escape, digging herself out, struggling with the weight of the earth surrounding her.

Giving up, allowing the darkness to crash over her. Waiting for death to come.

Count to fifty. Breathe. Breathe. Breathe.

That could have been her. She could have been covered in dirt and mud. Left to rot.

It should have been you. If you weren't such a COWARD.

Louise gripped the sides of the chair, feeling the pain enter her body now. The flashes of knives, piercing her skin, slashing across her chest.

She didn't realise she was talking out loud until a hand gripped her shoulder.

'Come on, Louise,' Shipley's voice said from above her. His hand was a steadying force, but held her by the shoulder with care, 'Let's get out of here.'

She forced open her eyes, blinking into the overhead light, allowing herself to be led away. She ignored the looks of the few detectives scattered around other parts of the room, just following Shipley's lead.

Mentally admonishing herself for allowing this to happen.

Twenty-Seven

Shipley brought her up to speed as he drove her home, now seemingly ignoring the state she'd been in when he'd arrived back at the office. Louise was more with it, back in the real world, rather than the one which seemed to exist only in fire.

She felt like a cliché. A fictional detective coming apart at the seams. One that could never exist in reality, yet everything about her situation felt all too real. The fact that she had found herself in over her head, suddenly desperate to be anywhere else, on any other case. Anything different, anything that didn't make her feel this way. She was collapsing under the expectation, its weight becoming too much to bear.

Shipley had led her out of the office, talking for their colleagues' benefit, trying to save face, she'd assumed.

'These long shifts,' he'd said loudly as he grabbed her by the arm. 'They'll be the death of you.'

Louise hadn't thought anyone paying any sort of mind to them would have bought it, but none of the others appeared to care what the new pair were doing.

'What's going on?' Shipley had said after he got her

through the doors, where she'd rested against the wall. 'What's the matter with you?'

She heard herself again, uttering lies; they sounded even worse now the car, in a colder light. 'Must have eaten something that didn't agree with me. Let me go to the bathroom a sec.'

Louise had guessed by the look he'd given her that he hadn't bought the lie. He didn't question her any more though, instead leaving her to it so she could dive into the bathroom. Collapsing at the sink area, propping herself up on the palms of her hands against the cold surface.

She hadn't looked up. Looked at herself in the mirror. Instead, she'd turned on the taps and splashed her face a few times. Removed a paper towel from the dispenser and wiped the water away.

Then she had gone back to her desk, mumbling to Shipley about going through the CCTV images a few more times, while secretly in fact reading as much as she could take in and process, from the folders about each victim they had discovered so far. A way of distracting herself from the feeling growing inside her.

The feeling that she shouldn't be anywhere near this case. She knew that without Shipley, she wouldn't even be there now. She would have walked away.

She couldn't leave his side.

That had been a couple of hours ago. Now, driving home, they were alone again.

Louise had accepted the offer of a lift without thinking. Not considering that it would mean twenty minutes in an enclosed environment alone with him. She cursed herself for leaving her own car at home that morning, and vowed not to make that mistake again. No matter how much another side of her wanted to be in that car, alone with Shipley. She had to forget that part of her existed. That there was something between them, something unspoken and raw.

It had been there for a long time.

She remembered when she had first met Shipley. The way he acted around her, as if she was something exotic. A young detective constable, fresh out of uniform and wanting a different life. He had recognised that, treating her a little differently to the way he treated others.

Louise had hated it. She'd wanted to be like everyone else. She'd wanted to be normal. Still did.

Now, he was talking about what he had learned in the hours he had been away from her side. The way Major Crimes worked, the people involved, how he had been accepted straight away. There was something endearing about the way he talked. The excitement exuding from him.

Also, worrying.

'So, they have loads more resources than we do,' Shipley continued, as he navigated the streets of the city. The traffic was lighter than it would have been a few hours previous, but there were still a fair few headlights blaring around them. 'They have profiles of each victim being drawn up, with an incredible amount of information. Nothing is left to chance. This is the way I've always wanted to work, you know. This is real detective work. Not the crap we usually have to deal with.'

'Do you think we'll be with them for the course of the investigation?'

'As long as we don't become deadwood, I think we'll be set. Then, who knows. Maybe we'll be able to transfer over to them. Show our worth and we could become invaluable.

We just need to find out who this guy is. That'll be the key. If we track him down and prove we can handle the big cases, they'll have to transfer us.'

'What's your plan then?' Louise asked, knowing Shipley would have something in mind. 'What should we do?'

'They think Rhys Durham is our best bet at the moment. Although the dates don't really match up. Unless we're looking at someone who was a serial killer aged fifteen.'

'That's what I've been saying, but I suppose it's not unheard of,' Louise replied, staring out of the passenger-side window at the blur of buildings as they passed by. 'He was obviously an angry young man. Druggies for parents, issues with the opposite sex and the legal age of consent.'

'I've been thinking about Jon Durham,' Shipley said, pulling the car slowly to a stop at some traffic lights. A couple crossed in front of them, seemingly arguing as they went. Then they both began to laugh, loud enough that Louise could hear the bark of it from inside the car. 'There's something not right with that whole situation.'

'What are you thinking?'

'Well, you saw those drawings, those messages. Then, there's the small fact of the pictures of the woodland area where we eventually found the bodies. That can't all be coincidence. He must have known something. I want to go through his room again, see if we can find anything else he might have noted down. Any more information we can get.'

Silence grew between them as they rounded the final corner and entered the short street where Louise lived. Shipley pulled the car over, parking just behind her own vehicle. She didn't get out straight away, instead turning to face him as he stared straight ahead.

'Look, about what happened back at the office . . .' Louise began, but Shipley cut her off.

'It's fine, you're probably just a little overworked or something. It's been a crazy couple of days for both of us. One minute we're investigating yet another domestic incident, next we're in the middle of a serial murder case. I've been feeling it as well.'

'You're hiding it better than I am,' Louise replied, smiling at Shipley. She couldn't hold it for long, though; it gradually fell from her face. 'I suppose you're right. It's not been the easiest time. Takes some getting used to, all of this. I'm not sure we're even ready.'

'We are. I know that for certain. I was getting bored rigid of dealing with the same cranks day in day out and so were you. This is a chance for us to move on. Both of us. You're a good detective, Louise. You deserve to be here as well.'

She didn't answer at first, allowing him to stare at her as she averted her eyes. They were inches from each other, but so far apart in so many other ways.

Louise moved closer, unable to stop herself any longer. Inches became centimetres, as he blurred in front of her.

He moved closer to her.

Louise felt his lips on hers, parting, and the softness of his mouth. His stubble scratched against her face as a slow kiss became something more. Hungrier. His hands were on her body, the flatness of his palms sliding around her shoulders and down her back. She caught her breath as he paused and held her.

She wanted him. The normality of the situation, rather than the irrationality of the past few days.

She wanted to feel normal.

His mouth found hers again, his hands moving lower down her back as she turned closer to him in her seat. She moved her hand to his face, then through his hair.

'No, not now,' Louise said, pulling away from Shipley. 'We can't do this.'

Shipley slumped back, nodding slightly to himself. 'You're right. I'm sorry.'

Louise smiled. 'Don't be.'

'Want me to pick you up tomorrow?'

Louise left the question hanging, trying to formulate the answer that worked best. She didn't want him to, preferring the silence of her lonely commutes. Yet, there was also a part of her that didn't want him to leave at all. That wanted to take him out of the car, lead him to her house, open the door and go inside. Leave reality behind for a few hours of peace.

'No, it's my turn,' she said eventually, turning towards him, unclasping her hands, which had been lying in her lap. 'I'm picking you up this time. Only fair.'

'I'm not going to argue with that,' Shipley replied with a laugh. It was a soft sound, not harsh and unyielding like the one he used around the other detectives. 'Spent a fortune in petrol coming back and forth here. Not that I mind, of course.'

'Usual time.'

There was a moment when Louise thought he was going to lean further forward, but he didn't move. Simply stared at her for a few more seconds, before she grasped the door handle and let herself out.

She didn't look back as she walked towards her door, hearing the car start up again and pull away. She pulled her keys out and let herself in, pulling the door closed behind her and dropping her bag in the hallway. She waited a few more seconds, then grabbed her car keys and phone, letting herself back out of the house.

Caroline was lying in the same position as when they'd last left her, propped up in the hospital bed, as if she'd been expecting Louise to arrive.

Maybe she had.

'Thought I'd drop in after this afternoon,' Louise said, pulling up a chair close to the bed. 'Didn't want you lying here alone all night again.'

'Something tells me you didn't exactly have much else to do anyway,' Caroline replied, the corners of her mouth turning up, but not smiling fully. 'It's fine. I'm not exactly tripping over visitors here.'

'Why is that?' Louise said, wanting to know the truth, even if she was sure she wouldn't actually get it. 'Why are you choosing to be here alone?'

'I told you, I'm not that close to anyone really. Not enough to have them see me like this.'

'I'm sure they'll understand. They'll be worried about you.'

'If they see me in this state, that's all they'll ever see me as. A victim. I couldn't deal with that. I won't be looked at that way.'

'And your family?'

Caroline thought for a second, then shook her head. 'I can't deal with them right now. They'll only find some way to make it all my fault.'

'You shouldn't take them for granted, you know,' Louise said, leaning on the bed with one hand. 'Some day, they might not be there for you to ignore at all. Then, you'll know loneliness.'

'Are you speaking from experience?'

Louise sat for a while in silence, thinking about how best to respond. 'You don't want to be alone, Caroline. No one should have to go through that.'

'Sometimes, it feels like I have to do this alone. That I'm paying for mistakes I've made, or something. Karma, you know? All my screw-ups coming home to roost. And if I can just get through this, I'll make up for them.'

Louise nodded, knowing the feeling all too well. 'I have these panic attacks, whenever I think about the past. It's like my body is trying to make me forget. I . . . I had one earlier. In work.'

'Really?'

'Don't worry,' Louise said quickly, holding her hands up. 'There's plenty of normal people working on this case. I'm just a small cog now in a massive machine. It doesn't matter if I lose my mind completely. There'll be twenty detectives who'll have already solved it all by then.'

'What happened?' Caroline said, ignoring Louise's attempts at keeping the mood light.

She didn't have to explain the question more – Louise knew what she'd meant. 'I don't know really. There was a fire, at a crime scene we found. It seems to be a trigger for something, but I don't know what.'

'Suppressed memory,' Caroline said, the words coming out quietly.

'Something like that.'

'I have a feeling I've been doing the same thing,' Caroline replied, fiddling with the blanket over her lap. 'Maybe they're a good thing.'

'I sometimes think my mind is trying to get me to remember something I really shouldn't.'

'Something bad. From your past I mean.'

'Yeah,' Louise replied, shifting in her chair. 'But I know enough to know it was bad, but I was okay. There was an accident.'

'What happened?' Caroline asked her again.

'My family. They're all gone. I was the only one who survived, but I don't remember most of it. Bits and pieces beforehand, but then it's like one day I was thirteen years old and I remember everything from then on. I had to move in with my grandparents. You don't want to be a teenager and living with a couple in their seventies, I can tell you that for nothing.'

'Your parents?'

'Dead,' Louise said and hoped that was as much as she would have to. 'All gone. Aunts and uncles, never met them, even if they're still around. I think my mum had a sister, but I never met her. Dad was an only child. His parents were dead before I was old enough to know anything about them. So, that left my mum's parents, and they tried hard, but they didn't last much longer after I'd moved out. They were old and I think raising a teenager sucked the rest of the life out of them.'

'I could tell you a similar story,' Caroline replied, smoothing down her blanket.

Louise knew she wouldn't, though. Something was keeping her from saying more, but she wasn't sure what it was.

'I joined the police pretty much as soon as I was able to,' Louise said, when the silence between them continued and became uncomfortable. 'I needed to do something, you know? Give something back or whatever.'

'Yeah, I know what you mean.'

'We will find whoever did this to you,' Louise said, leaning back in her chair. 'We're close.'

'I hope you're right.'

'You shouldn't be going through this alone. Give your mum a call. I'm sure she's worried about you.'

'I'll think about it.'

Louise sat there until Caroline's eyes began to droop, tiredness finally catching up with her, then left the room. It was after midnight and this side of the building had quietened; the corridors she walked through empty, as the wards settled down and allowed patients their fitful sleep. She imagined it would be just as crazy as it always was in A&E.

She stepped into the lift, resting her head against the cool metal side, straightening up as it came to a stop. Walked through an empty reception area and welcomed the almost icy blast of air that greeted her as she left the building. She stood for a few seconds, pulling her jacket closer around herself, watching someone light a cigarette. She wished she smoked. Something to take the edge off.

'Smile, love. It might never happen.'

Louise turned quickly. A scruffy-looking lad was leaning against the wall and smoking. He smiled at her, revealing a broken tooth at the front.

'What did you say?'

'Oh, don't be like that,' he said, shaking his head. 'I'm just being friendly.'

'Yeah, well, don't.' Louise replied, pulling her jacket closer and taking a step towards the car park.

'Stuck-up bitch.'

Louise stopped, her back still to the lad. She looked up and around, spotting the CCTV camera above the entrance. She stepped to the side until she felt certain she was out of its eye line. Then she stopped so he didn't see her close her eyes and begin to count.

She heard the sound of him moving along the wall towards her. 'Trying to be nice and that's the thanks you get.'

She reached three in her count, before she turned around and walked back towards him. She opened her mouth to speak, but her heart was racing now. The feeling in her stomach rising, the tremble in her hands, as if they were itching to be used.

Louise stopped a foot or so away from him. The stupid grin on his face seemed to be getting wider. She closed her mouth, looked away to his right and waited for his head to turn to follow her gaze.

Then, she raised her forearm and smashed it into the side of his head.

Twenty-Eight

They watched the news in silence, hearing the words but not really taking them in. Too busy looking at their phones to pay attention.

'It's trending on Twitter,' Karen said, making Tim shake his head at the ridiculousness of it all. 'Right there, see?'

Tim glanced up at the phone in Karen's hand, which she was shaking about in front of his face. 'It doesn't mean they're taking it seriously.'

'I'm telling you, there was always something about that story.'

'You think he's real?'

'I think you should listen to other people's opinions for once,' Karen replied, slumping back onto her side of the sofa. 'Keep an open mind.'

Tim scoffed at her, but closed the BBC Sport app he had been reading and opened Twitter. She was right. It was trending. Like that meant anything, but it still meant there were enough people out there talking about to make a dint in the usual rubbish talked about on social media.

He scrolled down some of the posts, reading stupid people's stories about the legend they had grown up with.

A brainless story from their childhood that people were trying to make into something. Various pictures of devil masks, attempts to scare others.

'It'll be some nutcase who just wants to make a name for himself,' Tim said, as the TV in the corner still flickered with breaking news banners and shadowy images from their city. 'He's not real.'

'I'm telling you, I saw him once . . .'

'You saw something, Karen, but I doubt it was the bloody Bone Keeper.'

'I know what I saw. We were in the woods by Formby and he was in there. Waiting for us. Ask any of the others. That's where he lived, inside the woods. He had marks on the trees that showed where he was or had been. Everyone knew about him round there. People would go missing and never turn up. We barely got away from him.'

'I'm going for a smoke,' Tim said, lifting himself off the sofa, so he didn't have to hear anything further from her.

They went to bed the same time as always. The cat safely ensconced inside; Karen didn't like him staying out all night. It didn't matter that he inevitably ended up on the bed, a dead weight between them. A living, breathing contraception.

Tim couldn't get out of this despair of a marriage if he'd tried. She would give him those sad eyes of hers and he'd relent. Anything to keep the peace.

He dreamed of a different life.

He dreamed of death.

Lying there in the darkness, he stared at the ceiling and wondered what he'd done in a previous life to deserve this. Turning over, listening to Karen snore, he closed his eyes and wished for the perfect dream. One that would wake him up hard and excited.

He couldn't remember the last time they'd actually gone to bed early enough to contemplate intimacy. He didn't miss it. Was actually thinking about taking up the big-chested girl in Accounts' offer. A quick fumble in the disabled toilets in work would provide some excitement, even if the guilt might eventually become too much to live with.

Tim was thinking of her as he drifted off to sleep.

When he heard the first noise, he was still not fully alert. The moment inbetween sleep and wakefulness. Confusion washed over him as he tried to work out if he was still asleep and dreaming, or awake.

It was a voice.

'You're talking in your sleep again, Karen,' Tim mumbled, his mouth dry enough to notice. He coughed and cleared his throat. 'If you carry on, I'm moving to the spare room.'

Karen didn't answer, but then she never did. He was more awake now, the creaking sound from beside him not bothering him. The damn cat again. Probably disturbed by his voice.

They had never got on.

He reached over, landing a hand on the glass of water on the bedside table. He brought the glass to his lips, sipping on the lukewarm liquid, which did little to quench his thirst.

He heard the sound again. He was becoming more awake by the second. Now he heard it properly.

It was whispering, in the darkness.

It wasn't coming from Karen.

The whispering grew louder, rhythmic and repetitive. Tim couldn't speak, couldn't move. Fear crawled around inside him and set up home. Words flew through his head, crashing into each other like moths on strip lights. He couldn't work out what was happening to him.

All bravado had gone. He had often thought he would be able to cope in any situation, used to defending himself growing up on a council estate in the middle of Liverpool. He had faced down the biggest bullies, rounded blind, dark corners when out in town at stupid o'clock in the morning. He had talked often about what he would do if someone broke into his house at night. How he would tackle them to the ground, get a few digs in while waiting for the police to arrive. No one could best him in a fight.

He had always thought that.

He had never known real fear. The terror of being awoken in the middle of the night, confused and disorientated.

While someone whispered in the shadows.

He couldn't move.

He couldn't move.

He wouldn't move.

The whispering grew louder. He could hear it now. Over and over.

You can do this. You can do this.

Do it now. Do it now.

His eyes were open as the shadow grew form and came towards him. He begged his body to move, to do anything. Fight or flight.

He did neither.

Instead, he lay there, paralysed with panic, fear, dread. Whatever it was, he couldn't move. Couldn't talk. He was rigid.

The bed became wet beneath his groin, as the shadow person now loomed over him. He could see its eyes, its mouth. He could see the clothes it wore, sense the smell of him. The square of his jawline, the hairs protruding from his nose.

The blackness of its breath on his skin, as it leaned over him.

He opened his mouth, but no sound came out. Saliva disappearing from his mouth, throat going dry. He could see better now, his eyes adjusting to the darkness.

He wished they hadn't.

He was unaware of Karen beside him. She had disappeared from his consciousness. The only things there in the room were him and the figure a foot away from him.

There was something in his hand, but Tim could only see it in his peripheral vision. He could only stare into its eyes, above him, studying him.

The movement came fast, before his brain had a chance to catch up with what his throat wanted to do. As he stretched open his mouth to cry out, to speak, to do something, the knife plunged into his neck.

Tim could feel the air cut out, a grunt of effort above him, as the blade plunged further in. There wasn't much pain at first; it was almost as if there was just something lodged in his throat, ready to be coughed up. His brain tried to make his body do that, but it didn't respond.

He felt pain suddenly, like a blast of wind as you opened a door. Bang, there it was. He felt as if he were screaming, but he couldn't hear anything. The knife was lodged in his neck, the thing above him still holding onto the handle.

And twist.

The pain became agony in an instant, as the knife

twisted in his neck. The handle moved upwards, cutting into him, as his vision finally gave up. Blurred, distant. His head flopped on the pillow as he bucked under the strain of the *thing* above him. A hand came across and laid him back down with little effort.

Tim was dreaming. That was all. The darkness of sleep came back to him. Drifting in and out of consciousness.

He was dreaming.

Of silent screams, of blood seeping out of him and onto the sheets he was lying on.

Of drowning. Not being able to breathe.

There was nothing else. Just endless, desperate gasps of non-existent air. Being swallowed by the waves, the eternal emptiness of the sea.

Nothing else.

He was nowhere. He was a nobody.

Tim was done.

He wiped a sleeve across his brow, but more sweat sprang up. He left the knife where he had plunged it into the neck of the man. The woman was still asleep, barely moving at all. He cocked his head, straightening up and dusting himself off absent-mindedly. He studied the slumbering form of the woman, wondering what to do next.

He knew what he had to do.

He knew what he *wanted* to do.

Twenty-Nine

Louise stared at the blood drying on her knuckles as she gripped the steering wheel and pulled into her road. She reached across and smudged the small mark away. Smiled to herself as she pictured the lad on the ground.

Even if he said anything – which was unlikely – having no witnesses or CCTV would have made it difficult to pin it on her. She didn't think it was very likely he would admit to being smacked around a little by a woman anyway. His ego would never survive that.

She still had the feeling coursing through her, that rose up after that first blow had landed. The relief, as she finally gave into what was always underneath her cold surface. The anger and rage that was always with her, unleashed for a few seconds.

There was a part of her that wanted to do it again. And again.

Louise pulled the car to a stop, adjusted the rear-view mirror and caught sight of her eyes in it. She turned away quickly, removing the keys and stepping out of the car. The street was quiet, as it always seemed to be late at night. It wasn't a cut-through to anywhere and it was far enough away from the shops and pubs that if anyone was walking past, they were going somewhere close.

She walked up to her front door, her breath catching in her throat now, as she thought of the darkness and silence that awaited her inside. Shook her head, opened up and let herself in.

Louise flicked on the hall lights and knew instantly that someone had been in her house. The air was thick with musk, a foreign aroma, not the usual one which greeted her. She stood still, waiting to hear any sound. Any betrayal of movement, something that didn't sound right.

She thought back to that morning, the routine she had gone through. She had locked every possible entrance, every window and door. There was no way anyone could have got in, Louise thought. Just as she always did.

No one could have got into her house.

She tried to think back to before she'd gone to the hospital a few hours earlier, but couldn't remember getting further than the hallway.

It was her mind playing tricks on her, that was all. Still in the heightened state it had been in all week. There was no way she could know if someone was in her house just from walking in and sniffing.

It wasn't possible.

She moved forwards, gaining more confidence with every step. Walked into the living room and switched on the light while the door was still opening. Looked around, to see if anything was out of place, if there was a sign that someone had really been into her house.

Nothing seemed out of the ordinary. Everything where it should be. Still, there was an unexplainable feeling that someone had been in this room. Someone other than herself.

She left the living room, making her way down the hall-way to the kitchen-diner. The house was only small, but it was good enough for her. She hadn't ever needed anything bigger than this, given she was on her own.

Louise flicked on the kitchen light, bathing the room in a warm glow.

She spotted it immediately. The thing out of place. There, on the small breakfast bar that separated the two halves of the room, was a small pile of something. The smell of it drifted her way – acrid and pungent.

Burning.

She froze half in and half out of the doorway, unwilling to turn around in case the person who had left them was standing behind her. She listened instead, waiting for a creak or a breath to appear.

There was silence.

Her feet finally broke the deadlock, moving across the room swiftly towards what had been left there.

A gathering of burnt pieces of wood, fashioned into shapes. Bundled together with what looked like vines. They were charred, the bark blackened and crumbling.

They looked like bones. Burnt and destroyed.

She swallowed a few times, her breathing becoming heavier as she stared at the offering. She wanted to slam a fist into it until all that was left was ashes, but her hands wouldn't obey. Instead, they moved towards the card that lay on the surface behind it.

Louise turned it over, reading the handwritten words on the reverse, hands shaking as she took it in, what it meant.

Time for you to come home Louise.
XX XX

Before

She was left there to wait, the seconds lasting an eternity. Staring into the void of the tunnel, the blackness growing in the circle, becoming all she could see. It seemed to pulse with an unseen energy, waiting, watching, alive with the possibility of swallowing someone whole. She wanted to get to her feet, move towards it and cross its threshold. Instead, she leaned to one side and the contents of her stomach appeared next to her.

'Ewwww, that's gross,' one of the brats said, her shrieking voice disturbing birds in the trees above. 'Lee, she's throwing up, look.'

'I can see that, you divvy.'

She ignored them, coughing and spluttering, as she dry-heaved a few more times until she couldn't any longer. Her eyes watered, stomach flipping over as she leaned back on her hands. 'Need to get Matty,' she managed to say, in the general direction of the two brats. 'He's in there.'

'Yeah, that's the point,' Lee replied, sniggering as he spoke. She wanted so much in that moment for him to have gone last, rather than Matty. Rather than her brother. Let this little idiot boy be the one. Not him.

'He'll be here in a minute and then you can stop crying like a little girl.'

She closed her eyes, wiping a sleeve across them to remove the moisture. She did the same across her chin, rubbing the sleeve against the ground once she'd done so. She turned back in the direction of the tunnel, wondering how long it would take until she heard the noise.

Expecting to hear screams. Agony.

She was convinced of it now. She knew what would happen to him in there. What had almost happened to her.

'There's someone in there,' she said, a growl of anger in her voice now. These two brats had led them to this place. It was their fault. If something happened to Matty . . .

'What are you talking about?' Faye said, hands on her hips, desperately trying to look older than her age. She looked exactly what she was. A little girl. 'There's nobody in there. We would have heard them.'

'I'm telling you, there's someone in there,' she replied, turning on them now. There was a sudden moment when she felt like a mother facing her two errant children. She was eleven years old, but felt thirty years older somehow. Ancient. 'I don't know who or what, but there's something in that tunnel and now it's going to get Matty.'

'It's him,' Lee said, making his voice deeper and more frightening. 'It's the Bone Keeper.'

'He'll slice your flesh. Your bones he'll keep.' Faye's singing voice lifted birds from the trees around them and into the darkening sky.

'Shut up, you stupid cow,' she almost screamed at the kid.

'Well, why don't you go back in there and save him then?' Faye said, drawing herself up to her full height, as if that was anything to be proud of. Faye looked even smaller to her now. A little waif, a stray. 'You're freaking out for no reason. Are you trying to scare us or something, because it's not working.'

Faye looked towards her brother for support, but he was looking past the two girls and towards the tunnel itself. She watched him for a moment, trying to read what was going on behind his eyes. She thought for a second that she saw something float past them, but then it was gone.

'We all have to go in,' she said. Her tone was firm, but even she could hear that there was no conviction behind it. 'We need to go and help him.'

'He'll be out in a minute, just keep your hair on.'

She ignored the little girl and concentrated on Lee, who had fallen silent and was simply staring at the tunnel. She could see he was shaping to speak, but something was holding him back.

'What is it, Lee?' she tried, hoping she hadn't read him wrong. 'What's in there?'

Lee looked at her as if she had just appeared there and he was confused by her presence. 'It's not real,' he said softly, his words almost dying on the breeze between them. 'It can't be.'

'What is it?' she replied, fighting the urge to cross the short space between them and shake the answer out of him. 'What is waiting in there?'

'It's in there.'

She had never believed the stories, even when they kept her awake at night. The idea of something like that existing was ridiculous, even to her young mind. She had gone along with this trek today because it seemed like a fun thing to do. Something to alleviate the boredom that had been threatening to overwhelm her.

'The Bone Keeper is going to get him,' Lee continued, his whole body beginning to shake. She could see that the bravado he had previously displayed was evaporating. What was left, was all that he was. A small boy, body growing faster than his mind wanted it to. He wasn't a teenager, but a child. Scared. Afraid. In over his tiny head.

'He's not real,' she said, but her voice betrayed her. She had been in there. Had felt it. There was something in that tunnel, something she couldn't describe. The smell, the feel of it. The air growing thicker, as if she had stepped into another world.

It had been too long. Waiting there, breath returning to a normal rate, allowing her thoughts to become more ordered.

She couldn't let this happen, she thought. There was just the two of them now. No more Mum and Dad. Just them. The two of them against the world. They were supposed to have each other's backs. Mum had brought a stranger into their lives, Dad had dropped them both as soon as he was able to. The only people they could count on were each other.

She couldn't move. She couldn't rush into that darkness and be by his side, whatever was in there waiting for him. Her feet were stuck to the ground, no matter how desperate she was to move.

'The Bone Keeper has got him,' Lee said, his voice shaking and wavering. 'That's it now. We're never going to see him again. There's nothing we can do. The Bone Keeper never lets you live. He skins you alive, so all that's left is your bones. No one ever finds your body. No one ever knows you've even gone.'

Lee continued to babble on. She turned away and ignored his voice. Stared at the tunnel opening, her jaw clenched as she waited for Matty to emerge. Behind her, Faye began to moan, then cry in a horrible fake way. She continued to stand and stare. Waiting, waiting, waiting.

She wanted to run in there. Make things different. Change everything that was going to happen if she didn't. Just her presence, her voice, might be enough. If Matty could hear her speak, could hear her voice, he might be okay.

Instead, she stood there and waited and hoped and prayed and did nothing.

The three of them. Waiting for what felt like hours, but was in reality only minutes. Standing, waiting, for her brother to emerge from the tunnel.

For whatever was in there to make itself known.

A few minutes, that was all that was needed.

'We can't just stand around here all night,' Faye said, trying to sound tough, now the crocodile tears had stopped. Her voice betrayed her. 'He's obviously having us on.'

Faye took a step towards the tunnel, but Lee put a hand on her shoulder. 'I'll go first.'

They shuffled forward in single file, only pausing for a second at the entrance. Then they started walking into the darkness again.

Silence greeted them, a certain stillness in the atmosphere that made the breath catch in her throat.

'Can you smell anything?' she whispered to the other two, ahead of her.

'No, what are you talking about,' came the response, but she could feel it now. Lingering there, settling around them.

'Matty?' Lee said, his voice barely above a whisper. 'Are you there? What are you doing?'

They followed suit, saying her brother's name over and over. Quiet at first, then louder as they grew braver, as they reached the middle of the tunnel.

Dull light came to them from the other side, a pinhole growing larger as they kept walking.

They emerged on the other side, back into the growing darkness outside. She waited for Matty to jump out on them, but nothing happened.

He was gone.

'Oh no . . .'

Faye was crying again, but she could tell it was for real this time. Lee didn't seem to be too far behind her.

She cupped her hands around her mouth and shouted Matty's name. 'Just come out. It's not funny now.'

Silence came back at her.

The panic was weak at first, but was growing stronger with each passing second. She tried to calm herself down, soothing words spilling from her lips.

'The Bone Keeper has got him,' Lee said, over and over, tears rolling down his cheeks. 'We woke him up and he's taken Matty. We have to get out of here before he gets us too.'

She didn't want to go. Leave Matty behind and let him be alone. Yet, she couldn't get that smell out of her nostrils – the noises she had heard in the tunnel – out of her mind.

She was scared. She wanted to go home. She wanted to see her mum. Her dad. She wanted to be in the warmth and comfort of the familiar.

She thought she heard a noise, stronger now.

She left Matty – out of sight, completely in mind – and followed the rushed footsteps of the other two.

Left him with the Bone Keeper.

Now

Thirty

Louise was standing in her kitchen on legs which threatened to turn to jelly at any second. Her own home was an enemy – but she was determined to rectify that swiftly.

First, she took the time to consider the card with her name written on it. Wondering why it had been left, why those words had been chosen. It couldn't have been from anyone other than him.

Him.

He was out there. He'd been in her house.

He wasn't real.

He was dead. Gone.

Yet he was the only person she could think of who would do this.

Louise placed the card back down carefully on the counter. The ink had smudged a little at the end of the last word, black bleeding onto the white card. She stared at it for a few more seconds, then left the kitchen.

She needed to know for sure.

At the end of her hallway, she turned on the upstairs light, then made her way up. She had two bedrooms, so she had turned the second one into a storage room. A menagerie of different items – presents from people she had no intention of ever using, bags of clothes which either didn't fit, or she would never wear. CDs she hadn't listened to in years. She passed over those and dug her way into the corner, finding the storage boxes she had put there when she first moved in.

Boxes which had followed her wherever she had gone.

She wanted to open them there and then, but resisted the urge. Instead, she carried them through into her bedroom, where she felt safe in the overhead glow of the light, and put them down on her perfectly made bed.

Louise looked at the open bedroom door, stood up and closed it. On the door ledge she kept the key she couldn't remember using before now. A remnant of the previous occupant. Now, she took it down from the ledge and turned it in the lock, sealing herself away.

She knew which box contained what she wanted, but she went first to the other one. Inside were memories of a past teenage life. What had survived over the years. Her journey through high school, various reports, her record of achievement. Some photographs of her grandparents and herself were buried further down. Some old faded school projects, corners curled and colours, in parts, now just a memory. A few Christmas cards she had handmade for them, similar ones for Easter and birthdays.

She set the photographs to one side, then closed up the box and pushed it away. The other box wasn't as heavy, but she still struggled to pull it towards her. It caught on the duvet cover as she tugged it her way. She reached over to the bedside table and picked up some nail scissors. They were small, almost blunt, but they would do the trick. She splayed the scissors, using the sharpest point to cut into the brown masking tape that was wrapped around the edges of the box. The tape snapped easily, meaning she only had to tear off one long strip along the top and the box was open.

A waft of unwanted nostalgia drifted into the atmosphere around her as the box opened. An old, musty smell, with hints of sickly lavender.

She reached in, taking the first item from the top.

Brought the T-shirt to her face and inhaled heavily. There was still a trace of his scent on the material; or was it her own mind making her think it was still there? Age would have destroyed that smell by now, she was sure – but still she breathed in, closing her eyes, and tried to remember when he had worn it last. That part of her memory remained cut adrift. Lost, forever. Gone, along with everything else that existed with them.

There wasn't time for this, she thought. To become lost in the annals of history. She should have got past all of this a long time ago, but still it lingered. Remnants of a time when she didn't know how evil the world could be, the anger and despair it could create. An easier time, when the only worries she had were minor.

She remembered walks through parks in the city – Sefton and Newsham were her favourites. She could spend an entire day in Sefton Park and still not cover its vast area. Could become lost and found in the space of a few minutes.

Her father, lifting her up in his arms, wrapping himself around her. She could still remember the touch of his hand on her shoulder, the way her mum looked at him.

Her brother, blond sandy hair sticking up in odd places, running ahead and fighting imaginary baddies. Kicking a football for a few minutes, before finding something else to do to capture his imagination.

They had been happy once.

She thought about fire. The flames appearing around her, the heat and smoke billowing into her room. Her body burned with the memory, her mind turning red and black.

She blinked and was back sitting on her bed in silence once more.

The T-shirt alone had been enough to send Louise back in time, but there was more in the box. She knew what else lurked inside, what secrets it held, but wasn't sure whether she could face them now. The only proof she had that they had existed, other than in her memories.

She had no choice – she had to keep going.

The photographs of her former life found their way into her hands.

She laid them back down, suddenly afraid of seeing them again. The fear of fully opening the door that had always been ajar. Just a crack, waiting to be kicked in and for the darkness to rush out.

Waiting for her to prove to herself that the childlike writing she knew was on the back of the photos matched that of the handwritten card lying on the kitchen worktop downstairs. Her writing, his writing. All of them, signing their names.

She found a photograph of her mum and brother in happier times, a third of it cut off, she assumed by her mother in a fit of rage of some perceived slight. The smiles on their faces, betraying the reality of what was to come.

Louise closed her eyes, seeing the blood, the smell of copper assailing her. The noise, the screaming. The panicked breaths, her heart beating madly against her chest. Hands shaking, unable to swallow, her mouth filling with saliva. Fear itching over her skin, confusion battling against her own mind.

She snapped open her eyes as the memory threatened to overwhelm her. She was sweating in the cool bedroom, breathing heavily. She could feel the memories still lingering, the same feelings as she had once had, still so easily brought back.

There was no way out. You can never escape your past.

She lay back down on the bed, the T-shirt containing his scent close to her face as she tried to forget the bad and remember the good that had preceded it. Thought back to a simpler time, of walks through the park, when nothing ever mattered. A time before she had become an only child. When her brother was still there, a little older than her, protecting her if she ever needed it. A watcher, keeping an eye out for her and anything bad that might happen. There to pick her up if she fell over, fussing over a skinned knee or elbow.

There when she needed him.

She remembered the arguments they had, the pettiness of children and the disagreements they had got into. The stupidity of it all now, as she looked back on them.

Louise would give everything she had just to argue with him one more time. To be exasperated by him in some way. To be annoyed, angry, irritated by his mere presence.

To not be alone anymore.

She closed her eyes, allowed the past to envelop her and keep her safe.

A time when she had everything and nothing bad could ever reach her. When evil hadn't yet made an appearance. A simpler time, when she hadn't known death or destruction.

When she had been normal.

When *he* wasn't back.

When the Bone Keeper had just been another story.

Thirty-One

Hazel Durham could hear him in his room, come back after all this time. Ready to be by her side again. It was a dream, come to life. The world changing as she slept, producing something she could never have envisioned happening.

Her prayers had finally been answered.

Jon had come home.

He was back.

She was stuck for a moment, torn between going to the room and finding him there and not wanting the feeling to end. Normal life returning and washing away the emptiness she had felt since her son had died.

The noise kept coming, growing into a cacophony of hopes and dreams made real. She could hear music now, which must have been what woke her up, she thought. She recognised the song – one that Jon had played often when he had sealed himself in his bedroom alone. Some indie band, with a weird name, she guessed. The tune was familiar, but she couldn't have spoken at length about the producers of it.

The music was playing now.

Jon was home.

Probably lying on his bed, his eyes closed, lost in the repetitive power of the same song playing over and over. In that moment, it didn't matter that she had seen his life-less body. That she had watched the coffin containing it lowered into the ground and dirt shovelled on top. It didn't matter that she had grieved for months over his death, until it had become more painful than the moment she had brought him into the world.

None of it mattered anymore. Just the idea of him being home was enough. She concentrated on that, as she stared into the darkness and built up the courage to make her way out of bed and towards his bedroom door.

Even as she woke up further, the feeling didn't dissipate. She had waited for this moment for so long that, now it was here, reason was not going to intrude on her mind. No rational thought. This was everything she had waited for, so now it was here she wasn't about to allow negativity to get in the way.

She stepped onto the landing, the music louder now there was no barrier in the way. She could see the light pooling around her son's bedroom door. Her heart was hammering in her chest as she crossed the few feet and placed a hand on the door.

She was ready.

She was smiling as she pushed open the door.

Her last smile.

At first, she didn't realise it wasn't Jon. She had built up this moment in her mind so much that reality took a few seconds to take hold. For some glorious time, she really did see her son lying on his bed, fully clothed, tapping one foot against the other in time to the music. She believed that was what she saw. She blinked a few more times, the music now much louder than she'd been expecting, her sense of smell taking over first.

Her son had that teenage-boy smell, as they all do, but this was something much worse. It was death, it was rotting flesh.

Whatever was in that room wasn't her son.

The room was dark, but she could still feel the presence of something in it. A black hole, the life sucked away from a part of it. An absence of humanity. She caught glints of shape and form, but couldn't comprehend them as anything solid.

'Hello, Hazel,' the thing in Jon's bedroom said, the inhuman voice low, growling, as the words spilled from its dark mouth. 'I've been waiting for you.'

Hazel wanted so much to speak, to shout and scream at this intruder, but instead her mouth formed a perfect O and stayed silent.

'You know who I am?'

There was a pause, where Hazel tried to resist the temptation to say his name, but it fell out of her mouth anyway. 'The Bone Keeper,' she said, her voice almost lost, as the words came out in a whisper. Her hands came up to her mouth slowly as if by themselves, as if they were angry with her somehow for saying the name aloud. Even as she realised that all the stories had been true.

The monster was real.

'You've been talking to people about me.'

She shook her head instantly, vigorously, suddenly fearful of what might happen to her if this *thing* believed she'd done him wrong. She could hear the noise as it lifted itself from the bed, yet she refused to look towards it. She looked at the floor, at her feet, willing them to move.

'Yes, you have, Hazel. He was trying to find me. He didn't have to look very far. I found him first. You've heard the stories about me. You know what I do.'

Hazel found herself nodding slowly in agreement, remembering the times she had sat around, making up scary stories with her friends. As teenagers, sitting on street corners, staving off boredom by embellishing tales to make them real. The Bone Keeper didn't have a name back then, but the stories had been the same.

'You're not real,' Hazel said softly, allowing herself to look at him now. 'You're not.'

'I'm here,' it said, drawing itself closer to her. Hazel could feel bile rising to her throat as the smell threatened to overwhelm her. She still refused to look up and confront whatever it was. That moment was coming, yet she was having to summon every ounce of courage and strength she had. 'You can see me. You can hear me. Doesn't that make me real?'

'Get out of my son's room,' Hazel said with a hiss. She felt anger rise up, overtaking the bile and fear which had been taking hold. 'Get out.'

She felt no reaction to her shout, even as it echoed off the walls. She had a sudden thought of her neighbours, whether they would have heard the music, her scream, and decided something was wrong. Whether they would call for help, if they would have recognised the sounds as something that required immediate intervention.

Or, as she guessed, whether they would grumble about neighbours intruding on their lives, turn over and go back to sleep.

'You know why I'm here.'

She felt she could suddenly see every part of it now, feel

everything emanating from the darkness. She wanted to stand up and banish the monster back into the shadows, back to hell or wherever it had come from. She wanted to defend herself, her home, the last memories of her son.

'It's your turn now.'

Her feet finally came to life, pivoting and rushing out of the room. A plan suddenly came to mind as she reached the top of the stairs, flinging herself downwards two at a time. She reached the bottom, fumbling on the side for her keys so she could unlock the door and get out of the house and onto the street. Scream for help. Her hands clamped around them, shaking as she found the right one and slipped it into the lock.

She had time to feel the silence behind her thicken as she turned the key, stepping back and pulling the door open. Cold air rushed towards her as she stepped onto the path, billowing around her shorts and T-shirt, giving her instant goosebumps. She kept moving forwards, making it to the end of the path before realising she had no further part to her plan. She risked a look back, slowing down as her bare feet felt the stones grinding into them.

It was there. She thought it was smiling at her.

She looked left, then right, then stopped with her back against the gate. It was an arm's length from her in the darkness of the street, the streetlights dim and creating endless shadows.

It was waiting, she realised.

She opened her mouth and screamed, the sound echoing around the small street.

It kept moving and was on her before she had a chance to do anything more.

Hazel could feel the pain, but it was almost otherworldly,

unconnected to her. All she could hear was the grunts of effort; all she could feel, something pawing at her body and then up around her throat. She had fallen to the ground, but couldn't quite remember at what point. There was wetness coming from her, as she made her hands move over the sides of her body, then instant pain as they found the wounds made in her torso.

She could look only into its eyes as her air supply was cut off. She could only struggle fitfully, with no real effect. She could feel her breath lodged at the bottom of her throat, her legs thrashing beneath her.

She couldn't hear sirens. She couldn't hear any shouts.

No one coming to help her.

No one coming home.

The fight began to leave her body, as it struggled limply. She could still smell death, above her. Around her. Taking her in its embrace.

She knew this was the end.

Her eyes closed and she could see her son. Smiling, as he had on occasion. Smiling at her.

Waiting.

She hoped he was waiting.

Hoped there would finally be a reunion, away from the monster who had taken them both.

Darkness fell over her, as she still thought of her son. Tinged in red and black.

Waiting for her.

Thirty-Two

Louise rubbed sleep from her eyes and tried to forget about the photographs. The handwriting on the card left for her to find. The burnt pieces of wood, still sitting in her kitchen untouched. She wanted to throw them away, never look at them again, but something had stopped her.

She knew it was the same thing that was stopping her from telling Shipley and everyone at the station what she had found.

How it connected to the investigation, if it did at all. There was no way it could. Just another part of the game. A door opening to the past that she didn't want to walk through and discover the truth of her life.

She thought of these things while looking at the body on the ground. Another victim. Killed the same night as someone had broken into her home and delivered her the past.

This was the new normal. *Her* new normal.

Louise mirrored DS Shipley, snapping on the blue forensic gloves that were swiftly becoming a part of her usual working life. Not that she had any intention of touching a single thing. Her mark was perhaps already on this scene, in so many ways.

Just breathe, keep calm, you can do this.

She hated the voice in her head now. Always placating her, trying to keep her on track, when all she wanted to do was scream her feelings out. Hide in a corner, covered with a blanket, until this was all over.

'Looks like it all happened in the one place,' Shipley said, giving Louise a little nudge. 'Stabbed her here, on the path, then by the looks of the marks on her neck, strangled her. Seems like overkill.'

They were back on the close they had visited only a couple of days previously. Now, it felt different, as if a dark cloud had descended above them, casting everything in a dull light. The atmosphere was thickened by tension as the residents had gathered nearby, all questioning what had occurred near their once-safe abodes. Death on your doorstep had a way of making you question your own life.

Louise could sympathise.

Only, they weren't supposed to come back.

Hazel Durham lay awkwardly on the ground, blood thick and dark surrounding her. Her greying hair was splayed out underneath her head, matted in parts as her life pooled into it. Angry red and purple marks were visible on her neck. Her eyes were open and staring upwards, as if she had looked towards the sky in her final moments. The once-white shorts and T-shirt she had been wearing were now torn and ruined, as the wounds beneath the rips in the fabric seemed to battle to reach out and be noticed.

'He wanted to be close to her,' Louise replied, squatting down and getting closer to Hazel Durham. 'Almost like he wanted to look in her eyes as she died.'

'This is personal then.'

'I expect so,' Louise said, standing up to her full height and facing Shipley. They were inside the forensic tent which had been erected around Hazel Durham's body, but not before enough people in the close had seen her prone body lying at the end of her path to mean quite a crowd had gathered. They had been shepherded away for the most part, but Louise could still feel their presence out there. Watching every movement in and out, hearing bits and pieces of information, making judgements. 'He's also used a knife on her, but it looks more rushed to me,' she went on. 'Still, I think it's the same guy.'

'I don't think there's any doubt about that.'

'Why her?' Louise said, stepping back from Hazel's body, carefully watching her step as she did so. Her entire body was covered, in order to keep the scene as forensically viable as possible, but she could see the para-medics' footprints in the blood which had pooled around the body. She knew Shipley would have the same pangs of guilt she was experiencing. As if they were somehow to blame for Hazel being killed and that by speaking to her, they had put her in danger. 'She didn't even tell us that much. It's not like he could have been annoyed with something she told us.'

'Maybe there was more to tell,' Shipley replied, nodding his head towards the house and waiting for Louise to follow him. 'Someone wanted to keep her quiet. Which leads me back to Rhys Durham. We still haven't found him and he's the most viable option for all of this.'

'The timing still doesn't fit in my opinion,' Louise said as they stepped into the house, which was now crawling with various uniformed officers and forensic techs. CSI would have the run of the place, but the main focus of activity was in the hallway and the path leading outside. They looked at each other and began ascending the stairs, knowing what they needed to see again. 'He'd be too young.'

'So, maybe he was a precocious serial killer.'

'Those bodies we found in the woods go back fifteen years. The stories about TBK go back even further than that. Are we really saying we have a serial killer who started as a baby? Or even as a glint in his father's eye?'

Shipley reached the top of the stairs and paused on the landing, turning towards her as she stopped on the last stair. 'Probably not, but those were only stories after all. Maybe they weren't true until someone made them so?'

She shrugged and waited for him to push open the door to Jon Durham's bedroom, then followed him inside. It was much the same as it had been the last time they had been there; the only discernible difference was that it was obvious someone had been inside and moved things around a little. The bed was no longer immaculately made up; instead the covers were rumpled and shifted to the side somewhat. There were muddy marks on the white sheet at the bottom of the bed, exposed by the duvet itself hanging off the side. The CD player on the bedside table was on, a digital display blinking a final track number in green. The small figures on a shelf had been swept over, the meticulousness of them now ruined. The wall display was still intact, left behind for them to study once again. Shipley had made his way over to it instantly and was looking at the pictures and notes, his head cocked to one side, taking it all in.

Louise took more interest in the CD player, lifting up the CD case perched on top of it with a gloved hand. It had already been marked up, fingerprints pictured and taken from it. She doubted that he would have left any behind. Whoever this was.

You know what it is.

'Shut up.'

'What?' Shipley replied, looking over his shoulder at her briefly. 'Did you say something?'

'No, nothing. It started in here,' Louise said, speaking to Shipley's back as he turned to study the wall again. 'Hazel was probably asleep and he waited for her to wake up.'

'Uniforms spoke to the neighbours first thing. One of them said they heard loud music around 4.30 a.m., they thought. Which fits into the timeline. What are you thinking?'

'He plays the music, lures Hazel in here, then begins his attack.'

'There's nothing in here that suggests there was a struggle though,' Shipley said, finally turning to face the rest of the room. 'I know, I know, the toys on the shelf have been knocked over, but that's not much. If you're fighting for your life, you make more mess than that. Same as the landing, the stairs and the hallway. Everything happens outside.'

'He let her get that far,' Louise said quietly, imagining herself in that position. Running for your life, while someone watched you, knowing your actions were futile. Perhaps taking pleasure in allowing you to think escape was possible. 'I keep coming back to the same question,' she continued, changing tack as the feeling grew too strong for her. 'Why her? What could she possibly have known that she wouldn't have already told us?'

'Information from this room led us to the woods in Speke. Maybe that was enough.'

Louise hummed in response, but didn't quite buy it. It felt like a loose thread that she couldn't help but pull. 'I'm not convinced.'

'We need this entire wall studied inch by inch,' Shipley said, turning back to face it once more. 'Maybe she interrupted him before he could destroy it himself, led him outside, and then he had to leave quickly or be caught. Why else would he come back?'

'You're probably right,' Louise replied, stepping alongside him and allowing herself to look at the wall once again. She recognised what was pictured there. The different areas of the city – of the entire county of Merseyside, if you wanted to be precise. There were pictures printed from the internet, mixed in with ones she imagined Jon had taken himself. Soon, they would begin combing the entire woodland around them, but for now they were still chasing their tails.

Trying to find someone who wasn't real.

'Then there's the question of Rhys Durham,' Shipley continued, tracing a gloved finger over one of the tendrils emanating from the devil mask. 'He's the prime suspect for all of these deaths. We need to find him. That'll be key to keeping us in the loop in this case. And beyond.'

That was the most important thing to Shipley, she realised. Staying involved. He saw this as nothing more than a large-scale investigation that he had stumbled into and was now desperate to stay with. Louise almost pitied him in that moment, but quickly thought about how she would have reacted in the same situation, without the baggage she was carrying.

She would have been holding the door open for him, then skipping through it herself.

'I don't think you have anything to worry about,' Louise said, replicating the soothing voice which was playing in her head more and more now. 'They wouldn't have sent us to this scene if they weren't keeping us on board. They know you're a good detective, you've already shown that much.'

Shipley shaped to reply, but then closed his mouth and only kept eye contact with her. There was a frisson of electricity in that moment, even with everything else going on around them.

Neither of them had mentioned what had happened in the car the previous night.

If only he knew. You can trust him. Just tell him. He'll understand.

She shook off the thought, knowing what his reaction would really be. Still, it would be a relief if she could tell him what she had found in her kitchen. Someone to share the burden she was carrying.

A uniform appeared at the door, clearing his throat to gain their attention. They turned in unison, Louise feeling a blush rise to her cheeks. She glanced at Shipley, who was also rosy-cheeked.

'Just thought I'd let you know,' the uniformed officer said, shifting uneasily on his feet. He was almost impossibly young, Louise thought, and winced a little at herself. He couldn't actually have been more than eight or nine years younger than her, but she felt as if she had decades on him. She wondered if he'd dealt with anything like this before, then decided that he probably had by now. It didn't take long being in uniform before you were confronted by death. 'Your DI has turned up. Looking for you both downstairs.'

Louise thanked the young lad, waiting for him to leave before she turned back to Shipley. 'We'd better get down there. Don't want to annoy our new boss.'

Shipley grinned in her direction, but didn't make eye contact this time.

She tailed him out of the room, waiting for him to take a couple of steps down the stairs before she followed.

Each step felt like a betrayal.

Thirty-Three

He washed his hands over and over, feeling sharp, stinging pain when he ran them under the tap. The knife he had used lay on the windowsill, blood drying on its blade. Light permeated the glass pane, stopping and being absorbed by the red and brown tinge.

He held his hand to his mouth, yawning again. His body felt empty, as if all the energy he'd once felt had been sucked out of him.

That was something he'd never expected. Exhaustion. Murder had wiped him out.

He giggled to himself, the noise of it echoing around the tiny bathroom. The idea of being something so hated.

At least he was something.

There's so many kinds of murder. The violent, spur-of-the-moment type. Unplanned and instant. Then there's the kind that is properly planned and thought out. All building up to the moment when you plunge the knife into someone's neck, or use your hands to choke the life out of a person. You can picture it in your head, every second of it, almost feeling as if it were real already. It is a poor substitute for actually doing it though, he thought. Nothing can ever match really ending some-one's life.

He knows what that feels like now.

He had become something. A thing to be feared, scared about.

The bodies entered his mind as he picked up the soap and began rubbing it into his hands again. He had left the bodies in the shared bed. He knew they would be found eventually, but there had been a second when he had hovered over the telephone, trying to decide whether he should call the police himself to make that discovery come quicker. He had decided against it, reasoning that it wouldn't be long before someone missed them.

They were there, now, as stark as reality in his head. Lying on the bed, as he watched the lifelessness of them. He had been stunned into silence by the stillness of them, how they had become blank shells in front of his eyes.

The way the air around them had changed and become empty.

There had been a few seconds, in the darkness as he stared at them, when he imagined he could see their souls leaving their bodies. Drifting upwards, past the ceiling above them and into the sky beyond. Joining the stars in the sky, taking their own place among them.

He had no way of knowing if that would have been their eventual resting place. For all he knew about the pair, they could have done terrible things in their lives. Maybe they were destined for a vastly different place than the one above.

He had wanted to go through their things, delve into their personal lives and discover what they were hiding.

The water running from the tap turned cold again as

he ran his hands under it, watching the stream run clear. At first, it had run dark, then had turned lighter with each wash. Now, there was nothing left. No trace.

After he had watched the couple for a while, he had opened a bedside drawer, looking through its contents. He'd switched on the lamp which that sat on top so he could see better. Nothing inside it had surprised him, or answered any of his questions. An unopened box of condoms, some medication, an old postcard and some odd bits of ribbon. He'd tried the other two drawers but found much the same. Nothing that told him anything about the couple.

Why did he want to know?

He should have run away immediately, he knew that. Staying there had only driven him towards bad thoughts and feelings.

He had left soon afterwards, ignoring everything else in the house.

The clothes he wore seemed cloying and restrictive once he was away from the scene. As if they had been made for someone else. He had broken into a run once he'd been clear of the street, to expend any last energy. He wanted it all gone, all the thoughts and feelings he had, the memories. He needed to keep moving, keep going. Not allow any of the events to catch up with him. To think about them too much, to dwell on them.

That wouldn't help him.

He had too much to do.

Now, in the bright, burning light of day, he couldn't get the image out of his mind. His hands around her neck, her eyes bulging out as she struggled to breathe. The knife lodged in the man's neck, the blood spilling out onto his gloved hands. He could almost feel it now, no matter that he had rubbed them raw under the running water.

He needed sleep.

He needed to hear the words again. The faded, mis-remembered ones he struggled to recall. Those that would appear when he closed his eyes and listened hard enough. Soothing tones, peaceful.

Flashes of red and black invaded his vision instead. The sounds and smells. This wasn't what he had expected. His balled his wet hands into fists and drove them against his eyes, wanting the darkness to return, but instead he could hear their voices. Their pleas for mercy. All of them, at once.

He believed he could see their faces, each of them in turn. All strangers to him. All of those bodies, now being dug up and found. Decayed, destroyed.

They blurred and merged into one face.

He couldn't get past the thoughts, the feelings, as he began to shake uncontrollably.

Thirty-Four

The clouds overhead had parted, allowing a dull sun to appear above them, as they made their way out of the house and to the waiting detective inspector. Louise had time to shed her forensic suit and gloves before they were pulled aside by their new boss, meaning she felt a little closer to normal. The DI was someone she'd met before, but never in this capacity.

Breathe. You can do this.

GO AWAY.

'Thoughts?' DI Locke said, barely giving them the chance to get to where he was standing. Louise imagined he didn't visit many scenes, which must mean this one had resonated back at the station. There were palpable signs of tension on the older man's face, which she guessed hadn't been there before this week.

'Looks like he gained entry through the back, then enticed her into her son's bedroom,' Shipley replied, almost standing to attention and speaking in a clipped tone. 'First confrontation was in there and then he chased her out to where she was killed on the path outside.'

'Where's the son?'

If Shipley was annoyed about the lack of insight into their work until that point, he didn't show it. 'Died a year ago. Suicide. It was his notes and photographs on TBK that led us to the woods down the road.'

'TBK?'

Louise had to turn away in order to hide her frustration. Shipley was more stoic than her, however, and continued without a pause.

'The Bone Keeper, sir. That's whoever this *person* is has been masquerading as, best we can tell. He put the woman – Caroline – in hospital earlier this week, leading us to here and then the woods.'

'Right, I see,' DI Locke replied, nodding his head. 'I'm familiar with the case up until this point. I didn't realise we were treating that aspect of it with such seriousness though.'

'Oh, don't get me wrong sir, neither are we . . .' Shipley started, almost tripping on his words as they tumbled from his mouth. Louise liked this part of Shipley least of all. She understood the urge to better himself, she just wished he could do it without sounding like so much of a sap.

'We need to take it seriously,' Louise interrupted before Shipley had a chance to finish the thought. Before she'd had a chance to think herself. 'It's . . . it could be important.'

'As far as I can see, we have a number of murders that have occurred over a long period of time. One man of interest, who would have been a glint in his father's eye when these stories about a monster lurking underneath your bed began. Let's not waste any more time on this Bone Keeper story. Someone is obviously playing a game. This woman who ended up in hospital, what else can we get out of her?'

The DI's question was directed at Louise, but Shipley spoke before she could. 'Nothing much, I imagine. Louise and I have spoken to her a few times now. She can't really remember much about the time when she was being held. We think she may have been drugged at some point. We're not sure on that one yet. We can try again, but it may be a waste of time.'

'What's her name?'

'Caroline Rickards.'

'You've looked into her background, all the usual stuff?'

'We haven't really been able to find out much,' Shipley said, shaking his head and looking towards Louise for help. She couldn't.

'Run her through the system. Properly. I mean forensically – I want a complete picture of who she is. See if she's been telling us the truth.'

'Yes, sir.'

'And all of this comes back to Rhys Durham. Not some ghost. We have a very real, very live suspect in him. Anything you do from now on is only to do with finding this man. Understand?'

Shipley hesitated, briefly, but it was enough time for DI Locke to shake his head and begin to turn away before continuing. 'I'll have my team go over what you've found out so far a little more closely. I think we can safely say he's escalating at this point. Hopefully he's left something behind here for CSI to find. Some kind of clue would be good.'

'Yes, sir,' Shipley repeated. Louise recognised the hard edge to his tone this time, even if DI Locke didn't seem to. 'We'll speak to the neighbours and secure any CCTV we can.'

DI Locke didn't answer him, walking away without another word. Louise turned to Shipley, eyebrows raised in mock surprise. 'Nice guy.'

'He's just doing his job,' Shipley replied, agitated and wringing his hands together. 'We'll have to get used to that type of thing if we want to stick around.'

Louise could feel herself becoming less calm by the second. The voice inside her had grown infuriatingly soothing, to the point where she was simply ignoring it entirely.

This was on her, she thought. This dead woman, all the others . . . it was her fault.

Which meant she had to do something about it, rather than standing around while these men measured their manhoods against each other's and battled for superiority.

'You okay nabbing a uniform and speaking to the neighbours?' Louise said, making a final decision. 'I'm going back to the station and getting a head start on tracking down this Rhys Durham. Keep in the good books with them lot.'

Shipley studied her for a few seconds before nodding his head. 'Okay, cool, good idea. We don't want to get left behind here. You go and do that, if you're all right with it?'

'Yeah, of course,' Louise replied with a smile, as if Shipley had thought of the idea himself. 'I'll check in with you later.'

She walked away, removing her car keys from her pocket, keying the automatic locking and not looking back. She slid herself into the driver's seat, then rested her head against the steering wheel for a second and composed herself. She closed her eyes as the voice insisted again:

Say something.

She wanted to sleep, put everything to one side and never think of any of it again. She was desperate for boredom again, a time when she didn't have to think about anything.

He's back.

Louise jumped as a loud knock on the window almost deafened her.

'Change of plans,' Shipley said, shouting through the glass. 'We've got another scene.'

Thirty minutes later, Louise pulled up near a semi-detached house, the street a similar scene to the one she'd just left behind. Shipley had beat her there by a good ten minutes, travelling with DI Locke, rather than her. Taking the opportunity to spend some quality time with the new boss, she guessed.

CSI vans were parked up. They were earning their wages today, she thought to herself. The crowd of onlookers was smaller here, a younger, more professional populace than in the part of the city she had been in earlier. Most would have been at work still, or were affecting the middle-class attitude which prevailed even here. *Don't get involved, not our problem.*

She still wasn't sure if she should be thinking the same. She left the car, making her way over to the house and flashing her ID at a uniform standing guard near the entrance. She spotted Shipley waiting for her near the front door and approached him. He looked up, studying her for a second before launching into a ramble.

'Another one,' he said, shaking his head at the incredulity of it all. 'Two, actually. Our guy had a busy night.'

'What is it?' Louise replied, already feeling that something wasn't right. 'Are you sure it's him?'

'Oh, yes, definitely,' Shipley said, nodding his head. She could see he was trying to keep a lid on his excitement, but he was struggling with it. 'Scrawled his name on the walls with their blood. It's him.'

'A couple, in their home?'

'Not just in their home, in their bed. Looks like they could barely fight back. The guy was stabbed in the throat, she was stuck in the heart and strangled. It's a bloodbath inside the room. It's everywhere.'

Louise shook her head, trying to process the information. 'And this happened last night?'

'Yeah, they were last seen around 6 p.m. Both didn't turn up for work this morning. Turns out one of them is in a car-share. She never misses it apparently, not without letting them know first. Someone got worried and managed to get hold of the girl's mother. She came round a couple of hours ago and found them both. Poor woman had to be carted off to hospital in shock.'

'This doesn't feel right, Paul,' Louise tried, attempting to make him see what she already knew. 'Hazel Durham, I can understand. Especially if it was Rhys. There's a personal connection there. But this . . . Who are these people? Are they connected in some way?'

Shipley sighed heavily, his hands finding his hips, fingers spreading out a little. 'What does that matter? Are we really going to start assigning any kind of logic to anything this nutcase does? All that matters is that we have two more murders, another scene, and possibly more mistakes made. It's getting worse, Louise. It's out in the open now. Which means this is the endgame.'

Louise kept silent, allowing Shipley to think he was still in control, yet the nagging feeling didn't leave her.

It strengthened further when they were allowed to see a glimpse of the bedroom. The bed, soaked with blood. The wall above it, spattered and dripping. The drawers on the floor, discarded and spilling their contents. Any other time, they would have categorised this as a burglary gone wrong, but Louise knew there was no chance of that happening now.

'We used to think he watched us as we slept,' a voice said from the stairwell. Louise tried to ignore it, but found that her attention wanted to be pulled away from the scene she was having to endure.

'My brother gave me sleepless nights for a week because of it. He hid in the wardrobe at the end of my bed and jumped out on me. I was in bed for half an hour before he did it, the little get. Dived out and shouted he was the Bone Keeper, come to get me.'

'That story got everywhere.'

'It was our legend, you know. Everyone had their own story about him. What do you think – is this him coming back?'

'It'll be some nutcase who *thinks* he's something else. That's all. Still, some scary stuff going on.'

Louise shook her head at the unseen men behind the voices, wondering if everyone would be able to dismiss it all as easily as they had.

You know he's dead. It can't be him.

She stepped back from the doorway, feeling the anger grow inside her anew. Her head snapped towards the uniforms whose voices she'd heard. They were standing on the stairs, leaning against the wall as if they didn't have a care in the world.

'You'd think he'd find someone a bit better-looking to go after though. Did you see the kip of her?'

Louise bristled at the words from one of the uniforms, then the laugh, shared with the other. 'Hey, you two, make yourselves useful and go and stand outside.'

'We're taking orders from you now?' one of them said, giving his mate a smirk. 'We're making sure no one comes up the stairs and messes up the crime scene, if that's okay with you?'

Louise smiled thinly and walked to the top of the stairs. She went down a few steps, until she was just above the one who had spoken to her. He still wore the same smirk, as her hands began to tremble.

'Look . . .' he just had time to say before she gripped him by the shoulder and pushed him down a step.

'Hey, hang on.'

'Get down there now,' Louise said, clenching the skin on his shoulder harder as the other uniform hopped down the stairs. 'I'm not going to ask nicely again.'

She pushed him again, watching as he stumbled and almost fell down the remaining steps. Gripped him by the shoulder, smiling as he shouted in pain.

'Louise?'

Shipley was standing at the top of the stairs, frowning at her, as she gently let go of the uniform's shoulder and allowed him to step back away from her, his feet almost slipping down the stairs, a look of shock still on his face.

'I was just . . .' She couldn't finish the sentence. She wondered how she had found herself there. 'Sorry.'

Shipley didn't reply, simply standing there as she looked back at the front entrance and the retreating men, then back up towards him.

'They were messing about . . .'

Louise stopped as she saw the look on Shipley's face, then the small shake of his head. He turned and disappeared from view as she stood on the staircase and rested her back against the wall. Closed her eyes and tried to breathe properly again.

Thirty-Five

He could smell the blood, staining his clothes and body.

He couldn't take it back. He couldn't turn back the clock.

He was the Bone Keeper.

He didn't want to be.

It had all seemed like the right thing to do a few days earlier. To do something different. Change his life and make it less ordinary. To not be normal any longer. All this time had led to that moment the previous night, but now it felt wrong.

Now, he could only see blood-red, smell death at every turn.

It wasn't supposed to be like this.

He slammed a fist into the wall he had been walking alongside, enjoying the feel of pain that shot through his wrist and up his arm. A guy walking opposite gave him a quick glance, but didn't return the stare he gave him back. That guy was safe. He didn't have to worry like he did. He didn't have to live with himself.

He was innocent.

He had gone back to the woods, hoping he could find answers there, but it was too late. It was a crime scene now. Bodies being unearthed, evidence found.

The voice . . . that was gone.

It wasn't supposed to eat away at him like this.

He had made a mistake.

He stopped pacing back and forth, picked the direction that led towards the city centre and started walking again. He passed the warehouses that dotted this part of the city's waterfront, abandoned and waiting to be knocked down or renovated in yet another rebuilding scheme. The tall buildings in the distance, another reminder of the life he had left behind. The one of normality and ordinary drabness.

There was only one place he had in mind.

He was going to be caught, he knew that now. He couldn't keep this inside him. He couldn't live with the faces of that couple in his head. The sounds they'd made, the expressions on their faces. The shock and surprise of finding him there, in their bedroom, just before he'd plunged the knife into their warm bodies.

The sound it had made would haunt him forever.

He wished he was brave enough to climb one of those tall buildings, go to the edge and throw himself down to the pavement.

He knew how much of a coward he was. That he would never have the guts to do that to himself.

Death would be too good for him.

He kept walking, picking up his pace as a single tear rolled down his cheek, as he remembered the night before. The air around him shimmered as exhaustion threatened to overwhelm him once again. He couldn't let that happen, no matter how much he wanted to crumple to the floor there and then. Feel the pavement against his face and shut his eyes.

The world was black, evil, dead.

He had killed the man first, thinking that was the right choice. Now, he knew why he'd decided to do that. What he wanted to do to the woman. Something he should never have thought about. He didn't want him to have to witness what he was going to do.

The Bone Keeper kept walking.

The reality of being Him now weighed heavy on his shoulders. An invisible load he was carrying without anyone knowing.

He reached the city centre within minutes, passing the Liver Building, the birds on top searching him with unseeing eyes. He could imagine their screeches of derision as they looked down on him, as if he were something unclean, dirty. He turned up the street towards the shopping centre, losing himself within the crowd within seconds.

He hated them all. They would never have to live with the screams of those who knew death was coming. They would never have to see their faces for the rest of their lives.

He passed first the Queen Victoria statue in the court square, giving the building a quick glance as he did so, knowing he would be returning to that place soon enough. Walked down the road, past the large department store at the entrance to the Liverpool One shopping centre, kept walking. He imagined he could feel the disgust coming off people towards him, as if they all knew what he'd done. How wrong he was. How bad. How filthy. How dangerous.

Gaming shops mixed with a restaurant or two, a discount store, an opticians, all going past in a blur, as he made his way to the place.

People were going to and fro in a haze, past the bank on one corner, the McDonald's opposite. A clothing store and an empty shell. He could smell fresh doughnuts from a green van a few metres away, people spilling out onto the pathway from a pub opposite. This was a main thoroughfare for shoppers into the city centre, away from the traffic, the roads. Simple paths, for simple shoppers.

The Bone Keeper stopped, fell to his knees a few feet away from someone in a terrible, and probably copyright-infringing, Mickey Mouse suit, holding balloons out to the odd child passing them by.

'You all right, mate?'

'You fallen over?'

He ignored the voices, allowing himself to rest for a few seconds. Knowing what had to happen next.

He took the knife from inside his jacket, holding it into the air. Some people had stopped in front of him, but he ignored their questions.

'The Bone Keeper's coming. The Bone Keeper's real. He doesn't stop. He doesn't feel.'

His voice cracked as he sang, volume increasing with every word until he was almost screeching.

'He'll snatch you up. And make you weep. He'll slice your flesh. Your bones he'll keep.'

People kept walking, just glancing down and giving him the once-over before they moved on. 'I'm the Bone Keeper. I'm here. I've killed people. I killed a couple in their beds last night. I'm the Bone Keeper.'

Someone out of sight clapped their hands, someone else

laughed. Others caught his eye, then quickly looked away. He waited for someone to stop him.

'I'm here. I'm waiting. I will do it again, unless you stop me.'

'. . . some nutter has got out of Ashworth.'

'Should we call someone?'

'There's a bizzie over there, he'll sort it.'

He waited, looking left and right for a sign of anyone coming for him. 'I'm a killer,' he tried again, his voice hoarse from the screaming. 'I'm going to do it again. And again. I liked it. I watched them die. I always do.'

He could see someone in uniform coming his way, speaking into the radio on his chest and staring at him. He held the knife higher.

'I killed them with this knife. It still has their blood on it. I can still smell it.'

The police officer was walking towards him more quickly now, as the Bone Keeper began to laugh and sing his song once again.

Thirty-Six

'Want to tell me what that was about?'

Louise was standing against her car, arms folded across her chest as Shipley asked her the question. Wishing she could answer him.

'We can't afford this . . .'

'Just, stop, okay,' Louise said, cutting him off before he could go on. 'I know how much you'd really love to be one of the top dogs in Major Crimes, but at the moment, we're in the same boat.'

'All right, calm down.'

'Don't tell me to calm down,' Louise said, the feeling inside her rising again. 'I'm perfectly calm.'

'Fine, okay.'

She breathed through it, waiting a moment or two before she could chance talking again. 'Look, I'm sorry. They were just standing around doing nothing. It's like they weren't taking it seriously, while two people lay on a bed just feet away from them, dead. They needed to be told.'

Shipley held up his hands in front of him, palms facing her, but didn't say anything. Louise began to say something more, before his phone cut her off.

'Really? Where? ... We'll be right there.'

Shipley pocketed his phone and turned to Louise with a smile.

'You won't believe this.'

'He's some crank,' DI Locke said, as Louise tuned back into the conversation that had been going on for the past few minutes now. She'd been an inactive participant in it; she'd left the talking to Shipley, hoping he'd recognise the task for what it was. A way of keeping the new bods out of the way, as the Major Crimes Unit began tightening its circle.

'I just need you two to take his statement and send him on his way once we have proof he wasn't involved.'

'Sir, isn't it just a waste of time though?' Shipley said, almost pleading with the DI not to be shuffled off to interview some weird guy who had decided to confess to something he couldn't possibly have done. His excitement had faded as quickly as it had arrived, once he'd been told of the circumstances behind the arrest.

'It might be, but we can't be too careful,' DI Locke replied, checking his watch for the fifth time since they'd been standing there. 'Look, just get it done and then we'll see where we all are. I imagine his story will fall apart pretty quickly. We've got a major press conference scheduled in fifteen minutes. I need to check in with the rest of the team beforehand.'

Shipley waited for DI Locke to leave them before turning to Louise. 'Bloody idiots. We bring this to them on a plate and now we're getting sidelined.'

'Not really,' Louise said, wanting to reach out and touch Shipley's arm. Soothe him. He didn't know the truth of all this. How pointless it would all be. He was simply trying to become something he couldn't, somewhere he didn't really belong. 'Look, we can get this done in an hour and be back before they know it.'

'I know what these nutters are like. We're going to be stuck listening to his crap for ages.'

'He was holding a knife he says was the murder weapon,' Louise said, reading the notes from the guy's arrest. 'It's being tested now, but results won't be back for a while.'

'It'll be his own blood, I reckon. Pointless, waste of time. We should be out there in the thick of it. Finding that Rhys Durham, talking to those people . . .'

Shipley trailed off, his anger and frustration getting the better of him, Louise thought.

If only he knew.

'Come on, let's get this over and done with,' Louise said, reaching up and giving him a quick pat on the shoulder. 'The quicker we get it sorted, the quicker we can get you back, super-detective.'

Shipley smiled in spite of himself, Louise accepting its warmth for a brief second before they set off.

They made their way down to the ground floor meeting the custody officers in the hallway which led to the interview rooms from the cells. Louise had sneaked her first look at the suspect at that point, unimpressed by what she'd seen.

After they'd led him into the room and sat down opposite him, she was even less impressed.

She busied herself with the recording machine as Shipley reeled off the usual spiel. His rights, his options. He had again confirmed he didn't want or need a solicitor, which hadn't surprised her. Attention-seekers usually didn't want to be interrupted by someone trying to protect them. She wondered if they should have the same care, but didn't think it was the time to bring that up.

He was young. That much was obvious just from looking at him. Far too young to be the man they'd been looking for. She expected Shipley had already made that observation, even if the man hadn't given the custody sergeant any more than his name when they'd booked him in. He had scraggly hair, unkempt and messy, which she suspected was his usual look, rather than just the result of spending a few hours on a thin mattress in a cell.

His clothes had been taken from him, sent for the same tests that would be done on the knife. She found herself looking for marks on his body where he could possibly have harmed himself, drawing blood to stain the black shirt and jeans he'd been wearing.

His cheekbones protruded from his face, jarring and pointed. Stubble on his face in random patches, as if he were still a teenager. Looking into his eyes, Louise could see he was a little older than she'd first thought, but he couldn't be more than twenty, twenty-one, she decided.

'Please state your name for the recording,' Shipley said, once Louise had given him the nod.

'The Bone Keeper.'

Louise could hear the waver in the youngster's voice, as if he'd prepared for this moment but, now it was here, he was unsure.

'And your actual, given name?'

The lad hesitated, as if he hadn't expected the follow-up question. 'It's . . . Steven. Steven Harris.'

'Why do you call yourself the Bone Keeper?'

'Because that's who I am. That's what I've been made into.'

Louise exchanged a look with Shipley. He rolled his eyes at her. 'And you're here to confess to a murder.'

'Not just one,' Steven said, more animated now. 'Loads of them. I did them all. That's who I am. I kill people.'

'Let's start at the beginning,' Louise said calmly. She tried to maintain eye contact with Steven, but he suddenly couldn't sit still. 'Why did you go to town today and begin this *confession*?'

'I couldn't stop seeing them.'

'Seeing who?'

'The two people in the bedroom. The man and the woman. They kept talking to me, telling me I had to confess to what I've done. It was the longest night of my life.'

'And who are these people, Steven?'

'I'm the Bone Keeper,' Steven said, his voice echoing off the walls around them. Shipley tensed up next to Louise, pushing his chair back a little. 'That's who I am now.'

'Okay, okay,' Louise replied, holding out her hands in front of her. 'Explain to us why you think you're the person who did this.'

Steven flashed a smile at her, his teeth revealed, stained and black in parts. 'Because I did it. I did it all.'

'This is a waste of time,' Shipley whispered, loud enough for her to hear but hopefully not loud enough to be picked up by the recording software.

'Tell us what you did exactly,' Louise continued, ignoring Shipley's remark.

'I waited and did exactly what I was supposed to do,' Steven said, his voice now measured, almost as if he were remembering it all as it happened. 'I stood in the garden, opened the door and went in. They were in bed. I went upstairs and killed him first. Then her.'

Louise pulled the crime scene report out, began scanning it in the silence. Very few details of the murder had been released until that point, but even a preliminary report had told her enough about the scene. The memory of it was still fresh in her mind, of course; it had only been a few hours. The day just felt like it had lasted a week. 'Tell me about the bedroom, what did you see?'

'There was a double bed, flowers on the duvet cover. Built-in wardrobes opposite. They both had bedside tables beside them. His had an alarm clock on the top of it. Hers had a lamp, and her phone. The carpet was like a beige-type colour. When I stuck the knife in his neck, he didn't make a sound. He pissed himself though. I could smell it.'

Shipley sat forward next to her as she listened, becoming increasingly wide-eyed. If he were making this up, he was doing a fine job of it. Louise pushed the file closer to Shipley so he could see the details. So far, Steven Harris hadn't missed a single thing.

'I wrote on the walls with their blood.'

And there was the confirmation. Shipley was sitting bolt upright now, a slow breath of air released from his mouth, as Louise tried to work out exactly what they were dealing with.

A copycat?

'So, you're the Bone Keeper,' Shipley said, glancing at the file and then back at Steven. 'Last night, you killed two people in their beds. Then what did you do?'

'I watched them for a while,' Steven replied, pulling one sleeve of his ill-fitting sweatshirt over his hand and stroking the side of his face with it. 'I don't know how long for. It was a long time. Too long. That's probably where I went wrong. I went back to the woods, but it wasn't quiet enough. I walked after that. Ended up in town. I need to make this all stop. I keep seeing their faces.'

'You didn't go anywhere other than the woods afterwards,' Shipley said, sitting back in his chair now, as if he'd finally had enough. 'Didn't go to the south of the city and do anything there?'

Steven shook his head. 'I killed those people. I've been there for others as well. The bodies you found in the woods near Speke, I knew they were there. I put them there.'

'All of them?' Louise asked, beginning to put the pieces together. 'How old are you?'

'The Bone Keeper is as old as the city . . .'

'Yeah, yeah, but how old are you actually?' Louise said, interrupting Steven before he could begin eulogising on the legend. 'When were you born?'

'I'm twenty-one,' Steven replied, a little despondently, as if he were on clearer ground when talking about anything else other than his actual life. 'But I feel much older.'

'Are you saying you killed and buried a body in those woods when you were five or six years old?'

Steven shaped to answer, then closed his mouth and didn't respond.

'Tell me more about the people you killed in that house. What street was it on, what did you see?'

'I've told you, I was there. I did it. And I'll do it again. And again. Unless you put me in prison now. Test the knife. It still has their blood on it. That's what I used.'

'What did you do to the woman, Steven?' Louise said, leaning forward closer to the younger man. 'Tell me about that.'

Steven shifted a little in his seat. 'I don't want to talk about that.'

'You read about the people we found in the woods, didn't you? And you got things a little muddled up, thought you could do something you've been wanting to do for a long time and pin it on the same person. That's the truth, isn't it? You've got nothing to do with those bodies in the woods. Have you?'

'Yes I have,' Steven replied, shouting at Louise now. She gave him no reaction, knowing that was what he wanted. 'I know all about it. We're all one. Everything the Bone Keeper has done, I have done. That's how it works.'

'Why did you kill them, Steven?' Shipley tried, as silence threatened to overpower them all.

Steven shrugged. 'I just wanted to know what it felt like to kill someone. Being the Bone Keeper helps me do that.'

Louise sat back, taking it in. The whole story. Shipley was already thinking Steven was a copycat, that was self-evident. It was difficult to think this was anything other than that.

Then she thought of the dark eyes that Nathan Coldfield's mother had spoken about. The familiarity of it, the knowledge that she had seen that type of eyes before.

The photograph in a box on her bed at home.

The same eyes peering into the lens, expressing nothing, as if a light had gone out and could never be repaired.

Thirty-Seven

Caroline walked out of the hospital with a destination in mind. The only one that made sense to her.

Back to the woods.

Not the ones from which she had barely escaped a few days earlier. She knew nothing remained there now.

Further north in the city.

It had been surprisingly easy to sign herself out. Against the doctor's wishes, of course, but it seemed like they were happy enough to let her go. An empty bed finally, which they could use for someone else they'd want to be rid of soon enough, she thought.

She had assumed the police would be told and have something to say about her leaving, but she was out of the door without any problem at all. Caroline wondered if she'd known this was the plan all along. That the reason she had used a different surname at work, and for the police, was because at some point she would need to disappear.

Caroline was her name, but Caroline *Rickards* didn't really exist.

She had wanted to be someone else for a long time. Had decided to do it and leave her past behind her.

Maybe it was simply so she didn't have to answer any questions about what had happened two decades earlier.

What she planned to atone for.

First, she had to do what she should have done a long time ago. Something she had allowed to fester.

If she was going back, she needed to see her one last time. In case she couldn't escape again.

As she left the taxi and stepped onto the pavement, there was a moment when she felt like walking away from it all. Abandoning everything and never thinking about what she would leave behind. There was a part of her that wanted more than anything to simply be able to do that. To live her life without a care about her past.

About why she had to go into those woods.

She took a deep breath and opened the gate at the end of the path, feeling the sting of nostalgia as she did so. The house in front of her, so familiar and yet so far removed from her life now. As if the memory had become a stranger to her.

She remembered standing at the end of a different path. Back when it all began. The feeling of loss, in the pit of her stomach. She couldn't have known then. No one could.

Caroline walked, twinges of pain in her stomach from the skin that was continuing to knit together and heal.

Knocked on the door and waited for it to open and her past to envelop her.

Thirty-Eight

They waited outside as Steven Harris was led back to his cell. They had tried to get more information out of him, but it became pretty clear that they weren't going to get much more viable information at that point. If talking in circles ever became an Olympic event, Louise would bet Steven could win a medal.

'He killed that couple,' Shipley said, shaking his head, then leaning back against the wall. 'I don't know what to tell you, sir, but I can't see how he would know what he does about that scene unless he'd been there last night.'

'Right,' DI Locke replied, one hand on the back of his neck, trying to rub out a knot, Louise thought. She could tell he wasn't going to forget their names in a hurry now. Shipley had got his wish.

'He's how old?' DI Locke continued, his voice almost pleading for some scrap of good fortune to suddenly come his way. 'Any chance he's older than he says?'

'He's saying twenty-one and I think he's telling the truth. If you're close up to him, you can see how young he is.'

'Plus, he's in the system,' Louise said, speaking for the

first time since they'd left the interview room and found the DI waiting outside. 'He isn't lying. He's too young.'

'And he confessed to the couple?'

'Yes. The whole thing,' Shipley said, looking over at Louise and then back at DI Locke. 'No doubt about it. But why would he confess to that, but not Hazel Durham on the same night?'

'Because it wasn't him?' Louise replied, moving a little to stand next to Shipley. It was quiet now, away from the main offices and the rest of the cells in the corridor. Steven Harris was back in his cell for now, but she didn't think he'd be there very long. 'You tell me. Any other signs of sexual assault on Hazel Durham? No. Only this one.'

'Meeting room, five minutes,' DI Locke said, shaking his head again, his shoulders seeming to sag even further. 'He's a copycat, that's all. But we'll still have to waste our time on him.'

Shipley shook his head as DI Locke turned away from them and walked away. Once the DI was out of earshot, he spoke to Louise. 'He's too young to be involved in any of them, surely? Unless TBK has a son he used to take on his murder trips into the forest. We can take his mugshot to the hospital, see if Caroline recognises him, but I think it's pretty clear. He's a copycat. An opportunist. One with a mental health problem, but an opportunist all the same. I'll put the report in on the interview once we've had him checked over again. I don't want his confession being thrown out because he suddenly decides to accept he's got problems.'

'So you don't think there's any link at all?'

'Do you?' Shipley replied, almost laughing as he spoke. 'He's just taken the chance to do something he's been thinking about for a long time. Turned out, he couldn't deal with the reality of raping and killing someone. I'm just glad it wasn't a complete waste of time. Now, we can get back to the real case.'

Louise didn't say anything, allowing Shipley to carry on believing the two cases weren't connected.

She didn't agree with him. Something told her everything was connected. That there was no such thing as coincidence. There was instinct. Her instinct. Telling her that nothing made sense any more, unless all of this was related.

Shipley walked away and Louise followed him back up to the main office of the Major Crimes Unit, still thinking about the week's events. How each murder, each discovery kept leading to the same places. The woods, where the stories about the Bone Keeper had begun long ago.

'Forensic reports are back on the initial bodies,' Shipley said, looking over his shoulder at her, before going back to reading from the scrawled notes on the large whiteboard at the end of the room. Everything was detailed there, each victim unearthed or found injured on the street. Her eyes found Caroline's in the photograph taken in the hospital bed the woman had called home for three days now.

'Eight bodies dug up now,' Shipley continued, turning back to the board. 'Most have even got names.'

'Adam Porter's mother was on television this morning,' a DC said, sidling up alongside them. 'Barely spoken to us, of course.'

'I imagine she blames us for his death,' Shipley replied, throwing a grin in the DC's direction. 'Still, if she's complaining to someone else, it gives us a chance to find who killed her son without any interference.'

'Problem is, it's sparked even more of that.'

Louise turned in the direction the DC was pointing, a television on the wall tuned to the news channel, a yellow banner running along the bottom of the screen. A reporter was on screen, speaking to camera from the city centre.

Where Steven Harris had been picked up by uniforms.

'Town is crawling with them now,' the DC said from behind her. Louise wished she'd bothered to learn his name, just so she could tell him to shut up. 'A bunch are outside as well. It's become the biggest news story around in less than a few hours.'

'A serial killer has that kind of effect.'

Louise moved closer to the television as someone reached across and turned the volume up.

'Yeah, they reckon it's this thing we all talked about as kids. Called it the Bone Keeper. I always said it was real. I had a mate who went missing after going into the woods. Never saw him again. Told him not to go in there but he didn't listen. Everyone thought it was just a silly ghost story, but what if he has been living in the woods all this time, just waiting—'

'Louise,' Shipley said, making her heart quicken a little. She tore her eyes away from the screen. 'They're waiting.'

Louise nodded and followed Shipley towards the meeting room, thinking of the reporters, the media, all converging on the city. Ready to ask their questions and unpick the story. Create their own, even. She knew they'd all be shielded from it, for the most part, but she could see the strain it was already placing on the detectives around them. The numerous officers who were now shuttling back and forth behind the scenes, being recruited from CID offices across the city, she guessed.

This was now the largest investigation the city will have seen in a long time, she thought.

Twelve confirmed murders, linked to one offender.

A serial killer, working for years without anyone knowing.

'All of the victims identified and found in the woods share a common history,' DI Locke said, addressing the gathered detectives in the meeting room as Louise and Shipley went in and sat down. She turned to look at him, rather than back at the open-plan office and the photos of the dead displayed there.

'Almost all of them?' DI Locke added, glancing at the DS sitting next to him.

'Almost.'

'Right, almost all of them. Adam Porter was different. Looks like he was just lost. Or something. The rest of them were all either homeless or living in refuges. Easily forgotten victims. That's probably why their disappearances didn't ring any alarm bells. No one was expecting them to be around for long.'

'What about the body found in the hut?' a DC sitting a row behind Louise said. 'Who was that?'

'Carl Groves,' DI Locke replied, after checking the file in front of him. 'Another local, staying at a hostel a mile or so away from Speke. Looks like he walked around a lot, according to the people spoken to there. A couple of the regulars there said he would walk as far as Hale some days. Looks like he walked past the wrong place. Now, we have a man in the cells below us, saying he killed the couple from last night. A copycat, by the looks of it. Our friends from Sefton CID have got a confession out of him, so they'll be boxing that off by the end of the day.'

Louise didn't avert her eyes from the DI as people turned to look at her and Shipley. She drifted in and out as the DI kept talking, explaining the entire situation as if they didn't already know it. Someone had killed twelve people, they didn't have anything other than a name in Rhys Durham, and someone not unwilling to go into people's houses and murder them out in the street.

'We are linking Hazel Durham at this time. Which brings us back to Rhys Durham. He's our man.'

Which would mean he killed people as a young teenager, Louise thought.

'He's escalating . . .'

There was a moment when she thought she'd actually sniggered out loud, but the fact that no one was paying any attention to her told her she was safe. It had become the new buzzword as soon as murders happened close together. Escalating. As if twelve people weren't enough, despite the length of time between the murders.

He escalated a long time ago, Louise thought.

'What about Caroline?' Shipley asked, breaking her train of thought. 'We can we talk to her again, maybe show her a picture of Steven Harris and make certain he's not involved?'

'That would be great,' DI Locke replied, shaking his head. 'But she checked out of the hospital a couple of hours ago. We're trying to locate her now. She wasn't at the address she gave when she was checked in.'

'Louise and I can do that,' Shipley replied quickly, giving her a nudge as he said her name. She nodded towards the DI for added effect.

'Yeah, good idea,' DI Locke said, turning away before he'd even finished answering. 'Finish up with Steven Harris first though.' He turned back to the rest of the room. Filled with bodies now, as the machine grew and the cogs Louise and Shipley represented grew smaller. 'Listen, I want feet on the ground. We've got enough resources now that we can use them more freely. Liaise with uniforms, go door to door. Someone, somewhere, will have seen something. That's how we usually find answers. I know there's a few of you going through CCTV, I want to know if you find anything. The entire area around Hazel Durham's house should be covered. Extensive statements taken. I don't want one stone left unturned . . .'

Louise tuned out again as DI Locke continued giving out the usual clichéd platitudes. It was obvious there was now more going on than she and Shipley were aware of. The investigation which had started with the two of them now involved a multitude of people she would never learn the names of, it seemed. They were a backstory now. Nothing important. She chewed on a fingernail as she considered what to do next.

Whether to think about the note back home in her kitchen and what it meant. If everything she knew about her past had been a lie until now.

The box on her bed, full of memories of a time she couldn't quite remember. Blurred and malformed.

Yet, she still had a job to do.

She needed to speak to Steven Harris.

She needed to be sure.

Thirty-Nine

Steven was sitting across from them once more, only this time he seemed even more diminutive, thinner and scared than he had earlier in the day. Almost as if life had begun seeping from him, leaving behind only a thin shell of a young man.

'Why did you go into the house?' Shipley said, continuing his line of questioning.

'To kill the people living there,' Steven replied, sounding as if he were answering something entirely different. Void of emotion, as matter-of-fact as if he had been describing what he'd bought on a shopping trip. 'The voices told me that was what I had to do. So I did it.'

'How did you get into the house?'

'I've told you this,' Steven said, tracing a circle on the desk between them with a finger. 'Why do I have to keep saying it?'

'How did you get into the house, Steven?'

'I'm the Bone Keeper. Stop calling me that. When we talk about these things, I'm the Bone Keeper. Not Steven. Steven would never do these things.'

Steven wasn't above talking about himself in the third

person though, Louise thought. The disassociation he had between what he had done and who he thought he was rang alarm bells for her. She knew what a lawyer would do with that information. He seemed to veer between having emotion and being blank. She knew guilt had driven him into the city centre and then into this interview room, but it almost seemed as if he was able to ignore it sometimes as well. Also, he had started adding this information about hearing voices, which she thought was a nice touch, but didn't believe in the slightest.

'Just explain again,' Shipley said, his voice as measured as it had been at the start. 'Please.'

'I walked into the house. Didn't need to break in. He . . . the man who lived there left the back door open after he finished smoking. It was easy. I just waited for him to finish and go back inside and walked in.'

'Where did you wait?'

'Just in the garden. Out of sight. No one ever saw me. Then, when I got inside, under the bed in their spare room.'

Louise thought about the small man, secreting himself easily in the garden. She'd only looked at it briefly, but could see how he had done so. There were a number of bushes at the back of the garden that it would have been simple to hide behind and be out of sight.

She thought about someone waiting underneath a bed in a room you barely used. You could never be sure who was in the one place you were supposed to feel safest.

The burnt pieces of wood on her kitchen worktop could attest to that.

'You waited for a long time,' Shipley said, staying professional and emotionless. She could imagine this would be released once he'd been found guilty at trial. Shown on true crime programmes endlessly, the lack of guilt playing to a crowd. Or, as she thought more likely, shown to a jury to prove Steven wasn't mentally competent.

'I had to,' Steven continued, taking a quick swig of the water he'd demanded before talking again. 'Otherwise it wouldn't have been right.'

'Why wouldn't it have been right?'

'That's not how the Bone Keeper works. I couldn't just go in the bedroom early, it had to be the right time. When they weren't expecting me to be there, otherwise he wouldn't be happy.'

Shipley didn't catch the slip, but Louise did. Shipley made as if to speak again, but Louise got in there first. 'Who wouldn't be happy?'

'The Bone Keeper.'

'I thought you were the Bone Keeper though?' Louise asked, as if it were just a throwaway question. 'Isn't that what you've been telling us? Why wouldn't you be happy with yourself?'

'I am now, but I wasn't before. That's what I'm saying.'

'Explain this to me,' Shipley said, cutting in again. 'I don't understand. Who is the Bone Keeper then?'

'Me.'

'But there's someone else as well? There's another one, who told you how to do what you've done?'

'There's many of them, all speaking at the same time. We're all doing the same work.'

Shipley looked at Louise, shaking his head slightly.

He didn't believe Steven, she thought. He had put it down to his hearing-voices declaration, when she suspected something else entirely.

Shipley was still talking as Louise considered what to

do next. The investigation was closing and she knew she wouldn't be needed for much longer. Which meant she could concentrate on what was happening to her.

Leave all this behind and see if the ghosts from her past had really returned.

Yet, she carried on listening as the interview began to go in circles again. Nothing new being revealed, Shipley becoming more and more exasperated as they went along.

By the end, there was no doubt in Louise's mind. Despite the obvious issues Steven Morris had, he'd been at his most uncomfortable when talking about one particular aspect of the crime.

'What did you do to Karen Marshall after you killed her, Steven?'

'Nothing.'

'Did you take off the duvet from her body, Steven?'

'I don't remember.'

'You do remember. I can see you want to talk about it, don't you? You want to tell us what you did after you stabbed her. Why don't you concentrate on that part for now?'

'Because I wasn't supposed to do that. I wasn't supposed to touch her in that way.'

'In what way?'

'I had sex with her.'

Louise felt the burn of anger in the back of her throat, as she thought about the utter absurdity of the sentence. As if raping a dying woman was just the same kind of sex as any other.

'She was still alive, wasn't she?'

'I didn't know. If I had, I wouldn't have done it until she was actually dead.'

As if that made it any better.

'Why didn't you want to do it, Steven?'

'He ... the Bone Keeper isn't supposed to do anything like that. He's supposed to be pure. I thought ... I thought if she was already dead it wouldn't matter as much. Now, he'll know. He always knows.'

'Who are you talking about?' Shipley said, becoming more exasperated again. Louise could already see the outcome with him. He wouldn't believe this version – Steven talking to another person, being guided by them. It was easier to think he was a copycat. Someone using the name to kill.

Yet, wasn't that what was happening anyway?

'No one,' Steven replied, withdrawing into himself once more. There was something so childlike about him that Louise couldn't help but wonder what had been done to this young lad. What had affected him so much to lead him to this point. Then, she thought of what he had done just over twenty-four hours earlier, and her empathy disappeared.

'Interview terminated at 7.35 p.m.' Shipley said, glancing towards her and rolling his eyes again. It was fast becoming his signature move, she thought. 'Let's get out of here.'

Louise didn't argue with him, even when he slammed his notebook closed and pushed his chair back with enough force to knock it over. She quietly cleared her own equipment away, trying not to look across the table at Steven Harris.

There was a pause as they waited for someone from custody to meet them and escort Steven Harris back to his cell. He sat quietly in the chair, staring at the table, seeming to contemplate its surface as if it was something new and unexplored. He looked up slowly, locking eyes with Louise as she sneaked a glance at him.

A small smile crept across his face. Louise glanced behind her, looking for Shipley, but he was moving away from them, staring up the corridor for someone to relieve them. Louise moved closer to Steven, gripping the side of the table for support.

She had the sudden urge to ask him the question that was still bothering her. 'Who are you?'

'He's coming,' Steven whispered, the smile still on his face. 'And there's nothing you can do about it.'

'You're not crazy,' Louise replied, hands shaking with anger. 'This is all one big act. You're going to spend the rest of your life in prison. Why?'

'Because he told me I had to. We do everything he tells us.'

'Who?'

'You know who,' Steven said, his voice different suddenly. More measured now, as if a light had been switched on inside him. 'I couldn't live with it – that's why I'm here – but he can. He has always lived with it. He wants you to stop ignoring him. To go and find him finally.'

'I've got no intention of doing anything,' Louise said through gritted teeth. She resisted the urge to reach out and slam his head against the table, but instead just gripped the edge harder. 'This is about the woman, isn't it? The one from the woods earlier this week. She escaped and it's all unravelling for poor Rhys.'

Louise turned to check Shipley wasn't listening, but he was still a fair distance out of the room, in the middle of the corridor. When she turned back, Steven was chuckling to himself.

'You don't get it. You don't know who she is.' Steven sat back further in his chair, a different man now. 'You don't know who Rhys is. But you know the Bone Keeper. I'm going to a hospital, not a prison. They'll think I'm mad. And you'll be dead if you don't accept who you are.'

Louise would have believed him if she didn't have any knowledge of the criminal justice system. Steven wasn't going anywhere other than prison. He might be able to pull the wool over Shipley's eyes, but he wouldn't be able to do the same to professionals. She let him think that though, not correcting him.

'Tell me ...' Steven said, folding his spindly arms across his chest. 'Did you like the offering – the message from him? I delivered it for him, before I killed those two people.'

Louise couldn't speak for a moment, trying and failing to work out exactly what she'd just been told. It made no sense on the surface yet, somehow, she knew it was true.

She had more of a connection to this case than she'd first feared. The burnt pieces of wood, fashioned to look like bones, should have been more important than the message.

There had always been this link to her past.

Now, she was in too deep.

She opened her mouth to ask more questions, but she was too late.

'Come on, Steven,' Shipley said from the doorway, seeming not to notice anything amiss. 'Time to go.'

She watched him leaving the room and being escorted away. He adopted the same lost look he'd been showing them for the previous few hours. Shipley shook his head as the young killer was taken away, then looked at her. A shadow crossed his features as he searched her face.

'You okay? You look a bit shaken up.'

Louise couldn't answer him.

Before

She could hear them down there, talking about her as if she weren't only a few feet away. Garbled voices, the floorboards beneath her turning normal conversation into something low and rumbling.

Anywhere else, she would have stayed where she was. At home, that was. She had never slept anywhere other than her own bed, in her own house, for any length of time.

That wasn't possible now.

Never would be again.

She pulled back the covers, disturbing yet another waft of the unfamiliar scent into the air around her. Sickly sweet lavender. She felt like she didn't care if the floor creaked underneath her feet, yet she still moved as slowly and softly as she could.

She wanted to hear what they were saying about her.

The bedroom door was open, as she'd demanded when they'd put her to bed an hour earlier. They didn't argue with her. Simply looked at her with sadness in their eyes, heads tilted to the side, as if they were dogs waiting for a treat. Concern written across their features.

There would be a lot she could get away with for a long

time, she realised suddenly. Rules would become strangers for as long as she could manage it.

She stepped out of the room, her right leg dragging a little, the bandage wrapped tightly enough to mask most of the problem. She made her way to the top of the stairs and heard their voices crystal-clear almost straight away. Dopey gets hadn't shut the living room door and they seemed to think they were talking low enough that she wouldn't hear. Or thought she'd already be asleep.

That was a laugh.

She didn't think she'd sleep properly for a long time.

'*What are we going to do though, Jack?*'

'*I don't know ... our best, I guess.*'

She could feel a nasty feeling rising inside her as she listened. Like she would be a problem for them. Still, it was a roof over her head for now, and she'd be out of there before they knew it. She didn't want to stay there any more than it seemed they wanted her to.

'*I just don't understand it. Why did it have to be all of them?*'

'*It was an accident. There's no reason for it at all.*'

'*Why couldn't it just have been him, though? Tell me that.*'

That horrible feeling inside her grew even stronger as they talked about him. They didn't know him like she did. They'd always hated him. She'd always thought that, but now she had proof. He wasn't ever good enough for them. For anyone. No matter how hard he tried, he was always the one in the wrong.

'*He was bad news. From the moment he arrived. I know it's bad to speak ill of the dead but ... I always said that, didn't I?*'

'You did.'

'And I was right, wasn't I? You can always tell. Some people ... they're just born bad and there's no coming back, isn't that right?'

'That's right.'

She was sitting at the top of the stairs, arms wrapped around her legs, listening as they discussed her family as if they'd known them. As if they had spent the time she had with them.

They hadn't done that, of course. She'd barely seen these people until now, when she'd had no other choice. She'd been left with strangers, while the rest of her family left her behind.

'She doesn't remember anything, you know. I've tried talking to her about things, but she just shakes her head and plays dumb. It's almost like she's lost the previous twelve years of her life. Other than little bits, you know. How do we deal with that?'

'She'll get better in time. It's a major shock, it'll take her a while to get over it. You've just got to let her get on with it.'

'Why couldn't it have just been him? There was always something about him, I'm telling you. You can tell by the eyes. His were horrible black things. Like a monster or something. He was bad.'

'Come on, we can't talk about him like that. We don't know that ...'

'Yes we do. It'll have started because of him. All of this. And now they're all gone and she's the only one left. And what if she's the same?'

She sat and listened, almost as if it were punishment for some unremembered crime she'd committed. There was nothing she could think of, just the pain inside her, wanting to be released. Wanting to come out and spread and infect and end the rest of existence.

She felt dead inside. A blank slate. The past erased, replaced with blurred memories of someone else's life.

A voice, inside her head, trying to keep her calm. Soothing her. Telling her everything was going to be all right.

That she needed to fight the urge to stand up, walk down the stairs, take a knife from the kitchen.

And kill the strangers sitting in the living room.

Just to feel something.

Anything other than the darkness growing and festering inside her.

Now

Forty

The backdrop was a dirty kind of beautiful. A cool autumnal breeze steadily blew across the group, as trees swayed and dropped leaves to the ground around them.

'This'll do, right?'

The guy holding the camera shared an exasperated look with his producer that he hoped the reporter standing a few feet away couldn't see. 'I think we need to be deeper into the woods, but I suppose this will be okay.'

'I don't want to get lost, that's all,' the reporter replied, brushing the hair away from her face with one hand. 'Place gives me the creeps.'

The cameraman shrugged and framed the shot once more. Behind the reporter, the river Mersey could be seen in the distance. Water stretching to the horizon and colliding with the Irish Sea, until it disappeared. Unkempt grass crashed into his legs as he continued to stare out at the sea through the camera lens. Watching, as the water tumbled and struggled against itself. Flashes of white against the grey, rising like mountains beneath the surface, angry and unforgiving. The sky grew grey above them, the wind picking up and ripping around his body.

'Okay, pick it up from after the intro,' the producer said, checking her watch for the fifteenth time in the past few minutes. 'Before we lose the light.'

The reporter waited for the signal and then began to speak.

'It's here, in the rural parts of the city, where someone using that old myth has been working unseen. There are a number of woodland areas in Liverpool, which belies its urban image. We're standing in one of the largest, located in the northernmost part of the city. While the woods where a number of bodies were found earlier this week were smaller, you can still really feel a sense of remoteness in them. As if you could disappear and never be found.'

The cameraman kept himself steady even as his senses picked up a shift in atmosphere behind him. He shook the feeling off, deciding it was just his mind playing tricks on him.

'The Bone Keeper is a legend many within the city know and have grown up telling each other. Now, it seems someone has been using this story in order to kill many people in woods just like these.'

The wind changed again, sending a shiver down the cameraman's spine. He glanced at the producer. She was still staring at the reporter, but her forehead was creasing as her eyes narrowed.

'Police are refusing to say whether they are using this information to inform what is now a wide-scale investigation. For people in the city however, this is just another part of a story that has shocked the entire city … we're repeating the word city in that line, Mo.'

The producer shook her head and made a throat-cutting

gesture at the cameraman. 'Don't worry, we'll fix that . . . did you hear something?'

The cameraman removed his headphones and looked to his left. 'What?'

'I don't know,' the producer said, looking past him to where the trees were thicker and more dense. 'Let's get this done and get out of here.'

The reporter didn't respond, instead walking slowly out of shot and towards a nearby tree. 'Was this here when we arrived?'

The cameraman looked to where she was pointing, trying to remember if he'd even looked at that particular tree when they'd set up their shot. They all looked the same, so he was sure he hadn't, yet the marks on the bark seemed fresh.

'That's . . . is that part of the story?' the reporter asked.

'We need to get out of here,' the cameraman said quietly, almost whispering as his heartbeat increased to a crescendo. 'Something feels very wrong about this place.'

The sky seemed to darken above them as they began to pack up, not saying another word to each other. The reporter was almost dancing from one foot to the other. 'Is there any other way out, other than back through the woods?'

'I don't know, do I?' the producer said, helping the cameraman move a bag up to his shoulder, then following him as he began to walk away. 'I don't know the place at all.'

The cameraman fixed his eyes on the direction of the road where they'd parked up – not that he could see the safety of the van now. It was a quarter of an hour's walk away, which suddenly felt like too far.

They could all feel the change around them as they

walked into the thick of the trees. The deafening silence, the smells of nature disappearing and being replaced by something acrid and pungent. It seemed like everywhere they looked, more marks appeared on the tree trunks around them.

He kept moving forward, ignoring the shuffling sounds in the undergrowth. The swiftly quietened squeals of pain behind him, as he refused to accept what was happening.

That he was walking alone now.

He blocked the noise out, refusing to believe what his senses were telling him.

He was the only one left.

The smell hit him, as he willed himself to run. To drop everything he was carrying and sprint for safety. Instead, he found himself slowing down, as his legs became heavy, as if he were walking through ever-thickening mud.

He didn't trust his ears, his nose. His taste.

Until the world turned black in front of his eyes and death revealed itself.

Forty-One

Louise left the station, driving past the growing hordes of reporters and TV cameras at the gates and onto the main road. She was caught by traffic lights at the first junction, and looked around. There was new graffiti sprayed on the wall to her right.

THE BONE KEEPER IS HERE!

She shook her head, pressing her foot down as the light changed and she could finally get past it. Her house should have been only a fifteen-minute drive, but even this early in the evening when people should have been off the roads, it was more like half an hour before she was finally pulling up outside her house.

Standing at her front door, key in hand, she paused and listened. Waiting for any sound to emanate from within and tell her someone had been in her home again. Was still in there. Her hand shook a little as she placed the key in the lock and turned, but when the door opened and she moved inside, she knew instantly she was alone.

It didn't stop her moving through the rooms one by one, looking for any sign that someone had been there.

Louise wanted to know who it was who had delivered the message; whether Steven himself had broken into her home before killing the couple in their beds. If this was all part of his plan to break her.

Yet, she knew it didn't make any sense.

'He was probably just watching you,' she whispered to herself, before the voice in her head had the chance to chime in. 'That's all it was.'

That didn't answer the question of who had sent them in the first place, though.

She made her way back upstairs and into her bedroom. The box she had moved there from the spare room the previous night was still lying on the floor, its lid open and contents visible. The card which had come with the burnt pieces of wood was lying on top, its black ink bleeding and message seeming to mock her.

She could almost smell the fire again. The way it burned and flickered, consuming everything in its path and destroying her life.

It was a memory that, most days, she tried to forget, but now she concentrated on the images. The time before she had become a different person. Louise felt her breathing becoming laboured as she sat down on the edge of the bed and closed her eyes. Smoke drifting up and enveloping her.

She couldn't remember.

It was always there, on the edges of her consciousness, but it was too painful, too real, to bring to her mind fully.

There was something about the blurred visage that was so real, yet she had tried talking about it with her grandparents on a few occasions and received nothing but shakes of the head and a changing of the subject. Her family were all gone and that was that. An accident. She was lucky to be alive. Nothing more to discuss.

They wouldn't talk about her family. Share memories, or tell stories. It was too painful and they were too British. Stiff upper lip and all that rubbish.

She wished she had pushed them more now.

The handwriting on the card was staring at her as she opened her eyes.

A flash, an image, crashed into her mind. Brief, fleeting, but there. Real.

Something had happened before the fire. An event she couldn't allow herself to focus on.

The woods.

She was thinking about the woods.

Louise closed her eyes and tried to calm her body. To remember. Picture every memory she'd had in her entire life and try to place them in order.

Don't . . .

There was the park. Sitting high on her father's shoulders, her mother walking alongside them. Her brother – further ahead, a stick in his hand that he was dragging along the concrete path. The sun above them, shielding her eyes from its glare.

Leaning against her bedroom door, listening to the shouts from her mother downstairs. Her brother sitting on her bed, his hands over his ears.

The sharp pain in her hand, as she punched a young boy over and over. A rat-faced little brat, his tears and snot splattering across his face.

Walking with her father, as he talked about the history around them.

Her brother . . . her brother crying.

Then, nothing. Only fire.

Her grandparents sitting next to her hospital bed. Telling her she was the only one left.

'Did that really happen?' Louise said aloud, into her empty bedroom. 'Did I make that up?'

She palmed her stiff-feeling face, trying to push life back into it, her eyes stinging from tiredness as her head began to pound. She had to keep going, no matter what.

Louise lifted the box up once more, removing each item and placing it on the bed beside her. Twelve years of her life, summed up in a few items. She discarded the rest, the remnants of her life once she'd moved into her grandparents' house. Looked at what remained from before that.

The few photographs of the four of them. Her family.

She traced a finger across their faces, in turn, pausing at each one.

Her brother, so different. Older, but more childlike than she had ever been. Fair-haired, a crazy mop on the top of his head. As if he had been dragged through a bush backwards. Wild, but smiling.

That smile.

Her mother, different in this picture than in an earlier one. Thin-faced, lined and cowed. Life had mistreated her.

Her father, a wide grin on his face, his arms circling her and his wife. Her mother.

She couldn't remember this time. This past life. If she hadn't known it was her, she wouldn't believe this had ever been her existence. That once, she'd been in a normal family. A normal life.

Until something changed everything.

There were a few more photographs, but she moved

them to one side to look at the handwriting again. A piece of paper, her writing at the top, small and neat. Her brother's below, followed by her parents'. A game of some sort, the scores and tallies marked in each column. She couldn't remember what any of it meant, but all of their names were on it. Written by each hand, as if they had been teenagers at school practising different surnames or autographs.

She looked at her name.

Louise

The way the S curved down, in an odd pattern. She compared it to the writing on the paper and saw an instant match.

In the top right-hand corner, someone had scrawled the date. Twenty-two years old and still surviving, kept in a box as if it could be important. Or, more likely, the only thing that had survived a fire.

A few photographs and this. All she had left.

It was a coincidence, that was all. Steven Harris had broken into her home the night before, knowing she was working on the case, and left the message to mess with her. Try to unsettle her. It was simply a fluke that his handwriting was similar to someone else's, that's all it was.

He was a psychopath, who wanted to kill and pretend to be someone else.

That's all it is.

She wanted to listen to herself, but something inside continued to scream. To try to be heard over the quiet and calm voice in her head.

Louise turned back to the other photographs on the bed, looking over them again. She could recognise certain places, even if she couldn't remember being there when the photographs were taken.

There was one of just the two of them, the last one in the row. She was looking at herself, aged eleven, no memory of herself at that point. Standing next to him, posing for the camera. Behind, brick buildings, half destroyed. Bushes growing over the brick, reclaiming the land. Empty windows, carved into the side, almost covered by moss and greenery.

The woods. She remembered the woods.

Her younger self stared into her eyes, seeing through the facade she put up. Almost judging her for what she had become.

Louise could feel her breathing become shallow as she stared at the picture. Her heartbeat increase, her throat closing, as she stared into the dark eyes looking at her from the picture.

The dark eyes Nathan Coldfield's mother had described Rhys Durham having. The ones that felt so familiar.

Ones she knew so well.

As she fell backwards on the bed, the woods took over her mind. The fire, the people. It all came together in one moment, overcrowding her thoughts, until she couldn't focus on any single thing. It was all a mess of images, feelings, emotions.

Hate, love, anger. Consuming her, until she could do nothing but scream into the empty room.

She knew where she had to go.

The house.

The woods.

Back to what the woods were hiding.

To discover what was hidden in her past.

Forty-Two

Caroline stood in the doorway, waiting for her mum to recognise her. It didn't happen as quickly as she'd hoped, but soon enough the confusion on her face turned into emotion.

'Caroline?'

'Hello, Mum,' Caroline replied, as the recognition settled and became resignation. As if her mum was waiting for her to aim a volley of abuse her way. Again. 'It's been—'

'A long time,' her mum finished for her.

Caroline opened her mouth to speak, but found she had no words. She tried to breathe through it, but it was too late.

All the emotion of the past few days, the hate and anger . . . the fear, it came out of her in one mess of tears.

'Oh, no, don't cry, love,' her mum said, pulling Caroline into her arms and stroking her head. 'It's okay. It'll all be okay.'

They stood in the open doorway like that for a few seconds. A mother and daughter, who hadn't spoken for years, now embracing as if that time hadn't existed. Caroline was a girl again. One who needed her mum, just for a few seconds.

Caroline allowed herself to be led into the living room, still snivelling like an idiot as she settled on the sofa. Her mum shut down the lid of a laptop, placing it on the arm at the other end. She felt ridiculous now she was inside, but she hadn't been able to help herself; seeing her mum and those doe eyes she possessed, had sent her into child mode without warning.

She shook it off now, or tried to at least. She needed to explain what had happened as calmly as possible, otherwise her mum would never let this lie. Caroline could hear her in the kitchen, doing what almost everyone of her age tended to do in a crisis.

'You still taking sugar?' her mum said, popping her head around the doorframe that led into the kitchen. 'I've only got sweeteners.'

'That'll be fine, Mum,' Caroline replied, smiling even as tears continued to cascade down her cheeks.

Her mum paused for a second, then disappeared again. Caroline wiped a hand across her face, clearing the dampness, looking around the room. It had been years since she'd last been there, but it hadn't changed at all by the looks of it. Still the same photographs on the wall, the same furniture and ornaments. Everywhere she looked, she could see her brother's face peering back at her. Before he'd become a teenager, older.

Then, suddenly, they stopped.

Dead.

That's what she believed now. That what she had tried to do had been a waste of time. She winced as she leant for too long on her side. The wounds would heal, but the scars would be there forever. A reminder, if she ever needed it.

'I've just made a quick cup rather than a pot,' her mum

said, coming back into the room. She placed a cup on a coaster next to Caroline, then stood over her. Studied her, hard. Looking over every inch of her, as if she were considering every mark, every scratch, every bruise on her daughter's body.

'What happened to you?'

'I'll get to it, Mum, but I need you to sit down first. Please.'

Caroline's mum hesitated for a second, then came over slowly and perched herself on the edge of the sofa next to her. She turned, hands clasped together in her lap, and waited for Caroline to speak.

'I tried to find him, Mum,' Caroline said, suddenly stuck for a way to explain what had happened. 'I . . . I thought I could find him.'

'Matthew.'

'Yes,' Caroline replied, even though she knew it wasn't a question. 'I've been looking for him for a long time, Mum. I never gave up on him.'

'None of us did, Caroline,' her mum said, a little defensively in Caroline's eyes. She could already see why she'd not mentioned anything to her before. This defensiveness was always there under the surface with her mum – that was Val Edwards all over. Her mum. Still worried that people thought she'd given up on her own son after he'd disappeared.

'That's not what I mean, Mum,' Caroline continued, glancing at the cup of tea next to her, then turning back to her mother. 'I just want to explain what happened. I went to find him.'

'Matthew?'

This time it was a question. 'No . . . well, yeah, but I

mean . . .' Caroline sighed, trying to get her thoughts in order. 'It's real, Mum. The Bone Keeper is real. And it took Matthew.'

Another thing Val Edwards could do well was show no reaction to surprising new information. Her face remained passive, as if Caroline had just told her something of no consequence at all.

'I met someone who knew all about it, who said he could lead me to where it stayed hidden. I shouldn't have trusted him, but I was getting desperate. He . . . he hurt me. Bad, Mum.'

'What happened? Did he tell you what happened to Matthew? Where he is?'

Caroline breathed silently for a few moments, preparing herself. 'I think he's gone, Mum. This thing . . . it's a monster. It was there. Back in those woods, over the water on the Wirral. In that tunnel. It wanted Matthew, but not to just do what it tried to do to me. It'd been waiting there for someone like him.'

'How do you know all this?'

'I tried, Mum, I really did,' Caroline said, feeling the tears beneath the surface again. She swallowed them back, or tried to at least. She had to get through this. Then decide what to do next. 'I went to these woods, near Melling. It was waiting for me there. It tortured me for hours. It . . . it sliced into me. Into my skin. It was going to kill me. It said it would chop me up and hide my bones.'

'So you would never be found . . .' her mum whispered, a hand moving slowly to cover her mouth. 'But it's not really a . . . *devil*?'

'I don't know what it is, but yes, it's all true. The stories they used to tell, when we were younger – it exists. I think it has for a very long time. I tried to ask it what happened to Matty, I really did, but it wouldn't answer me.'

'How did you get away?' her mum said, a frown appearing suddenly on her face. 'How are you here?'

'I don't know,' Caroline said, moving closer to her mum. 'I got away somehow.'

'Tell me what's been going on,' her mum replied, holding Caroline's gaze now, confusion still etched on her features. 'From the beginning.'

'You know what happened in those woods. The ones on the Wirral, twenty years ago. That's the real beginning. But, I've never told you everything about what happened when we went through that tunnel . . .'

'You were playing a game, with the other two. They said that's where the Bone Keeper lived and you were all going through it.'

Caroline started to nod, then stopped herself. 'I heard him. In that tunnel. The other two didn't, but I did. And I let Matty go in there. It's my fault. I should have gone back for him.'

'It's not your fault . . .'

'It is,' Caroline said, her voice reverberating around the room. 'I know it is. We waited and waited, long enough for Matty to be taken from us. Then, we ran from those woods.'

'Darling . . .'

'Mum, we left him there. He's gone and it was my fault.'

Forty-Three

It was growing darker outside as she pulled up on the street outside the house. The area hadn't changed much in the years since she'd last been there, but as she'd driven towards it, she couldn't help but notice the subtle differences. The way traffic lights had appeared out of nowhere, suddenly added to the roads without her knowing. A few new housing developments dotted about the large village, new shops and storefronts.

As Louise had got closer, the changes had become less noticeable. The road leading towards the woodland had been relaid at some point, she assumed, but apart from that, everything seemed to have the same feel about it, she thought. Then wondered where the memory was coming from.

The traffic had been heavier nearer the village centre, but it had thinned out palpably now she was on the outskirts of the town. It had been years since she'd been there, but she remembered the way as if it had only been a day or two.

She didn't really remember living in the house, even as familiarity crawled over her skin.

Louise turned off the engine, leaning forward and looking

towards the place they had called home for just over a year. She wondered how they had been able to afford it, but then, she knew her dad always had money stashed away in places.

She couldn't remember why she knew that.

Formby was always known as the posh part of the city. Where people's lives were vastly different to those in the southern towns, where unemployment was higher and less investment had taken place.

Louise closed her eyes as a memory hit her. Visiting somewhere nearby, when she was much younger. Around four or five, she guessed. Standing on the beach, her bare-feet in the sand. Her mum, snapping at her brother in the back seat. Dad, driving, one arm dangling out of the window holding a cigarette. Ignoring them all, the shouts and screams seemingly not affecting him at all. Letting her mum sort out the noise, while he tuned them out.

She could see it all clearly now. Sitting behind her dad, looking at the strong arm in front of her.

Louise opened her eyes, trying to remember more but failing. She guessed her mum was behind those trips. The few photos she still had showed walks in Sefton Park, in woodland dotted around various parts of the city. All for good reasons, she imagined her mum had thought. Healthy exercise, for what was fast becoming a sedentary generation.

She wondered if that was why she avoided the woods even as an adult. If she had tried to forget her past all these years. Another way of not remembering what had happened.

There was a streetlight near the car, a dull glow emanating from it. The street was quiet as she got out of the car, closing the door as quietly as possible behind her. She took a few steps forward, stopped, breathed in and out for a few seconds, then continued.

Within seconds, she was standing outside the house.

Louise stared at the windows, the stone adorning the outside, the front door, the small patch of grass. Waiting for something to emerge. Another memory. She closed her eyes, hoping that would help, but nothing came.

She shifted to her left, walking alongside the house, looking for anything that would spark further memories, but it was dull and lifeless. It looked newer than the ones next to it. She imagined it would have been rebuilt, after the fire had torn it apart until there was nothing left but a shell.

She wished she knew more about what had happened afterwards. About who had repaired and replaced her old life.

There was a car parked in the small driveway, which meant someone lived there. The house had recovered and new people had moved in. She wondered if they knew what had happened there, all those years before.

If they could tell her.

Behind the house, she could see the trees, a couple in the back garden, as she moved around to the side of the house. She continued moving until she was on the road that led into the woods.

A flash then. Something there, on the edge of her mind. She tried to hold onto it for a little longer, but it was gone.

Louise turned back towards her car, imagining driving away and never facing this again, but something continued to drive her on. As if there was something pulling her towards them and she was a willing recipient.

Now she was there, she wasn't sure what her next move should be. Whether to allow it to happen. Whether she wanted to know.

Yes you do. You need this.

'Shut up,' she whispered to herself, but she kept walking, down the small lane, towards the thicker woodland which her old home backed onto. She passed a sign, pausing to read its letters, hoping they sparked something.

Formby Nature Reserve

The wind picked up again, rustling in the trees that bordered the small lane. They grew thicker the further she walked, until the lane had almost become a tunnel. The lane ended abruptly and she turned to her right, knowing there was a golf course in that direction, wishing that she was going to stroll to the great expanse of perfectly manicured greens.

To her, the city had always been as large as it had wanted to be. Enough hidden parts to never really be understood. To her left, one of its better-kept secrets.

She began walking into the woods.

There was a great expanse of bare land; what had once been green and luscious was now light brown and broken. Overgrown and uninviting. She imagined it had been a quad bike playground until recently, the owners of the land eventually becoming tired of the destruction and allowing it to grow neglected. Uniforms being called out constantly, as the town pulled together to get rid of the unwanted. She followed a narrow mud path away, into the thick treeline ahead of her, moving on instinct as she was swallowed into the dense woodland where the path ended.

Louise kept walking, moving deeper into the denseness, trees becoming closer together, until all she could see around her in the dull evening light was trunks, fallen logs, and small patches of actual ground. The earth beneath her was uneven, rising into small slopes in parts, as she picked a spot in the distance and walked towards it.

Her body seemed to know the way, as if it had been waiting to guide her there. Her eyes were telling her that it all looked the same, and yet she was taking turnings as if she knew them.

She was moving on instinct, putting one foot in front of the other and trusting this base part of herself. The terrain grew thicker, the breeze coming off the river – hidden away behind the thick treeline – disappearing as she walked further, the forest taking hold second by second. She stopped to take a breath, forcing herself to ignore her greater thoughts.

Why was she there?

What was she doing?

She leaned against a thick tree trunk with one hand, feeling the old bark crumble in her grasp. Her chest tightened, throat constricted, as if the further she moved into the woods, the greater became her body's desire to leave. She closed her eyes, counted her breaths in and out, feeling herself calm with every exhale. Opened her eyes and removed her hand from the tree, wiping the stuck shards of bark off against her leg. She continued walking, stepping over the large, exposed tree roots on the ground.

The air had become still as she'd travelled further into the middle of the woods, only the sound of her laboured breathing disturbing the quiet. No small animals scuttled around her, no birds nesting in the trees. It was almost as if they had decided to avoid this place along with anyone else.

Louise found the first marking a minute or two later. A

small, inverted cross, carved into a tree. That was quickly followed by two, then three more, different markings, all small and unnoticeable unless you were looking for them.

She stopped to look at one, tracing a finger into the carving, the smoothness of the indentation.

A memory of doing the same. A long time before.

She realised she'd been waiting to see these markings. She'd known they would be there.

She stopped, looking around her for something familiar and spotted a small ridge around twenty metres to her right. She crossed the short distance, her shoes disturbing leaves and mulch as she walked. As she reached the ridge, she could already smell the familiar aroma.

Down a couple of feet, almost completely camouflaged from view, was what she had been looking for.

She could smell death on the air, the same odour which seemed to linger in the other woods in the city. Louise trod more carefully now, watching her step as she walked slowly down the ridge towards the small, brick ruin of a building. It was a rudimentary shelter, and crumbling in places, but it had lasted for years.

She had a couple of seconds to wonder if there were bodies buried underneath her feet here as well. Quickly discarded the idea.

It wasn't him. It couldn't be.

A perfect hiding place. One which was well hidden, barely known about, despite this being a nature reserve. There was a moment when she thought he wasn't there. That the aroma of him had just settled on the area and couldn't be shifted all that easily. She could feel his presence, something deep inside her that called out, being reflected from an unseen force.

He was in there. After all this time. A place he had retreated to, years earlier.

After.

You have to walk with me now. We have to move on from here. You have to come with me into the woods and live your new life. Become just like me.

She had resisted and he had disappeared. Dead, in her mind. Leaving her alone.

Breathe, Louise. You're here. Now ... what do we do?

She didn't have to think about the question for long, as the air changed around her and the darkness took shape and form.

'Hello, Louise. It's been ... too long.'

Forty-Four

They were sitting at either end of the sofa, sipping quietly on their cups of tea, as if she'd just popped in for a visit. A silent visit, but one that had the semblance of normality nonetheless.

Underneath the surface of supposed British awkwardness, Caroline knew there was more that had caused the silence to settle over them. She looked towards the window, ignoring the television in the corner for a few seconds, before deciding that perhaps it was the icebreaker they needed.

'Who would ever think Liverpool would see this kind of thing.'

'Seems like you'd know more than most.'

Caroline watched the screen for a few more seconds, then turned to the window again. Outside, the light was dimming, as it became grey once more. Flowers sat on the windowsill, lilies. She frowned at them for a moment, then turned back to her mum.

'We should go to the police. Tell them everything.'

Caroline's mouth was open; she'd been preparing to speak before her mum had jumped in and broached the subject.

'It's the only thing that makes sense,' her mum continued, placing her cup down on the cluttered coffee table in front of her. 'If you know more than you've told them, you should . . .'

'Mum, that's not going to work.'

'Why? If he's out there . . .'

'That's just the thing,' Caroline said quickly, interrupting her mum before she could finish the thought. 'I don't know anymore. I'm not sure what to believe.'

'Maybe this was someone different to who took Matthew. Another bad man.'

'He knew too much.'

'Who was in that tunnel?'

'I don't know,' Caroline replied, placing her own cup down on the opposite end of the coffee table. She spied the letters sitting underneath the detritus covering the surface. Unopened bills, stacked up. 'It had to be him.'

'What happened in that tunnel?'

'I don't know, Mum.'

Caroline placed both her palms against the side of her face, rubbing her temples with her fingers. There was pain behind her eyes now, tiredness taking hold. Also, the fact she couldn't answer any questions with real answers. She just wanted to give the only true response, but knew it would sound ridiculous in that room now.

Caroline thought of the police detective, Louise. The only real visitor she'd had while she was in hospital. The questions she had asked, the way she'd opened up about her own life. She had thought there was a possibility that Louise might take her seriously, but even then it would be paled by her job. She was a detective, not a ghosthunter. When she'd checked herself out of the hospital, she had taken Louise's card with her, a mobile number scrawled on the back.

Twenty years she had carried the story of what had happened when she'd gone into the woods with her brother. She wondered now why she had waited so long, whether it would have made any difference in the years that had passed since to his plight.

It had been her fault. She had been protecting herself from what was the painful truth.

She had chosen her own life over his. Left him alone in those woods, never to be seen again. Now, in the stark and painful light of a new day, she wished she hadn't said a word. Wished she had never tried to find him. Wished she had never left her old comfortable life.

She would still have all her original skin, for one. She grimaced at that, looking down at where her torso bulged under the thin material of the T-shirt she was wearing. Bandaged up and left to heal. The scars left behind would be a constant reminder for the rest of her life, that sometimes . . . sometimes things are better left unknown.

'Something was waiting in the tunnel,' Caroline said finally, glancing at her mum for a moment, then away. 'Waiting for Matty.'

'Waiting for him?'

'The tunnel we all went through, in those woods. Something was in there when I walked through. It had been watching us from the moment we entered the woods. Waiting for its chance. Going through that tunnel was it. Only, it thought I was him at first. It tried to get me. That's why I knew something was in there. If I'd turned and run back out, then Matty would still be here.'

'It?'

'Whatever, I don't know. It was *something*.'

'The Bone Keeper,' her mum said, her voice quiet now. Fear wrapped within each syllable.

'I heard it.'

This was the first time she'd said this aloud, but it didn't shift the weight she'd expected it to. Instead, the words hung between them, like a cloud of cigarette smoke in mid-air.

'You heard the Bone Keeper?'

Caroline shook her head, wondering if that was actually true or not. Whether, in fact, it was a lie. It was still as it always had been – a story passed around fearful children, from generation to generation.

Yet, there was something out there, in those woods.

'We went back through that tunnel, but we couldn't see anything. The other two kids went off, scared – they ran back home, but I stayed there a few seconds longer. I heard him, Mum. I heard Matty's voice. It was in that tunnel. He was crying, scared. I didn't know what to do. I wanted to run back in there and help but I . . . I couldn't move.'

'We looked in the tunnel. He wasn't there.'

'I left him there, Mum. I left him there and that was it. He was gone. If I'd gone back in on my own, maybe I could have saved him.'

She could still remember that part, more clearly than any other, twenty years later. Standing at the edge of the tunnel entrance, shivering against a non-existent cold. Frightened. A scared, petrified little girl.

Caught up in a silly game gone wrong.

'I probably stood there for a minute, but it felt like an hour. I heard him cry. I heard him shout for me . . . for you. Then, silence. I've never forgotten that dirty, horrific silence. I ran away. Back to you. I left him there, all alone. I couldn't help him.'

Caroline could still see that tunnel in her mind, the smallness of it masking what lay within. The ordinariness of it, as if she had expected an evil place to have a sign indicating it to be so.

That's the thing about evil. It never announces itself. Just festers and lives among the normal. The clean.

'About six months ago, someone came into the shelter,' Caroline continued, her eyes settling on the television as the yellow breaking news ticker slid along the bottom of the screen. More people reported missing, more crime scenes found. Helicopters in the sky and police vehicles swarming the city. 'He was talking about the Bone Keeper. Saying he'd met someone who could take him to the actual, real monster. Everyone was calling him a liar and all that, but I listened. I followed him one evening, seeing where he was going, and he went into these woods. I found out later who he was meeting. A man called Rhys. I watched what they did. In those woods. I had to be sure. I had to see him.'

'See who?'

'The Bone Keeper. Whatever took our Matty. My brother. I wanted to see it, smell that same smell I did in that tunnel. I needed to know if this was just a silly game, or whether it was real. I saw it there. I saw symbols carved into the trees, appearing out of nowhere. I could smell it even from the distance I was. It stank like rotten meat, like death.'

She could feel the tears coming back now, as she remembered what had happened next. The mistake she had made in trying to stop him herself.

'Why didn't you tell me what happened?'

'I thought you'd blame me for not helping. I thought it was a trick. That he would just come back. I was scared. I didn't know what to do.'

Her mum seemed to accept what she said, even if the lines on her forehead creased in confusion even further.

'So, Matthew could still be out there?'

Caroline didn't answer, only thinking of the man she'd known as Rhys. The man she'd originally followed, calling him that and nothing else. This *Rhys* and his eyes, as he'd stood over her. The cries of the man lying further away, dead within hours. She'd had to listen to his final breaths as the knife sliced into his skin.

The smell of death, permeating the atmosphere around them both.

'He's still out there, Caroline,' her mum said, edging along the sofa towards her. 'And I know it.'

Caroline looked at her mum, then across the room to where she was staring. At the flowers on the windowsill. She cocked her head, then lifted herself up, grimacing against the shooting pain across her stomach she did so. Made her way over to the windowsill, picking up what looked like twigs that were lying there, abandoned almost. A card lay at their side. She picked it up, reading the words carefully, twice, three times, then turned to her mum. She could feel her heart beating against her chest, the same feeling she'd had as she was lying on the ground, waiting for death in those woods.

'Who sent you these?'

'They're from Matthew. He's coming back.'

Caroline could feel her hands begin to shake, as her breathing became constricted. 'This isn't from Matty. It can't be.'

Forty-Five

Louise couldn't place the voice and the familiarity she had felt with each word. The memory of it, gravelled and deep.

The safety she felt in its presence.

Years and years. Time just spiralling away into nothingness, her past a blurred memory, another life, another world. Enough experiences since that time to replace the old ones.

She was a different person now, yet she could have been eleven years old again. Transported back to that time she couldn't quite remember, yet which felt so memorable now.

A slight breeze rippled through the leaves, stinging her eyes, which were wide open, unblinking. She closed them briefly, feeling the wind rip through her hair, waiting for it to settle again. She was far enough away from the coastline now that the smell of saltwater had dissipated, but she imagined she could still taste it in the air.

'You remember this place?' the voice said, hidden among the earth, the leaves. The darkness.

'Who are you?' Louise replied, speaking in the general direction of the voice. She couldn't be sure. Wouldn't allow herself to be. She glanced at the ruins of an old building, seeing the graffiti on its bricks.

'You know who I am,' the voice said, now coming into full form. The shadow took shape, until she could see him entirely. Dressed in ragged clothes, a long coat that covered almost his entire body. Dark, almost black in colour. A thought came into her head unbidden, about this person always being adept at camouflaging himself. That he had so much experience in doing so, not just here, in his natural habitat of the woods, but even in his personality and the way he presented himself.

He didn't look like a real person. He was an apparition almost, as if he was just a part of the surroundings. A part of the night.

He had fooled them all. For so long.

'Say my name.'

Louise hesitated, still not sure what exactly she was doing there in those woods. How she had found this place, what had led her there. Every instinct screamed at her to run, to get away from there, but she couldn't move.

'You have two choices, Louise. Either you accept who I am, or you arrest me.'

She could feel the smirk behind the words. She laughed, before she caught herself and stopped it escaping her mouth. She couldn't help it. The situation was simply that ridiculous, she thought.

Her, a detective.

Him, a serial killer?

The memory sparked to life then, when she thought those words. Of being eleven years old and walking through these woods. Him, alongside her.

They were hunting. Something. She wasn't sure.

He had left that message for her, knowing it would bring her back. She found it difficult to accept that there was anything more than that. Just a coincidence. That was all. He had hidden away in the woods behind their old house for all this time, making her think he was dead. Yet, everything within her was screaming the fact. It was who he was. What he had always been.

Was that who he was?

It had taken a long time, but she now recognised him for what he was at his core.

Evil.

'What would you do if I did arrest you?'

She could see parts of him now which were still recognisable, but she couldn't trust her memory. She couldn't trust reality. She imagined something built into the ground itself. Buried underneath the ruins, she guessed. Where he felt most at home.

Louise knew him. What he was capable of, given the opportunity.

'I don't think that would be a very good idea,' he replied, no joviality to his tone now. 'How would you explain my being here? What you let me do?'

'I thought you were dead. All of you.'

'You always knew. Right from the start of this. You knew who I was and who was responsible. Right from the very beginning. As soon as you saw those marks in the woods and heard the name.'

'It would be your word against mine. Who are they going to believe ... a detective, or a sick, sadistic killer?'

'Is that what you think of me? That I'm evil?'

'What else is there to believe?' Louise said, now circling around him as he stood there unmoving. 'Isn't that why I'm here? Isn't that why you broke into my home? You leave me alone for years and then suddenly return when bodies are found across the city. What am I supposed to think? You knew what I was going to discover. What you've been doing all these years. You killed her. Hazel Durham.'

'She was fun. You would have enjoyed the way she ran,' he said, something new in his voice now. Pleading, as if he were hoping she wouldn't reject him now, at the final hurdle. 'I have a life to protect.'

'Yeah, a life where you kill people.'

'It's not as simple as that, Louise,' he said, annoyance gone now. Back to his usual tone of pity and patronising. 'Nothing ever is. We don't live in a world of black and white. It's grey. It's always grey. You know that better than anyone.'

'Tell that to the families of Adam Parker, Nicola Borthwick, Greg Hall, Carl Groves . . .'

'No . . .'

'Jon Durham,' Louise finished, spitting the name out towards him. 'Couldn't even kill him yourself, could you? Had to drive him to it. Because he knew exactly what you were.'

'Enough,' he said, his voice dark and echoing around them. Louise stopped moving, closer to him now. Close enough to see deep into his eyes, the dark orbs they had become. What they had always been. Lifeless, without soul. She could see the black underneath his skin, the mud which was almost a part of his features now. He could still make her stop dead – the power he still held over her . . . it frightened her.

All these memories, now suddenly in her mind, as if his mere presence had been enough to break down the barriers she had created over the years. Saving herself, so she didn't have to face what she came from.

'You don't understand,' he said, more measured now. 'Poor Louise. I know you've been through a lot. If you can just let me explain, you'll know why you're here . . .'

'No,' Louise said, firmly but without raising her voice as he had done. A minor victory, but she could see his features fall a little, which made it feel more substantial. 'I can't let this go on.'

'Yes, you can. You know that's the answer. What you've been searching for all these years.'

'And you'd know what I've been doing all this time?'

'I know more than you realise.'

Louise didn't say anything for a few moments, trying to formulate a response that didn't sound as empty as the threat she wanted to throw at him.

'Tell me why,' she said finally, risking another step closer. She could see him more clearly now, his features, marked and changed over the years since they'd last stood this close to one another. The lies and broken promises thick in the air between them. 'Why did you let me live thinking you were . . . gone?'

He had been the Bone Keeper. Always. Another thought that sprang up out of nowhere, without prompt. Yet, the information meant nothing to her. She felt cold inside.

'I had to go, Louise,' he replied, turning his back on her now. 'The fire gave me a way out. To get back to where I belong. To where *you* belong. You should have come with me after. That was the right way for you.'

Louise ignored the last part. 'All these years I've carried the belief that I was alone. That I was the only one left. Why?'

'It was better this way.'

The wind whistled around them, as the sky darkened further. Louise could feel the familiar feeling growing inside her now. The one which she tried hard, so often ,to ignore. The hatred and anger, like a black ball of pus in her stomach, bubbling and craving attention. To be released.

'And you were him. All along.'

'There is no *him*. Just me. You know why I'm here. Why I've always been here. You feel it too.'

'I don't understand . . .'

'Yes you do, Louise,' he said, cocking his head to one side and seemingly studying her anew. 'Some of us have a need to play sports, or become lawyers or politicians. You wanted to protect people, so you joined the police. We all have our callings.'

'And yours was killing people?'

'It's more than that, Louise,' he said quickly, standing taller now. The small clearing began to feel as if it were closing in around them. Louise could feel it become tighter, more constricting. 'So much more. I'm free. I own my life. My story. No one can stop me.'

'You sicken me.'

He laughed, deep and repellent. This was the real him. It had always been there, hidden away from her and all those who had known him. That's what it felt like now. She had glimpsed the person behind the facade he'd worn like a mask. This was him.

His laughter came to a sudden stop. 'What else can I be?' he said, his features turning in an instant. 'I can't be like all the people out there. Mindless drones. That's not me. It's not you. Tell me, do you feel good when you lock up the bad guys? Like you've done something right? It's pathetic. You were always better than just being a cog in the machine. That's what *you've* become. Just someone else shuffling paperwork around, taking away people's freedom. We're all just animals, Louise.'

She hated the way he said her name. As if he owned it. 'You've lost your mind. You're sick. Let me help you.'

'You can't help me. None of you ever could. This was always me. You were a distraction. All of you were. All you ever did was try and stop me from being all I could be.'

'You were never this. You've become something else. This isn't the real you.'

He moved closer to her and she realised she could no longer move. Stuck to the ground, as he grew nearer, the stench of him coming along.

It's death. He stinks of it. It will rub off on you. You'll never be able to get it off your skin. It'll stain and scar you just the same.

'The real me? Is that what you want to see? Is that why you came here?' he said, coming to a stop a couple of feet from her, staring into her eyes. She couldn't help but hold his stare, becoming lost in the blackness there. 'You didn't come here for that. You came to find me. Well, here I am.'

'Years I spent thinking you were gone. All that time ... you were here. Letting me live with what happened alone.'

'It was for your own good ...'

'That wasn't for you to decide,' Louise said, her voice now echoing around them. She could feel a lump at the back of her throat, as she blinked away the tears forming in her eyes. 'Why? Why would you kill them? What have they ever done to deserve this?'

'You should know better. We're all evil. We all have that capacity within us. I bet you've got the same feelings now.

You would love nothing more than to kill me yourself. To wrap those pretty little hands around my throat and choke the life out of me. You're a detective. I bet you've sat opposite the bad people before. You will have felt the same then. That the world would be a better place if you just removed them from it. You ever wonder where that feeling comes from? Here's the nasty, dirty little secret … we all want to be killers. We all want to do the things I've done. You know that's true. You know how you feel, deep inside, locked away like all the memories you've kept hidden all these years. That's why you're here now.'

'You're wrong,' Louise said, her voice barely above a whisper. She could feel him almost on her now. His warm breath on her face, the air between them disappearing into nothingness. 'I could never do what you have done.'

'Just give into it,' he replied, his teeth showing as he opened his mouth and smiled. 'You know that's what you want.'

Louise screwed her eyes tightly shut, shaking her head. Her breathing grew shallow, her chest tightening. She could sense him looming over her, as her legs became weaker.

'No, you won't do this to me,' Louise screamed, birds lifted into the air above them at the sound, unseen but she imagined their wings flapping in unison as they escaped the hell she had stumbled into. Her eyes had snapped open, spittle flying from her mouth. 'You won't have me. I won't do this anymore. You're nothing. You're no better than any other scum. And I'm stopping this now.'

She didn't see him move, just a blur as the darkness shifted and then she was on the ground. A bolt of light flashed through her back, as her head smacked into the earth and made her vision shake. An arm went across her throat, cutting off her air supply, before she had a chance to react.

'Don't move,' he said above her, his mouth wide, revealing blackened, rotting teeth. 'This will hurt less if you just allow it to happen.'

She bucked beneath him, grasping at his arms, trying to prise them away from her chest and throat. She dug her nails into any soft flesh she could find, but he didn't react.

It's not supposed to be like this.

SHUT UP!

Louise battered against his arms, her hands balled into fists, as she gasped for air that wasn't there. She could only look into those pools of darkness which lay where his eyes should have been. She tried to shake her head, but he used his free hand to keep it pinned to the ground. She continued to pound at his body, his arms. Anything she could.

'It'll be over soon, Louise,' he said, his words coming to her on a wave of haziness. 'I didn't want it to end this way. I thought you'd see sense. That you could join me, like the others did.'

She could feel herself drifting away, so she redoubled her efforts.

It's too late. You should never have come here.

She couldn't allow this to happen, but her fight was becoming useless. He was too strong for her, too powerful.

Too experienced.

The stories she had heard as a child had become his. He had personified them, made them his own.

He had become the monster.

Now, he was killing her as well.

Forty-Six

They were sitting in silence, almost waiting for the next part of their lives to unfold. Her mother had stopped suggesting they go to the police now, which pleased Caroline. There was no point, she had told her over and over.

She played with the card with Louise's number written on it, twirling it in her hands. She had hidden the truth from Louise – from them all – and she wondered if they had seen through her lies by now. She didn't think it was possible, but it wouldn't matter soon anyway.

'He's coming home.'

Caroline's mum had said that after she'd read the card and tried to tell her mum who it was really from. Not Matty, but something else. Something that could arrive at any moment.

He was coming.

'It can't be him, Mum,' Caroline said, trying to break the silence that had festered between them for an hour or so. Both staring at the unfolding events on the television. 'He's . . . he's not out there.'

'Look at the writing,' her mum replied, without breaking her gaze from the screen and the increasing horror it was reporting. 'It's his.'

Caroline didn't need to look at it again. The scrawled writing, almost illegible. Childlike in so many ways.

'That's his handwriting. Look at the way he writes *mum*. The way the M curves up and around. That's him.'

She left her seat, almost banging into the coffee table in her haste. Caroline heard footsteps pounding up the stairs, then overhead in the bedroom. She stared at Louise's card again. Wondering.

'Here, look,' her mum said, thrusting one of Matty's old schoolbooks into her face. She opened the pages and began tapping at blurred words Caroline couldn't read. 'That's it, right there.'

Caroline didn't say anything, unable to summon the energy. She wanted to forget. More than anything.

Another part of her knew she couldn't turn her back now.

That she would have to go back at some point.

They settled back into silence – her mum, waiting for a son who was long gone to return; Caroline waiting for what was coming their way. Caroline wanted to get out, out of her mother's web of depression, which had now grown around them both. Sitting in the living room, watching the twenty-four-hour news channel, waiting for it to tell them more about what was happening in their city. Every time she moved, she could sense her mum tensing, fear exuding from her every pore.

'Just wait,' her mum had said the last time she'd attempted to talk about leaving. 'He'll be here soon.'

Caroline was stuck, not wanting to explain again that Matty wasn't coming back. That they never came back. That once you're gone, you're gone. It was never the same afterwards.

He was never going to come back and be the son she wanted, even if he could. It had been too long.

'Are we supposed to sit here all night and wait?' Caroline said, trying to make her mother see the futility of it all. Trying to make her see sense.

'He's coming, you'll see.'

Caroline knew she had made a mistake in telling her mum what had happened to her. In coming back to this house, this life. She had escaped once, away from this nightmare.

She should never have tried to find him. To bring him back.

The wind picked up, chimes dinging away outside. She could feel the darkness out there and it reminded her of the woods. The way the wind had howled through the trees, almost deafening her with its hostility. In the darkness, with the trees and earth all around, things became much more apparent than they ever had in the light.

She thought she could still feel his breath on her. The way he moved. The way he touched her.

She had managed to get out, but it felt futile now.

Caroline's eyes were transfixed by the television screen as her mum left her side and made her way into the back room. The unfolding news, becoming more and more unbelievable as it went, the scattering of events, the increasing number of scenes of interest.

The videos.

It was becoming too much for her to bear. The way her nightmares had become real.

'*Sky News has received this video, which shows something in the woods . . .*'

She stared again at Louise's number on the card, then

made a decision. Reached across and picked up her mum's mobile phone and began keying the number. As she was about to hit the call button, she became aware of something happening in the other room. A sharp intake of breath, a mumbling, an escaped cry. She tore her eyes away from the phone screen, just in time to see her mum talking to herself as she reached out to the door handle and turned it.

'He's here, he's come back.'

She became rigid with fear, as she saw the figure in black in the space outside the door. Rose to her feet, without realising. 'Mum, don't open that.'

They don't come back. They never come back.

He could see them inside, waiting patiently for his return.

He wished it was always this way.

He followed instructions carefully.

The Bone Keeper had shown him the way. Made him in his own image. Showed him the light and the darkness.

Taught him to kill.

This was the end of the story. The last chapter. Tomorrow, he would begin a new story. Away from there.

A different place. New and exciting.

He wouldn't be able to be the Bone Keeper anymore. It would require a new start. Every city, every town, every village … they all had their own Bone Keeper story. It would just take a little time to discover what it was and then consume it.

Become the myth.

That was the plan for them all. A final night of violence, in this city where they had all been born, then a fresh start.

The air was beginning to still now, its howling and violence quietening. He looked to the sky, the grey of the clouds against the dark night. It would rain soon, he thought.

He enjoyed the rain.

The two women were inside, sitting on the sofa in the living room in silence, staring at the television in the corner. He imagined them taking in the information being shown, the different stories being told.

All those people.

All those bodies.

He could see Caroline. The marks on her face, the wince as she moved. How close he had been to killing her.

He remembered her best just before dawn. The soft light playing across her face, the soft rustle of the leaves beneath her body almost like a lullaby, soothing her sleep. She had been both beautiful and horrifying in equal measure.

He moved with the grace of someone used to living their life in the shadows. Never seen. Never noticed. He had spent years living this life, invisible to all until he decided to reveal himself.

The air was becoming colder around him, but he didn't notice it. Instead, he watched and he waited.

Decided on his next move.

Caroline and her mother had to die. So they could continue to live.

He was saving her.

He took in a deep breath of air, as if he had never tasted anything as sweet and good before. Prepared himself to taste the stale air he knew resided inside the house before him. He imagined it swirling around in front of him, flowing in a thick and slovenly manner.

He preferred the freshness of the air in the woods he called home.

The mother stood up, said something to Caroline, then crossed the living room and went into the back room. There was a difference between the two connected areas, carpet in the living room, wood floors in what looked like the dining part of it. These all led to a large bay window, floor to almost ceiling. It covered most of the outer wall, the door in the middle bordered by a wall-length window-pane at each side. It had given him an uninterrupted view inside, right through into the front of the house where they had been sitting in their silence.

He shifted a little, watching as the mother crossed to the windows. He could see into her eyes, the pain that lay there, the hurt. The lines that creased her face, the sag to her skin and body. He imagined her grief like a weight, bearing down on her shoulders, so she was only just able to carry it around. He could see it was becoming too much for her, that it was too heavy now.

He watched as she paused at the door, looking out into the garden. He stared at her, thinking of all the things she had lived with. All the things she had lived without.

There was a moment when he could see directly into her eyes. His locking with hers, even though she was simply staring into the darkness. There was a connection there – a bond they shared, without her ever knowing.

A familiarity.

He had something inside him she missed with every fibre of her being. A part of him she would recognise, think of as part of herself. He could almost feel her thoughts, her feelings.

He moved now, quickly, without sound. He could feel himself almost gliding across the surface below him, a straight line towards the door where she stood. She didn't see him at first, as he continued to blend into the darkness with ease.

Her face changed as he emerged in her line of sight. At first, she stepped back in shock, as he came to a stop just beyond the glass that separated them. Then she stepped forward again, her hands shaking as she lifted them to her face.

He smiled.

This was the moment he had waited for. The look she was giving him now, as if she had recognised him. As if he was everything she had been waiting for.

As if he were the son she had been missing.

The son who was long dead.

The first victim of the new story. When the Bone Keeper had returned.

He remembered sitting in the darkness, listening to the story, unable to tear his eyes away from the older man. He had been so young then, a decade or so earlier, but he had absorbed every word.

He had been offered a way out of his disgusting life. His drug-addicted parents now long forgotten. It had been in those woods that he'd been born.

He could see her mouthing silent words, hands still shaking as she shook her head and began to cry. He motioned towards the door with his head and she complied.

Opened it and welcomed him inside.

Forty-Seven

Louise could only see spots of black in her vision, her mouth open, her tongue becoming dead and useless. She continued to fight, unprepared to simply give up and allow him to take what he wanted. There was no way she was going to let that happen.

Not without exhausting every possibility.

She straightened her legs out, then brought them towards her body knees first, driving them into the small of his back. He shifted a little, the arm he had across her throat moving a few inches over and away for a moment. That gave her the chance to suck in one breath, which gave her renewed energy. She did it again, then once more, hearing a satisfying noise of pain from above her.

She knew she wouldn't have long to escape. A million thoughts were running through her head, colliding with each other until they became one indiscernible cacophony of noise. In that moment, it didn't matter what her history was, her past, her future. It was one moment in time, everything coming down to her.

Then, she couldn't breathe again, her air supply cut off

by his arm across her throat once more. He bore down, trying to use his whole weight to keep her trapped. She struggled to move, his attempt to keep her prone, dormant, almost working.

Their eyes were locked together as she continued to bash her arm against his biceps, his neck. He moved his head, dodging her blows with ease. She looked into those eyes of his, dark and soulless yet in so many ways familiar, and narrowed her own gaze. Pleaded with him, without being able to say a word.

He smiled at her through matted hair around his mouth, baring those disgusting, rotten teeth and gums of his. She remembered another time – another smile. One which had made her happy. Made her feel safe. Now, it had become twisted and deformed.

This was not the same person she had known.

She closed her eyes, summoning one final burst of energy.

Her knees drove into him, a satisfying thump directly into the area that was always the most effective target on a man. And that's all he was. Not a monster, not some kind of ogre. Just a human being.

That's all he was.

He gave a sharp intake of breath, then became sound-less, the weight he had been applying to her neck slowly diminishing. He moved slightly and she didn't think twice, pushing against him and slipping out from underneath his body.

Louise didn't look back, getting to her feet and taking off down the first path she saw. She commanded her body to run and it responded without question, moving through the trees as if she were suddenly a light-footed gazelle. Branches snapped against her body, her face, as she moved through the thick brush, each foot pounding into the ground, arms pumping at her sides. She could almost hear him following her with each step she took, a roar of anger somewhere in the distance, gaining with each passing second.

She stumbled on a fallen branch, losing her footing and twisting over on her ankle. A sharp jolt of pain flashed up her foot and into her calf as she fell to the ground and instinctively clutched at her lower limb. She looked around, expecting him to be pushing himself through the trees behind her, but could only see the broken path she had made as she ran.

Louise lifted herself up, her hands now almost black, caked in mud and God knew what else. She continued moving, not prepared to chance him either giving up or being unable to find her. He knew those woods better than she ever could, so she continued onwards, trying to find her way out. With each step pain coursed through her foot, but she tried to ignore it, limping on as swiftly as she was able.

A few moments later, she broke through the treeline and out into the open field where she'd arrived earlier, which already felt like a lifetime ago.

She was a hundred metres or so away from the actual path that led into the woods, but she felt safer already. In the distance, she could see lights, the road. Signs of life.

People.

She slowed down, risking more weight on her ankle, which she could almost feel swelling up beneath her.

It could have been broken. Then it would have been over.

Louise continued to stumble down the lane, which she knew led to where she'd parked her car. Paused for a second,

looking behind her, expecting him to be there. Only trees
and the lane could be seen. Calm, untouched. No one rushing up to take her, there in the open.

He was going to kill you. You. Why?

Louise shook her head, driving the voice out, not willing to think about that yet. First, she had to get to her car,
then away from there as fast as possible. After that, she
wasn't sure, but then she didn't think her decisions could
be trusted at that point.

She kept moving, crossing the field in a minute or so and
hitting the path that connected to the one leading to the
car parking area. She could feel the salt air on the breeze
now. She welcomed the normality of it.

A man passed her, being pulled along by a cocker spaniel
on a lead. She turned her head away from him, shoving her
hands in the pockets of her jacket, but she saw the quick
glance and frown he gave her. She didn't stop, hoping he
didn't call her back. Ask if she was okay, a polite concern
to his voice.

He kept moving.

Louise limped slowly to her car, then bent over and
pretended to fix her shoe as someone else passed by. Once
they were out of sight, she reached behind the back tyre
and removed the small fob and attached key.

Within moments she was inside the car. She wondered
for a brief second if her foot was going to be in any state to
drive – and then the reality of her situation hit her.

She couldn't breathe properly, gasping for air, her heart
hammering against her chest. She could feel his weight on top
of her once more, choking her, stopping her moving. It was
as if her entire body had been placed in a vice that was slowly
being tightened until she couldn't be squeezed anymore.

Louise screwed her eyes shut, gripping hold of the steering wheel and allowing the voice to soothe her.

Just breathe. You're okay. Just remember to breathe slowly. In, out. In, out.

Hands clawing at her skin, ripping into it, burning flesh. Lying in the ground, a hole, dirt shovelled on top of her, coming too quickly for her to avoid. Being swallowed by the earth, wrapping itself around her, enveloping her, becoming a second skin.

You can do this.

There was only darkness in her vision and the sound of her laboured breathing surrounding her. Yet, she knew that was preferable to the unconsciousness that it could have been. She held onto those sounds, feeling reality slipping back into sync with her mind.

Louise opened her eyes and they were immediately drawn to the clock on the dashboard.

Just under ninety minutes. That was the entire length of time in which she had arrived, parked up, walked into the woods, then escaped them.

It felt much longer than that.

Anger took hold then. Bubbling and then boiling away inside her, until she couldn't hold it back any longer. It came out in a scream, which echoed around the inside of her car. Her fists pounded the steering wheel, then she leant forward and smacked the dashboard. Moved her clenched hands and struck the door to the side of her, hair falling around her face as she breathed in and started pounding the dashboard again.

Ringing. She could hear ringing, coming from the outside world.

She wanted to kill him. Wrap her hands around his

throat and choke every last scrap of pathetic life out of him. Slide a knife into his chest, his stomach. Cut every artery she could find. Take an axe to him.

When she was done, her breath came in short pants, her heart hammering against her chest.

The ringing continued.

She moved the rear-view mirror, examining her face and neck. Apart from dirt marks, new lines, smudged black make-up around her eyes, she didn't look too far from normal. Even paler than before maybe, but she didn't think she would draw many looks on the way back.

Her neck was bright red, marked, but she didn't think it had been bruised or anything that would last too long.

'The day's looking up,' Louise said to herself, a sad smirk appearing on her reflection's face.

The ringing kept on.

She blinked, finally realising it was real, and reached across to the passenger footwell, where she'd chucked her work phone. Brought it to her face, expecting to see Shipley's name on the screen. Instead, it was a number she didn't recognise.

'Hello?'

'It's me.'

It took Louise a moment to place the voice, then it came to her. 'Caroline?'

'Please, you have to come. He's here.'

'Where are you?' Louise said, cradling her phone into her shoulder and turning the key in the car.

'I'm at my mum's house, please, you have to come now.'

'Where is it?' Louise could hear something in the background crashing, a scream. Then the line went dead. She took the phone away from her ear, redialling the number that had called her, but it rang for a few seconds before cutting to voicemail.

'No . . .'

She ended the call, looking out at the road, trying to work out what she should do. On her phone screen, numerous notifications.

Missed calls and a text message from Shipley.

Louise pressed on his name and waited for him to pick up. 'Paul . . .' she said quietly, hoping her voice didn't betray her now.

'Where are you?'

Louise shook her head at the gruff response, yet it allowed her to shift into professional mode one final time. 'Listen, it's not important. We need to get to her.'

'Where are you?'

She sat forward in her seat, looking around the car to make sure there was still no one watching her.

Tell him.

She couldn't tell him.

'It's Caroline, she's in danger,' she said, ignoring his repeated question. 'You have to find her.'

'We've already done that, that's why I've been trying to get hold of you.'

'Great, she's just called me and she needs someone there now.'

'You'll never believe who she is. Remember that kid who went missing in the woods over the water, about twenty years ago? She's his sister.'

Louise didn't remember, but couldn't interrupt Shipley.

'Anyway, we think there's a link between that disappearance and why she was in those woods.'

'Okay, so you'll go over to her mum's house?'

'Yeah, no problem. Need to find her and work out why she lied to us anyway. Are you coming?'

Louise looked over her shoulder, back into the darkness there. Then at the road ahead of her.

'Not right now,' she said, then ended the call before Shipley could argue with her. She looked at the house she had parked near, all that time ago. Memories now flooding back, as if all along the key had been those woods.

Him.

She made a decision.

Let the handbrake down and started driving away.

Forty-Eight

Caroline dropped the phone to the floor as the man came into the house, moving alongside the dining room table, his elbow knocking into a bowl and sending it crashing to the ground. Caroline screamed, but he showed no reaction, continuing his path towards her mum. A cold rush of air came in, bringing with it the smell of death. She gagged on it, bending over as it hit her, sending her back to those woods. The thing above her, hurting her.

The pain.

'I can't believe you're home. You've come back.'

Caroline reached out, but was too far away. Way too far. She had to get herself together, forget the memories, the pain. She had to save her mum from the monster.

It wasn't her son.

'Mum, come back here,' Caroline said, too quietly. Her mum didn't react, only cocking her head slightly, as she stared at the stranger in her dining room. 'Mum, that's not him. It's not Matty.'

She moved across the room, ignoring the cries of her body to stop. The dining table was between them as she reached the back of the room, the man now coming into full view.

'Look, Caroline,' her mum said, turning to her, her face bright, smiling for the first time she could remember. 'He's come home.'

'Get away from my mum,' Caroline said, ignoring her mother and looking at the thing that had entered their home.

'What are you saying, Caroline?' her mum said, confusion sweeping over her face. She stepped towards her still, glancing at the thing in her house, before turning back to Caroline. 'It's Matthew. He's come back to us.'

'That's not him. It never was. Matty has gone. Get away from him, Mum.'

'No, it's him. Why are you doing this?'

He was now standing close to her mum, looking at Caroline, the same sick smile playing across his face when he'd held her in those woods. The overpowering aroma of him, seeping into her every pore. Her mum was still looking up at him, a frown crossing her face, then disappearing as fast as it had appeared.

'Get away from her,' Caroline said, her voice a hiss now. She wasn't going to let this happen. Not now. Not here.

'Caroline, stop it,' her mum said, cold as ice towards her. She could see her searching his face, looking for familiarity and seemingly finding it. 'Where have you been, son?'

The thing reached out a gnarled hand, her mum mirroring him. Caroline slipped around the dining room table, but she wasn't quick enough. He gripped her mum's hand, softly at first, but she could see the grasp getting tighter. His other hand shot out and grabbed her by the arm, pushing her back on the other side of the table and towards the living room.

'No, don't,' Caroline screamed, as she watched the thing

lift her mum off her feet and throw her to the floor. She moved quickly, rushing towards it, before stopping as she saw what was in its hand.

'Stop,' Caroline tried, pain shooting through her again.

She watched, helpless, as her mum looked towards Rhys Durham, tears in her eyes. Then the knife appeared, seemed to leap forward and into her mum's chest.

'No ...'

She tried to move, but her legs wouldn't obey. Buckled underneath her, as she tried to cross the room and stop him.

Caroline watched the knife come back again and screamed as the man turned towards her. He came forward, smiling. Lifted her off the ground and smashed her head into the wall. She fell to the ground again, seeing his boots move back towards her mum as her vision turned to black.

Shipley pulled the car to a stop outside the house. A normal-looking semi-detached house, in a quiet street. The front garden was overgrown, but it didn't look that bad. He'd been to worse places. He'd tried calling Louise back numerous times, but she wouldn't answer. He'd sworn at his phone, then phoned through to the station to find out Caroline Edwards's address. Her mum's address as well, just to be sure. Louise had told him to go there and when it turned out he was only a few minutes away, he decided to just go round.

She was going to be the death of him, he thought. He'd learned more about her in the past few days than he had in the three years previous. Still, he knew, there were things she wasn't telling him. About her past.

He knew this case had brought up memories she'd wanted to keep hidden inside her. There were stories about her, always told when she was out of earshot. How she was prone to 'snap', as they put it. He hadn't seen it himself, but knew it was possible. The job can do that to anyone.

And then there was the fire. He'd looked it up, unable to help himself. She'd been found almost dead, outside her family home, the only survivor.

Shipley got out of the car, walked up the path and then stopped in his tracks at the door. He listened for anything unusual, but couldn't hear anything at all.

At first.

He began pounding on the door with a closed fist, shouting as he did so. He could hear noise from inside now, furniture crashing, a woman's cries, the thud of bodies on the ground. He looked around, wondering how on earth he could get into the house. Pulled his radio from his pocket and shouted into it.

'DS Paul Shipley, requesting backup immediately.' He reeled off the address and then looked back towards the window.

They didn't have time.

There was another crash inside. He stepped back and flung his boot at the door. It didn't move. He tried again, swinging with all his strength, landing his foot against the bottom half. It buckled a little, but not enough. He was panting already, still shouting to the people inside.

'Police, open the door.'

His hand slipped to his belt, removing the baton there, then extended it out. Took a step back and swung it at the small pane of glass next to the door. It cracked, splintering in a spider web. He didn't pause, swinging again and smashing the glass, the shards flying into the house. He thrust his hand inside, searching for the lock; he found it and grasped the key. He twisted it and pulled down the door handle.

He didn't think, simply pushed his way inside and started in the direction of the noise. The living room was to his right, the door closed, the sounds louder now. Shipley stepped forward and opened the door, taking in the scene. It was only a small room, but it felt like a black hole, drawing him in and swallowing him whole.

Two women. One older than the other. The younger one at first glance seemed to be simply sitting on the floor, but when Shipley took another step forward, he could see the blood running down her face. He recognised her. Caroline. The woman from the hospital, her face still bruised and yellowed. Her eyes were closed, her head resting against the wall – where it had hit it, Shipley guessed.

The older woman was lying on her back, a man in black crouching over her, a knife in his hand. Shipley saw the blood, pooling on the ground around her, and he didn't blink. Didn't pause. He threw himself forward as the knife plunged again into the woman's body.

Shipley stopped and swung the baton over his head, faintly aware of his own cry as he crashed it into the head of the figure holding the knife. He felt the impact throughout the entirety of his arm, a shockwave of pain travelling up and into his shoulder. He ignored it, swinging again and hitting him in the shoulder this time.

The man rocked on his feet, listing to the side, grunting as he did so. The woman beneath him groaned, tried to move but didn't seem able to. Shipley fixed his eyes on the man anew, watching as he fell to the side and then tried to lift himself up.

'Can you move?' Shipley said to the woman, still keeping his eyes on the man as he moaned and shook his head. He crouched down next to the woman, laying a hand on her shoulder. She flinched at his touch, but shifted a little.

Shipley grabbed hold of the woman's shoulder, tried moving her away, but she was like a dead weight. He moved his eyes to the other end of the room, where Caroline still sat, eyes closed.

Then back to the figure in black.

The man had his back to Shipley, but he could see he was struggling to his feet. Shipley moved around the woman, closer to him, ready to strike again. The man got up on one knee, then collapsed to the floor again. He could see the wound he'd inflicted on the side of the man's head, the hair there matted with blood. More blood rolled down and onto the black of his clothes, mixing with the blood spray from the woman's wounds.

Shipley lifted the baton above his head, waiting, wanting to see the man's face.

'Come on,' he cried, his breath slow and heavy. 'It's over. Lie down on the ground.'

The man shifted again, turning to face Shipley, who cocked his head to one side, studying the other's face.

Rhys Durham stared glassy-eyed up at Shipley, his face clouded with a growing stain of blood. Hair sprouted out in odd ways from his face, not the full beard Shipley had been expecting. His hair was long, dark, dank. He was older, of course, than in the photographs Shipley had seen, but he was still recognisable.

Shipley got to his feet and stood over the man, breathing

heavily. Rhys Durham lay at his feet, the blood from his head wound pooling around him. His eyes opened and closed. His breath was still coming out in rasps.

'I bloody caught him,' Shipley whispered, almost laughing at the idea.

He turned to where Caroline was still slumped against the wall, and kneeled down in front of her.

'Caroline, wake up, it's Paul. Detective Sergeant Shipley. You have to wake up. It's over.'

Shipley placed a hand on Caroline's shoulder just as she opened her eyes slowly. Her pupils widened as she recognised the man kneeling in front of her. Shipley guessed that he was the last person Caroline had been expecting to see.

'Wha— where's Mum?'

'She's over here, she's hurt. I need you to stay calm, okay? Police are on their way. I'll get an ambulance as well.'

'What about ...'

Caroline couldn't finish her question. She was looking at the broken figure in black lying close by. He was still moaning and making guttural noises, but was clearly unable to move.

'It's okay, he's not going to hurt you,' Shipley said, standing back up and moving towards Rhys Durham as he pulled his phone out of his pocket.

His hands were still shaking, adrenaline still rushing through his veins. He could feel it inside him, spreading through every part of his body. It was intensely satisfying.

'Ambulance ... Same place ...'

Shipley jumped at Caroline's scream, then turned to find Rhys Durham on his feet, stumbling, almost bent over at the waist, towards him. His heartbeat came to a stop, as time seemed to slow down.

Rhys roared as he threw himself at him. Shipley stepped to one side, bringing the baton down across the back of his shoulders as Rhys crashed into a coffee table that had been upended and shoved aside.

This time, he didn't move. Didn't make a sound.

Shipley felt his heart start beating madly against his chest once more. He shook his head, looked up at Caroline, who was still.

'Don't just stand there,' Shipley said, looking around for something, anything, that might tell him what to do next. 'Get out of the room.'

He bent down and lifted Val Edwards, dragging her into the hallway. Tried to work out how to keep Rhys Durham incapacitated without inflicting any further damage.

Shipley wanted to sit across from him in an interview room.

'Make sure your mum is okay,' Shipley said, stepping away from the women and leaving them in the hallway. In the distance, he could hear approaching sirens.

He stepped back into the living room, half-expecting Rhys Durham to have escaped out of the back door. A horror movie villain, with one last scare in him.

Instead, he lay on the floor where Shipley had left him. Blood on the floor, mixing in with the older woman's, coalescing into one large pool.

Shipley gripped Rhys Durham's arms and held on tight.

It was only human. He was only a man. Not a monster. Not a myth.

Just human.

He wanted to call Louise. Put her mind at rest. It would have to wait. Instead, he tightened his grip.

And waited for the cavalry to arrive.

Forty-Nine

Louise was on the road north when her phone rang again. She glanced at the screen, knowing it would be Shipley's name that showed. She considered throwing the damn thing out of the window, but decided she wanted to hear his voice one more time.

'Hello.'

'We got him.'

She could hear the barely constrained excitement in his voice. She couldn't help but smile, as it filled the car around her, enveloping her in a warm embrace. 'Are they okay?'

'The mum has been stabbed a few times, on her way to hospital now. Lost a lot of blood, but she's alive for now. Caroline will need a few more days' recovery.'

'Good news for now then.'

'It was Rhys Durham,' Shipley continued, as if he hadn't heard her talk. 'We were right all along. Thing is, there's been a couple of other incidents this evening as well. Kids in the woods, that sort of thing. We think there's a couple of copycats out there. Taking the opportunity. The whole force is up the wall with everything going on. Hopefully it'll get under some control soon.'

Louise listened, thought about the copycat narrative and then rejected it. Now, she felt she understood what was going on. What had happened. What had been happening. Pieces of the story began to slot together, her past and present finally coalescing, so she could comprehend it all. He wasn't the only one. The man she had known wasn't the only one. He had been the first. That was all. He was the one who had started the entire story. Taken an apocryphal tale and made it real. Whether by design or accidentally she wasn't sure, but that's how it had ended. When he had walked into those woods all those years before, maybe he hadn't expected to take on the persona of the Bone Keeper, but that was what had eventually happened.

He wasn't just a killer. He wasn't just evil.

He was more than that.

He made people in his image.

'Make sure they find every single last one of those people in the woods,' Louise said, as she approached the motorway that would take her the rest of the way. 'It's important.'

'Are you on your way still?'

Louise hesitated, wondering how to answer the question. 'Listen, I . . .'

'I've got to go, Louise, but give me a shout when you arrive. It's because of you that we caught him. We've got some celebrating to do. Together.'

She tried to reply, but the phone had already gone dead.

The thought of what she had left behind in the woods came to her. That man. What he had become.

He wouldn't stop now.

It would begin again. A new story. A new legend.

More death.

It was clear to her now. She had a choice. She could continue driving north, to the Lakes or further. Resign from the police and start a new, even more hidden life.

Or, she could turn the car around and go back into those woods and stop another story beginning.

She could end it.

Keep going. We're free. No one knows. You can keep driving and never have to face him again.

'Shut up . . .'

You can't win. No one can. What are you going to do, kill him?

Louise shook her head, her hands shaking even more now.

That would make you exactly like him. That's what he wants. They'll still know. You're a killer. Just like your dad. Just like your father always was. Keep driving.

'No.'

Louise pulled the car over into a lay-by at the side of the road and watched her hands judder on the steering wheel. Felt the familiar constriction in her chest and knew what her future would hold if she continued running away.

'No more hiding,' she whispered to herself.

This is how it ends.

She thought of the man in the woods. Her father. The man who had carried her on his shoulders as a child. Had read her bedtime stories. Who had been perfect.

For a while.

Then, the man he had become. Withdrawn and distant. Angrier, quick to shout, completely unlike he had been before.

She thought she knew the reason. He had tried to be normal. To have a family, to be just like everyone else. It hadn't worked though. He was always something else. Something he eventually couldn't keep inside anymore.

Memories were flooding back now, as she continued to drive into the darkness. Flashes, here and there. As if her mind had produced a flick-book of everything she had repressed for all this time and was now trying to show it to her all at once.

Louise didn't know what had happened over the years. How many of the people they had found buried had been his work and how many Rhys Durham's. It didn't matter. It was all the same. They were one person.

They were both the Bone Keeper.

That's who her father had been. Who he was.

This wasn't for anyone else to know. It would only make things worse than they already were. If there was any future for her, any light to be found, he was the only one left to silence.

You're just like him.

She retraced her journey, as the time slipped away from her. Evening had become night, total darkness only lit by the headlights of her car.

Back to the same woodland she had only hours earlier escaped from.

In a way, she had always known it would end there. When she had been left alone, thirteen years old and afraid, her grandparents had taken her in. She had never met any of her father's family – she wasn't sure they even existed. She had become an adult, knowing only that her family was gone. Now, she could see how they had protected her from the truth. Encouraged her to forget what had come before, so all she was left with was flashes of someone else's life.

Back into the woods he loved so much.

He wanted to make her like him. That was the answer. More memories started to push to the surface. She tried to resist. Failed to.

They had walked into those woods often in the year before she was left alone. Just the two of them.

He had seen something in her.

She knew the truth.

She was supposed to be like them. Like Rhys Durham and Steven Harris. Probably more, she guessed. Disciples, followers. She was never going to be like those people.

You're already like them. That's why you have to run. He'll win in the end.

The journey passed in a blur, buildings thinning out as she reached the north of the city. She wondered if they would be able to deal with the aftermath. If Shipley would be more involved now, considering he had been the one to stop Rhys Durham.

She wondered if she would be around to see how it all panned out for him. Whether there could have ever been a future for them.

There was part of her that hoped she wouldn't be around to find out. To feel that disappointment which seemed inevitable.

That this was the end of her story as well.

It was almost 1 a.m. by the time she pulled up on the same street as earlier in the evening. She didn't hesitate, getting out of the car as soon as she'd removed her car keys, almost being blown back by the force of the wind. There, on the coast, it was harsh and unforgiving. Inside the woods would be different, she thought. She pulled her jacket around her and began to walk.

The path led her into the woods, but then she was on her own. She walked with purpose, the clouds parting and allowing the moonlight to shine above her, illuminating the way enough for her to see. Soon enough, she didn't need it anyway– she could see and smell the light to follow.

Burning, being carried on the breeze towards her. The wind wasn't as heavy, now she was surrounded by the trees and brush. It had become colder, her jacket not thick enough to prevent the cold tearing through, making her shiver as she walked into the middle of the woodland. It was only on the periphery of her mind, though – she was single-minded now.

She had to reach the middle.

She had to reach him.

And then what? What are you going to do?

There was a crackling sound now, smoke drifting towards her, reaching out and passing through her body. Like fingers, tendrils which wanted to touch her. Cover her and smother her. Consume everything in its path.

She was close now.

On the ground, branches of a past long forgotten littered the way. Trees which had fallen where they'd stood, left to wither away and die. Time had stripped them bare, leaving only memories of what they had once been. She imagined sepia tones of light, cascading from them and glowing. The beauty found in nature. Above her, the trees that had survived the years were dormant. What would be stunning in sunlight was now charcoal black, looming over her as if they were ready to swallow her. They had lost their vibrancy, their life, becoming simply lifeless sticks of nothingness.

She could hear the fire crackling and spitting. The glow ahead had grown, orange and red in the distance. She wanted to jog, to run, but her ankle still protested underneath her, a reminder of what had happened only a few hours before.

Flashes of red in her vision. Darkness clouding her eyes.

Louise kept moving, snapping branches underneath her feet as she walked. They danced on the ground, lifting up as she passed them, their sounds becoming tuneless, as she broke through the treeline and into the clearing.

She stopped at the edge, her jaw pulsing, mouth closed. She didn't want to breathe in, scared it would be the last normal breath she took before the sight of the fire brought on another attack.

She knew it wouldn't, somehow. As if that part of her life was now beginning to dissipate, as the memories of her past returned.

He was sitting near the fire, his head down on his chest. She could see his hands, clasped as if in prayer. She could see how he might be thought of as non-human. The way he blended into his surroundings, becoming a part of the darkness. She walked closer, careful with her step as she made her way down the small ridge, almost slipping on the damp earth. She came to a stop opposite him, the fire between them. It was larger than she'd anticipated as she'd made her way to him. Bits of driftwood piled in the middle, other things underneath. The wind picked up, the flames flickering and then calming. Something came dislodged from underneath, coming to a rest a few feet away from her. A photograph, almost completely destroyed.

'You came back,' he said, that voice, so changed by the years. 'I knew you would.'

He was burning it all, she thought. Her past. His past. What had survived and had been taken into the woods by him all those years before. It was all in the fire.

He was destroying everything about him that was a link to his past. He was watching the last remnants of humanity turning to ash.

'Why?'

He looked up at her now, his eyes black in the light from the fire. 'I was ... I wasn't ready.'

'I never thought you'd hurt me. I'm yours. I have your blood inside me.'

He chuckled softly, as if she had told him an old joke. 'You do. That's not enough.'

'It should be.'

'I need to tell you a story, Louise.'

Louise waited for him to speak, a calmness rushing over her as she stood near the fire. The warmth from it soothed her, filling her body with peace. It was almost silent now, her mind quietening, ready to discover the truth. Of him. Of her. Of their past.

That's why she was there.

She needed to know.

'I failed you,' he said, his voice changing to a more familiar tone now. Not quite the one she remembered from being a small child, when he read to her at bedtime. It was softer than before though. More human. 'When you were younger, you didn't understand what was inside you. What I had passed down to my daughter. The anger, the resentment, I should have recognised it. I did ... eventually. I just didn't want to accept it. I had worked for so long not to be that person any longer. Seeing it in you, it made me realise I could never escape the need.'

'I'm not like you.'

'You know where the story of the Bone Keeper began, Louise?' he continued, as if she hadn't spoken. 'Right here. In these woods. This is where I was born. Not literally, of course, but my story began here, when I was young. The other kids, they didn't understand what I was, why I did the things I did. They left me alone, to find my own way. I did.'

'Do you have a point?' Louise said, resisting the urge to sit down and allow his words to ease her mind. 'None of this explains anything that's happened.'

'You always were eager to rush. I saw that in you at a very early age. You were constantly wanting to be ahead of what other kids were doing. You wanted to climb higher, run faster. Your brother was four years older than you and still struggled to keep up sometimes.'

'And they're dead. Because of you.'

He turned his head slightly, listening to the silence, it seemed. He looked at her, a ghost of a smile appearing across his face. 'I always wondered if you'd remember. Whether you carried the guilt. I knew afterwards that you were gone. That you were broken. I hoped you would be able to use what you did that night. That in the end, we would sit near a fire and find common ground. Instead, you seem to have forgotten it completely. Maybe that's for the best.'

Louise could see the fire now, the beauty of it, the control you could have over something so devastating. A spark of memory, of a match striking alight in darkness, her eyes gleaming in its heat.

'Do you think about them? Do you feel anything for them?'

Louise didn't answer him, lost in the fire now. A dream returning to her. A recurrent one, she hadn't experienced for a long time. Then, her grandmother coming into her bedroom, late at night. Holding her tightly, as she wailed and cried.

She thought about fire.

As she did so often.

She had blocked all of this. Thrown herself into her career. Made that her life. Didn't think of what she had gone through.

What she had done.

'You never had any feelings for them. You lack that same thing I do. Empathy. Compassion.'

Louise scratched at her thigh. The scar there that refused to fade. A reminder. Only she didn't want to remember any of it.

'It was an accident ...' she said, her voice a whisper, almost lost in the flames.

'You lit that fire, Louise. You killed them both.'

Fifty

'No.'

A single word. It was all she had. It wasn't enough.

It was the only word she could get out. Her mind was running at speed, thoughts and memories fighting for her attention.

'No,' she repeated, hoping it *could* be enough.

'Is that all you can say?' he said, the smile now gone, replaced by a blank expression. She couldn't read him at all. Never had been able to. 'I thought there would be more of a reaction.'

'You're lying.'

'You know it's true, Louise.'

'Stop saying my name.'

'They died in their beds, never knowing it was you who did it. You watched it happen. You stood and marvelled at it, knowing what was going on inside the house. Do you remember that?'

'Yes . . . but it wasn't me who did it. It was an accident.'

'No. You know the truth, don't you? That's what you're here for, isn't it? The truth? I wouldn't lie to you about this. I couldn't. If I wanted them dead – and believe me, there were more than a few times I considered it – I would have done it a lot cleaner than you did. There wouldn't have been a trace of them left. No one would have ever known what happened to them. I have been very careful over the years.'

'I couldn't do that,' Louise said, her mind betraying her and feeding what she thought was a lie. Had to be. Yet, there were images, sounds, she couldn't process properly. 'I'm not like you.'

'You keep saying that, but it's not true. You're just the same as me. What did you think, that you could join the police and become the good guy? That you could turn your back on your true self and never think about it? That's not how real life works.'

'I'd remember it,' Louise whispered, but even then she could sense he was right. That she had blocked out parts of her life for years. A way of dealing with what she had done, what she was. That little voice which spoke to her – now silent – had been attempting to make her see, but she had ignored it. 'Why would I do that?'

'You wanted to hurt people, things, animals,' he replied, as if it were the most normal thing anyone could ever want. He repulsed her, but she was now ensnared by him. Trapped in his words.

'I caught you once,' he continued, reaching out and poking the fire with a long stick. 'You had your hands around the throat of some young girl who lived in the street. I had to use all my strength to get you off her. Poor kid was so shaken up. Took every skill we had to get her parents to agree not to phone the police for that one.'

'You're lying,' Louise said, but she could see the girl's eyes now, the fear in them, the way her neck had felt beneath her own small hands. The power she could feel from what she was doing. It flooded back to her now, a perfect scene in her mind.

'You remember it all. That's good. Think about it. You'll never be the same again.'

'I'm not evil,' Louise said, her voice now a croak, hitching and scratching at her throat. She shook her head. 'No. No. I'm not like you. I'm not.'

'I never wanted this life for you, Louise,' he said, standing up finally and walking towards her. She took a step back, as he continued to come towards her. 'I didn't want that life anymore. I wanted to be normal. That's why I married your mother. Had two children. Still, the urge, the *need* was there. Inside me. I killed someone a year before Mum and Martin died. Some homeless guy nobody would miss. It felt so good, to allow myself to be that man again. It was as if I had been missing an arm before that day, then suddenly it had been reattached. I was whole again. I knew it wouldn't be long until I had to leave you all. Remember when we would walk through these woods? You knew why we were doing it, but I never needed to say a word. The marks – my marks – we made in the trees. We were preparing to come home. That night . . . that night changed everything. I thought you would finally accept what you had to become, but you couldn't. Not then. I came back here, to these woods, and I hoped for some time you would finally accept that this was where you belonged. I became the Bone Keeper again.'

'It was an accident,' Louise said, feeling a tear fall down her cheek. She wiped a sleeve across her face, taking another step backwards. She remembered it now, the moments before, the panic, the fear. She could control it. Setting fires had become her favourite hobby. She remembered watching the flames dancing, the power she felt with it.

She thought of the curtains in the living room. The Zippo lighter her mum had, kept hidden in the kitchen. Smoking out the back door, so as not to do it in front of her and Martin. Her brother. He was older than her, fifteen or sixteen. She could see him perfectly. Always had been able to. She remembered not being able to sleep, the thought of the lighter within reach downstairs playing round and round in her mind.

Louise had never allowed herself to think about what happened that night. Not fully. Only afterwards, the feel of the heat and the sound of the house burning inside. The cold outside, as she stood watching the fire.

Now, she could see herself, creeping down and playing with the curtains in the living room. Hating the colour of them. The trip she had taken with her mum to buy them, made to think she would have a say and then being overruled.

Flicking the lighter and watching the flame catch them, the noise it made. The excitement she had felt. Watching, as the flames spread around the room, until she had to get out. The burning sensation, as her pyjamas caught light, burning her leg, before she managed to get out of the house and roll on the grass outside.

'I never wanted them to die . . .'

'Stop lying to yourself, Louise,' he said, only a foot or so away from her now. She could smell him, the cloying aroma assaulting her. His face was aglow, the fire still burning beside them. 'You know what you are. I wanted you to be. I waited for you. I came to these woods. I killed again and again. The story of me taking hold once again.

Local kids, spotting me in the woods, creating more lavish parts to the story.'

'I don't want to hear this.'

'You need to. And I know you want to know. I knew if that woman was found near those woods, you would be involved in the investigation. I couldn't just come to you, understand? I needed to put you in this place again.'

'Rhys Durham . . .' Louise said, shaking her head at the incredulity of it. 'He's what, your pet project?'

He smiled, sick and sweet. 'Every body buried in the woods is a mistake. A failure. I spent years trying to replace you, before I realised that it couldn't be done. I found a few people. Young men, lost and directionless. I gave them the purpose I should have given to you. I made them into something more than they could ever have possibly imagined. Gave them the tools. You have to understand what people like you and me are. We're saving these souls, while also keeping the darkness within us happy. Taking them to the wonder of death, away from the horror of their lives.'

'You made them into killers. Steven Harris, Rhys, who knows how many.'

'Steven was never right. Not like Rhys. He was the only one who came close to what you're going to be,' he said, his face darkening suddenly. 'He has become more than I ever thought he could be. It took him time, but he can go off on his own now. Become his own story. Leaving just the two of us to become even greater.'

'He's dead,' Louise said and enjoyed the reaction she got from this lie. His face fell, sank into itself. She could feel the pain she had caused him. 'I warned them. That he was going to Caroline and her mum. They had to kill him. To save Caroline and Val Edwards.'

'They needed to die . . .'

'Not tonight. I stopped him. Steven Harris isn't dead, but he may as well be. He's in a cell now, waiting to be charged for two murders.' Louise took a small step forward. 'He raped the woman, did you know that? He broke into their homes and killed them in their bed. Raped her while she was still alive. Did you teach him that?'

'No . . . that wasn't supposed to happen. I never told him to do that.'

'Well, I guess you're not as good a teacher as you thought. You ever wonder about the others, *Dad*? Were they always ones who needed saving, or did your little boys sometimes kill because they wanted to? Because they wanted to feel powerful? The women they killed, maybe they were just like anyone else, any other man given a bit of power. Maybe they did that to them all.'

'They're not like that.'

Louise didn't flinch as his voice rose in volume, bouncing off the trees around them. 'I'm not like you. You could see that even then. I saw through you. I saw what you were. That scared you, didn't it? That I was more powerful than you could ever be. It didn't matter how many people you brought into these words and murdered, you couldn't even deal with your own daughter. A little *girl*. That frightened you. You were petrified that I would come after you next.'

He shrank back now, as Louise stepped closer to him.

'You're weak,' she said, enjoying the way he couldn't look at her now. The way he seemed smaller, more insignificant. 'You could never control me, like you thought you controlled them.'

'He never controlled me.'

Louise spun, the new voice from the darkness behind

her pausing her heartbeat for a second. Her breath caught in her throat as the shadows began to speak.

'He didn't have to. I wanted this.'

Louise squinted past the glow of the fire to the trees beyond, as something shuffled out of the night there.

'Is she with us?' the voice said, scratched and low. 'What should I do with him?'

'Who is that? Who is he holding?'

'Please, just let me go,' the man said, struggling against this new acolyte of her father's. 'I'm just a cameraman. I won't tell anyone you're here, honest.'

'Put him with the others.'

Louise turned back to her father, lines creasing her forehead as she tried to understand what was happening. 'Others?'

'You thought it was just you here, in these woods? Louise, you know better than that. This, is one of my "pet projects" as you call them. The guy he's holding . . . he could be your first.'

The lad – as he came closer, she realised he was no older than twenty – continued moving forward out of the shadows, as Louise stepped back and tried to keep the two men in her vision. He came into the light from the fire and she saw the man he was guiding into the clearing. Light glinted off the knife in the young lad's hand, its point resting against the back of the man's head. He had finally fallen silent, the fight leaving him. He turned his head slowly in Louise's direction, but she couldn't see the expression on his face. She was almost glad of that. She didn't want to see the fear in his eyes, the slackness of his features as he came to terms with what was happening.

She couldn't let this happen.

'Let him go,' Louise's shout echoed around the woods, but her father didn't flinch. 'He's not important. You have me. He's got nothing to do with any of this. He's nobody.'

'You came back here because you knew this was your destiny.'

'Let him go. Please.'

Her father looked across at the lad pushing the man along, then back at Louise. She hoped he could see how much she needed to be listened to.

'Kill him.'

Her body had already reacted before she knew she had heard her father's words. She turned to see the young lad taking in the order. Her legs were moving her towards him before she realised. Time slowed for a second or two, the world blurring around her as she sprinted to where they were standing. The fire burned beside her, as she skirted around it and to the other side, as the lad smiled at her, holding the knife in the air.

The man struggled against him, but as Louise got closer she could see that he was overpowered. The battle already lost, beaten out of him. Blood on his face, his arms flailing with little effect against the lad's grip.

She was a few feet away when she realised she was going to be too late. That it was futile.

Keep going. You can stop this.

Louise watched as another Bone Keeper thrust the knife in his hand into the man.

Fifty-One

Louise came to a stop a few feet from them, her breath coming in short bursts, unable to comprehend what she was seeing. She felt as if she could smell the blood exiting the man's body as he slumped slowly to the floor at their feet.

She wasn't fully aware that she was screaming; it seemed like distant noise as she walked towards where he had fallen, as if she were walking through a sea made of blood. 'No . . . no.'

He had fallen on his side, *the* side. Where the knife had entered him. His eyes were closed, his breaths short and almost imperceptible. She watched the rise and fall of his chest, only faintly aware of the laughter coming from above where she knelt. Louise held the back of his head, willing him to open his eyes, but they remained closed. His breathing became more laboured as a drop of blood seeped from his mouth, visible in the glow of the firelight.

The laughing continued as she laid the man's head carefully back down on the ground. Wiped a sleeve across her face as the world shifted back into focus, her senses returning. Something stirred inside her, the anger, the darkness within her, spreading through her veins and pouring over her like a second skin. Louise stood up slowly, a guttural noise building inside and then escaping from her mouth without warning.

The lad flinched a little at the sound, as she stood up fully and faced him. 'You killed him.'

'And you're next,' he replied, the grin fading, replaced by an empty expression as he went glassy-eyed, focusing on where she was standing. 'No more games.'

Louise clenched her teeth, her fists closing as she finally allowed the rage to take her over. Let the floodgates open, her body reacting as she allowed the fury that had always been there, waiting, to be set free.

She moved towards him as he raised the blade above his head again, closing the gap between them swiftly. She ducked as he lunged, shifting to one side of him and dodging the first blow. He turned quickly, his arm coming around him first, slashing at the air she had just been occupying. She was breathing heavily, but every part of her was awake. She could see every movement he was making, waiting, watching.

Something raw and animalistic within her took over.

He came at her again, but this time she was ready. She sidestepped to her left as he thrust the knife towards her. It missed by millimetres, but she didn't check her momentum, grasping his wrist and forcing it back.

In one movement she drove his arm upwards, towards his chest, the knife in his hand following.

She missed.

The knife entered his throat, just under his chin. He stepped back, but Louise followed him, sweeping his legs out from underneath him and falling with him down to the ground.

Louise fell on top of him, her weight pressed against his arm, as the knife went further into his throat. His eyes were wide with surprise as she screamed into his face, spittle flying from her mouth and landing on him. His hand was still clasped round the handle of the knife, but now he was trying to pull it from where it was firmly lodged.

'How does it feel, hey? How does it feel?'

Louise kept her weight on him, both hands now covering his own around the handle, saliva raining down on his face as she screamed. She watched his eyes widen more, his legs kicking underneath her begin to slow; his face begin to turn a different colour, before he finally stopped moving.

Her hands were white in the glow of the fire, as she slowly released them and allowed the anger to subside a little.

Until she heard the sound of hands clapping behind her.

'I am so proud,' her father said, sounding as if she had just won a race on sports day, or brought home a painting from school. 'I knew you had it in you.'

Louise didn't speak, standing up to her full height without turning to face him.

'This was what I wanted,' he continued, his voice carrying over the crackle of the flames between them. 'Now I see it in you. That same feeling. That darkness. I knew it was there. Do you feel it? Do you feel that power? It's always been there. You've become something else now. You'll never be the same. This is it. You and me. No more failures. I've worked hard to replace you, but it never worked. You're me.'

Silence fell on them as he stopped talking. Louise could feel her breathing start to quicken, become shallower. Her heart pounding still, as she looked towards where the man was lying on the ground. Prone, unmoving.

She closed her eyes, breathing deeply through her nose as she remembered the look in the young lad's eyes as she'd forced the knife deeper into his throat. She could feel the calmness come over her.

Now she knew how it felt to kill someone.

Louise turned, opening her eyes and looking at her father. He was smiling, black and yellowed teeth revealed, noticeable even in the dull light between them.

'It's time, Louise. You're ready.'

She didn't speak, simply walked slowly back to where he was still standing. He hadn't moved the entire time. Her heart rate increased as she imagined him watching what had just happened in front of him in the space of a few minutes. Impassive, turned-on, enjoyment? She didn't care.

'There's two more behind those trees, Louise. We can start tonight. Leave your old life behind and start again. I will teach you. How to release that anger, that rage you feel. Channel it into doing good. It'll never hold you back again.'

She allowed his words to wash over her, concentrating on putting one foot in front of the other, making her way around the fire back to him. She didn't break stride as she came to within ten feet of him.

Nine.

Eight.

Seven.

Six.

'I'll never be like you,' Louise said, a sick smile appearing across her face. 'But I will make sure you can never hurt anyone again.'

'I've been doing this a long time. Don't make this mistake again.'

'You're nothing. You're pathetic. I'll kill you as easily as I did your *protégé*. You watched him die.'

Louise felt a wave of pleasure course through her as her father reacted to the words. A slight twitch in his neck, as the verbal blow landed.

She came forward another step, fists clenched at her sides. He took a step towards her, as a crack from the fire made her flinch.

She didn't see the blow coming, just a blur of movement, then she was on her back, looking up at a clear sky, wondering how she'd ended up there. Confused, disorientated. She had underestimated him. Again. Her view was blocked suddenly as he roared above her, then crashed down on top of her. She could feel his weight crushing her chest, his hands slipping around her throat.

'This time, you don't get free,' he said, spittle falling from his gritted teeth and onto her face. She could almost feel it burning her skin, infecting her with his poison. She bucked, grabbing hold of his arms and trying to free herself, but he was stronger. Much stronger. Now she knew how she'd escaped before – he hadn't really wanted to kill her then.

He did now.

'We could have been something, you and me. I thought we were the same. But you're just like them. Out there. You have my blood inside you, I thought it would be different, but you're just like them. Why won't you listen to reason?'

Louise couldn't breathe; his hands were locked around her throat, impervious to her struggle as she battered his forearms, her fingers as she tried to prise at his. He dodged her attempts to land a punch on his head, on his face. When she did land a blow, it had no effect.

This was him, this was the Bone Keeper.

She tried turning, squirming underneath him, but his full weight was on her and she couldn't move more than an inch. She could feel her grip on consciousness slipping, darkness creeping into her vision.

Her arm fell to her side, landing on something.

'I'm sorry it's come to this, really I am. But I've got to start again. I hoped you would be able to join me, but I can see that's not going to happen.'

Her hand slipped around the thing on the ground beside her. She lifted it and flicked her wrist.

He didn't see it coming.

There was a soft thunk as the baton she had brought with her this time – but then dropped when the second *protégé* had arrived – landed at the back of his head. His hands slackened around her throat a little as she hit him again.

And again.

And again.

She extricated herself from beneath him, crawling across the ground away from him, as he shook his head and came for her again. Louise ducked his first blow, striking him in the knee with the baton. He let out a cry, but didn't stop moving. Simply turned in her direction again and let out a scream and dived for her.

She moved to the side, hitting him again, in the thigh this time. He lost his balance and she didn't have to think what to do next.

She raised the baton as he was about to fall and struck him in the temple with all the force she could muster.

He teetered on the spot, almost pirouetting in a circle. His face sank into itself, his eyes glassed over, like a drunk in the street.

Then, he fell face first into the fire.

She moved towards him, baton poised over her shoulder ready to strike again, but it was too late.

He was ablaze, still unconscious. He lay there for a second. Then another, as the fire took hold, burning through his clothing. His hair was fast disappearing.

Louise counted.

The agony of the fire destroying him snapped him back into consciousness. Ate at his skin, turning it red, then black. His screams filled the night.

It was too late, Louise thought. In those seconds, she imagined it all leave her body. The hate, the anger, the fear. It all dissipated from inside her and lifted from her shoulders. A burden gone.

She hoped.

She watched him burn.

After

The waiter smiled at Caroline as he placed the condiments on the table, but then the smile deserted his face as his eyes narrowed in recognition. She turned away, dropping her hands into her lap, yet still returned the smile. Even as he turned his back and left her.

'That happens a lot,' Caroline said, shrugging towards her from the opposite side of the table. 'Like I'd give him one anyway.'

'People are weird,' Louise replied, a small chuckle escaping her. 'I bet you'd get loads of strange ones if you put it on a Tinder profile.'

Caroline laughed, but it was empty. Louise picked up the salt shaker, twirling it in her hand. 'And your mum's okay?'

'She will be,' Caroline replied, placing her hands back on the table between them. 'No more surgeries, which is a good thing. She's loving the scars, reckons we should call ourselves the scar twins. Says it give her character. I told her no one will see them, given where they are. She just winked at me.'

Louise laughed for real now, and felt relieved when

Caroline joined in. It died down quickly though, as the weight of what they shared fell over them once more.

'How are you?'

'I'm okay, I guess,' Louise replied, nodding her head slowly. 'What about you?'

'If he hadn't turned up, I don't know what would have happened. I can't begin to thank you . . .'

'*He* saved your lives,' Louise said, talking over her and staring into her eyes. 'You don't need to thank me.'

'He would never have known to come if you hadn't thought quickly.'

Louise nodded again, more surely this time. Bit down on her lower lip, enjoying the sharpness of the pain. She couldn't tell Caroline that it should have been herself in that house instead of Shipley. If she hadn't been elsewhere.

'He's a hero,' Caroline said, her voice soft but firm with conviction. 'As are you.'

Louise didn't say anything, knowing it wasn't really true. Caroline didn't know what had happened in those woods. No one did. She had told the police who arrived after Shipley at the bloody scene in her mother's house as much as she did know. How Shipley had saved them, after she'd called Louise. It was no wonder they thought she was a hero. Given what had happened elsewhere in the city that night, they hadn't been much interested in the veracity of her account when she had emerged hours later.

They'd just been glad to see her alive.

How did you know to go there?

'How many did you find?'

Louise thought for a moment, knowing the information was all over the media. She guessed Caroline had ignored it all, gone into a safe bubble and decided none of it mattered.

'Three dead, two people arrested and charged. Two saved in Formby woods, where ... where I was. Two dead suspects. All those alive claiming to be the real Bone Keeper. We think it had become something of a cult.'

'You knew something, didn't you?'

Louise didn't answer her, staring at the salt shaker in her hand. A flash of heat crossed her face. She changed the subject. 'How did you find him?'

'It took me twenty years, but I finally found someone. Nathan. He came into my work talking about the Bone Keeper, that he'd seen him in those woods. He had been spoken to, by Rhys, about what could happen in the darkness there. All I got was the location and the name the Bone Keeper. That was all. I watched him for weeks. I wanted answers.'

'Did you get them?'

'Not really. They still haven't found him, but I'll dig up that woodland myself if I have to. He's there somewhere.'

Louise nodded, knowing the discovery would be coming soon enough. More graves had been found already in the woods in Formby. Another circle of bodies they were guessing was an older site. The entire land was being searched now; a total of twelve bodies had been recovered from there, all told. All that death, no one ever knowing it was there.

She thought of her dad, training those men, those boys, to become like him. Trying to replace the hole he felt should have been filled by someone else. Seeing in them something he recognised in himself.

In her.

That desire to kill. That anger and rage. She felt Matthew had resisted and had been killed because he didn't want to become like them. *Every body buried in the woods is a failure,* she heard her dad's voice say, and thought that was the closest to the truth she could get. All of them a possible replacement for her. Louise didn't know how to approach that side of the story with Caroline. Whether she and her mother would ever talk about it. She knew they would have questions that could never be answered.

'I really thought he was still alive,' Caroline continued, looking towards the exit. 'That's why I kept going. I never gave up on him.'

Louise would never know her whole story. What had happened all those years ago, why she had kept the lie from the detectives when they'd visited her at the hospital. She could hazard a guess, but didn't feel the need to.

Caroline had wanted to be someone else. That was the reason for turning her back on her mother and changing her name all those years before.

'You knew something,' Caroline said again, waiting for an answer.

Part of Louise wanted to give it to her, but she kept silent. That was one part she wasn't willing to discuss. 'I've heard the stories since I was a kid. Went hunting for him myself, when I was a teenager and thought I was invincible. I think I saw something once. Then, obviously, when we were led his way by Nathan Coldfield's mother. He wasn't exactly hiding away.'

The lie came easily. Louise wondered if the man in the woods – her father – would ever be identified. His DNA hadn't been on file until now. His fingerprints had never been taken before he'd been destroyed in that fire. He was a stranger to all.

And the fire had made him unrecognisable. A broken and burnt skeleton of a man.

She felt she knew what had happened now. Everything in the past few days designed to drive her back into her past. To come home, to him. To finally become what he'd always wanted her to be.

That had been his plan.

'Well, he thought he was untouchable. Rhys . . . he was an animal in those woods when he had me.'

'You're remembering more now?'

'Bits, here and there. I wasn't lying when I said it felt like he was inhuman. That's how it felt. Maybe I'd been expecting a monster and my mind somehow made sure that's how he looked.'

'How did you really get free?'

Caroline shrugged again. 'I don't know. I just remember bits of the night. I tell you one thing, I don't think he was the only one there. Maybe some of the others turned up. I just remember a face above me, all blurry. It was dark, as if it were covered with something. His hair was long, like Rhys's, but he was smaller I think. Does that sound like any of the other ones you arrested?'

Louise nodded calmly, but felt her heart quicken. She placed the salt shaker back down, moving her shaking hands down to her sides.

Her father had been there that night and set Caroline free. She had no doubt now.

She knew why.

It was the beginning of her father trying to get her back. Just as she'd thought. He was tired of the replacements. He wanted the real thing. He wanted the monster he thought he'd created when she'd been born. Someone who would be just like him. Passing down the flame of death.

'Mum thinks it was Matty,' Caroline said, shaking her head at the thought, then raising her hands in front of her in a 'maybe' gesture. 'I don't know. I thought I heard his voice at one point, but it was old and full of anger. It couldn't have been him. I know he's gone. It would be nice to think he was looking down on me, even after all this time. Saving me from myself. I'd like to believe that.'

'Then you believe that,' Louise said, reaching out and laying her hand on top of Caroline's. 'There's nothing wrong with thinking we have a guardian angel watching our backs when we do stupid things.'

'Believe me, I'm never going back to the woods. No forests, no trees, no large parks. Not for a long time.'

Louise chuckled, removing her hand from Caroline's. She believed the woman would be able to go back to some semblance of a normal life. That the events would fade, the way all memories eventually do. Soon, it wouldn't be real to her.

She hoped she was right.

'So, you're really going?'

Louise looked over the table at Shipley. His eyes were boring into hers. Caroline had left an hour earlier, replaced quickly by him. 'For now, yeah. I have to get away for a while.'

'I don't understand.'

'I don't need you to,' Louise replied, then slipped a hand over his. 'This is just something I have to do.'

'I'll be waiting for you. When you come back.'

Louise smiled, but she didn't believe him. He was moving forward, away from the quiet life they had led alongside each other.

'We never talked after . . .'

Louise held up a hand and shook her head. 'We didn't need to. We both know what that was. Just two people under pressure, looking for some comfort.'

She could still remember the feeling, as their lips had met in the car. The hunger and desire she had felt at that moment. The knowledge he returned those emotions as well. It could have been more, Louise thought, but she wasn't sure they would have ever been truly happy. Normal. Maybe that was something she had to accept. That for her, there was no normal.

There was so much she could never tell him.

Could never tell anyone.

'It was more than that for me,' Shipley said, then went quiet for a moment, knowing her mind was already set. Protecting himself. 'Keep in touch?'

'Of course,' Louise said, then lifted her hand. They both rose from the table and she allowed his arms to encircle her.

'See you soon.'

Louise left him there, walking outside into the winter sunlight and getting into her car. She sat there for a moment, holding the steering wheel, and breathed. Nothing felt heavy anymore. There was nothing holding her back. The guilt would never leave her, but she could live with that.

Maybe the anger and hate would be there, like a dark passenger she couldn't always control. Yet, for the first time, she felt she could see the possibility of light. Of learning to accept her past and move on.

The scars would remain, but perhaps that was okay. Maybe she needed to remember what she'd lived through.

A different kind of normal.

She placed the keys in the ignition and turned the engine

over. Glanced to her right – to see Shipley running over. He stopped next to the car. She pressed the button to slide down her window.

'I have to know,' Shipley said, a little breathless, one hand resting on top of the car. 'What happened in those woods?'

Louise looked towards the road, then back at him. 'The end of the story, Paul.'

Then, she drove away.

Heading south, leaving the city's woods behind her.

Matthew

He still remembered the tunnel. Hidden deep in those woods. The soft ground underneath his feet, the sounds coming from the darkness.

The echoes.

The rage.

The smell of death.

He remembered watching his sister go through first. The faint sound of her voice. He hadn't known then what lay inside – that would come a few seconds later. At that moment, he had simply thought she had scared herself and that was what he could hear.

A few seconds later, he met him.

The Bone Keeper.

Now, Matthew Edwards walked through the forest, the sounds of leaves crunching under his feet filling the air around him. Some lifted off the ground ahead, as the wind carried through the branches.

This would be his new home.

Back then, he had resisted at first. Tried to get away as strong arms lifted him into the air and carried him back out of the tunnel. The stench of the monster, filling his nostrils and clawing at his skin. Something going across his mouth, a hand or a paw. He didn't know then.

He didn't know he had been watched for a long time.

The Bone Keeper had forced him to be still, using his weight against him, even as his eyes screamed at the emerging figures of his sister and the two others. Then back into the tunnel, where his only shout was clamped down by a dirty hand.

The words began then. The stories.

His life.

The Bone Keeper had shown him his true self. The one he had tried to hide away. His feelings – and lack of them. The anger he felt inside and couldn't control.

Matthew had killed his first victim a year later. Aged fifteen, but unaware any more of time as a concept.

He remembered the tunnel.

He remembered the way the man's flesh had felt in his fingers, as he used the knife to slice into him.

Matthew was his old name – one forced on him without his consent. Now, he was who he was supposed to be.

He was the Bone Keeper.

Still, some part of him thought of himself as Matthew. Matty, as his sister called him. He had wanted to watch her die in those woods. Screamed at Rhys to finish the job. He wouldn't get the chance now. He was long gone. He imagined they would still be looking for him, still hoping he would come back.

They never come back.

Rhys had failed. He wished they were dead, so he wouldn't have to think of them ever again.

The woods were thick and dark, tree trunks at every turn, rising up into the sky and providing shelter. The expanse covered hundreds of acres, a distance he still couldn't comprehend. Larger than any he had worked within before.

He removed the knife from the sheath on his hip and began carving the symbols into the brown of a tree. Exposing the flesh beneath the bark and creating a new mark.

The terrain was unfamiliar, yet he knew it wouldn't be long until he knew every part of these woods.

Soon, they would talk about a monster who hid in this forest.

The Bone Keeper would live again.

He would begin a new story.

Acknowledgments

As always, this book wouldn't be in your hands right now without the support of so many people. Here are my heartfelt thanks to as many of them as I can fit into these pages.

To the Chamber – Eva, Nick, and Jay. You three are what get me through the good and bad days in this thing of ours.

To my PodBro, Steve Cavanagh – thanks for coming up with that amazing idea of how we should spend our Sunday nights talking for hours about nonsense. I don't have much more fun than when we are giggling like fools. *So, Steve, how have you been this week?*

My agent – Phil Patterson. Thank you for always listening to me drone on. After five years, I imagine you understand at least 40 per cent of what I say with this accent. Also to agents Sandra Sawicka and Luke Speed, for everything you do with foreign rights and TV/Film.

My editor – Jo Dickinson. She made this book approximately 156 per cent better. Always a calm presence, which is great when I can't see the wood for the trees (which in this book, full of woodland settings, was of great help). Jo is simply awesome. She makes me a better writer every single day.

The team at Simon & Schuster – Emma Capron, for her fantastic editorial assistance. Jack Smyth, for his incredible cover and new look for my books (the man is a genius), and the bestest publicist ever, Jess Barratt. Jess is one of the most hardworking people I've ever met. A superb person.

Sarah Hughes at Waterstones Liverpool One – for her general awesomeness and being one of my favourite friends. Thanks for letting me become the Scouse Parky.

All the reviewers, both bloggers and print who have taken a chance on the books so far and supported them, you have my unending appreciation.

Liz Barnsley and Kate Moloney – for reading early versions of the book and casting critical eyes over it. Thank you so much for the words of encouragement.

Craig Sisterson – who won an auction to name a character for charity – he chose his dad, so I hope he enjoys who he became in the book. Your son's a good bloke, Peter.

My family – for always being my biggest champions.

Finally, Emma, Abigail, and Megan. My world. All of this is for you three. I love you.